ALSO AVAILABLE BY DANIEL KIRK

NOVELS
The *Elf Realm* trilogy
The Low Road
The High Road
The Road's End

PICTURE BOOKS
Library Mouse
Library Mouse: A Friend's Tale
Library Mouse: A World to Explore

ELF REALM

The Road's End

DANIEL KIRK

AMULET BOOKS

New York

Library of Congress Cataloging-in-Publication Data

Kirk, Daniel.
The road's end / by Daniel Kirk.
p. cm. — (Elf Realm ; [bk. 3])
Summary: Fourteen-year-old Matt, Tuava-Li the elf, and Tomtar the troll continue their race to the North Pole to try to save their worlds, but unexpected horrors await whoever journeys beyond the Gates of Vattar.
ISBN 978-0-8109-8978-8 (alk. paper)
[1. Elves—Fiction. 2. Trolls—Fiction. 3. Fairies—Fiction. 4. Magic—Fiction.] I. Title.
PZ7.K6339Ro 2011
[Fic]—dc22
2010038752

Book design by Chad W. Beckerman and Melissa Arnst

Printed and bound in U.S.A.
10 9 8 7 6 5 4 3 2 1

ABRAMS
THE ART OF BOOKS SINCE 1949
115 West 18th Street
New York, NY 10011
www.abramsbooks.com

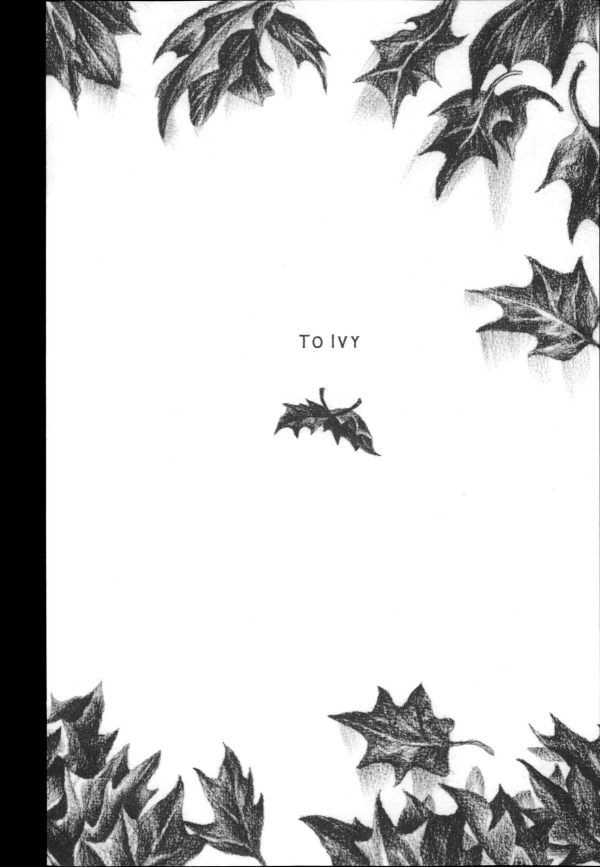

TO IVY

O Mighty Yggdrasil, with branches
As plentiful as the windows in the dome of night,
And leaves as abundant as the people of your tribes,
shelter us in your eternal embrace and bless us
always with the bounties of your seasons.
—FROM THE PAPYRUS OF GUIKUD, OLD LUNAR ERA, 14

'Tis the courage of Elf, Troll, and Human
united in common cause
that will heal the wounds of the worlds
and awaken us from long and troubled dreams.
May we each harken to the call of the Goddess
and spread her eternal Word,
awaiting our salvation in the rebirth of our Holy Tree,
as Winter awaits the coming of Spring.
—FROM THE SCROLL OF THAGR, OLD LUNAR ERA, 48765

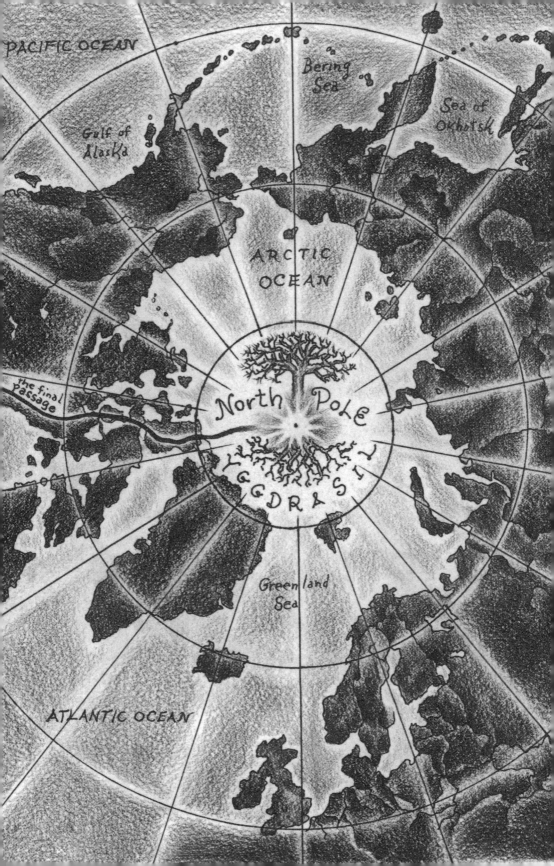

The Road's End

1

THE SCREAM WAS BRIEF; Asra was grateful for
that, at least. From the other side of the wall she recognized
surprise and anger in Macta's final shriek, but not pain. Not real
pain. Wouldn't it hurt to have one's soul devoured? A sliver of
moonlight worked through the bars of the high dungeon window.
The Princess crouched like a child in the feeble glow, head in
hands, with her back to the damp stone wall. Her matted hair
hung over her face, and though she'd squeezed her eyes shut,
she'd been unable to block out Macta's scream. It still rang in
her ears. She shuddered but felt a tinge of relief that the deed
was done; if she could believe that shape-shifter Jal-Maktar's
promise, she herself was in no immediate danger. Jal-Maktar
had vowed to eat only one soul, and Macta had, more or less,

volunteered. Now that chapter of her life was closed for good; a book best put aside and forgotten. But what new horror might open up in its place?

Asra's descent from Princess to prisoner had been swift. When she left the forest with the Human girl, Rebecca, she honestly believed they'd be able to waltz, carefree, into the palace of Helfratheim. Now Asra was trapped in the bowels of that distant fortress, with no more hope than a mouse at the bottom of a well. Rebecca was gone. Macta, her relentless suitor, was dead. Asra guessed there was no one alive who knew she was here except for Jal-Maktar. She could rot in the vaulted chambers of this prison, and no one would ever suspect a thing. Her only chance was that Jal-Maktar might help her escape. She'd probably be forced to pay him for his favors with some part of her body, some piece of lung or liver, but so be it. She would do anything, sacrifice anything, to get away.

Asra's eyes blinked open at the sound of approaching footsteps. In the dim light, she was shocked to see that Jal-Maktar was still impersonating King Macta. He *had* to have known how much this would hurt her! It would have been so easy for him to change his shape to something less emotionally charged. Jal-Maktar could, after all, become anything, anyone at all. "Is this some kind of joke?" Asra hissed. Then she noted that the figure shambling toward her was not dressed in royal finery, but was as battered and disheveled looking as Asra herself. The figure's right arm was missing, and there were Bloodstains on his torn shirt. "Why would you choose to appear like this?" Asra demanded. "Does it please you to wound me? Now that you've killed Macta, must you go on pretending to be him?"

"He's gone." The figure let out a choked laugh. "Jal-Maktar is gone!"

Asra felt faint; she dreaded the words she knew were coming.

"His time ran out before he could take me. You heard him say that he had to work fast, don't you remember? I kept him talking, and his time in this world ran out. He's gone! He's disembodied, once more. He can't hurt either of us; he can't hurt anyone, anymore. We're safe, Asra! What were the chances of that?"

"You—"

"'Tis I," said the figure, and in the feeble light Asra could see the glee in his eyes. "'Tis I, Macta! I'm alive, Asra, I'm alive!"

Macta drew the little book from his pocket, found a bit of charcoal, and squatted on the floor. In a trembling hand he began to write. "I'll calculate the odds, if I can. I'll make a bet as to the chances of us getting out of here! Luck is with us again, Asra. I can feel it!"

Asra's spirits sank at the realization that, once again, she was trapped with the Elfin prince who, not that long ago, had nearly become her husband. How could fate be so cruel? She got to her feet and pressed her body against the wall, as if she could dissolve into the stone. "Then it wasn't you who screamed?"

"No, no," Macta giggled, almost hysterical. "It was that monster Jal-Maktar. When he looked down and saw himself disappearing, he let out a roar, but that's all. There was nothing he could do; he was completely helpless!"

Helpless, like me, Asra thought, struggling to rein in her growing sense of panic. Macta's scratching in his little book was driving her mad. "Stop that!" she cried. "Stop!"

Macta looked up, eyes wide. He wasn't used to being told what to do. Asra glared at him. "Put away your stupid book, and think for a minute. You grew up in the palace above us. Isn't there any way out of here?"

The moon, its pockmarked face pale and full, hung sullenly over the towers of Helfratheim. Prashta, head of Dockalfar Security Operations, was in the midst of his speech. He stood in the high tower window, explaining to the citizens why the thousand Human children had not, in the end, been sacrificed to the Gods, according to Brahja-Chi's Acquisition. He said that the Gods were appeased merely by the *offer* of the sacrifice, and that the heavenly hosts had made it clear there was no need for the plan to be carried to its Bloody conclusion. The risk of contamination from the foul Human children would have been high, after all, and the Gods' love for the Elves was far, far greater than their thirst for Human Blood. How comforted the Elves should be, Prashta assured them, to know that he was there to relay the glad tidings of the Gods!

4

"What of our Mage, Jardaine?" a peasant called from the crowd.

"And our King!" someone else shouted. "Why are our leaders not here to speak to us?"

Prashta cleared his throat. The only thing he knew for certain was that Brahja-Chi had died at the hands of the shape-shifter, Jal-Maktar. It seemed likely that Jal-Maktar and Jardaine were still together, plotting their revenge against him and the Council. He had no idea what might have become of Macta. Nervously he fingered the medallions around his neck. "Jardaine and King Macta are understandably tired after the events of this busy day and have retired to their quarters. Rest assured that all is well in Helfratheim, and that the Gods are smiling down on each of you, grateful for your love and devotion. Good night, gentle Elves, and may you rest peacefully this night beyond the Gates of Vattar."

Prashta turned from the tower window and wiped the sweat from his brow. He'd be lucky if his flimsy wall of lies and evasions got him through the night. "Guards," he called, as half a dozen Elves in maroon uniforms snapped to attention, "I want you to find Jardaine and bring her to me."

The guards hesitated; one of them stepped forward and bowed his head. "Sir," he gulped, "if Jardaine is with that shape-shifting monster, our weapons will be no match for—"

"Our weapons are the best in all the realm," Prashta bellowed. "Each of you take a Dragon Thunderbus, and do what must be done. If Jardaine resists arrest, shoot her. Shoot Jal-Maktar, too."

In the grand ballroom upstairs, Jardaine and her underling Nick the Troll were hurriedly moving chairs from the plush carpet so that Becky could lie down. Fire Sprites flickered in their sconces, casting shadows into the high rafters. Becky yawned and sat down on the carpet. Jardaine glanced at the girl with an anxious grin. "We'll have this cleared away in no time," she said. "You'll get a good night's sleep, and tomorrow we'll begin our preparations to leave for the Pole."

"How long do you think it will take?" Becky asked wearily. The Elf's name was on the tip of her tongue, but she couldn't quite recall it. She lay on her side, with the mossy carpet pressed against her cheek. "I've forgotten what to call you," she murmured.

"You can call me Astrid," Jardaine said, "and my friend's name is Nicholas."

"I prefer Nick," the dark-haired Elf piped in, "like how I arrived *in the nick of time*!"

"How long will it take before we can go after my brother?" Becky asked. "If those Elves, Tuava-Li and her Mage, want to hurt him, we'd better hurry."

Jardaine turned and swept across the carpet to where Becky lay. "I know how worried you are," she said. "But we must be properly prepared for the journey. While you sleep, we'll work

JARDAINE AND BECKY 🍂

on acquiring the maps, cold-weather provisions, weapons, and the Arvada for travel. We'll be on our way as soon as we can."

"There's something else," Becky said. "Princess Asra, she's my friend, and she's here, in the palace somewhere. Do you think you could find her and tell her I'm okay?"

"*Asra,* you say?" Jardaine said through gritted teeth. "You know an Elfin Princess called Asra?"

Becky nodded. "Uh-huh. She's my best friend."

"I'll look into it," Jardaine said, "and if she's here, I'll do what I can to find her for you. In the meantime, though, I want you to close your eyes and not give it another thought."

"Thank you," Becky said with a sleepy smile. "I'm really glad to know that there are Elves like you, who want to help people."

Nick moved the last of the chairs into the corner of the room, and Becky stretched out on the carpet. With a gesture from Jardaine, the Fire Sprites drew their flickering light down to a dim glow. Becky was already asleep by the time Jardaine and Nick exited through the massive ballroom doors and hurried down the corridor. "How does that child know Princess Asra?" she said anxiously. "And why would she call the Princess *her best friend*? If Macta and Asra are still alive, they have the power to completely destroy our plans, Nick. We've got to get out of Helfratheim before the girl finds out what's going on."

"Jal-Maktar struck Macta and Asra with his fist, and they vanished in a puff of smoke!"

"Aye, but he didn't kill them. He said he was going to deal

with them *later.* He sent them somewhere else, that's all. For all we know, the three of them could be conspiring against me, right now."

"Halt," a voice cried out. "Stop where you are, both of you!"

Weapons clattering, a handful of Imperial Guards squeezed together, midway up the stairs. Their eyes darted around, knowing that if Jardaine were here, Jal-Maktar might well be nearby. Jardaine sneered down at them from the banister. She wasn't sure which of them had dared to bark orders at her; they all looked equally fearful and wary. "Fools, don't you know that Jal-Maktar is right behind me? Which of you will order *him* to stop?"

She put a hand on Nick's shoulder and whispered, "I'm going to conjure up the image of one of Jal-Maktar's monsters. It takes an enormous amount of energy to do this. Hold on to me, in case I lose my balance. I can't afford to fall down."

Nick complied, thrilled that his Master had confided her weakness to him. Jardaine pressed her eyelids shut and bowed her head. She pictured a huge, tar-skinned creature with a dozen bobbing heads, and with a sharp exhalation of breath she sent the image of the monster into the minds of the guards cringing below. Jardaine's knees buckled as the guards shrieked and turned on the stairs, panic-stricken, and raced for the exit. She opened her eyes and realized that Nick still had his arms around her shoulders. She could feel his hot breath on her cheek. "Let go of me," she hissed and pushed him away.

"Are you all right?" Nick asked.

"Aye," Jardaine said, stiffening. "Prashta's stooges are gone, aren't they?"

Nick's eyes were wild with delight. "How did you do that, my Mage? There was nothing there, but the soldiers ran like frightened rabbits! Can you teach me to make monsters with my mind?"

Jardaine snorted. "Bah! 'Tis magick, not for the likes of you. Don't get too excited, though. The soldiers will be back. Prashta will send them with reinforcements next time, and I may not have the strength to fool them again. We've got to get over to the techmagick labs and see if they have any weapons I can use against Prashta's forces. My bag of tricks will take us only so far!"

The pair met no further resistance between the palace and the Techmagicians' labs. The door, deep in shadows, was ajar. "Is anyone here?" Jardaine cried.

There was no response. Jardaine turned toward the narrow doorway in the corner. "We don't want any surprises," she said, starting up the staircase. "We'll take the back way. Prashta's troops could surprise us at any moment."

On the second floor they entered a glass-walled room, stacked with mechanical gear. A ghostly blue glow came from a box propped on a table. Cables snaked their way from the back of the box, down the table legs, and across the floor. In the gloom Jardaine could see a figure in a lab coat cowering under the table. "Come out of there," she commanded. "'Tis no use trying to hide. Let me see your face!"

"Your Hi-Highness," the Elf stammered, creeping from his hiding place. "I mean, Your Grace, I mean, my Mage! I am at your command!"

"Indeed you are," Jardaine said. "Though I'm the Mage of Helfratheim, I have enemies within the palace. I've come in search of weapons with which I may defend myself."

The Techmagician gulped. His best weapons were already in factory production, and there was little that remained in the Experimentalists' labs to share with the Mage. He placed a trembling finger on his chin and gazed around. Then he crossed the room, reached into a vat of liquid, and fished out a ceramic rod. A thin, segmented worm was coiled around the tip. He held it up for Jardaine to see. "Touch the end of this device to your enemy's flesh," he said, "and they'll be shocked, as if struck by lightning. The worm holds an electric charge for twelve hours."

"Indeed," Jardaine said, wrinkling her nose. "Is it lethal?"

The Techmagician shrugged. "That depends on the length of contact."

Jardaine took the device in her hand. "What else?"

"What else?" The Techmagician's heart was pounding. "Ah, there are protective medallions, which you could wear around your neck. They'll prevent your enemies from approaching you and inflicting harm. . . ."

"I am interested in *offense*, not *defense*," Jardaine said.

"Perhaps I should look beneath the tables here to see if any of your cowardly associates are still hiding there. Perhaps there are others who will prove more useful than you!"

The Techmagician backed away. "I'm alone, ma'am; the others all went to witness the ritual in the courtyard!"

"And why did you remain here?"

"I'm squeamish about Blood, my Mage."

"What about books, then? There's no Mage's library in all of Helfratheim. Have you got books of spells or curses? Something that doesn't require hardware?"

"As it happens," the Techmagician said brightly, "there is something of a library here!"

He moved to the end of the table and stood in the glow of the strange vertical box. Any Human being would have immediately recognized it as an old computer monitor; but the Elf and the Troll had never seen such a thing, and they were transfixed as the Techmagician pushed some small rectangular buttons and an image appeared on the screen. "By the Gods," Jardaine whispered. "Spells and curses, enchantments and conjury, right before my eyes. What manner of magick is this?"

The Techmagician chuckled, scrolling down a long list. "'Tis *Human* magick, or at least a version of it. We stole it from them, and adapted it to our own uses. We can find out just about anything we want to know concerning the Human world, and some of us have been using the device to compile information from the Elfin libraries you're interested in, my Mage."

"Stop," Jardaine ordered, as the Elf scrolled down the list of magick spells. "Right there, it reads, *methods for using mental energy to conquer an enemy with the power of the mind*—that's what I want! Show me how it's done!"

The Techmagician pressed another button and a detailed description materialized on the screen, laying out the method by which one could send bolts of pure mental energy into the brain of an enemy. Jardaine glanced warily at Nick. "Step out into the hall," she said. "This information is privileged, not for you."

The Troll shuffled dejectedly from the room. Jardaine peered into the computer monitor. Silently she digested the words she read. Once she was certain she'd memorized the spell she looked away, mouthed the words, then checked the screen once again to make sure she had made no mistakes. "Does this magick work from afar?" she asked the Techmagician.

"Ma'am, it depends on the mental powers of the one uttering the spell!"

"Then I'll have to see for myself," Jardaine said, narrowing her eyes at him.

"Please, my Mage," he cried, backing away, "have mercy!"

"All right," she said with a sigh, "I won't use it on you! But is there a way to minimize the effect?"

"According to our tests, permanent damage can be avoided by leaving off the last four lines of the text."

"Very well!" Jardaine turned her gaze to the door and uttered the spell she'd memorized, being careful to stop before she'd recited the last four lines. There was a sound like a sack of grain hitting the floor. She raced to the doorway and peered into the darkened corridor, then went to Nick's side and slapped his cheeks. "Nicholas, wake up," she cried, "wake up!"

The Troll opened his eyes and groaned. Every muscle in his body was aching. "Are you all right?" Jardaine asked. "You must have fainted from the stress of the evening. Here, see if you can get up!"

"I don't know what happened," Nick said. "I thought I was standing next to you in the lab, looking at that box of blue light, and the next thing I know, I'm out here in the darkness, and you're slapping me!"

"You remember nothing else?"

"Nooo," Nick grumbled.

Jardaine turned again to the Techmagician, who stood trembling in the doorway. "I'll take your lightning rod," she said, "for what it's worth. But what I *really* want is all the information I saw revealed in your magick box. You must copy it for me. I'll be back before morning to pick it up. Do you understand? 'Tis a simple task, but if you fail, I will have your head on a pike."

"My Mage," said the Elf, moving toward another machine made of metal and plastic, "Human magick makes it a very simple task, indeed. With a push of a button, the words will write themselves on sheets of paper, which I feed into this device. 'Twill be ready in no time!"

Jardaine nodded, then turned toward the stairway. "Come,

14

Nick. We're going to pay a little visit to Prashta, and see how fast he's willing to get us out of here."

Prashta lay in the bed of his apartment in the Western Tower. Anxiety did not let him rest. His wife had prepared a tincture meant to bring sleep. Her own portion of the pungent liquid had sent her to the Gates of Vattar in record time; her husband, however, tossed and turned. Before retiring for the night he had stationed guards both outside the door of his apartment as well as in the foyer of the great stone building. Soldiers were still searching for Jardaine, Nick, and Jal-Maktar. They were advised to be on the lookout for King Macta and Princess Asra, too, in case they were still alive. It was the thought of Jardaine, though, that kept Prashta squirming uneasily between his silken sheets. She'd been ordered to leave Helfratheim immediately, but now that she'd been appointed Mage, she'd never willingly give up her position. A torrent of doubt swept through Prashta's mind. If Jardaine and that shape-shifting monster Jal-Maktar forged an alliance of their own, Prashta knew he and the Council would be doomed.

Jardaine and Nick huddled in moon shadow behind the bushes surrounding the apartment tower. Nick saw the guards, more than a dozen in number, and a sinking sensation came over him. He'd chosen sides, and he was more certain by the minute that he'd chosen badly. Jardaine knelt behind the bushes, mouthing the words to the incantation she had learned. One by one, the guards began to fall.

Jardaine stepped up to the fallen guards and grinned. It had been far, far easier to strike them down with bursts of mental energy than it would have been to plant an image in their minds of Jal-Maktar in one of his hideous guises. Nick dragged the guards away, then held the door wide so that his Master could slip inside. Smiling coyly, she aimed the point of the Techmagician's lightning rod at Nick's cheek, then handed it to him and swaggered inside. "I'll save three of the guards upstairs for you. Make sure they're out cold, then tie them up."

Outside Prashta's apartment Jardaine and Nick quickly did their work. Inside, Prashta reached for his wife, who had been snoring at his side, and realized that her half of the bed was empty. He turned his head to see Jardaine looking down at him, a smirk on her face. "Wha—" he started.

"Don't bother calling for help," Jardaine snapped, knowing that Prashta would try to alert the guards stationed outside. "Your henchmen are sleeping on the job."

Prashta's wife was bound to a bedside chair, and she was gagged to prevent her from screaming. "Whatever you want, Jardaine," Prashta said, trembling. "I'll give whatever you ask."

"Indeed you will," Jardaine said, holding the lightning rod close to Prashta's wife. "I need an Arvada and a flight crew. I need maps that will guide us to the Pole. I need provisions—food and water for three months' journey."

"Three months?" Prashta cried. "What makes you think—"

Jardaine held the tip of the lightning rod so close to Prashta's wife that a blue spark jumped to her quivering flesh. "Three sheets of royal stationery, Nick," Jardaine said and gestured to Prashta's writing desk. "Paper and pen."

Prashta sat up in bed. With trembling hands he wrote letters to the captain of the Arvada, the Guild Hall mapmakers, and the Secretary in charge of provisions, ordering them to fulfill all of Jardaine's demands. He slipped the notes into envelopes. "Will you leave us in peace now?" he pleaded.

There was a groan from just outside the door; the guards Nick had shocked into unconsciousness were waking up. "We'll leave you in peace," Jardaine said, "when we're sure the letters have been delivered and that you haven't betrayed us."

Nick severed the vines around the guards' wrists, while Jardaine kept the lightning rod handy. "Deliver these letters," Prashta said to the guards. "Return with formal replies as quickly as you can. Our new Mage is to have all the resources of Helfratheim at her disposal."

"And don't try anything heroic," Jardaine said, holding up a handful of hair she'd clipped from the heads of the guards while they were unconscious. "I can use this to cast spells on you that will make you wish you'd never been born."

"She's not fooling," Prashta said. "Just do what I ordered, and hurry back!"

Nick opened the door for the guards to leave. They stepped over the fallen bodies of their fellows and hurried down the hallway.

"Where is King Macta?" Prashta asked cautiously.

"That's none of your concern."

"I spoke to our people this evening," Prashta said. "I told them that you and Macta had retired to the palace, after a long day."

Jardaine nodded. "Very well. I'd feel reassured to hear news like that."

"We'd make a good team, you and I," Prashta said. "If you were my ally, instead of my enemy, perhaps we—"

"Too late," Jardaine interrupted. "What's done is done."

"Where is Jal-Maktar?"

"He's tending to my affairs," Jardaine lied. "He'll come to my aid at a moment's notice if I encounter the slightest resistance from you or any of your cronies."

Prashta's wife, behind her gag, was squealing, desperately trying to speak. "*Shhhhhh*, my dear," her husband soothed. The door of his apartment hung open and a sliver of light fell upon the guards piled in the hallway. He knew what Jardaine would likely do next, and there was nothing he could do to stop her.

Before long the guards returned with written reassurances that all of Jardaine's requests would be met. Nick slipped up from behind and touched them lightly with the lightning rod. He moved so fast that the guards had no time to protest, and they fell without a sound. At a nod from his Master, Nick brought the lightning rod to Prashta's wife, still gagged and trussed in her chair. Prashta offered no resistance when it was his turn. His face, in fact, bore a look of relief when the device touched his neck and flashed blue against his pale skin.

Jardaine wrinkled her nose at the scent of ozone and stepped out of the room. Nick turned to follow, but she blocked his exit. "Wait. You're not finished with that rod. Shock them again, just to be sure."

Nick's eyes widened. "You don't mean—"

"I mean you'd best not question my orders," Jardaine interrupted.

The Troll nodded and turned back into the bedroom.

"Make it fast," Jardaine called. "There's much to be done! I must pick up the spells from the techmagick labs, and then I want to see to it that their doors are closed forever. Once we're gone, we don't want them coming after us!"

2

MATT, TOMTAR, AND TUAVA-LI hurtled, arms outstretched, through the Cord. The three of them had been heading north for hours. Matt couldn't stop his mind from drifting back to the fate of his parents and sister Emily. He had no way of knowing that they were free, safe and sound, and back in the human realm; but if he'd known what had happened to Becky since he'd left her in the woods outside Ljosalfar, he'd have far more reason to worry.

Matt tried to distract himself by imagining what the landscape was like aboveground—if there were people, and towns. He wondered how far north they'd managed to come. He wondered what the repercussions had been in the human world after the horrible sacrifice in Helfratheim. He wondered if he'd ever get to

Helfratheim to rescue his parents and baby sister, after planting the Seed from the tree at the North Pole. His mind bounced from feelings of hope to despair, and after a while it was too much to bear.

Tuava-Li flew behind Matt, in fierce concentration, watching for any sign that he was sinking into sleep or a stupor. She couldn't afford to lose him now. On occasion she spoke to him in thoughtspeak, so that he would stay as sharp and attentive to his surroundings as he possibly could. With no sleep and little food, and nothing in their field of vision but the endless length of gray, even Tuava-Li and Tomtar, accustomed to travel in the Cord, were having a hard time staying alert. It was time to take a break. When Tuava-Li felt the elevation rise and saw a feeble yellow glow in the distance, she gestured to Tomtar and called out to Matt. *Prepare yourself. We must get out of the Cord and rest, clear our heads with talk, and food, and fresh air.*

Matt and Tomtar shifted their arms and banked to the right, allowing Tuava-Li to pass by. The color of the Cord they'd been traveling through was little more than a dull beige, like the inside of a tree root, but there was a faint warm glow ahead that let them know there was sunlight outside. Tuava-Li clutched the wall of the Cord and flung her body into the pulpy mass. With one sharp fingernail, she drew a line through it, and climbed out. Air spilled from the opening with a loud *whooosh*. Matt and Tomtar gripped the wall with their fingers and pushed with their feet. They found the slit, and followed Tuava-Li out into the open air. Matt was crawling on his hands and knees. After so many hours in the Cord, his tongue felt thick and dry, and his ears were ringing. His body still felt like it was going a hundred miles an hour. On solid ground he felt awkward and clumsy; it was a strange sensation. In the Cord, he and his companions had learned to move together as elegantly as birds in flight. He sat down and looked around. The Cord rose out of the earth like the knuckle of an enormous finger, ten feet wide and thirty or more feet in length.

Tuava-Li was already smoothing the cut she'd made, sealing the opening with gentle strokes of her fingers. The Cord was healthier here, more resilient than other tributaries she'd seen lately, even when so much of this one was exposed to the elements. But the fibrous skin did not immediately heal itself, and it bulged and flapped as the hot, damp wind blew through it. "Where are we?" Tomtar asked.

"It's obvious," Matt said with a sigh, "it's clear as day. We're in the middle of nowhere!"

A rocky plain spread out before them on all sides. Long brown grass clung to the ground in patches, and a few bare trees stood in the distance, silhouetted by black hills. There was no sign of civilization, no trace of Human hands on the landscape. Neither, however, was there any sign of Faerie life. The sky was gray and streaked with yellow, and there was a strong wind from the north. The air was far colder than it had been in Pittsburgh.

Tomtar shivered. "I hope we're near the North Pole!"

"Me, too," Matt said. "I'm beginning to wonder what we're supposed to do when we get there. We don't have coats, or boots, or anything! We've got to find a town where we can buy some gear, or we'll be frozen solid before we find that magic tree at the top of the world."

Tuava-Li drew the hair out of her eyes when the wind whipped it across her face. "The Gods will provide," she said. "They always do."

Matt sighed in frustration, but without the anger that had eaten at him before. "I've said it before, and I'll say it again, if there are any gods out there, they'd want us to take care of ourselves, Tuava-Li. You honestly think the gods have time to worry about our little troubles?"

"Is there any food?" Tomtar asked.

"You misunderstand," Tuava-Li said. "Our troubles aren't little. Our troubles are the troubles of the world, and the Gods watch our every move with great interest. They must, for the future depends upon our success. We must succeed in our efforts, and yet without their help, we'll fail. Let us see if your tattoos have changed!"

Matt pulled up his shirt. "Wow," he exclaimed. "Usually I feel all tingly when they change, but I guess I was distracted in the Cord. What *is* that?"

"Elves," Tuava-Li said, closely examining Matt's torso. "Nooo, children. I think they're Human children. Holding hands and spinning in a circle."

Matt sighed. "What is that supposed to mean? My body's turned into a kids' book illustration. Is it symbolic, that we're acting like children, not being responsible enough, smart enough? We're doing everything we can!"

"Can we think about it while we're looking for something to eat?" Tomtar pleaded.

Matt yanked his shirt back down. Then he took off his pack and rummaged around through the pockets. "I had a few almonds," he mumbled, "unless I ate them already."

"Fungus?" offered Tuava-Li, drawing a gnarled, dusty-looking root from her own pack.

"You bet," Tomtar said, reaching out a hand. He was already drooling in delight at the prospect of having something—anything—in his belly.

"Give it to me," Matt said with a sigh. He pulled his knife from his pocket, and holding the fungus against a rock, cut it into three equal strips.

"'Tisn't fair," Tomtar said, munching on his piece. "Matt, you're bigger than Tuava-Li and me put together; you should have gotten a bigger piece for yourself!"

"It isn't fair that all we have to eat is fungus," Matt said. "Eat up. I'll find something else!"

Matt, hoping he might find a berry bush or some edible-looking plant, took a few tentative steps across the rock-strewn ground. "Whoa," he cried, bending over, and bracing his hands on his knees. "I'm dizzy!"

"Go easy," said Tuava-Li. "Balance is hard to maintain when one's been traveling long in the Cord."

"Tell me about it," Matt said. "Or maybe — don't. Just help me find something to eat, guys!"

"Be careful," Tuava-Li warned. "I'm not certain where we are, but the Human realm is full of poisonous plants."

"And the elf realm?" Matt asked. "Poisonous plants there?"

"Mushrooms, puffballs, scurvy grass, those are all safe," Tuava-Li said.

Other than the distant trees, there were only stunted bushes with brown leaves clinging to withered twigs. "Look here," Tuava-Li said, slipping her pack from around her shoulders and bending by a low bush. "'Tis whortleberry. Look for blue-black berries and small oval leaves. These normally ripen in August, so we're lucky to find any now still on the branches."

"Luck of the Chosen Ones," Tomtar said with a grin, plucking some of the berries and stuffing them into his mouth.

"Chosen to suffer," Matt said, nibbling a few of the berries and wiping the dark juice from his lips. "They're not bad, but we can't make a meal out of these things. Tuava-Li, we've got to find something more substantial. I'm completely starving."

Tuava-Li got up and walked away, keeping her eyes on the ground. "If we're far enough north, the reindeer eat the bark of the arctic willow and ground birch. We could probably eat that, too, if we had to. We could look for lichen, crowberries, many things."

"There's a stream over this way," Matt said.

"Then we might look for something called *Archangelica*. 'Tis a tall plant, Matthew, sometimes it grows as tall as you. The leaf stalks are tender, and if there are any flowering stems, I've heard the Elves of the North find them delicious when prepared in a soup."

"Soup!" Tomtar said excitedly. "We could get some water from the stream, build a fire, and cook the greens!"

"If we had anything to put it in," Matt grumbled, walking along the water's edge. He stepped carefully, as the stones on the bank were slippery, and he didn't want to fall into the freezing water. He waved away the tall grass and peered into the burbling stream. There was something moving in a shallow pond, where the rocks had blocked the passage of swift-moving water. "Hey, you won't believe this. There's a fish trapped over here!"

Tomtar scampered over to take a look. The fish was easily a foot long, and its gray back was spotted with white. "We should move the rocks," Tomtar said, "so it can get back into the stream. It's probably trying to reach the sea!"

Matt shook his head. The fish was sluggish, and its dorsal fin rose out of the shallow water. "I don't want to do this, Tomtar, but I've got to eat. You should go over there with Tuava-Li."

"No, Matt, we can—"

Tomtar looked on in horror as Matt dug his fingers beneath a football-sized rock and hoisted it over the fish's head. He dropped the rock, then jumped back. Ice water splashed over his clothes. "It's survival, Tomtar," he said apologetically, wiping his face with his sleeve. He reached into the stream and moved the rock. Then he pulled out the limp body of the arctic char. "Sorry, fish! Ends justify the means. Circle of life, you know. I just hope I can remember what to do; I helped my dad clean fish last summer at a lake!"

"At the very least," Tuava-Li said, "you must express some gratitude for the poor creature's life."

"I was getting to that," Matt said, holding the limp body in his hands. "I'm sorry, fish, that your time on earth is done. I'm sorry that I need your life force inside me, so that I can continue my journey and achieve my goals. I am grateful for your sacrifice."

Before long the three were squatting in front of a fire. Tomtar had gathered twigs for kindling, and Matt found some gnarled branches to build a framework where he could cook the fish. He opened one of the matchbooks he'd taken from Mrs. Babcek's kitchen, back in Pittsburgh, and soon there was a roaring blaze in the midst of a circle of smooth, round stones. The skin of the fish popped and sizzled as smoke coiled in the cold morning air. Tuava-Li kept her eyes averted from the body of the fish, impaled on a sharp stick. "You don't have to eat it," Matt said. "You, either, Tomtar."

"I didn't say anything, Matt," Tomtar replied.

"I know you're both vegetarians, or whatever, vegans, if that's what they call it in elf language. It's just that if you want

me to be strong for this journey, I have to have some protein in my belly. Humans starve to death eating just berries and twigs and grass."

"I didn't say anything, either, Matthew," Tuava-Li said. "Animals in the Human realm eat one another to survive."

Matt snorted. "So you're saying I'm an animal?"

Tuava-Li shook her head. "Let's not fight! I meant predatory animals from your own world: bears, and tigers, and the like."

"And owls," Tomtar offered.

Matt added, "And hawks."

Tuava-Li threw him a look. In owl form, her own Mage often hunted for living food. She did it to balance and ground the energies inside her; she did it to keep her chakras in a more perfect relationship. Tuava-Li, herself, had the power to become a hawk. Though she hadn't yet required the sacrifice of a living creature to eat, she knew it was only a matter of time. "I know, Matt, I didn't say anything. I didn't complain, I didn't judge, I didn't do anything."

"Something always has to sacrifice itself so that something else can live," Matt said. "Even plants have lives. Fruits and vegetables don't want to die, do they? And even vegans have to eat vegetables."

Matt prodded the fish with a stick, to see if it was cooked, and it fell in chunks into the fire. "No!" he cried. He leapt up, stomping on the glowing coals, and used the stick to push his blackened supper out of harm's way. He ate his meal in silence

🍁 TOMTAR, MATT, AND TUAVA-LI

as his companions sat and watched the flickering embers. "You know," said Tuava-Li, "this journey is all about sacrifice."

Tomtar asked, "What do you mean?"

"Each of us has sacrificed our time," she answered thoughtfully. "We've risked our plans for the future, maybe even the rest of our lives, if things do not go well, for the hope of a greater good. Sacrifice is in our nature. 'Tis natural that we do it. 'Tis right that we sacrifice ourselves on the altar of the good."

"I don't think so," Matt said. "Don't forget that elf mage who just sacrificed a thousand human children for her gods! She thought she was doing the right thing, but you can bet those kids weren't too happy about it. It's barbaric and disgusting, what she did."

"I won't argue with you," said Tuava-Li. "Better that we make our sacrifices without coercion. Better that we give of ourselves freely."

"Unlike this fish," Matt said, chewing. "He didn't know what was coming. And when he found out, he had no options. It was too late to try to get away. He died, so I could eat."

Tuava-Li sat before the fire, thinking about the sacrifice Matt was going to make when he got to the center of the earth, the sacrifice of Blood to nourish the Seed of the mighty Adri. He, too, didn't know what was to come. Tuava-Li wondered whether Matt would make the sacrifice willingly, or if it would be up to her to wield the knife when the time came. *Surely the Goddess wouldn't demand that of me,* she thought with a shudder. Many things might change before they arrived at their destination. She only knew that the sacrifice had to be made, as it was in ancient times, and she didn't dare tell Matt what was going to be required.

"Matt, can I taste a piece of that fish?" Tomtar asked timidly.

"Sure," Matt said. "I'd feel guilty eating it all by myself."

"And I'll feel guilty for what I'm about to do," Tomtar said sheepishly, holding out a hand.

Tuava-Li got up from the fire and stalked away, annoyed and disappointed in Tomtar. "She'll be fine," Matt said. "You know how she is." To Tuava-Li he shouted, "A troll's got to eat, doesn't he?"

The Elf stopped a short distance away and bent to look at a thick clump of grass. She reached into the dense growth, and using all her strength, dragged something out.

"What is it?" Tomtar asked.

Matt shrugged. "Can't say!"

As Tuava-Li turned, it was plain to see that she was laboring with the weight of a large animal skull. "Tuava-Li, what are you doing? Let me help!" Matt cried.

"D'you think she wants to bury it?" Tomtar called after Matt as he jumped up and hurried to Tuava-Li's aid. Back in the countryside near Pittsburgh they had stopped to perform small ceremonies for all manner of roadkill.

"A bowl," Tuava-Li said. "For cooking soup."

"Wow," Matt said, examining the bleached skull. "You'd use it for that?"

"The animal is long dead. I wouldn't be consuming its flesh."

"Must be some kind of moose," Matt ventured. "Caribou, or musk ox, or something. I wonder how long it's been here?"

"Let's take it to the stream, to clean it," Tuava-Li said. "We can fill it with water there, and I can heat up the water and cook some of the leaves and twigs we've found. 'Twill be nutritious, if nothing else."

Carefully Matt arranged some stones around the fire so that the skull could sit above the flames. The three of them gathered herbs and greens, and once Tuava-Li had sorted out the questionable ingredients, they cooked them in the great white basin of the dead herbivore's skull. Tomtar said a blessing, thanking the animal for the gift of its cranium, thanking Mother Earth for the gift of her plants, and thanking the Gods and Goddesses for their bounty. When the soup was hot they swept the embers from beneath the skull. Then they took turns sipping from the smooth edge.

"So," Matt said hesitantly, as the warm broth sent relief all the way to his fingers and toes. "Any ideas about my tattoos?"

"Children are the hope for the future," Tuava-Li speculated. "Perhaps the tattoo is meant to suggest that we shouldn't give up hope."

"The children were dancing," Tomtar suggested. "Maybe it means that we need more music! I could play my flute, if you wanted."

When he thought of children, Matt's mind naturally drifted

to his sister Becky, and then to the rest of his missing family. It felt like a long time since he'd seen them. "What do you think Jardaine is doing to my parents right now?"

Tuava-Li and Tomtar knew as little as Matt; all they had to go on was speculation. Still, Tuava-Li ventured a thought. "You shouldn't worry about them, Matthew. Jardaine will be afraid of your parents. They're Humans. They're big. They'll be a mystery to Jardaine and the others in Helfratheim. The Elves will want to keep their distance, because they'll fear contamination."

"What about my baby sister, Emily?" Matt asked. "Will they be afraid of her, too? What if she was part of that sacrifice?"

"Matt, I'm sure they're all right," Tomtar said. "Don't you remember when Tuava-Li told us that your family is worth far more to Jardaine alive than . . ."

Tomtar felt uncomfortable at how close he'd come to saying the word *dead*. "Well, she'd want to keep them safe, and healthy, so that she could learn about Humans, and what they do, and what they need to live, and things like that. You know, it doesn't do any good to worry about them. You're doing the best you can!"

Matt's hands rested on his knees. Tomtar laid his own small, square hand on top of Matt's and patted it gently. Matt sighed. Not long ago, he'd never heard of the Cord, of Helfratheim, or Alfheim, or Ljosalfar, or any of the other places that now loomed large in his mind. He hadn't believed in Faeries, Elves, or Trolls, and his sheltered teenage life was gloriously dull and predictable.

Now his world was turned upside down and inside out. He was clinging desperately to hope, but it was like trying to keep a kite flying in a hurricane. It was stupid to think life would ever be normal again; but he didn't dare let himself settle on that conclusion. He knew, instinctively, that Tomtar and Tuava-Li would do anything in their power to keep him from giving up.

When they had finished their soup, Matt asked the question he was afraid to ask himself. "What do you think, guys? Am I crazy to keep hoping that everything will work out okay?"

Tuava-Li shook her head, leaning back from the skull. "There's nothing saner than hope!"

Matt nodded. "What do you think, Tomtar?"

The Troll smiled reassuringly and laughed. "Like you said, Matt, *clear as day*. I believe in *you*! Would you like to hear some music now?"

"If you want," Matt said, getting to his feet. "But I've got to put out that fire before we leave."

He used the animal skull to carry water from the stream and doused the dying embers. As the sound of Tomtar's flute was carried away in the wind, Matt and Tuava-Li covered the embers in dirt. "Come on, guys," Matt soon said with a shiver. "We've got an appointment at the North Pole!"

3

PRINCESS ASRA WAS HOARSE from screaming.
Macta was, too. At first, believing it was likely that a passerby
outside the high window would hear their cries, Asra had swallowed her pride and climbed onto Macta's shoulders so that she
was closer to the source of light. She was very nearly able to see
outside. There was no sound to indicate any traffic in the winding
alley. She knew that even if her cries from the dungeon were
heard, there was no reason to think that whoever it was would
seek help for the poor souls locked inside. Helfratheim had been
built for prisoners, and many Faerie Folk, no doubt, spent their
last days locked up here, crying pitifully for aid that never came.

Macta did his best to balance the Princess on his shoulders,
but his terrible wound made it difficult for her to perch there for

long. He gasped with the pain of it as her heel ground into his flesh. When he could take no more, they took turns calling for help through the crack around the old wooden door. It led, as far as they knew, into a darkened corridor in the bowels of the palace; but there was always a chance that a guard might pass close enough to hear.

Asra pressed her fingers into her ears to blunt Macta's hoarse cries. She had to give him some credit, though. He was louder than a howling Goblin. Once his voice gave out and all that he could emit was a hoarse croak, it would be Asra's turn. Until then, she knew, it would be best for her to rest. "What a joke," she muttered to herself. Her thoughts were like leaves washed downstream, battering against one hopeless conclusion after another. Who, she wondered, had survived the debacle upstairs in the palace with that shape-shifter Jal-Maktar? Jardaine, Brahja-Chi, the Council of Seven, Becky, too, hung in some kind of limbo for Asra. They were neither alive nor dead. All that remained was Macta's awful wailing.

Macta began to cough. He fell to the floor of the dungeon. He was done; he could scream for help no more. Asra got up slowly and went to stand over him. She could barely straighten herself for the gnawing hunger in her belly. "'Tis useless," she whispered hoarsely. "No one's around to hear us. Otherwise, we would have driven them completely mad by now."

"I'm so hungry," Macta said. "I'm going to lie here on the stone and die, and there'll be nothing left of me but a skeleton."

Asra tossed her dirty hair. "'Tis a pleasant image to entertain,

Macta, but I won't let you give up so readily. Let me climb on your shoulders again, by the window. I believe there's a little voice left in me yet."

"I'm done," Macta groaned, rolling onto his back. "I'm all used up."

"You're insufferable," Asra said, "and my ears are ringing with your moaning."

At that moment Macta turned his head. There was an almost imperceptible scrabbling sound along one of the far walls. "A mouse?" he cried. "A rat, perhaps?" He leapt to his feet. "We won't starve, after all, my Princess!"

Asra caught sight of movement in the gloom. The rodent hurried along the wall, hidden in shadows, and Macta jumped up in hot pursuit. "You never fail to find new ways of disgusting me," Asra said.

"We'll have to eat it raw," Macta said, "but I'll save the sweetest parts for you, my dear. I shall lay out its innards like a banquet, and we will dine together. 'Tis better to live together than to die together, isn't it?"

Macta lunged for the mouse and it rocketed out of sight. "*Nooooooo!*" Macta cried. "You belong to me, little one!"

Asra saw Macta disappear around the corner where, not long before, he had followed Jal-Maktar. She heard Macta's feet shuffle, then stop. There was a long moment of silence before he said, "Asra, come here. I want to show you something! Luck may be smiling upon us once again."

"If you caught that rodent, you might as well know now that I'll have no part of consuming it," Asra said. "I'd far sooner die with my lips clean of such an insult than survive another day to descend into depravity with you."

"Descent may be our way out of here," Macta said. He was on his knees peering at the floor when Asra came around the corner. "What do you—"

"A drain," Macta said, looking up. "The rodent ran down into a drain hole here on the floor. Look—it's an earthen passage, beneath the stones, not just some little pipe. 'Tis big enough for us to crawl through. There's corrosion around the opening. One of the stones is cracked. If we can lift these slabs away, the passage may lead somewhere else in the palace, or perhaps outside. I'm sure of it! Where else would wastewater go?"

"A sewer," Asra said. "You want me to follow you into the sewer! 'Tis a fitting metaphor for my life." She bent to see how badly the mortar around the stones was decayed, and dug a fingernail into the powdery mass. "If the strength of three arms can move these, then it will be done."

"Wait," said Macta. He reached into his pocket, drew out the book he used to keep track of his gambling, and rested it on his knee. "I want to make a little bet with myself first!"

As he searched for a bit of charcoal in his pocket, Asra struck the book with the flat of her hand. It skittered across the floor. "No more of that, Macta. I can't bear it anymore. No more making bets with yourself or anyone else. No more scribble scrabble in your little book! No more gambling. You're done with that forever. Do you understand me?"

Macta looked up at the Princess. Her eyes burned with an intensity that made his skin tingle. "I do," he said. "I understand, Asra, I do! If you wish it to be so, then that is the way it shall be!"

Together they wedged their fingers beneath one of the stones at the edge of the drain. "On the count of three," Asra said, keenly aware that her shoulder and Macta's were pressed together in common cause.

Macta looked into the eyes of his beloved and winked. "I'll bet you ten dratmas we can do it!"

"I wasn't joking," Asra said icily.

4

THE AIR THUNDERED around Becky as the massive
Sprite twitched its tail, and the Arvada lifted from the ground.
Flat on her back inside the cab, Becky felt herself slide
backwards as the craft made its jerky ascent. Jardaine and
Nick were with the crew at the foredeck, belted safely into their
seats until the Arvada reached cruising altitude and leveled off.
Jardaine cradled a basket in her lap. Inside were the papers
from the Techmagicians' lab, documenting the myriad ways of
using magick to disarm a foe. On the floor next to her was a
stack of birch-bark maps of the northern hemisphere of the
Elfin world. "Hunaland," she shouted over the Air Sprite's din,
"we long to see you!"

The Arvada pilots used the concentrated force of their will

to move the Air Sprite through the sky. Three of them sat in a circle at the front of the cabin, eyes narrowed in single-minded intensity, as other members of the Air Squad kept watch in the front window or pored over the details of the maps. "'Tis a fact that the kingdom at the top of the world is cloaked in magick," one of them said. "I don't see any way of getting around that. The maps may take us to the right coordinates, but unless we can peer through a cloak of invisibility, I fear we'll see nothing!"

"O ye of little faith," Jardaine said in exasperation. "I'm a Mage, and I have powers of perception you cannot begin to fathom. When we reach our destination I shall see the boughs of the great tree, Yggdrasil, towering over the North Pole, and we shall enter the gates of Hunaland as heroes!"

Becky was alone at the rear of the craft, where the seats had been hastily removed to accommodate her. She was afraid, and lonely, and when her elbows and toes bumped the walls of the cab she drew back, panicking at the feeling of being trapped in the metal box. She had no real sense of the scale of the task she was about to undertake. She had no real notion of what it might be like to endure confinement for many long, uncomfortable hours, passing through the clouds toward the North Pole, because she had never done anything remotely like it before. She'd never even flown in an airplane. Becky had faith in Jardaine's promises, because the enormity of the monk's lie was beyond anything Becky had ever heard before.

She gulped anxious breaths as the air pressure changed

around her, and thought about Matt. Was he safe? Certainly, if Tuava-Li and Tomtar meant to sacrifice her brother to the Elfin gods, they'd make sure he was kept from harm until the moment when they would . . . what? Stab him, cut him apart, like she'd read in a book about the ancient Mayans or Aztec priests? Chop off his head, like the Iraqis did to that newspaper reporter she'd heard about on television? Or would it be some kind of horrible magick that would paralyze his heart or stop him from breathing? Becky wished her friend Asra was there to console her, to give her hope. She let out a single, choked sob. With trembling fists, she banged helplessly on the sides of the cab. She gasped and cried again.

A moment later she caught a glimpse of Jardaine making her way along the cabin wall. "Where were you, Astrid?" Becky cried. "You said that when we got off the ground, you'd tell me what you'd learned about Princess Asra!"

Jardaine could see the fear in the child's eyes. "Dear one, I know 'tis hard to lie here like this. Just try to remember that you're doing a good thing, a heroic thing, and you are very grown-up, very grown-up indeed to make this sacrifice for your brother. Now you must calm yourself. You can breathe, you can! Repeat these words: I am strong, I am capable, I choose the path of truth. Can you say them with me?"

Becky said the words, as her fingers and toes tingled and beads of sweat ran down her forehead and into her tangled hair. "I am strong, I am capable, I choose the path of truth."

"There, there," Jardaine said. "Whenever you feel small and afraid, say those words to yourself, and they will protect you and make you strong. Will you remember? Nothing happens in this life unless 'tis first a dream. You must picture your brother, your mother and father, your younger sister, in some safe place, some happy place, where you are all together. You must visualize things the way you want them to be, before you can begin the work of making your dream come true. Do you understand?"

Becky squeezed her eyes shut and nodded. Somehow she felt a surge of hope. "In the name of the Mother and her Cord, may all be well," Becky said.

Jardaine raised her brow in surprise. "Now where did you learn an expression like that?"

"From my best friend, Princess Asra. Please tell me what you found out about her!"

Jardaine gave Becky a kindly smile. The girl's trust in her was built on a fabric of lies, and Jardaine had to be certain that every string was carefully woven. There must be no holes, no gaps for the truth to show through. Until last night, she hadn't given much thought as to how Becky had arrived at Helfratheim. She assumed that the girl was just one of those brought in Brahja-Chi's Acquisition. Now, though, it all made sense. The girl must have come with Asra and Macta. She must have been taken from her companions and thrown into the cage with the other Human children before Asra and Macta

43

entered the palace. But why would Asra, who hated Macta, have appeared at the palace with him in the first place? Why were they working together? What had they been planning? Jardaine knew the girl would reveal as much as she knew. "Your Princess is safe, child," she lied. "I didn't see her, but the leader of the Council of Seven informed me that she's well and planning her return to Ljosalfar."

"But she's not welcome there," Becky said. "I should have tried to find her last night. I should have let her know I was all right—she's probably worried about me. Maybe she could have come along with us! I know she would have wanted to help Matt, too."

Jardaine nodded. "I asked the Council to let Asra know you were all right and to tell her that you still had important business to take care of. There would have been no room in the Arvada for any more passengers, my child. 'Tis for the best that the Princess stayed behind. No doubt you'll see her again upon our return from the Pole!" Jardaine squeezed Becky's hand. Her own hand was doll-sized, able to grip no more than two of Becky's fingers. Still she gave a reassuring squeeze, suppressing her disgust at such intimacy with a Human. "Did you and Asra travel together to Helfratheim?"

"Yes," Becky said, "we came together." She tried to sit up a little. When her head banged the inside roof of the cab, the massive Air Sprite let out a grunt of disapproval. Becky flinched.

"Don't mind that," Jardaine said. "The creature can't hurt us. Go on! Tell me what happened!"

Becky lay back again and turned her head to Jardaine. "We came with Prince—I mean, King Macta. He's in love with her, you know, but he's kind of crazy. When he came to us in the woods his arm was, well, it was nearly torn off. Asra had to cut away what was left of it, so that the infection wouldn't spread and kill him. She saved his life, so that we could get to Helfratheim and . . ." Becky was suddenly overcome with images of the pen full of children that had been trapped in the courtyard. "Astrid, what did you do to stop the sacrifice?"

Jardaine shook her head impatiently. "We'd been working behind the scenes for quite some time to put a stop to it, Rebecca. But what about Macta? What was he—"

There was a blinding flash of light, and the cab jerked. Becky and Jardaine felt a blast of heat through the brass walls. There was a smell of singed hair; Becky's fingers flew to her head. Her eyes were wide with fear. "What's happening?"

There was another powerful jerk, and Jardaine lost her footing and tumbled to the floor. She grabbed Becky's leg and held on as storage bins, bundles of rope, and emergency gear tumbled into the corner. Amid their own screams, they could hear shouts of anger and surprise coming from the control room up ahead. The giant Sprite roared. It turned in the air, and for a moment Becky and Jardaine could see what was happening through the portal windows. There was another Air

Sprite, another Arvada—no, two Arvada—approaching from the south. The Sprites were not easy to see; they were gigantic, yet translucent, and the clouds in the sky were visible through their pale hides. The brass cabs beneath the Sprites gleamed in the sun. They were closing in, getting bigger by the second. Suddenly one of the Sprites opened its enormous mouth and a long blast of fire shot out.

Becky saw the ball of flame hurtling toward her. She screamed as the Arvada shuddered, dropped, dodging the fiery ball, then rocketed out of harm's way. Jardaine was crawling back to the control room. "Astrid, don't leave me!" Becky screamed.

The three Arvada were locked in a firefight. The pair of attacking Sprites opened their great maws, ejecting plumes of flame, trying to bring down Becky's Arvada. "Why are they attacking?" Jardaine screamed at the pilots as she pulled herself into the foredeck. Nick, cowering in his seat, turned guiltily away from Jardaine. Abruptly the Sprite shifted again. Jardaine toppled over one of the pilots and practically landed on Nick's lap. She grabbed his ears with both hands, and her enormous eyes burned into his. "Did you kill Prashta, as I commanded? Only the Council of Seven could have ordered Arvada to strike us down. Only Prashta could have given the command!"

"I'm s-sorry, my Mage," Nick stammered. "I swear, I thought they were dead, I thought—"

"So you failed to obey my orders?"

Nick was whimpering. "My Mage, I did as I was told, I swear, I thought they were dead!"

"Weakling!" Jardaine shrieked. She tugged on Nick's ears as the Sprite roared and pitched again, and then her body swung against the window. "Bring the ship down," she yelled. "Bring it down; there's a clearing in the woods ahead, I can see it!"

"But we'll be a sitting target," one of the pilots cried.

A fiery blast shot past the cab, and the Sprite, overhead, roared with pain. "After King Valdis's Arvada was shot down," the pilot shouted, "the Techmagicians worked out ways to toughen the Sprites' hides. But the beasts can't take this kind of heat! On the ground, we'll have no protection at all! We'll be doomed!"

"We're not going to stay in the cab, you idiot," Jardaine yelled. "Take us down, now!"

Dodging another burst of fire, the Air Sprite turned. The cab skimmed the treetops, denting and scraping the metal underbelly, and a moment later it reached the center of the clearing. It hovered there with the damaged cab dangling inches above the ground. The shadows of the two enemy craft swept across the field. Jardaine was the first to open the door and leap onto the matted grass, followed by members of the royal Air Squad. They dragged the ship's long tethers behind them. "Don't tie it down," Jardaine shouted as currents of air

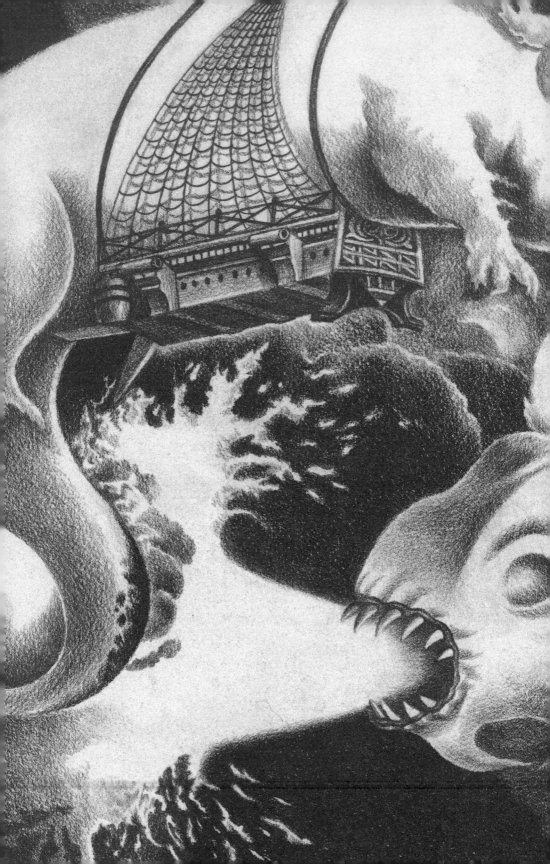

swept around them. "Let the Sprite loose — 'twill fight better without the weight of the cab hanging from its belly!"

"Aye," cried the squad leader, knowing they'd never be able to capture the Sprite again.

One of the beasts in the air turned its head downward and opened its jaws. A gush of flame erupted, reaching all the way to the clearing. The blast tossed Jardaine and the others onto the grass as the column of fire chewed a hole in the earth. Meanwhile the windows of the Arvada cracked and smoked, as Becky shrieked inside. "She'll be burned alive!" Jardaine screamed. "Get her out, now!"

Above the cab the Sprite swung its tail furiously back and forth until the harness stretched across its back snapped and fell away. With a mighty bellow it launched itself into the air, cutting a wide arc around the other two Sprites. It turned its head and belched a river of fire at its attackers. The air crackled with smoke and heat. Flaming cinders, burning chunks of the Sprite's flesh, fell like rain. Crewmembers managed to turn the release bolts on the side of the cab. Becky pushed with all her might. The cab wall flew back and knocked the Elves to the ground. She rolled onto the grass, got to her feet, and scrambled for safety among the trees. Nick cowered beside Jardaine as she stood in the middle of the clearing, gazing skyward. Her robe billowed around her, snapping in the wind. "Come," Nick pleaded. "We must find shelter, before —"

"Hush," Jardaine spat. "Can't you see what I'm doing?"

From the relative safety of her hiding place Becky watched the battle in the sky. Smoke was everywhere, and the swishes of the Sprites' tails, and their monstrous belches of flame, turned the air into a crazed patchwork of flashes and flares. Leaves fell from the trees, shaken loose by the bellows of the great airborne monsters. The ground itself rumbled. Becky watched her new friend Astrid standing in the field, commanding the freed Sprite. The air flashed with light. The freed Air Sprite aimed a gust of fiery breath at one of the enemy craft, and the flames caught hold. The enemy Sprite bellowed in pain, its translucent hide erupting in a sheet of fire. The Arvada sank toward the roof of the forest. The Sprite twitched and coiled as it burned. Becky thought she saw small figures leaping from the red-hot cab, their parachutes burning; they were too high in the air to survive the fall.

Jardaine stood in the grass with her arms extended, her eyes closed. All her strength was concentrated into exerting control over the remaining enemy Arvada. The great Sprite, so full of power and tension in its harness in the air, suddenly seemed to soften. Its turn was almost graceful as it descended toward the clearing. A roar of triumph came from above. The freed airborne Sprite, no longer under Jardaine's influence and no longer facing attack, swished its snakelike tail. It turned in the smoky air and sped away.

When the first of the royal Air Squad of the downed Arvada thrust his head out the door of the cab, Jardaine was ready for him. She had already spoken the words of magick, and it took but a moment for a writhing mass of energy to form in her mind. Then she sent it, like a psychic cannonball, hurtling at her opponent. The Elf fell before he could raise his Dragon Thunderbus. Again and again she fired her psychic burst, until the crew of six lay dead inside their cab. "What's going on, Astrid?" Becky cried. "What happened to the Elves?"

The monk could not answer, for all her energy was spent. She dropped to her knees and fell facedown in the grass. "No," Becky cried, "not you, too!"

She hurried from her hiding place and rushed to Jardaine's side. Nick was already there, turning Jardaine's body so that he could see her face. He slapped her cheeks like she had done to revive him, back in the techmagick labs. "Stop," Jardaine sputtered helplessly. "Stop that!"

"My Mage, I was so worried about you. Are you all right?"

"Of course I'm all right," Jardaine muttered, turning onto her hands and knees. She weaved uncertainly from side to side and Nick hovered over her, afraid she might fall down again. "The Gods have smiled on me and send me good fortune for our journey," Jardaine said. "'Tis just a bit of vertigo that makes me weak."

Jardaine glanced up and saw that Becky was completely stricken. "Don't be afraid, my child. I can see now that only one of those Arvada was trying to attack. This one, here, has come to save us. Isn't that right, Nick?"

The Troll snapped to attention. "Of course, my Mage, of course! The Elves landed their ship here on the grass next to us, so that we might be rescued after our own Arvada crashed. Fortunately the enemy ship was shot down. I don't understand, though, what's become of our rescuers! They lay about as if they're, as if they're —"

"I pray that their hearts have not given out," Jardaine said, getting to her feet. She stood, leaning heavily on Nick, her fingers tense against his arm as she smiled at Becky. "Elfin hearts are not as strong as one might think, you know."

Jardaine called the flight crew from her own ruined Arvada to move the bodies out of sight. Then, while the Air Sprite twitched impatiently, they hauled their provisions into the empty cab and prepared for flight. "If there was ever any doubt as to the importance of our journey," Jardaine announced, "if there was ever the slightest hesitation on our part that we were undertaking a truly historic, nay, more, a blessed pilgrimage, today's events have proven, beyond the shadow of a doubt, the eternal wisdom of this venture to Hunaland. The Gods are truly with us, and from behind their heavenly veil, they look upon us with pride and encouragement. All of you may feel justifiably proud of your contribution to our quest to save the Human boy, Matt, from the wicked Mage Tuava-Li and her accomplice, Tomtar."

At the mention of Tomtar's name, Becky felt a stab of pain in her heart. Despite her hatred of Tuava-Li, she had a soft spot for the Troll with whom she'd spent so many hours playing, laughing, and drinking tea.

The Air Squad turned the massive bolts on the side of the Arvada and opened the hatch so that Becky could enter. "Come, child," Jardaine said. "Here is your place of honor. Be glad to sacrifice your comfort for the sake of the salvation of your brother! 'Twill not be long, now, before we reach our destination."

5

HOURS PASSED UNDERGROUND, maybe days.
There was no way for Matt to tell anymore just how long he,
Tomtar, and Tuava-Li had traveled in the Cord. The only light in
their subterranean passage was a kind of twilit incandescence,
rippling the inside of the tube in a faint, milky glow. Matt's
companions seemed little more to him than black shapes
moving at his side, indistinct smears of darkness in the harsh
Underworld winds. At times Matt would perceive a speck in
the distance, no bigger than a fly or a gnat. He would watch the
shape grow larger and larger, until finally, when it looked like
the blackness was a void about to engulf him, a voice would
cry, *Watch out!*

He'd draw in his shoulders as he ripped past a protruding

branch, or another lonely traveler, or a moldering patch of Cord. *Watch out!*

Matt could no longer tell who, if anyone, was speaking. Nothing seemed real anymore. Maybe it was all nothing more than his imagination, filling in that yawning chasm, that void, which the Cord created in his brain. He was a bird riding on a breeze; he was a fish in a river. He was sheer movement. His head was a bullet, cleaving the air in two. At the same time, the tempest propelled him from behind, sent him careening forward, cocooned in wind, enveloped in air. The sound of it was a relentless throb, steady and insistently monotonous. His awareness had slipped into a featureless haze, and there it hovered. *It must be like this when you're still in the womb,* he thought. *You just float there in an ocean of sounds and light, and nothing's sharp or clear enough to really see, to grab on to. It's like I'm floating in a vat of—what's that called? Amniotic fluid? And I'm waiting to be born. It's like . . .*

Don't drift away. Tuava-Li's words appeared in his mind, more crisp and distinct than anything his senses told him. He wondered if the words were perhaps his own, or if all this was just a dream. He thought he heard someone singing, far away in the murky distance. *I'll take the high road, and you'll take the low road, and I'll reach the North Pole before you. . . .*

"What?" he cried aloud. "Was that you singing, Tomtar?"

"Nooooo, 'twasn't me. I didn't say anything!"

Stay awake. Stay focused. Stay strong.

I'll take the . . .

Matt shut his eyes and saw a black speck. Something was approaching; the speck was growing. He opened his eyes and there was nothing. *Relax,* he said to himself. He closed his eyes again, and the blackness was larger. A thick, oily fog seemed to come at him, ready to soak through his clothes, his skin, his soul. The odor engulfed him; he couldn't breathe.

Stay awake. Stay focused. Stay strong.

Suddenly he was in the back of the family car, and his dad was outside, filling the tank. *Oil.* He was in a classroom, looking out the window as workers poured fresh, steaming tar on the playground. *Oil.* He was riding a bus and the reek of the exhaust made him so sick he fell to his knees on the floor of the bus, and he threw up, and the wall between the worlds started coming down, and a river of blackness shot out of his mouth and filled the bus. *Oil.*

Every thought that arose in his mind was like a seed sprouting in a field of green, a tender new plant basking in the golden sun. Each tender leaf was turning black—withering, rotting. Everything living on this green earth was turning black. *Oil.* Matt's eyes were closed, and yet he saw sky. It was full of roiling clouds, black and heavy, and the rain that fell in great greasy globs was poison. The sky was full of oil; his nostrils burned with the stench of it.

Wake up, Matt! Wake up! You're drifting away! Something's wrong up ahead. We've got to stop! Move to the side, and grab hold of the Cord!

Matt felt his body turning before his brain could register the peril in Tuava-Li's command. He saw his hand reaching, as if in slow motion, for a fistful of the rubbery membrane. Above him the Cord was pale. Below him, darkness. There was a subtle bend in the Cord as it listed downward, and in the distance the blackness was complete. Inky fingers reached up the walls. It looked to Matt like he and his companions were dropping into a great bucket of black paint, but it smelled like a spill at the filling station.

Pain exploded in his jaw. There was a flash of light, and a splatter of black. Tomtar's shoe hit Matt before it sent a shower of pitch across his face. As the Troll caught hold of the Cord and his body swung around, his leg came up drenched. "What is it, Matt?" he hollered.

"Oil, tar, I don't know!" Matt grabbed the Cord and pulled himself backwards, against the wind. He saw himself drowning in the foul black liquid.

Tuava-Li's entire body was pressed into the wall. "Follow me," she ordered.

The three of them crept laboriously toward the roof of the Cord, like they were working their way around the inside of a barrel. With each grip of their hands, their fingers came away black and greasy. The oil in the Cord was seeping up the walls. Tuava-Li extended one stiffened finger and drew a sharp nail along the roof of the passage. Noxious air gushed from the opening. Following the Elf, Matt dragged himself free, clutching Tomtar's sleeve. Cold, fresh air struck them like a blow as they tumbled from the Cord and landed on a bed of gravel, dusted in snow. Matt got to his feet, blinking. He'd lost control of his own senses in the Cord, and because of it, he'd nearly lost his life. He was too shaken up to speak.

The exposed length of Cord was a swollen hump, no bigger than a car. The torn flap fluttered in a field of white. Where the snow ended a black plain rolled out, extending all the way to the horizon. "Is that the ocean?" Matt cried into the wind.

The sky was a leaden slab. In the distance he thought he saw a trio of old-fashioned sailing vessels, with sails and masts like the *Niña*, *Pinta*, and *Santa María*, the ships he'd seen in pictures in school. He felt like he'd slipped back in time five hundred years. There was something primal, something fierce and uncivilized about this place. Then he realized that what he thought were masts were in fact cranes and derricks, and the ships were actually metal platforms, rising up out of the water on immense steel legs. Matt squinted into the wind and saw that the metal was rusted and bent, that the oil platforms had been abandoned to the elements.

Tomtar stumbled over the rocks and stood next to his friend. His trousers, blackened with oil, clung to his legs. There was litter strewn on the ground, washed up from the ocean: plastic bottles, rope, rusted cans. "What are those things out there, Matt?" he asked, pointing and shielding his eyes from the harsh, dry snow that fell like cinders. His jacket billowed in the wind as he hugged himself to stay warm.

"I think they're oil derricks, Tomtar."

"What?"

Matt struggled past the dizziness and nausea to find a way to explain it. "They're like, factories, Tomtar, they're portable factories, on the surface of the water. Corporations, companies, they set them up to drill underwater and look for oil. If they find it, they pump it up and fill ships with it, and haul it back to civilization. They use it to fuel cars and trucks, and burn it to heat houses in the winter."

"I don't see any Humans out there," Tomtar said.

Matt shook his head. "I don't, either. There aren't any people, or ships, or anything. Maybe they already got all the oil they could, and they left the rigs behind. It makes me wonder if their drills, out there, punctured the Cord we were traveling in. Maybe that's why the Cord was filled with oil."

Tomtar blew into his hands. "We're just lucky we got out in time!"

"You call this lucky?"

"Well, we didn't drown."

Matt squinted into the sky, then looked at his friend and shrugged. "We didn't drown, but this is a dead end. We're probably still a long way from the North Pole. What are we going to do now?"

"I could play my flute a little," Tomtar said, drawing his wooden instrument from the corner of his pack. "That always cheers me up!" He lifted the rod to his lips and began to blow.

The sound was thin, and the notes wavered and fell away in the wind.

"I don't know, Tomtar," Matt said. "Maybe you ought to save your energy. We might be needing it."

"How do you know this isn't the North Pole, Matthew?" Tuava-Li asked, stepping up from behind. She'd been trying to smooth over the rip in the surface of the Cord. Her hands were wet and sticky with oil, and she held them awkwardly at her sides.

"Well, just look," Matt said, pointing. "Too much water. I can see chunks of ice out there, bobbing in the waves, but we've still got to be pretty far from where we want to go. I know there's global warming, and all, but the North Pole is at the top of the Arctic Ocean, which has been covered in a mile of ice for thousands of years. When we're near it, we should be able to walk there. Though we'd freeze to death, first."

Tomtar's breath was a silent gust of vapor. "I don't want to freeze to death," he whispered. He clutched the flute tightly in his chapped hands as doubt crept over him. "What if the Goddess abandoned us, like the Humans abandoned their machines? We can't survive out here! The Cord is ruined, and we can't travel over ground like this!"

"The Goddess will never abandon us, Tomtar," Tuava-Li said consolingly.

Matt stared down at the Elf. "Do you think there's another Cord around here that's moving back in the direction we came?

We could head back for a while, find some kind of tributary, or something to take us north again. We can't stay here. Maybe we should split up to look for a Cord. There has to be another, doesn't there? Somewhere?"

"Let us see your tattoos, Matthew," Tuava-Li said. "Perhaps they've changed again and can give us some guidance."

Matt's cheeks reddened. "It's freezing out here, Tuava-Li. I can't take off my shirt. Why do the gods always have to communicate with hidden clues and symbols and things you have to interpret, anyway? If they're so all-powerful, why don't they just shout down from the heavens and say what they've got to say?"

"'Tis not up to us to understand the ways of the Gods," said Tuava-Li. "They speak to us with every breath we take, though, if we but know how to listen. 'Tis our duty to hear, and obey. Now, may we see your tattoos?"

Matt let out an exasperated sigh and yanked up his shirt. "There," he said. "Make it quick, okay?"

Tomtar and Tuava-Li drew close and studied Matt's chest as he shivered before them. "The children are gone," said Tuava-Li. "But I don't know how to interpret this. Tomtar?"

The Troll shook his head. "I've never seen anything like that before. Is it a bear?"

Matt looked down and tried to make sense of the round, smooth shape with the two black spots for eyes. Behind the creature there were flashes of green in a black field. "Well, I hope we don't run into one of these, because I've never seen one in my whole life. I think we're on our own, this time. Tuava-Li, can you change into a hawk when it's this cold outside?"

"Of course I can," she replied. "'Twill be hard to stay airborne when there are no thermals to keep me aloft, but if it pleases you, Matthew, I can look over these hills and see if there's any sign of another Cord."

"It pleases me," Matt said.

Tuava-Li quickly shed her clothing and began her transformation. Facing away from the wind, she quickly sprouted a coat of brown and white feathers, lifted her kestrel wings, and flapped into the air. Matt and Tomtar watched her work her way across the snow-flecked sky. High overhead she made a slow arc, peering down with her fierce kestrel gaze, surveying the harsh landscape. "What do you think, Matt?" Tomtar asked.

"Well, I can tell what *you* think," Matt said, looking at the anguish on his friend's face. "I'm worried, too. I have a bad feeling that coming here was a mistake—a really bad one. We need food, clothing, and shelter just to survive up here, and if we don't get out of this weather, we'll freeze. I thought that Cord would take us all the way to the city at the North Pole. I guess I was wrong, as usual. Back in Pittsburgh, the jewels we're carrying were worth so much that people would kill for them, but up here, they're not worth a dime. Before long we'll be wishing we could trade them all for a hole in the ground or an animal skin to curl up in."

Matt glanced around. Where the rocks peeked out of the

snow, red and green lichen spread like spattered paint. Tufts of tough grass climbed out of thin drifts, curling like fingers in the wind. A few bare trees dotted the far horizon. "It's late September. This must be the first snow of the season up here, otherwise all the grass would be dead."

He bent and stroked one of the clumps of grass, and as he stood up he caught movement out of the corner of his eye. "There's something down there, Tomtar, look! Do you see what I see?"

Tomtar got to his knees to peer at the ground, where grassy knots crept from rocky crevices. Matt said, "There's mice under there—little mice, hiding under the rocks and plants!"

Hundreds of rodents were barely concealed in the fissures and clefts, partially blanketed by snow. "Wait a minute," Matt said. "They're not mice, they're lemmings, they have to be! They live in the north. They'll be hibernating soon. Maybe we're closer to the North Pole than I thought!"

"Are you going to eat them?" Tomtar asked, only half joking. "I don't imagine that's what we saw in your tattoos."

"I thought we were alone out here," Matt said. "It's weird how life adapts."

"Do you think they bite, Matt?"

"Lemmings are crazy, Tomtar. Did you ever hear what they do? They go nuts and stampede over the edge of cliffs, and wham, no more lemmings!"

Overhead Tuava-Li was circling back, flapping hard against

the wind. She spread her wings and swept behind a rocky outcropping, where she could change back to her Elfin form in private. Tomtar hurried to lay her clothing at her feet as her beak and claws drew back into her skin, and the feathers lightened and then dissolved. "Well?" Matt asked as she stepped into view. "What did you see?"

"I thought it was Faerie Folk, at first," Tuava-Li said, gasping for air. "Then I realized it was children. Human children, Matthew, five of them—like the ones that were in your tattoo. They're approaching the ridge now, and if they keep moving, they'll be here in a few minutes."

"If there are children," Tomtar said excitedly, "they must have homes nearby. There must be a town, with some place for us to get warm, and eat, and plan what we're going to do next!"

"Aye," said the Elf. "There's a kind of village about a mile from here. Matthew, you'll have to convince the Humans to take you back with them. We need to find shelter."

Tomtar was practically jumping up and down. "We don't want Humans to see us! Should we chew some *Trans* to make us invisible, just in case? I've got them in my *Huldu*."

"Find them," Tuava-Li said.

Tomtar's hands were shaking with cold and excitement as he rooted around in his pack. When he pulled out the *Huldu*, all the little wooden chips that were infused with Faerie spells fell from the open sack. Tomtar tried to grab a fistful as they scattered on the frozen ground. "Oooh, now look what I've done!"

Tuava-Li and Matt bent to pick up the chips before the wind carried them all away, but their fingers were stiff and numb. "Too late to find the right ones now," Tuava-Li said. "Just stay behind Matt, and we'll hope for the best."

"Nowhere to run, nowhere to hide," Matt said with a shrug. "Guess I'm about to make some new friends!"

Over the ridge, crossing the bleached horizon, five dusky figures came into view.

6

Asra and Macta were no strangers to darkness. They had followed Becky through the subterranean tunnels of an abandoned coal mine, where even their sensitive Elfin eyes were ill equipped for the depths of gloom. It was not darkness that made their crawl through the sewers of Helfratheim so terrible; the thing that made the slimy brick passage beneath the palace so unutterably loathsome was the smell. Even when they perceived a glimmer of light at the end of the tunnel, it was the dank, appalling odor of putrefaction that overwhelmed them. Macta recognized the smell as the rotting waste of the slaughterhouse where meat for the palace was processed.

When they heaved aside the grate over the drain and climbed into the empty chamber, Asra and Macta were both dripping wet and reeking of gore. Wordlessly Macta led Asra from the slaughterhouse. As they crept into the courtyard, they heard a scurrying sound around the corner of the building. "Stop," Macta hissed, holding his one good arm in front of Asra.

"What is it?"

There was a growl, and a whimper, and something small slunk from one shadowed corner to another. Then a pack of Goblins raced into the clearing, their fangs bared, their muzzles curled in warning. Their eyes, sharp with cunning, darted from the shadows to Macta and then back again. Their nostrils sniffed the air; no doubt they smelled the odor of rot on the two Elves. "They think we're their next meal," Macta whispered.

The ribs of the Goblins protruded from their furry hides; their lean muscles tensed as they waited to see what the Elf was going to do. One false move and the creatures would attack. "I've seen these creatures," Macta murmured. "They're wild. They live outside the fortress, eating the refuse the townspeople toss over the walls. With all the chaos in this place they must have gotten inside. They're starving. Look, what's that?"

A small Goblin, no more than a pup, limped out of the shadows and headed a little too slowly toward the shelter of the slaughterhouse door. The pack growled, lunged after the pup, and Asra cried in horror. "They've been hunting it! They're going to rip it to pieces!"

"AAAAARRRGH!" Macta screamed at the top of his lungs. Wild-eyed, he sprinted across the courtyard. The pack of Goblins reared back in surprise and alarm as the pup scurried past Asra's legs and raced into the slaughterhouse. They backed away, turned tail, and ran. Macta followed the retreating pack until he came to a corner with a view of the palace, where he stood just out of sight and watched them disappear. Then he hurried back to Asra's side. "Where's the pup?"

"It ran in there. Don't go back inside, Macta, I beg of you, 'tis revolting."

Macta entered the building. "Here, boy," he said in a soothing voice, peering into every corner of the slaughterhouse, "come here!"

Outside, Asra was getting nervous. If anyone had heard Macta's scream, the two of them might well be in danger. It was imperative to get out of the open as soon as possible. Macta came to the doorway with the little Goblin cradled in the crook of his arm. The ugly, misshapen creature was slurping the slaughterhouse blood from his cheek, and Macta giggled in delight. "You saved the beast," Asra said, "isn't that enough? Put it down, Macta, and get me to the palace. If I don't get this gore off me soon I'll go mad."

"He's coming with us," Macta said. "He reminds me of my old Goblin, Powcca. I'm going to keep him."

Asra sighed in exasperation. "Whatever you want, Macta; please, let's just get out of here!"

Stealthily they hurried from the slaughterhouse to the palace kitchen, sneaking around corners and slipping through

doorways, avoiding the eyes and ears of any of the guards that remained on duty. They headed to Macta's private apartments, which he hadn't visited since the fall of Alfheim. "Quiet, boy," he whispered to the Goblin pup, as it whimpered in his grasp. "Just a while longer now."

Macta flung open the door and gazed around. Sunlight spilled through stained-glass windows; the room was calm and quiet. He was glad to be home again, though his memories of the place gave him a stab of melancholy. He put the pup down on the carpet and it limped beneath the nearest settee. "Make yourself at home, boy," he said, then turned to Asra with a smile. "I'll lock the door, so that we're not disturbed, then I shall run you a bath!"

When the tub was full Macta left the Princess alone to scrub away the filth of their journey through the sewer. He found something for her to wear—a plain dress that had belonged to one of his servants, Herma or Holda. He stood next to his bed and considered how many of the truly important figures in his life were dead. Powcca, of course, was gone. His father, his servants, his friends and relatives, and several of his enemies, as well . . . gone. He felt lucky to still be alive, and he felt positively blessed to have Princess Asra in the next room. *What are the chances of that?* he said to himself. *A hundred to one? Five hundred to one? After all that's happened, she's still with me. If I believed in the Gods, I'd say that they're smiling on me. But all I believe in is luck . . . and love, of course.*

 # Macta and Powcca

Macta went to coax the Goblin pup from under the settee, and found that the creature had discovered an old chew toy that had belonged to Powcca. The pup gnawed furiously on the leather knot, growling contentedly. "Good boy," Macta cooed, "good boy, you're all right, you're all right!"

When it was Macta's turn to fill the tub, Asra waited quietly in the sitting room, lost in her own thoughts. She had longed for adventure, she'd longed to be more than just a Princess, with no responsibilities. Now she longed for peace and normalcy. *'Tis odd how things work out,* she thought.

Macta was quick to scrub away the grime of his long journey. When he was finished he dried himself with a fresh towel, pulled on some clean trousers, and brushed his hair. He applied powder as best as he could manage with only one arm, shaved the wispy hair from his chin, and spent a few minutes before the mirror examining the dreadful wound at his shoulder. His flesh was still swollen and inflamed, though the healing process had finally begun. After a brief search he found some strips of cloth in a basket near the oaken tub. He tried unsuccessfully to tie a bandage around his shoulder, hoping to cover the wound so that it would not be injured anew. Frustrated, he called to Asra. "There's something I have to ask you, Princess. Could you help me with my bandage? I know it must repulse you to see me this way, but I cannot do it by myself."

Asra sighed as she came around the corner. "Give me the cloth, Macta, I'll do it."

She gave the wound a gentle prod with the tip of her finger. "Does that still hurt?"

"Your touch brings me nothing but the most exquisite pleasure," he said through gritted teeth.

"Liar," Asra said. "As King, you must have a personal physik. You should see him as soon as possible. After all that filth we had to crawl through, we'll probably both be deathly ill from infection."

Macta shook his head. "All that business about the curse of Blood and contamination is just superstitious nonsense. The Mages who spread that drivel are living in the dark ages. Aye, we got dirty, but it means nothing. We're clean now!"

Asra wrapped the dressing around Macta's shoulder and gave the end of it a tug.

"Perhaps I could convince you to stay in Helfratheim," Macta said, wincing, "just to keep an eye on me and make sure I don't get into any more trouble."

"You'd like that, wouldn't you?" Asra said, as she knotted the end of the bandage and stood back. "Dream on, mighty King. I want you to find out what's become of my friend Becky, now that Brahja-Chi's game is finished. I want you to see to it that an Arvada's prepared to take Becky and me back to Ljosalfar. I have no intention of remaining here any longer than necessary."

"I needn't remind you that I came within a hairbreadth of giving my life for you," Macta said.

"Nooo, you needn't remind me, Macta. My gratefulness for

your generosity is exceeded only by my profound boredom in your company. Can we go now, and find your Council of Seven?"

Macta had pulled on a clean shirt from his wardrobe, but discovered that he could not button it with only one hand. "Please," he said, "the buttons?"

Asra sighed and set to work. "Couldn't you have found something that was easier to put on?"

Macta gave a shrug but said nothing. Asra was surprised to discover, as her fingertips brushed his chest, that she no longer felt the same revulsion she'd once had for Macta. She realized it was her resolve to not accept any more of his bad behavior that gave her strength and allowed her to remain affable in his company.

"There's something I want to say to you," Macta murmured, as the Princess fastened the final button at his collar.

Asra shook her head. "I won't be your servant, and I won't be your friend. I know what you profess to feel for me, but that's only an illusion, Macta. You never *loved* me. You don't know what love is. You're fixated on an image that has nothing to do with me. You're addicted to your unfulfilled desire, your longing, and that's all. You're a romantic fool, I can see that now. Perhaps you're not evil, as I thought you were. You're careless and insensitive, and you're a smug, egomaniacal bully, but you're just an Elf, in the end—a confused, wretched mess of an Elf. You think you know me, Macta, but you don't. And you never will. Aye, you saved my life. But I saved yours, too. So why don't we just call it even, and go our separate ways?"

Macta grabbed Asra's hand and stared into her eyes. "My heart has always belonged to you, to do with as you will. If you choose to toss it into the fire, or abandon it by the side of the road, my love remains undiminished. You wound me, though, when you say you know more about my feelings than I do. You have no real conception of my feelings, because it's plain that you don't share them."

Asra pulled her hand away and stepped back. "Enough! Come now, let's pay a visit to your Council. I won't rest until I know Becky's safe."

"I don't dare leave the Goblin here alone," Macta said, getting down on his knees and stroking the little creature's fur as it lurked beneath the settee. "Help me tempt him out, won't you? I'll take him with us. 'Tis the only way."

Prashta and the other Council members were gathered in their chambers when the guards stepped aside so that Macta, holding the little Goblin close, and Princess Asra could enter. Black-robed and hunched, the Council clustered in a circle, like crows absorbed in their own frantic pecking. "All hail King Macta," the guards shouted, and the Council members jumped in alarm.

Prashta bowed and put on an oily smile. "My King, we were unsure of your whereabouts, after Jal-Maktar dispatched you and the lady to—well, we weren't sure where you were! 'Tis such an enormous relief to know that you're alive and well! We've been discussing an important matter of state, but that conversation can wait, now that you've arrived! What, pray tell, are you holding?"

"I'm calling him Powcca," Macta said, lifting his chin imperiously, "in honor of my old Goblin. Asra and I, as you can see, are both well; but that fiend Jal-Maktar is gone for good. I have dispatched him to the netherworld from whence he came. Do not mention his name in my presence again!"

Macta slipped into a seat and sighed. "I have returned, Prashta, and I'm in command. Now what is this matter of state you mention? Are you so helpless in my absence that already my kingdom is in jeopardy from new enemies?"

The Council members exchanged furtive glances. They had not expected to see Macta alive again, and each had secretly been relishing the sweetness of supreme authority. With no King or living heir, all power in Helfratheim would have gone to the Council. Now that Macta was back, however, their role would revert to the mundane task of carrying out the King's commands. The suddenness of their loss of status made them sag as they stood, disheartened, before their Master.

"Allow me to explain," said Lehtinen, Director of Operations. "A major problem has developed in relation to the new Mage, Jardaine. I believe you know her well!"

"Aye, I count Jardaine the vilest of my enemies," Macta said, nuzzling the Goblin with his chin, "for she was once my ally. Her crimes are too many and too foul to mention. What has she done now?"

"Jardaine has done her best to ruin us," Lehtinen said. "You have no idea how close she's come to succeeding. She set fire to the techmagick labs. The building complex is completely gutted! Ongoing experiments in biogenetics, plasmatology, and psychotometrics are lost. Weapon development has been set back, irrevocably. Records have been damaged, prototypes destroyed!"

"Jardaine nearly killed me, and my wife, as well," Prashta said. "She forced me to sign papers providing her with one of our Arvada, along with its crew, maps, and supplies. If not for the incompetence of that Troll who follows her everywhere, I wouldn't be speaking to you now."

"Once I was informed of Jardaine's traitorous actions," Lehtinen said, "I authorized a pair of Arvada to overtake her on her way to the North Pole and bring her down. The Arvada have not yet returned, however, and we fear for their safety."

Macta shook his head. "The North Pole?"

"That's where Tuava-Li's headed," Asra said, "with Tomtar and Becky's brother. Jardaine must be following them! What's she trying to do?"

"Jardaine is a menace," Macta said. "In all the world there's no greater threat to my authority. She must be stopped. Send more Arvada after her, and when she's captured, bring me her head. Tell me the names of her allies in these villainous acts!"

"Sire, she traveled with a Troll called Nick and a Human female," Lehtinen said. "The guards told us that she's the child who accompanied you and the Princess on the night of your arrival in Helfratheim."

"What?" Asra cried. "It can't be. Why would Becky go with Jardaine? It makes no sense!"

"Macta, there's no way to stop Jardaine," Prashta said, his jowls shaking. "The rest of the fleet of Arvada was sold to our allies on the promise that they would be used to help us fight a war with the Humans. Since the labs have been burned, we can't prepare any more Air Sprites for flight. We're completely helpless!"

Macta's face darkened. "No Arvada? None? You gave them all away? Without my authority?"

Lehtinen's eyes darted back and forth between the King and the Princess. "Sire, forgive us, but we did not know if you were alive or dead. You have to understand the debt we incurred, preparing for battle with the Humans; it was astronomical. Promises were made, deals undertaken, that had to—"

"What about Becky?" Asra asked. "Did it appear that she left of her own free will to travel with Jardaine?"

"As far as can be discerned," Prashta said, anxious to avoid further discussion of the loss of Arvada, "Jardaine and her fellow traitors are trying to beat another group of three, who hope to reach the North Pole and acquire the magick Seed from the mythical tree that grows there. We assume they believe this will cure the ills of the Cord, according to legend."

Macta snorted. "Hogwash!"

"We must stop them," Asra said. "Becky's in danger. I don't know what Jardaine said to her, what she promised her, but she would never have gotten into the back of one of those things again, I know it. Not unless she was forced. Macta, please, you've got to do something!"

Macta smoldered. His fury with both Jardaine and his Council engulfed him, overshadowing his delight that Asra was begging for his help. It took a supreme effort of will to calm himself enough to formulate a strategy. "Prashta," he asked, "how long will it take to get back one of our Arvada? I'll gladly authorize the purchase, just so I can personally go after Jardaine and bring her to justice. 'Tis not enough that the witch must die—she must die by my own hand. She's the one who's responsible for the loss of my arm, the burning of Alfheim, my father's and Brahja-Chi's deaths, and the near ruin of my own kingdom. I despise her, *I loathe her,* and I shall not rest until my blade tastes her Blood. If she thinks she can escape my wrath, she's sadly mistaken!"

"I shall send messages right away," Prashta said, "to the effect that the King of Helfratheim wishes to purchase an Arvada, as soon as possible. I'm sure we can have you airborne in just a matter of days, my lord!"

"Days?" Asra cried. "That's far too long!"

"Make it sooner," Macta said. "My fiancée appears to be the only one here who understands the urgency of this situation."

"I'm not your fiancée," Asra said. "But if you're going to

stop Jardaine, then I'm coming along, to make sure that nothing happens to Becky."

"Indeed," said Macta, his eyes wide at the prospect of his great good fortune. He had always thought that he was at his absolute best when on some sort of mission. Now Asra would be at his side to witness his discipline, his valor, and his victory. Jardaine would die by his hand. And with any luck, when this was all over, Asra, sweet, sweet Asra, would finally be *his*. The Goblin pup squirmed against Macta's shoulder, so he knelt and let the creature down onto the floor. It limped over to the nearest piece of furniture and lifted a hind leg. "Bad boy," Macta said, as a yellow puddle grew beneath the feet of the new Powcca. "Bad, bad boy!"

7

DO YOU KNOW THE HISTORY of the Arvada?" asked the captain, attempting to make small talk with Jardaine, as they sat in the steering deck and sailed high above the Canadian forests. He'd realized that it might be to his advantage to have the Mage on his side, after all. He was uncertain as to the extent of her powers and did not want to be on the receiving end of her wrath. He was well aware that Jardaine must have done something dreadful back in Helfratheim; otherwise, the only two Arvada left in their kingdom would never have been sent to find them and launch an attack. He had witnessed the life go out of the original Arvada crew like snuffed candles, and Jardaine, with her witch's powers, had to have been responsible. It would be best to give the impression of being open and friendly, as long as he was careful.

A pair of Aeronauts sat next to the captain in plush window seats, surveying the passing landscape. Adepts at psychic messaging, they sent coordinates to the trio of Telekeneticists, who were settled on a carpet at the center of the deck. Together they directed their commands to the mind of the Air Sprite, which modified its weaving path through the sky.

Jardaine was hunched in her seat. She was studying a large parchment map, spread like a blanket over her lap. When she shrugged distractedly at the captain's question, he took it as an invitation to continue. "The Arvada, you know, was an invention of the Techmagicians of Helfratheim. As such, it combines advanced technology with elements of ancient magick. The first step in the process is to capture and breed a pair of common Air Sprites. The offspring are genetically modified in the lab so that the natural limits of growth are extended a thousandfold. They grow quickly from tiny creatures to beasts of truly immense proportions."

"Fascinating," said Nick, gazing first at the captain and then at his Master.

The captain, too, looked for a response from Jardaine, but she had not yet warmed to his pleasantries. "Examined in spectral light," he continued, "the Sprite, which is naturally translucent, resembles a kind of slug or primitive newt. Because of its molecular substance, it's lighter than air. The rudimentary nervous system of the creature allows for easy motor manipulation by Elfin Telekeneticists. These are Aeronauts, specially trained in Etheric Perception, as well as the magickal art of guiding external matter with internal commands. This is the training I've undergone, by the way."

Jardaine glanced up. "Indeed," she said curtly, then returned her gaze to the map.

The captain smiled, pleased to have elicited a response.

"How did you know what the giant Sprites would be good for?" asked Nick.

"Ah," the captain replied, "weapons technology, like all warfare planning, is a kind of game. 'Tis all about planning ahead, preparing for contingencies. We grew the Sprites to a suitable proportion to haul brass cabs through the air. We built the cabs large enough to accommodate a dozen Elves, to be carried by the Sprites over long distances. We figured the Sprites could transport equipment more efficiently than moving it over ground, or in gondolas that traveled in the Cord. Sprites could be used to drop explosive charges from high altitudes. But then, when the Techmagicians spliced in genetic material from Fire Sprites, the offspring acquired the ability to breathe fire. Each Sprite is now a formidable weapon. You've already seen a demonstration of that, I'm afraid!"

Nick glanced at Jardaine, still busily studying the map, and sensed that something was wrong. Whatever was making her agitated, it might be best to ignore it, for now, and perhaps her mood would pass. "Where does the name *Arvada* come from?" he asked the captain, glancing nervously back and forth between the two of them.

"In one of the ancient Elfin tongues, *Arvada* meant 'eagle.' To Macta's father, King Valdis, Arvada seemed a fitting name for a craft that was swift, stealthy, deadly, and when seen from below, quite majestic in appearance. It's beautiful, don't you think?"

"Aye," Nick said, swallowing, and glancing again at Jardaine. Her brow was furrowed, her fierce attention directed at the map.

"This is madness," Jardaine spat, leaping from her seat and tossing aside the map.

The captain sat back, wide-eyed. Nick stiffened, waiting for the explosion of rage that was Jardaine's trademark. She glared through the bow window at the expanse of undifferentiated forest that spread in the shadow of the mighty craft. Then she kicked the map. "I can't make any sense of it. How do you navigate with garbage like this? These maps of yours must have been drawn before any of these trees were saplings."

"You must be still," one of the Aeronauts said, his voice distracted and dream-heavy. "The Sprite is meandering westward, and we must correct its course, or risk losing time. Captain, your attention?"

Jardaine spun her head around and glared at the Aeronauts. Too late, Nick realized that Jardaine saw him staring at her. "What are you looking at?" she hissed.

Nick cleared his throat. It was terrifying when Jardaine directed her anger at him. "Nothing, my Mage," he said. He stared dumbly at the images imprinted on the brass walls of the cab. There were figures there, birds, insects and mythical flying things, dragons, and hippogriffs, as well as Pixies with delicate wings and beautiful, smiling faces. Intricately woven in a decorative pattern, the flying creatures filled the pictorial air with motion, frozen in time. Nick felt a stab of longing for his own Pixie friends. In a moment of pride, selfishness, and ambition, he had left them behind. Now he wondered if it had been the right decision.

"Well?" Jardaine said darkly.

"I—I was *admiring* you, my Mage," Nick replied, flustered. He dared to look up for a moment and found that she was still glaring at him. "I've observed that even when your . . . your uncertainty about a subject is exposed, you still manage to convey authority!"

Nick was not lying; he did truly admire Jardaine's confidence. He could only wish that he believed in himself with just a fraction of the self-assurance Jardaine possessed. "Say what you mean," Jardaine ordered. "You dance around an answer like a foolish child."

"What I mean is," Nick said haltingly, "if I didn't know how to read the maps, I'd be afraid to say anything, for fear of making a fool of myself. But you, my Mage—"

Jardaine was half out of her seat. "You're saying I don't know how to read maps? You're calling me a fool?"

Nick blanched. "No, my Mage, that's not it at all. It's just that—"

"There," interrupted the captain, swiveling his chair around.

He rubbed his eyes; it took time to readjust to normal conversation as he withdrew from communal-mind navigation. "The course correction is complete. Am I to understand that you wish to learn something of the Aeronaut's art, Jardaine? 'Tis a discipline few are equipped to master, but if you're willing to try—"

"I want to know how *you* navigate," Jardaine grumbled. "I'm not sure I can trust you to take me where I command, when these maps reveal nothing of our progress."

"Well," said the captain, "we navigate by the passage of the sun through the sky, by the stars at night, by the landmarks we pinpoint on maps like the one there in your hand, by compass and sexton, and by intuition. Our training makes us specialists in many exalted arts. There is no single method by which we determine the proper course, but we make our way. Such are the skills of the Aeronaut."

Jardaine struggled to contain her fury. The captain was speaking far too casually with her, as he might to someone of his own station. He made no attempt to show the proper respect. She thought he ought to realize what it meant to speak to a Mage, one of the most important and powerful figures in all the land, and yet he did not. "Then you claim to have magickal skills," she said. "Perhaps you think that your gifts are like those of a Mage," she said. "But did you see how I controlled the actions of the Sprites that attacked us? The force of my will brought the Arvada down, killed its crew, and allowed us to sail freely again. Can you honestly say your skills compare with mine?"

"I didn't realize this was a contest," the captain said, pride overshadowing his caution. "All Aeronauts are experts at a high level of Etheric Perception, even those who are our enemies. Those pilots from Helfratheim who followed us, for instance, sensed our heartbeats, even at some distance. They felt the tension in our hurry to depart, not to mention the heat generated by our Air Sprite. They knew our location long before our cab was visible in the sky. We felt their approach, though we didn't sense the danger immediately. Do you wonder why?"

Jardaine lifted an eyebrow.

"We didn't sense the danger," he said, "because you gave us no reason to believe we had anything to fear from anyone, Jardaine. 'Twas your secrecy that almost cost us our lives. And as for your great powers, I can't help but wonder, if you can so readily control the behavior of an Air Sprite, why didn't you stop the attackers in midair? Surely you didn't mean to put all our lives at risk . . . did you?"

Jardaine stiffened with rage. She leaned into the captain's face, her eyes like coals. "How dare you question me? I'm your Mage, don't forget, and your life is in my hands! I've had enough of your casual familiarity. When you address me, don't call me by my given name. I am *my Mage*, or *Your Highness*. You'll speak only when spoken to, and you'll treat me and my companion with the respect we deserve!"

"Astrid," the worried voice boomed from the aft of the Arvada. "Astrid, I need you!"

"Now what," Jardaine growled. "How long must I endure her incessant whining?"

Nick and the captain exchanged glances. Jardaine struggled to keep her balance as she descended portside, headed into the hold. "I'm coming, child," she soothed.

Becky was doing her best to remain calm as she stared up at the ceiling. It was a blank screen for her to project her thoughts and worries upon, and her worries were many. She thought of her parents, and prayed they'd made it back home with her baby sister, Emily. Of course they'd be worried sick about Becky, and probably with good reason. She considered how absurd it was for a girl, not yet ten years old, to attempt to save her brother's life. The Elves and Trolls were the grown-ups here, and though they were as small as dolls, Becky knew how powerful they were. Among them were her allies, and her enemies. They were her world now, and she would have to deal with their promises and their threats. She would have to deal with the facts, no matter how she might feel about her chances for success.

Outside of the captain's quarters and the steering deck, the Arvada was not so well appointed. Becky lay on a cold metal sheet, where her body constantly bounced against the hard, unyielding surface. The air was thin, and cold, and it was difficult to breathe. Columns of sunlight shot intermittently through the round porthole windows as the Arvada made its way through clear sky and cloud. The air outside rumbled with the nauseating movements of the Sprite, and it made Becky afraid that she was going to vomit. At the same time, she was sick with hunger. "Astrid," she called again.

"I'm right here, child," Jardaine said, and gave Becky a reassuring pat on her sleeve. "You look unhappy. Tell me what's wrong!"

At the sight of the Elf's concerned face, a tear rolled down Becky's cheek. Jardaine stepped back. She was repulsed and wary at her proximity to the girl's bodily fluids. "I'm hungry," Becky said. "I think I've got to get something in my stomach, or I'm going to be sick."

"Then I'll see if I can find something for you to eat, my dear," Jardaine said. "Stay right here."

As she turned away Jardaine winced at the absurdity of her remark. Of course the girl wasn't going anywhere; she was completely under her control. To have to cater to the girl's needs like this, however, was loathsome. "What have I become," she muttered to herself, "a serving maid?"

Jardaine went to the galley and found a crewmember that could help her carry a sack of vegetables and fungus back to the hold. Becky found it difficult to eat, lying down, but she had no other choice. She chewed and swallowed the bitter paste of roots and herbs. "Astrid," she said, grimacing with the astringent taste in her mouth, "tell me how we're going to do it."

"Do what?"

"You know," Becky said, "save Matt. I know we're going to the North Pole to find him, and save him from Tuava-Li, but how are we going to do it? I've been thinking about this a lot. Tuava-Li has powers, you know. She can stop Matt from coming with us, when we tell him the truth. She's not going to let him go too easily. Shouldn't we be planning what we're going to say, what we're going to do to stop her, and get Matt back? And since we only have this one Arvada, how are we going to get Matt home?"

Jardaine smiled, masking her irritation. "You think too much, child. I didn't tell you, but I trained as a monk, just like Tuava-Li did. I have powers of my own, and Nick is strong, too. Once we confront Tuava-Li and tell your brother the truth, she won't be able to stop him from returning with us. And it will be easy for the pilots to send back a message that we need another Arvada. Don't worry, child, this is a job for the adults to handle. You'll be there, when the time comes, to help convince your brother that he's been deceived by Tuava-Li and Tomtar. Until then, you should rest and try to be calm. I know 'tis not comfortable to travel like this. You've been a brave girl; very, very brave. Now I want you to repeat after me, *all will be well.*"

"*All will be well,*" Becky said.

"That's right, *all will be well.* I am strong, I am capable, I choose the path of truth."

Becky repeated the lines, trying to find solace in them. "Now," said Jardaine, "whenever you're feeling tense, or worried, and you can't stop your mind from thinking too much about the task that lies before us, just say those words. 'Twill help to calm you down and bring you peace."

"Can you tell me again where we're going, when we get to the North Pole?" Becky asked.

Jardaine stole a quick glance out one of the porthole windows. She couldn't wait to get back to the steering deck, and the stack of maps, spells, and incantations she'd left on the floor. She was worried what Nick might be learning, if he dared to read through the papers given to her by the Techmagician. "Hunaland," she said. "We're going to Hunaland, where the great tree, Yggdrasil, grows. Under normal circumstances, strangers aren't welcome there. The monks there use their magick to shield the place within a wall of mist. Though the branches of the tree reach into the heavens, 'tis not easy to spot them, even from the air."

"Then how will we find it?" Becky asked.

"We will find it because it is *right* that we find it," Jardaine said. "The Great Goddess is good, and wise, and as long as she is watching us, our efforts will succeed. Trust me, child. *All will be well.*"

"*All will be well,*" Becky repeated.

Jardaine turned to leave.

"Astrid," Becky said, "there's one other thing. I'm sorry, but I have to go to the bathroom."

Jardaine caught her breath. "My child," she said, wild-eyed with fury, "I'm so sorry, but what can we do? You'll simply have to wait until we reach our destination. It can't be too much longer now. The Arvada is a fast-moving craft, and the winds are at our backs. Please be patient."

Becky sighed and shook her head. "You don't understand. I can't wait!"

"In that case," Jardaine said, sucking in her cheeks, "I'll see what I can do."

Back on the steering deck Jardaine rifled through her stack of spells and incantations. "There must be something here," she muttered. "Some bit of magick, something. I don't want to hurt the Human, but she can't make a mess of the Arvada. If we have to make a special stop, 'twill set us back again. I don't want to lose any more time."

Nick contemplated the wisdom of saying anything to Jardaine in her current agitated state, and chose his words carefully. "Is there anything I can do to help, my Mage?"

The thought had already crossed Jardaine's mind that if Nick were to look at her catalog of magick, he might memorize some bit of information he could use to hurt her, should the opportunity arise. But the thought of what would happen in the hold if she didn't find a quick solution made her risk it. "All right," she said, handing him a fistful of papers. "The girl has to relieve herself. Find something to stop it."

The pair of them searched the reams of documents in frantic desperation. "I've got something," Nick finally said. "If you give the girl a pinch of bitter elm mixed with horse root and the juices of three Death's-head moths beneath the light of a new moon, she'll lose the power to move her own extremities."

"Where would I get Death's-head moths this time of year?"

Jardaine snapped. "And what good would it do if she couldn't move? She could still make a mess out of the Arvada, and then what?"

"Here's another," Nick said. "It has magick words and everything! It's for turning any solid into a gas."

"Let me see that," Jardaine demanded, grabbing the papers from Nick's hands. Her lips silently mouthed the words of the spell as she read. Then she scowled and shook her head. "Noooo, 'twould not be good to fill the girl with vapors."

She threw the papers onto the floor and leapt from her seat when Becky's voice rose from the hold. "Astrid, we need to stop! You have to take me down to the ground!"

"Well," she cried to the Aeronauts sitting in the warm glow of the bow window. "Didn't you hear her? We've got to land, now. Make your command to the Air Sprite. We'll all be taking a little break."

"But, Jardaine," said the captain. "Look below! There's nothing but trees for miles around us. There's no place to land!"

"Then make a place," Jardaine said. "And do not address me by that name. Haven't I already warned you once? Have your Air Sprite burn a spot for us to land!"

The captain clenched his teeth and reluctantly sent the message to the trio of Telekeneticists, who then translated the message to the Sprite. Becky squirmed uncomfortably in the hold as the great Air Sprite lowered its head, unhinged its translucent jaw, and spewed forth a torrent of flame. A broad swath of forest was instantly vaporized. Trees surrounding the smoldering patch of scorched earth burst into flames, as their leaves leapt up in a withering dance. The Sprite circled the tract of land, then came around and opened its mouth again. This time it let out a fearsome gust of hot air. The noxious wind blew through the clearing and swept away every bit of seared debris and blackened woodland detritus. "Nothing's too good for our Becky," Jardaine said, staring out the window. "Bring us down!"

8

THERE WAS NO TIME for Tomtar and Tuava-Li to
hide. There was no time to chew on the *Trans* that would have
rendered them invisible to all eyes, so they had to take their chances
and assume that the approaching children, like most Humans,
wouldn't even see them. They stood shivering behind Matt as the
strangers drew closer. There were five of them, and none looked
old enough to go to school. They were dressed in colorful parkas
with fur-lined hoods, mittens, and boots. Their laughter was sharp
in the freezing air; Matt was taken aback at the sound, now that
he'd been spending more time with Faerie Folk than Humans.
Still, he knew that these kids were his ticket out of the danger
and the cold, so he smiled and waved as they hurried to meet him.
"Just stay behind me," he said to his companions.

The children spread out as they drew closer and surrounded Matt, Tuava-Li, and Tomtar. Then they reached out and took one another's hands, closing the circle. They were speaking a language Matt didn't understand. He introduced himself awkwardly, then asked, "Can you take me to your parents?"

The children's wide, dark faces were wreathed in smiles as they began to move, forcing Matt, Tomtar, and Tuava-Li to move along with them. "They're leading us someplace," Matt said. "Do you think they understand what I'm saying?"

"Clear as day," Tomtar said, "or . . . not!"

"I think they can see us," Tuava-Li murmured, as she made fleeting eye contact with one of the children. "They don't look frightened. Maybe this isn't the first time they've seen Faerie Folk!"

When it was plain that Matt and the others were headed in the right direction, the children let go of one another's hands and raced ahead. They were still laughing and shouting and pointing over their shoulders at Tomtar and Tuava-Li. Matt's teeth were chattering by the time they reached the village. It wasn't much to look at, but the sight of the trailers, aluminum sheds, and barracks-style cinder-block buildings was paradise. On one side of the village was a long, sandy beach leading to the ocean. Looming in the distance on the other side were snow-covered mountains. In between there were steel-roofed sheds on wooden stilts, water towers, trucks and ATVs in various states of disrepair, and chain-link fences. Telephone and light poles dotted the landscape.

The children led Matt and his companions to a small shingled house built on a platform of plywood and 4x4s. They hurried up the steps, gesturing for their guests to follow, and flung open the door. In a flash they were all jostling to be the first inside, tugging on Matt's sleeve to drag him in, too. The children were laughing and shouting. Though they didn't touch Tomtar or Tuava-Li, they made it clear that they wanted the trio to enter the little house together. Tomtar always preferred being outdoors. He looked alarmed as he was swept toward the door. Since his pants and shoes were still soaked with oil, he slipped off his shoes and left them on the deck before stepping into the house. He looked around for any signs of danger; it was risky to leave personal belongings where someone could use them to cast spells or curses on their owner. It was risky, too, however, to be rude to a host when one was in desperate need of help.

The house was dingy and cramped. Plastic toys littered the worn carpet, and the furniture was a hodgepodge of overstuffed sofas and straight-backed chairs that all faced a large flat-screen TV at the corner of the living room. In the opposite corner there was an outdated computer perched on a desk, and sitting at the computer was an elderly, overweight woman. Her snowy hair was pulled into a tight knot at the back of her head. She heaved herself out of her chair and hobbled past the mob of children, reaching out her hand to greet Matt. "Welcome," she said, "welcome to the end of the world. I'm Mary Suluk."

Matt held out his hand, wondering why she behaved almost

as if she'd expected his arrival. And what did she mean by *the end of the world*? Did she mean *the top of the world*? When he shook her hand it felt small and hard, like a block of wood. "I'm Matt," he said. "Pleased to meet you."

"What brings you here, son?"

Matt didn't know where to begin. "Well, I'm—I guess I'm kind of lost. What's the name of this . . . village?"

The children were peeling off their gloves, coats, and hats. They hurried to hang them on a rack by the door, then returned to wrap their arms around Mary, clinging to her flowered dress, burying their faces in her soft belly, and shyly peeking out at their visitors. "We call it *Aujuittuq*. That means 'the place that never thaws out.' That used to be true, but now I'm not so sure we're not going to have to change our name. Where you from, son?"

"Uh, I live—or, at least, I lived, in Pennsylvania. That's in the United States."

"I know where Pennsylvania is," Mary said with a humorless smile. "You're a long way from home. Maybe you should get your friends over here for a proper introduction, and tell me how you managed to get so far north!"

It was the first time that the woman had acknowledged the presence of Tomtar and Tuava-Li. Obviously, just like the children, she could see them perfectly well. Obviously, too, the sight of Faerie Folk was neither strange nor alarming to her. The children were staring, wide-eyed. They weren't surprised, though; they were mimicking their guests. One of them tugged at the tips of his ears and pranced around, which made the others giggle. "Stop that," said Mary. "Don't be rude."

"Do they speak English, too?" Matt asked. "They were all talking in some other language when they brought me here."

"They speak Inuktitut. Then English in school, as a second language."

"Wow," Matt said, then nodded toward his friends, who still hovered behind his legs. "This is Tomtar, and this is Tuava-Li. I didn't know for sure if you'd be able to see them, you know? We're trying to get to the North Pole. I'm not really sure what to say. This is all really strange. The kids found us out by the beach, and they seemed to want to bring us here to meet you. Do they understand what we're talking about?"

"They understand enough," Mary said. "I send 'em down to the beach every afternoon to look for folk like you, just in case."

"In case of what?"

The woman smiled. "I run sort of a day-care center here for some of the families where the parents are workin'. Not that there's much work to be had." She wrapped her heavy arms around a boy and girl and gave them a squeeze. "These two are my grandkids!"

Tomtar, still standing behind Matt, grinned mischievously and wiggled his fingers at the children. When they turned their faces into the woman's breast their muffled laughter spilled out. "You want a glass of water?" Mary asked, prying herself away from the children. She went to turn on the television. "It's about all I got to offer. Drinking water's precious around here, these days. We've been scrapin' it off the glaciers and storin' it in tanks up the hillside a ways."

"Look, I don't mean to sound rude or anything," Matt said, following the woman to the kitchen. "Anybody else would be running out of here, foaming at the mouth if they saw my friends. How come the sight of an elf and a troll doesn't bother you at all?"

Mary chuckled and lifted a plate for Matt to see. "Look what I found! Do you think your friends would like a little *muktuk*? It's air-dried. The kids gobbled up most of it, but there's a few pieces left."

Matt looked at the brownish chunks on the chipped plate; they looked a little like fried pork rinds. "What's *muktuk*?"

"This kind is narwhal. You can also get it from beluga, but we like the narwhal blubber. Try it, it's good!"

Matt was reluctant, but his stomach gnawed with hunger. He reconsidered and took a piece. "Thanks. I'll give it a try, but Tomtar and Tuava-Li are vegetarians."

"You won't survive long up here without eatin' meat," Mary said.

Matt chewed the leathery blubber, which tasted like jerky and a little like nuts. He nearly swooned with pleasure as the juice ran down his throat. "They get by," he said. "Look, this has been a really strange journey for me. I didn't choose to come here. It's all been just an accident, really, and I'm not the kind of person who . . . well, what I mean to say is, I've met people who know faerie folk, and they always have some kind of, you know, some kind of game they're playing, and I usually end up the one who's being tricked. So when I meet somebody who can see elves and trolls, and acts like it's just the most normal thing in the world, I get a little nervous."

"You three didn't have anything to do with all those kids that got kidnapped and taken into Canada, did you?"

"No," Matt said, his eyes wide. "What did you hear? I guess it was all over the news. Probably all around the world!"

"Eh, just a lot of Faerie mischief, as far as I could see," Mary said, waving her hand. "It's always been the same. At least, in the end, they let the kids all go! It could have been a heck of a lot worse."

"What?" Matt said. "You mean they weren't . . . killed?"

"Noooo," Mary laughed. "Maybe the Faerie Folk were just tryin' to make a point. Everybody's fine, for now."

Tuava-Li stepped quietly into the room and stood in the doorway. Behind her, the television blared. Mary filled a small glass from the tap and set it on the edge of the table for Tuava-Li to take. "No need to be nervous," she said. "I'm just an old lady. I don't bite. They call me an elder, when they're tryin' to be polite, 'cause I've seen a lot of things in my day. I'm spirit-wise, though. I've seen your kind comin' and goin' since I was a little girl; I just never knew what to call 'em. Now back in summertime—we call it *Aujak*—the kids found a couple of Faerie Folk out beyond the ridge. They'd been travelin' north in that big Cord out there, and they plowed straight into the oil slick. They managed to get out, but they were lyin' on the ground and coughin' up black stuff when the kids found them. We cleaned 'em up as best we could, like you'd clean up a seabird or a turtle after a tanker spill. Didn't do much good, though."

"Then you know about the Cord?" Matt asked.

"Sure do!"

"The Cord's not safe to travel in anymore," Tuava-Li said. "We only used it because there was no other way to get north."

"Ain't nothin' safe anymore," the woman said. "The whole world's comin' apart, and it's too late to do anything about it."

"The Gods are looking out for us," Tomtar offered, stepping into the doorway. "We're on a mission!"

"A mission, eh?" Mary said. "Ya know, the Inuit have always known somethin' about your kind, goin' back thousands of years. There aren't too many of us anymore who can still see the nature spirits, though. Your Cords come up out of the ice and snow, and most Inuit haven't got a clue they're even there. Here, look at these."

The woman gestured to a window ledge, where small carvings made of bone and white stone stood in a row. The sculptures were of soft, rounded, ghostlike figures with heads and arms, and dots for eyes. "I made these. A few of us here make carvings, and there's a woman who sells 'em for us down in the city."

Matt's heart pounded. The figures were exactly like the

one tattooed on his chest. "What are these supposed to be? What do they mean?"

"They're spirit guides," Mary said. "They help folks in need."

"They're . . . really nice," Matt said, trying to suppress his excitement.

The woman shrugged. "As a matter of fact, our people used to build shrines around the places where the Cords rise out of the ground. You can still see some of 'em out in the wilderness, if you go far enough. There used to be a lot of 'em out on the pack ice, before the temperature started to rise. Now the ice is breakin' off in chunks bigger than Texas. Thank god there's snow on the ground again, and *Ukiassak's* finally here."

"*What's* here?" Matt asked.

"Early autumn," Mary said. "Dark season'll be here before you know it. Anyway, the shrines were marked with stones and carved wooden frames. We got experts nowadays claimin' that the shrines have somethin' to do with the way the Inuit used to hunt. But they don't know anything."

Tuava-Li craned her neck to get a closer look at the carvings. "You say that there were Faerie Folk here. Have they gone?"

"You might say that," the woman answered. "They didn't make it, after they'd been soaked in oil and lay out there on the tundra, sick and starvin' for days. We kept it to ourselves, of course, and buried 'em out on the plain. You know there are derricks still out there from when the oil companies tried to run a pipeline? They gave up, because of the shiftin' ocean ice, though they'll probably try again in a few years when the ice is finally gone and they have easy access. They'll pick our bones clean, I swear! This weather's gonna bring this world to its knees. It's changed our whole way of life already."

"Uh-huh," Matt said. "Global warming."

Mary gave him a look. "You might not feel it in Pittsburgh, but up here, it's tearin' us apart. I guess it ain't so nice for your Faerie Folk here, either. You'll be next, Max, believe me."

"It's Matt."

Mary nodded. "Anyway, since *Aujak*, I send the kids out once a day to see if anything's doin' with that Cord. That way, if anybody gets spat out of there and we find 'em soon enough, I figure we can probably do something to save 'em."

"We're all right," Matt said. "We saw the oil in the Cord in time to get out. But my friend here has it all over his pants, as you can see."

The woman looked at Tomtar, who was soaked from the knees down with black goo. "I took my shoes off," Tomtar said apologetically.

"We need food," Tuava-Li said. "We need supplies to help us to travel north. We need cold-weather gear. If you know where we can find another Cord that goes north, we'd be happy to pay you for anything you can do to help us."

"Pay." Mary laughed. "You don't look like the type to carry a big wad of cash in your pocket. Lord knows I could use a few dollars, but I'm not gonna take it from you. You're on a mission, after all. Hopeless, doomed to fail, like all missions these days, but still a mission." The woman peered into the living room at the children, who were hunkered down in front of the TV screen watching cartoons. "I don't know what's gonna happen to us," she said.

"We've got to reach the North Pole," Matt said to Mary. "You're right, we don't have money, but we have something you can trade for money. Our world isn't the only one out there, you know. There's a faerie world, an elf realm, and there's a tree up at the top of the world. We're going to get a seed from that tree and plant it at the center of the earth. It's going to make things better for the faerie folk. It's going to make their world strong, the way it used to be."

"Used to be?" Mary said with a touch of scorn. "Son, we used to have all the caribou we wanted to eat. We used to have char, and beluga, and we took tourists around to shoot polar bear. The ice shelf out there was five thousand years old. Then one day it just dropped off. We lost three-quarters of another ice shelf, and just this summer we lost enough ice to make three of your New York Cities. The bears are starving, and the lucky ones are going to drown before the last of the seals is gone. Don't worry about saving the Elf world, worry about saving your own! Really, you should turn around and go back where you came from. There's nothin' you can do up here."

"'Tis a shame you feel that way," Tuava-Li said. "But this is our *destiny*. If you can help us, we'd be truly grateful, but if you cannot, we'd be happy if you could tell us where we might find food and shelter tonight. We're not prepared for cold like this."

"Seems to me you're not prepared for much," Mary said. With a deep sigh she got out of her chair and walked slowly into one of the dark rooms at the back of the house. She flicked on a light, and Matt and Tuava-Li could see her bending to tug a trunk out from under a bed. When she returned, she had some worn-looking coats, mittens, and boots in her arms. "These belonged to my kids when they were little," she said. "I was savin' 'em for the grandkids, but they don't want my old stuff, anyway. Everything's gotta be new, new, new these days. Their mama works down at the co-op, and their dad, he runs cargo planes, when there's work. So I'm gonna give these to you."

She dropped the clothing in a heap on the floor, and Tuava-Li reluctantly stepped forward to finger the fur that lined the jackets and mittens. "You'll have to go by the co-op and see about buyin' somethin' your size," Mary said to Matt. "They've got a few rooms for rent there, too, and you could stay the night, if you've really got money. I'll see if my daughter can get you a break on the room. You can eat there, too. I suppose you're hungry, the way you scarfed down the last of my *muktuk*."

Truck tires sounded on the gravel road outside and Matt tensed when he heard the back door of the house creak open. Tomtar and Tuava-Li moved behind the kitchen cabinet and crouched there in the shadows. "Don't worry," Mary said in a low voice, "it's just Joe. He wouldn't notice an Elf if one was sittin' on his chest and singin' hallelujah."

A man stepped into the narrow hallway and set his rifle down in the corner. Then he took off his coat and hung it on a hook. "Company, Joe," Mary called, and looked at Matt. She leaned in and spoke in a whisper. "I'm gonna say your dad's a scientist up here, doin' research on climate change or somethin', and that you took off from school to give him a hand."

When he ambled into the kitchen, Matt saw that the man wasn't much taller than he was. He was stocky, with a broad face and a mop of black hair, and tired brown eyes. He looked wary when he noticed Matt standing by the table. "This is Matt," Mary said. "He's come in from the U.S. to help out his old man."

"Oh, yeah?"

"Uh-huh, workin' up at the Pole, and writin' up some research for school. Isn't that right, Matt?"

Matt nodded.

Joe held out his hand and Matt shook it. "He's stayin' down at the co-op," Mary said, "and Joan called and asked me if I could give him some local history. I guess everybody figures I'm the expert around here."

"Does he talk?" Joe asked.

"I talk," Matt said.

Mary went to the refrigerator and got her son-in-law a can of soda. He slumped into a chair as she popped the lid and placed it on the table. "I guess you didn't shoot nothin' today."

"Nah," he said, and took a long drink. He wiped his mouth on the sleeve of his sweater. "Couldn't find a caribou interested in bein' our dinner."

Mary smiled and turned to Matt. "One of them big animals will feed our whole family for two weeks."

"I'd have taken a seal, but the pickin's are scarce out there. You ever shoot anything?" Joe asked Matt.

"Uh, yeah." Matt remembered aiming a red-hot rifle at the Air Sprite that breathed down fire all around him. He remembered what happened after he pulled the trigger and decided it would be best not to provide too many details. "There are a lot of hunters in my family."

Joe took another swig of his drink. "It's hard finding enough ice to stand on. Pretty soon I'll have to do all my huntin' from a boat, like it's summer year-round. I guess there's always char."

"You know the kids don't like fish," Mary said.

Joe shrugged. "Beggars can't be choosers."

Matt pressed his lips together and nodded. He was wondering how long he could keep up this charade.

"How you gettin' north?" Joe asked Matt.

"I, uh—"

"His dad's gonna come down and get him, isn't that right, Matt?"

Matt swallowed. He didn't like having to make up so many lies on the spot; it would be hard to keep his story straight. "Yeah, pretty soon now."

"Don't worry, Joe," Mary said, "business will pick up in the spring." She turned to Matt. "Joe does some business flying cargo down to Resolute in a Twin Otter. Once in a while he gets a job takin' hunters or scientists from one place to another, but now that summer's gone, the work's dried up. You know the sun's goin' down pretty soon, and there won't be light again until the end of February. Most of the scientists have already headed home."

"What's a Twin Otter?" Matt asked.

"What's a Twin Otter?" Joe repeated. "How'd you get here, kid? Had to have been a Super King, or a DHC-6 Otter."

"It's an airplane," Mary said. "Workhorses of the Arctic, isn't that right, Joe?"

Joe finished his soda and got up. "I'm gonna get the kids and head on home, that is if I can pry 'em away from the TV."

When he'd gone into the living room to collect his children, Matt cast a quick glance at Tomtar and Tuava-Li. They were still standing behind the counter, and their faces were anxious. "Let me help you with the kids' coats," Mary said to Joe and left the kitchen.

When she returned Tomtar was pacing nervously. "My friends get a little uncomfortable if they spend too long in a— well, in a building made for humans," Matt said.

"Okay, you want to go," Mary said. "I understand. It's gonna be cold tonight. I'll call my daughter and tell her you need a room. Your friends gonna be able to tolerate that, or do they have to be outdoors?"

"I think if they're asleep we'll be okay."

"You said you have money?"

"I have . . . I have jewels, from the faerie world, but they're jewels pretty much just like ours. Diamonds, emeralds, rubies, stuff like that. I was hoping we could trade some for money or supplies."

Mary's eyes widened. "Nobody will even believe they're real, if you show 'em around. Let me see!"

Matt opened a sack of jewels and spread the gems on the table. Mary examined them carefully. "There's gonna be more folks comin' by to pick up their kids, any time now. Look, I've got some money saved up. Wait here."

Mary disappeared into her bedroom again and came back with an old wooden cigar box. She lifted the lid and withdrew a pile of bills. "This is my retirement, if I live long enough to retire. I'll take your word for it that these jewels are real. I'll trade you the money, for the sack."

"I don't know," Matt said, glancing over at Tomtar and Tuava-Li. "I'm sorry, but we just want to trade in enough jewels to get the supplies we'll need to get to the North Pole. How far is it from here, anyway?"

"You can't reach the North Pole from here. Not on foot; it would take you months. There's too much water out there, and thin ice, and hungry polar bears, and you're just a kid. Whole teams of experts get lost or drown out there, and you don't know anything. Listen. Tomorrow we'll find out what it'll cost to fly you to Ottawa, or somewhere else you can connect to home. I'll give you the airfare in cash, in exchange for . . . let's see."

Mary moved the jewels around on the tabletop. "I'll take these stones. Just five little rocks, okay? Nobody's ever gonna say I don't have a good heart. I don't want to see you get hurt out there, and I know you will, if you keep on with this notion of reaching the Pole."

"You don't understand," Matt said. "I don't have a home to go back to. My parents were abducted by elves, and my house was burned down. I've got to get to the North Pole to take care of this business with the seed, and then these guys are going to help me get my parents back. I can't fly anywhere. I've got no passport. And do you honestly think I can get seats on an airplane for faeries?"

Mary frowned. "I don't know what to say. I'll call my daughter, and we'll get you set up for the night. Tomorrow you can come back here and we'll discuss our options. Okay? Just don't tell anybody about the jewels. Let me give you some cash in advance."

Matt looked to Tomtar and Tuava-Li for approval, then nodded. They were going to have to trust this woman to help them; there was no other choice. Mary picked up her telephone from the counter.

Ten minutes later the travelers were out on the gravel road. Tomtar and Tuava-Li were dressed in their new cold-weather gear, and Matt shivered in his thin jacket and jeans, his shoulders hunched and his hands jammed into his pockets. He looked up at the gray sky and wondered what time of day it was; the sky already looked darker. Fat snowflakes drifted down as the trio plodded along the gravel road toward the Inuit Co-operative. "Why do you think my tattoo shows the same kind of thing that Mary carves?"

"I think *Mary's* our spirit guide," Tuava-Li said. "We were meant to find her, and she was meant to help us on our way. The tattoo is proof, that's all. The Goddess always provides!"

"I wonder if we pass anybody, if they'll see the two of you," Matt mused.

"They'll see our clothes and assume we're nothing but Human children," Tuava-Li said. "'Tis such a small village, compared to Argant, that we'll draw attention no matter what we do."

"Then when we get to the co-op," Matt said, "you just stay outside until I get the room settled. I'll come back and get you when I'm sure nobody's looking."

Tomtar pointed. "There's the place she told us about!"

The building was low and flat, with a steel roof and a few windows peeking out on each side. There was a wooden sign hung above the door. "Garden spot of the Arctic," Matt read aloud.

"A real garden?" Tomtar asked.

Matt laughed. "Dream on!"

The co-op was a general store, motel, and Laundromat all rolled into one. Mary's daughter gave Matt his room key. He carefully led Tomtar and Tuava-Li inside, and left them on the bed while he went to look and see what kind of coat they might have in his size. He brought back a big plastic sack filled with gear, and some food for himself and his friends. They ate it on the edge of the bed while they watched TV and listened for news about Brahja-Chi's Acquisition. Sadly, there was nothing more specific than what Mary had told them already. There were no new revelations to report, and the coverage was reduced to aimless and hysterical speculation about terrorists and child predators. Experts were marched in front of the cameras to talk about post-traumatic stress and why authorities considered eyewitness accounts from children to be less than reliable.

Matt felt strange watching the programs. Something very important had happened, maybe the most important thing that had *ever* happened to Humankind, and yet it seemed like the Acquisition was quickly becoming yesterday's news. The worldview shared by most Humans did not allow for the possibility of Faerie abductions. People wanted to forget what they did not understand, and return as quickly as possible to whatever made them comfortable. For another half hour they watched reports from a TV station in Ottawa—traffic, weather, a burglary, an apartment fire, and a heartwarming story about a woman who had rescued some kittens from an abandoned building. Most likely the FBI, the army, or the police were doing something to find out about what had happened, but they were keeping it to themselves. No matter how much TV Matt watched, he realized he would learn nothing new.

The three of them were exhausted. Matt switched off the television and suggested that they go to sleep. Tomtar begged him to leave the window open, just a crack. Then he curled up on a blanket on the floor and pulled his knit cap over his eyes. Tuava-Li knelt to say some prayers, then lay sideways at the foot of the bed with her arms crossed over her chest. Matt pulled the blankets up under his chin. He was freezing. The temperature outside had slipped below zero, and with the window open, he felt like he might as well be sleeping outdoors. As he fell asleep he thought of his tattoos and wondered if they would change again during the night. Images of Green Men and great figures made of gleaming jewels marched through his dark and troubled dreams.

9

MACTA WINCED AS the Techmagicians attached the mechanical arm to his shoulder. There were straps and bands to hold it firmly in place, but the fabric covering the wound was rough, and the new skin growing there was tender. "Be careful, fools," he cried. "You're hurting me, and I'm not in the mood for any more pain. Just picture your heads on the end of spikes, rotting in the sun, with crows pecking out your eyes." He smiled, soothed somehow by the image his words conjured up. He gazed into the corner where his new Goblin pup was busily gnawing a bone.

"Tell me, Prashta," Macta asked as the technicians worked diligently on his arm, "what have you arranged for my Princess to do, today? A little sightseeing, perhaps?"

"Asra is under house arrest, as she was yesterday and the day before that," Prashta said matter-of-factly. "I've explained all this to you before. If she were to get out among the people, it would only raise unpleasant reminders of your failed wedding and the death of your father in the Arvada."

"*Simple* and *stable* are our code words, Macta," said Lehtinen. "Order must be maintained. Luckily the rabble is easily distracted. We've been handing out food and cold-weather clothing to the poor all week. We've got to keep their minds off Brahja-Chi's failed Acquisition. 'Twill be best if Asra entertains herself, until the time's come for your departure."

"Don't talk to me of failure," Macta said. "You fail me if you ignore my wishes. You could devise some amusements for the Princess, certainly. Bring in some troubadours, a theater troupe, a circus! Give her a tour of the palace. Show her the Crown Jewels, let her try something on. Remind her that someday all these things will be hers. Give me more time to go and visit her! You monopolize my every moment with your nonsense."

"Your Highness," said one of the Techmagicians, "you must pay attention. There are muscle groups in your shoulder that you must exercise if the new arm is to work properly. I've prepared a chart for you so that you may practice. There's not much time before your speech to the people, and you will want to appear as hale and hearty as possible."

Macta squirmed on his stool. "I'm heartier than I've ever been. My heart is full of hate, and my soul is crying out for revenge.

Once my dagger pierces Jardaine's black heart, I will once again breathe the air of freedom and peace. Do you understand?"

"You're not going to get revenge, Macta," Prashta said. "Remember, the official story is that you're going to plant the Seed of the Adri and save Elf Realm from disaster."

Macta sighed deeply. "The citizens of Helfratheim aren't the kind to fall for silly stories. And yet you want me to tell the people that Jardaine and I are going to the North Pole to relive the adventure of Fada and save the world. Right?"

"Correct," Prashta said. "No one knows that Jardaine has already gone, so the story will not be doubted. You'll kill Jardaine when you find her, and plant the Seed yourself. The glory will be yours and no one else's. We'll spread the account throughout the realms that Jardaine gave her life in the service of her King, and all will remember her with fondness and gratitude."

"What if I come back from the North Pole and the Cord continues to deteriorate? What then? My tenure as hero will be short-lived, indeed. Everyone will know that we lied or simply failed!"

Prashta and Lehtinen looked at each other. "We've concluded," Prashta said, "that Jardaine would not have undertaken such a mission, risked so much by attempting to assassinate me and stealing our Arvada, without a very good reason. We believe that she's correct, and that the fulfillment of this quest will indeed save our world."

"Do you care to place any bets on that?" Macta said

incredulously. "You've never struck me as the religious type, you two. There are no Gods, and there's no way to save the Cord. 'Tis that simple. We stand to win everything by coming to terms with the fact that things in this world are going to change, no matter how much everyone else is in denial. We must take advantage of the trends, while others wander around, helpless and full of silly stories."

One of the Techmagicians slipped a needle into Macta's left arm, just above the elbow. *"Oooow!"* he cried.

From the exposed end of the needle a thin tube coiled. A flaccid sack full of green liquid hung from a stand at Macta's side, and the fluid slowly drained through the tube into his arm. "I don't know why I can't just eat, like any normal Elf," Macta said. "I don't trust needles and potions, any more than I trust magickal spells or the pair of you."

"Sir, if you wish to regain the weight you lost during your ordeal," said the Techmagician, "we must supplement your diet with intravenous fluids. The magick infused in the potion, on the other hand, is purely precautionary. We don't want you to get any infections."

"Don't talk to me of other hands," Macta said, trying to make the stiff mechanical fingers do his bidding. "This is impossible. Besides, Powcca will be terrified of me when I wear this wretched thing . . . won't you, Powcca?"

The Goblin looked up from his bone, growling as a group of black-hooded monks arrived in the chamber. They knelt at Macta's feet, and their lips began to move in a silent chant. Prashta had brought them from a neighboring village to assist in Macta's healing. Though he and the other Council members had never before put their faith in the Gods and Goddesses of the old religion, they saw no point in taking chances. "Now what are *they* doing?" Macta said condescendingly.

Powcca got up and limped over to the monks, sniffing their robes and grunting. "Try to be open-minded, if you can," Prashta said. "Mages and monks can effect very powerful magick when called upon to assist in matters like these. Jardaine and Brahja-Chi had capabilities the rest of us could only dream of. Magick plays an important part in most of our laboratory's best inventions, as you well know. The melding of science and spirit, body and mind—"

"The real and the pretend," Macta said, "and what do you get? This nonsense is overrated. My father never placed any stock in monks and Mages, and neither should you, Prashta. You're aware that Helfratheim didn't even have a Mage until that traitor Jardaine showed up with her shape-shifter. Now *he* was a source of power, Prashta, and he didn't have to cast any spells or burn any herbs to get what he wanted. He just reached out and took it."

Macta was exasperated. His shoulders flinched, and the mechanical hand sprang from his lap, striking him hard in the jaw. *"Awwww!"* he cried and rubbed his chin with his good hand. "Listen, you two, this is what I'm talking about. You act like you're in charge here, but you're not. *I* am. My father didn't find it necessary to stand before his people every time somebody fell down and got a scratch. He came and went whenever he pleased, and it didn't seem to put the kingdom in jeopardy. Now you tell me I have to go out there on the ledge where Jal-Maktar impersonated me, and let everyone know that the kingdom is in good hands. I was wounded in battle. I gave my arm to help my people; they should be proud and moved to hear of my sacrifice. 'Tis *all* about sacrifice, you know. It's what you plan for Jardaine, isn't it? That Human boy Tuava-Li's taking to the Pole is going to be sacrificed, too, for the good of all. The *legend says* that's what must happen! The boy will be a hero. His name will live throughout time in all the Faerie realms. Art will be made to commemorate his sacrifice, sculptures showing his wounded body, with the heart removed and the red Blood spilled like wine. People will speak of Jardaine's great heroism and sacrifice, too. The thought of it makes me want to vomit."

"No, Your Highness," cried the Techmagician. "You mustn't do that; 'twill interfere with your nourishment!"

"I didn't mean it literally, you fool," Macta growled. He seethed at the monk's relentless chanting and the abuse he was forced to take from the Council leaders. He tensed his shoulder again, intent on making the arm move as it had before. He turned his body toward Prashta and when the wooden fist on its framework of rods, trusses, and vines flew forward, it struck Prashta in his flabby belly. "Aha!" Macta chortled as the old Elf doubled over in pain. Powcca pranced and barked at the sight. "Perhaps the arm is good for something after all," Macta said. "Come, Prashta, stand a little closer and let me do that again."

Lehtinen said, "We're not amused by your juvenile antics! A kingdom is an effective machine only if its parts operate in harmony."

"'Tis much like your artificial arm, sire," said one of the Techmagicians. "The oily nectar conducting the signals from your shoulder run through the machine parts like Blood through veins, insuring fluid movement of all the components, building upon bioelectric signals transmitted from your brain."

"Right," Prashta said. "One part means nothing without the others. A kingdom is nothing but a well-greased machine, and you are just another cog in that machine, Macta. Your father knew how it works. You must learn to control your ego and lust for power."

"Until I strike Jardaine down and get my sweet revenge, every waking moment will be nothing but misery for me, Prashta. Ego and power lust have nothing to do with this. I only attempt to honor the memory of my father, and seek justice for my people and my kingdom."

"Not bad," Prashta said. "Honor and justice . . . We'll make sure that goes in your speech!"

There was a frantic knock at the door. Powcca leapt up, snarling and scraping. "See who's there!" Lehtinen said.

One of the guards scurried to peer through the peephole

in the ornately carved door. "'Tis only one of the household servants, sir," the guard said. "From the wing where Princess Asra's being held."

"Let him in," Macta commanded, getting up from his seat.

The stand attached to his arm rattled, and instinctively he reached out with his mechanical hand and grabbed it so that it wouldn't topple over. In delight he gazed at the hand as the servant bumbled into the chamber and cried, "Princess Asra has escaped, my lords. She's gone!"

Asra's exit from the palace hadn't been particularly difficult. Her eager young handmaid, always busy flirting with the guards, had unwittingly provided enough of a distraction for Asra to slip away unnoticed. Another gang of guards had been huddled by the side doors, engrossed in a game of knucklebones. The Princess sauntered into the brisk morning air, and no one challenged her freedom. She didn't stop to consider that those whose carelessness had allowed her to escape would probably be hanging from the gallows by the end of the day. With her plain dress and her hair in a simple braid, Asra disappeared into the crowd. She looked hardly worthy of a second glance, and that was just the way she liked it.

The square was abuzz with the usual midmorning clamor, jostling crowds, vendors hawking their wares, all the hustle and bustle, the sights and smells of market day. Fruits and vegetables, herbs and spices, candles, knitwear, books, charms, rugs, pottery, and a thousand other commodities were displayed in booths throughout the square. Asra thought that Helfratheim might not be without its charms. Here, at least, the fear and trepidation that filled the palace seemed absent. Faerie Folk went about their business, buying, trading, and selling what they could, for that was what they did to survive and, with any luck, to prosper.

Asra was dressed in another of the plain garments that had belonged to one of Macta's servants. Though the dress had been laundered and pressed, there was still something disturbing about wearing another's clothing, especially since the original owner was dead. All Elves were inclined to believe in the principles of contagious magick, wherein any two things, once in contact, remain in contact forever. Therefore, Asra felt a peculiar sense of urgency about finding something new to wear. She had a few coins in her pocket, secreted from the handmaid's bag. If she could, she would buy another dress — something a little more cheerful, something with a little more personality than what she had on . . . something that did not have the faintest whiff of mortality about it. She could see shops along the edge of the market square, and there must be more of them along the narrow streets that ran down the hill. The rows of buildings looked charming and full of promise. With their steep tiled roofs, high chimneys, gleaming crystal windows, and cheery displays, the shops seemed to call out to Asra and draw her closer. The boutiques seemed virtually guaranteed to have something that would suit her sense of style, as well as her meager budget.

The ceramic bell over the circular entryway tinkled invitingly when Asra opened the door of a shop and stepped inside. The proprietor was a trim Elf in a snug green suit, standing behind a glass-topped counter. His eyebrows rose languidly at the sight of the Elfmaid in her plain frock. "Aye?" he said. One glance told him that a sale would not likely be forthcoming.

"Good morning," Asra said, gazing around at the elegant dresses on display. She walked casually among the racks of garments woven from linen and silk, and saw one with a fitted bodice and sleeves. Richly colored threads were sewn through the dress, making a pattern of dragons in flight. She was curious about the cut of the garment. She was also curious as to what the cost of the dress might be, but she was uncertain of how to ask the proper questions without appearing rude or common. As a Princess, Asra was accustomed to having her clothes custom-made and fitted. As an Elf, she was loath to try on an item of clothing that someone else had tried on before her. Garments in a shop like this were meant for the daughters and wives of the merchant class. They were mostly loose in style, and meant to be belted to fit. The dress Asra held in her hands, however, was another matter.

"That's not for you," the proprietor said. He eyed Asra coldly, judging her not only by the quality but the style of her hand-me-down dress. He was annoyed that she had somehow found her way into his store.

"I beg your pardon?"

"Have you tried the stalls in the market, ma'am? Artisans there do wonders with felt and nettle fabric. I have no doubt you'd find it more . . . affordable."

"But I'm interested in this dress," Asra said, stroking the edge of the fine and expensive fabric. "I'm wondering about the fit."

"That's not really the question!" The Elf took the dress from Asra and hung it back on the rack. "The clothing in this establishment is meant for the affluent and well-heeled. One does not simply come in here and take things from the rack."

"I see," Asra said, bristling. "'Tis plain you don't know who you're talking—"

She clenched her jaw and realized that it would be best to turn around and go. "Thank you," she said. "I'll try the market."

Head down, Asra fled from the store and clomped along the cobblestone street. She was indignant, livid with anger and frustration. Suddenly she was overcome with the desire to keep walking through the gates of Helfratheim, find a Cord that led away, and disappear. What did her quest matter? Who needed Macta Dockalfar and his Arvada, anyway? Who needed Becky?

Asra knew that each time she traveled in a Cord she risked injury or death. She knew that there were few these days that were foolhardy enough to take the chance. *Still*, she thought, *what was there in life but risk? What was there, in the end, but the certainty that her luck would run out, one way or another?* She passed a shop with a painted wooden hand hanging above the doorway.

An old Elf stood inside the window, gesturing to Asra. She was a Saga. The crone's face was painted black and white, and her clawlike hands ruffled a well-worn deck of cards. The smile she gave Asra was leering and toothless. Asra stared for a second, recalling that other Fortune-teller she had met in Ljosalfar and later followed to Storehoj. It seemed like a lifetime ago when the Saga had explained to her the card called The Hanged One. Asra had thought the card meant that she was about to die. Then the Saga had told her that it meant she would reach her destiny only through surrender.

Asra lingered for a moment, then turned away from the old crone in the window and stalked away. *Surrender,* she thought. *Surrender to what?* She came to the market square again. She wasn't thinking about her clothing anymore. She wasn't thinking at all, she was raging. She lurched past a stall with a hideous display of animal carcasses hanging from hooks, the pelt of each wretched creature stripped away to reveal muscle and bone. Asra had never eaten the flesh of a living creature, and the very thought of it was an abomination. Suddenly there was someone at her side. "Where are you headed in such a hurry, lass?" asked the handsome Elf in the spattered apron, who walked just a little too closely to Asra. She could feel the warmth of his body, and she wrinkled her nose at the smell of him. He was a predator, she thought, and she was like a rabbit, all her senses on alert.

"None of your business," Asra muttered. "Leave me alone."

"And risk never seeing your pretty face again?" the Elflad

said. "I am at your service, fair one, but you ask too much of me when you tell me to begone!"

"Please," Asra said, looking into his face. His eyes were blue, and clear, and for a second Asra thought she might have been too quick to judge him.

"Please what?" he said.

"Just . . . just leave me alone," Asra said, scanning his Bloody apron and turning to go. Her life certainly needed no further complications.

"I know you," the Elflad said with a cocky grin. "I know you from somewhere. I never forget a face. Does your father deliver meat to the market? Perhaps he knows my father! Does your mother clean out the stalls?"

"Of course not," Asra said haughtily, turning once again to the stranger. "My mother is the Qu—"

She managed to catch herself in midsentence. "My mother brings in eggs from our farm outside the gates. Now I beg your pardon, I'm here with my father, and if he finds me talking to a lad like you, he'll be happy to poke out your eyes!"

"I knew I'd seen you before," the Elf called, watching Asra go. He thought she was probably lying about her father, but it was better to be safe than sorry. "I'll take a dozen of your eggs—no, two dozen! Bring 'em by the stall first thing next market day; that way you'll be sure to find me there!"

Asra hurried on through the market, having decided that it might be best to return to the palace before someone recognized her. As she approached a fruit stall she saw an Elfmaid, no more than half her age, sneaking a pomegranate beneath her apron. The girl slinked away with her prize, and the vendor, busily arranging goods, seemed not to notice. Then the vendor's young helper, an Elflad in a soiled cap, shot out an arm from behind a rack of persimmons and grabbed the girl. She cried out, but the boy wouldn't let her go. He threw her to the ground, swearing, as he reached into the girl's clothing and pulled out the stolen fruit. "I knew it," he cried in triumph.

A moment later the vendor, too, was on top of her. "Thief," he cried, "thief, you'll lose a hand for what you've done. Guards! Guards!"

As the Elfmaid struggled, tears ran down her cheeks. She was too weak from hunger to fight, and she soon gave up squirming in the boy's grip. Asra watched helplessly. She saw that the girl's clothes were dirty and worn, and despite her youth, there were black spaces in her mouth where teeth ought to have been. Before many others had gathered around to watch the spectacle of the palace guards beating the girl and dragging her away in chains, Asra drew close to the fruit vendor and spoke into his ear. "How much for the pomegranate? I'll pay for it. Just let the girl go."

"You must be joking," the Elf snorted. "She's a criminal, and she must pay!"

"I'll pay," Asra said, and withdrew one of the coins she'd been saving to buy herself a new dress. She held it out for the vendor to see. "This should be enough to purchase a dozen pieces of fruit. What do you say?"

The Elf grabbed the coin and shoved it into his pocket. "Let the ruffian go," he called to his assistant, and the Elflad got up reluctantly and wiped his hands on his trousers.

The Elfmaid leapt to her feet and vanished in the crowd. Asra shook her head and stalked on. *This place is horrid*, she said to herself. *How dare they treat one another this way! No wonder Macta turned out like he did, after spending his entire life in this cesspool.* She was just approaching an awning by the next corner when the Elfmaid whose life she'd saved stepped into her path. The girl looked up at the Princess with malice, cocked her head, and spit. "You think you're better than me?" she taunted. "You think you can just buy your way out of trouble? Life ain't that simple for some of us, sister. Stay out of my business, if you know what's good for you!"

Asra's mouth hung open. "The audacity," she managed to say, "the unmitigated gall!"

The Elfmaid turned on her heels and disappeared once more into the hubbub and confusion of the market. Another pair of Elves, carrying a small animal tied by its feet to both ends of a wooden stake, jostled their way past the Princess. "Be off," one of them cried. "You're blockin' the way!"

Asra looked over the heads of the crowd and the peaked stalls to the palace looming in the distance. Flags snapped on the turrets as chill breezes swept across the dull sky. Somehow, she longed to be back within the walls of that grim place. She felt in her pocket for the remaining coins and vowed that her next move would be wiser than before. She had to focus, she had to rise to the occasion; she could not allow herself to be brought down by the perverse misery of this place. She had to be prepared, more than prepared, when the Arvada took her to the North Pole in search of her friend Becky. She found a stall with simple, utilitarian clothing made of cotton and wool. "I need to dress for cold weather," she told the proprietress. "I need leggings, trousers, a jacket with a fitted bodice and sleeves, and a felt cap."

Asra chose an outfit that would allow for multiple layers of clothing, topped with a hooded cloak made of wool. It took all the remaining money to pay for the garments, but when she turned toward the palace of Helfratheim with a large sack draped over her arm, she felt confident and in control of her life. The feeling was novel to her. It fit her, however, like a new suit of clothes.

10

JARDAINE'S ARVADA NEARED the Pole. Casting
its shadow over the Arctic Ocean, it suddenly trembled and
lurched forward. The flying contraption gained altitude as
well as speed. Squeezed inside the cab, Becky felt herself slip
to the aft. Her head banged the brass wall behind her. "What
is it?" she called out fearfully, and Jardaine heard her all the
way in the quarterdeck. "What's wrong?" Becky cried louder.
"Astrid?"

"Not again," Jardaine groused and got up from her seat.
She stumbled to the portside, grabbing on to the rigging
that stretched like a spiderweb along the wall. She waited
impatiently for the cab to stabilize and stared glumly at the
hatch separating her from the girl.

"We've slipped back into the Faerie realm," the captain said, trying to sound calm and to keep Jardaine in good humor. "The Sprite always knows when the quality of the air changes, and it can't contain its joy. That's why the velocity and altitude increase, though it's only momentary, until the pilots rein the Sprite back in. Its emotions aren't complex, but they're quite powerful and hard to control. Not the smoothest ride, but 'tis fast and reliable. Like riding a dragon, you might say."

"I would never say that," Jardaine grumbled. "Dragons don't exist. But there's something else. I smell burning! Are we being attacked again?"

"Nooo," he answered. "We sense no fear or trepidation from the beast; we'd know if there was imminent danger. There *is* something in the air, though. Dark clouds, ahead!"

Nick sniffed as he gathered up his playing cards. "'Tis not burning flesh but burning wood. A forest fire, perhaps?"

Jardaine shook her head. "Look out the window, fool, there are no forests down there. There's only ice, and snow, and black water. Wait . . . there's more ice, now, than when we were over the Human realm! Strange — where would smoke come from?"

"Astrid, what's wrong?" Becky cried again. "I smell something bad!"

"I'm coming!" Jardaine hollered. She turned to the captain. "Why don't you tell your so-called pilots to make the Sprite go higher? That way we'll get above the smoke."

The captain shook his head. "The air here is already thin.

'Twill be better to pass through the smoke than try to rise above it."

Jardaine flung open the hatch and stepped down. There was even more smoke in the hold than there had been on the quarterdeck. "I'm here," she rasped, tears stinging her eyes. "Don't be afraid, the fire's not on the Arvada. Take shallow breaths, and we'll get the Sprite to lift us up out of the smoke."

"How much longer until we reach the Pole?"

"Not long," Jardaine said. "The Aeronauts have been studying the maps and they feel we're getting very close, now. We just have to get past this—"

There was a jolt, and the Sprite tumbled downward. Jardaine fell hard against a crystal window and cracked it. Shards of glass fell as smoke rolled into the cab, and her robe billowed out into the frigid air. She caught herself. Gripping the brass window frame, Jardaine clung with all her might. She was slipping through the gaping hole. Becky pressed her hands against the top of the cab and pushed her feet against the fore, hoping to stabilize herself. But she fell to the side, and the weight of her body pressed Jardaine to the wall. *"Aaaaaarrrrrggg!"* the monk screamed, just as the Sprite righted itself and flew forward again. Though none inside the Arvada could yet see, the Sprite had collided with an enormous gnarled branch, reaching from the trunk of a tree as tall as a mountain. Many other twisted boughs stretched, barely visible, from the smoke. The monks in the city below worked their magick so that Hunaland, and Yggdrasil, the mighty Adri, were cloaked from afar. Only as the travelers drew close did the tree finally become visible to the naked eye.

The Sprite had been bruised, but not punctured. It flicked its tail and made a wide circle around the periphery of the tree. Because the Sprite was a translucent being, keeping a safe distance from branches that were barely visible, much of what could be seen at this distance was smoke. "Look!" the Aeronauts cried, pointing from the window of the quarterdeck. "I think . . . I think I see the tree, the great tree!"

From the hold, with its small round windows, Becky and Jardaine could finally see the tips of the sun-bleached branches reaching toward them. There were no leaves on the tree. There was no fruit, at least none that was visible. The tree looked dead, and it was now obvious where the smoke that filled the sky was coming from. Rising from countless sacrificial bonfires along the streets of Hunaland the smoke swirled, curling into the heavens, as arctic winds caught it and dragged it across the sky. "We're here!" Becky cried, oblivious to the dismal look of the place. "We're here, and we can find Matt and bring him home!"

"Aye," Jardaine said, pressing her forehead against a crystal window and staring glumly. If the tree were dead, she realized, if there were no fruit, and no Seed, then there would be no quest, no hero's journey, nothing but failure, embarrassment, and shame, once again. *At least if I fail,* she thought with grim satisfaction, *Tuava-Li will fail, too.* "We're here, Becky," she said with a mannequin's smile. "We've reached our destination!"

The Arvada circled the legendary tree for a while, while the Aeronauts assessed the best spot for landing. The longer they gazed in the direction of the tree, the clearer its dimensions became. Its enormity was far greater than any of them had imagined; though they all knew the myth from the days of their youth, it was difficult to believe that the tree was really as big as it appeared. Its higher boughs, reaching toward the heavens, disappeared in the atmosphere. Around the base of the trunk the city of Hunaland curled, like a blanket around an old Elf's legs. Becky and Jardaine peered down through the smoke-clouded windows of the Arvada. They had stretched a piece of tarpaulin over the broken window to keep out the bitter cold, but the temperature in the hold had dropped precipitously, and their teeth chattered as they peered out through the gray haze. From above the town was a patchwork of snow-covered roofs. The streets were densely packed, and everywhere hordes of Faerie Folk clustered around bonfires. "What are all those little fires for?" Becky asked.

"Smoke signals to the Gods and Goddesses," Jardaine answered. "Or maybe they're simply freezing! If they weren't desperate, they'd never risk lighting fires under their Sacred Tree."

With high stone walls enclosing both the city and the roots of the tree, there appeared to be only one way in or out; and yet there were no visible roads leading to or from the gates of the fortress.

"I must go and speak with the captain," Jardaine said to Becky.

Becky shivered uncontrollably. "Astrid," she stammered, "I—I'm so cold!"

"I'll be back as soon as we've landed!"

Since the Arvada had entered the Faerie realm once again, the black seas and thawing ice floes of the Human realm had been replaced with a vast sheet of white, brilliant and blinding. If the ice were thin, the Aeronauts speculated, it would appear gray to the naked eye. But since the ice looked thick and solid, they decided to bring down their craft just outside the gates. The Arvada landed with a dull thud, followed immediately by a sharp report, like the crack of a rifle. A black line zigzagged across the ice and disappeared in the distance. When the crew climbed down the rope ladders and went to anchor the Arvada in the ice, they found puddles of frigid water pooling around the base. The ice creaked and groaned with the tension of the ropes, straining from the hooks affixed to the underside of the hovering craft. "So the ice here is just a step behind the Human realm," Jardaine said to the Aeronauts as she exited from the cab and made her way carefully down the brass steps. "It's all melting." Swathed in fur, with her eyes shielded from the sun by tiny goggles, Jardaine paused and made a sweeping gesture with one gloved hand. "Soon Hunaland will sink beneath the waves."

"I was under the assumption that Hunaland was situated on solid earth," the captain said. "In the Human realm the North Pole is an unfixed point over a frozen sea, but now it seems that *our* world has taken on the properties of theirs. Why else would there be a film of ice over water here? How could a tree stand without soil to hold it up? What would all that salt water mean for the roots?"

"Salt water would gnaw away at the roots," Jardaine said, stepping cautiously onto the ice. "Perhaps that's why the tree is dead."

"If the tree is dead, there will be no fruit for you to pick, no Seed for you to plant."

The captain's words buzzed annoyingly inside Jardaine's head as she turned to face the crew. "I don't like this," she said. "The Elves here must have seen our Arvada circling overhead, and yet they've shown no reaction—neither a gracious welcoming committee with parades and banners to greet us, nor soldiers at the battlements with arrows to fire upon the strangers. Nothing at all. There are no paths, roads, footprints, or anything outside the gates. Look at them!"

The twin doors at the entryway were made of wood so old and rough that it might as well have been petrified. Surrounding the doors were ornate carvings: hundreds of figures, engaged in the act of gathering, sowing, and planting seeds. Larger figures, immense, muscular figures with multiple arms like tree branches, blocky heads, and thick trunks, were set into niches in the walls. The carvings were worn from exposure to ice and wind, but the expressions on the sculpted faces were unmistakable. They were joyful. They were at one with their world and at peace with themselves. Atop the gate was an immense two-headed figure, with bushy leaves growing from its hands and arms. These carvings of Tree Faeries contrasted poignantly with the barren branches of the once-mighty tree, Yggdrasil, looming above. Through clouds of smoke it appeared to be nothing but a jumble of petrified limbs. Plumes of fresh smoke lifted through the branches like souls of the departed.

"Look at the gates," Jardaine said. "I think they're just for show. I don't believe they've ever been opened."

"Then what would you suggest?" the captain asked, shivering. His nose dripped into his drooping gray mustache. "We can't stand out here much longer without freezing to death!"

"Go and release the Human from the hold," Jardaine ordered, and a dozen Aeronauts raced across the ice, glad for the opportunity to move around. "Don't forget, she calls me Astrid, and so should you."

"You don't really look much like an *Astrid*," the captain said, wiping his nose on his sleeve.

"What does an *Astrid* look like? Now listen. Nick and the Human will accompany me when we enter Hunaland. You and your crew will remain with the Arvada, until you receive further orders from me."

The captain nodded, delighted to know that his time with Jardaine was nearly over. Once she was out of his sight, he planned to untie the Arvada and set off for home, despite her orders.

Jardaine reached into her pocket and withdrew a folded piece of paper. "'Tis one of the spells I got from the Techmagicians at Helfratheim," she explained, her thick gloves making it hard to unfold the paper. "'Twill raise the girl's body temperature from inside her, so she doesn't die out here."

When it was clear that the captain was not going to comment, Jardaine glanced up at him. "You presumed that I didn't really care about her, didn't you?"

"I never gave it any thought," the captain replied. "The Human is your business, not mine. My job was to bring the three of you here, and I've accomplished my mission."

Jardaine frowned. "Your duty is to follow my commands, sir. And your mission is far from over, believe me!" She looked down at the spell printed on the paper, mouthing the words. Then she glanced up at the captain again. "Not only that, but anyone with half a brain would be inspired by my compassion! My thoughts are only of Becky's well-being. It isn't every day you meet an Elf who cares so deeply about a Human."

When the Aeronauts loosened the screws at the back of the hold and dropped the long brass flap so that its edge struck the ice, Becky squirmed out of her prison. She was so stiff with cold that she could barely stand when she finally got her legs out of the cab. "Dear one," Jardaine soothed, "we have no cold-weather clothing for you to wear, but I will cast a spell that will keep you warm until we are inside the gates. Now stand straight, and close your eyes."

Becky did as she was told, though her knees were knocking and her teeth chattered. "Hurry, Astrid," she said, then added, "p-p-please!"

Jardaine read from the crumpled page. *"Naum sole au folla,"* she began, absently contemplating where this spell might have originated. She didn't recognize the language and wasn't confident about her pronunciation. Surely the spell must have come from a place with a cold, northern climate. *How does it work?* she wondered. *Appeal to invisible spirits? Projection of will? A few circling Fire Sprites would probably do the job just as well, if I had them.* "Juae cvarollan, et tamey tvvorin."

She looked up at Becky; it was obvious the spell had had no effect. The girl was hunched over, her arms wrapped tightly around herself, her cheeks and nose red with cold. *I'll try it again,* Jardaine said to herself. *I must have the pronunciation wrong.*

"Are you sure your eyes are closed tightly?" she asked Becky.

"I'm s-s-sure!"

Jardaine concentrated more deeply on the words this time as she pictured a microscopic world inside her, where tiny orbs of energy spun faster and faster, generating heat. She knew she had to *feel* the spell as well as simply repeat the words.

She imagined leaping flames consuming a fireplace log. She thought of Alfheim, her own homeland, burning. *"Naum ſole au folla, Juae cvarollan, et tamey tvvorin."*

Becky's rigid expression dissolved as she opened her eyes and looked down at her feet. "You did it," she said in amazement. "Astrid, you did it! It's like warmth creeping up my legs, like I'm standing on something hot. But I'm not, am I?"

She stepped back, to see if her sneakers had left melted tracks in the ice below. "There's nothing there. Where is the heat coming from? Oh, I opened my eyes! Is it all right?"

"Of course, child," Jardaine said. She tingled with pleasure that the spell had worked. It gave her confidence that the other spells she had taken from the Techmagician would be equally effective. "Come now. Becky, and Nick, we're going to look for another entrance to Hunaland. These gates are not meant for us, I'm sure of it."

The Captain of the Arvada rolled his eyes. What could she be thinking now? His face was numb from the cold as he called to his crew. "Back inside the ship, lads, there's no need for us to wait around out here and freeze!"

"Just a moment," Jardaine commanded, stepping close to the captain. "You have my permission to go and warm yourself inside your ship, but I order you to keep the Arvada moored here until our return from the center of the earth. Do you understand? I am a Mage with many powers, and if you choose not to obey me, I shall call upon all of the forces at my disposal to seek vengeance. Your death will not be a pleasant one, I assure you!"

"But of course," the captain said obligingly, quite certain that he would never see Jardaine again. He'd already made up his mind to leave the North Pole as soon as she and her crew were safely out of his sight.

Jardaine led Nick and Becky along the length of the fortress wall.

The air was smoky, but the black clouds drifting above the walls carried away most of the fumes and ash. "What are we looking for?" Nick cried, stumbling over the lumpy ice. "We didn't see any other entryways from the air. We might spend an entire day tramping around this fortress and see nothing, and then we'll be right back where we started!"

Jardaine struggled to rein in her anger. The image of herself that she'd been creating for Becky's benefit was an illusion of kindness and patience. "There's something odd about this place," she said thoughtfully. "I wouldn't rely on what we think we saw from above, as we were looking through tree branches as well as smoke! There's much we might have missed. Have faith in my intuition, Becky and Nicholas, there will be another entrance — I'm sure of it."

Nick pressed his lips tightly together. He knew that whenever Jardaine called him by his full name, she was angry. It was foolish of him to have questioned her judgment, especially in front of the girl. "Then I'm sure, too," he murmured.

Ten feet above the icy ground, a decorative frieze, running the entire length of the wall, was cut into the stone. Becky tried to make sense of the carvings as she passed. It seemed odd that so many of the sculptures seemed to be about farming, sowing, and harvesting, when everything around was covered in ice. Every twenty feet or so they passed a carved column, depicting scenes of animals and Faerie Folk. Between the columns were niches, like small doorways, in which stone figures stood. The borders of the niches were decorated with stone snakes, braided together in long coils. The carvings were so lifelike that Becky imagined the figures might jump out at her. She began to feel anxious. "Astrid, do you think we'll be able to catch up with them?" she asked. "I mean, Matt, and Tomtar, and Tuava-Li? Do you think they already have the Seed, and they're headed underground? Are we too late?"

"Don't worry, child," Jardaine said. "Just have some faith in me, and all will be well. Remember? Say it with me now. *All will be well.*"

"All will be well," Becky repeated, as Jardaine reached the end of the wall. As she stepped out of the shadow and into the sunlight, the wind caught the corner of her coat and shook it like laundry on a clothesline. Jardaine didn't stop or turn along the wall. Instead she walked straight ahead. Becky slowed her pace, confused. She was about to say something when Nick put a finger to his lips. "Best just to follow," he whispered.

Once Jardaine was a hundred paces away from the wall,

she turned around. Holding up one hand to shield her face from the sun, she looked back. She studied the row of columns and niches and searched for any irregularities in the surface. Midway along the wall there was an empty niche with no figure inside. Though a strong shadow darkened the small archway, she could tell that the color streaking the inside was more brown than gray. "Look there," she said, pointing.

"What is it?" Becky cried. "What do you see?"

"A doorway, sweet one," Jardaine replied. "'Tis the door through which we were meant to make our entry. If I'm not mistaken, there will be Elves waiting to welcome us on the other side of that wall. Come!"

Jardaine stalked purposefully toward the niche. Nick and Becky followed. As they drew closer it was plain that Jardaine had been right; before them was a concealed wooden door, barely big enough for Becky to crawl through, but a door nonetheless. Surrounding the door were small geometric carvings; Becky thought it looked like a depiction of a maze, with twisted passageways and little paths in between. She touched the time-worn stone, letting her finger trail along one of the paths. Jardaine paused in the shadow with her back to Becky and Nick. She took a deep breath and knocked three times. Almost immediately a collective gasp rose from the countless Faerie Folk waiting inside. "They're here!" a faint voice exclaimed from within. "The people from the wingless b-b-bird have come to *our* door!"

The door creaked open. A gust of warm air poured over the trio of visitors as they stood stiffly in the cold; the sensation made each of them weak at the knees. Inside the gate, there was so much activity that it took a moment to register everything that was going on. Elfin guardsmen in long green coats flanked the door. The lower half of their faces were covered with sheer masks, but their eyes bulged in surprise. At the sight of Jardaine, Nick, and Becky entering through the gate, they fell to their knees and bowed their heads. Beyond the guards, a crowd of viridian-robed monks parted. They, too, dropped to their knees, forming a sea of green with an open channel down the middle. The path led to the massive trunk of Yggdrasil, looming in the smoky distance. Obscured in spirals of scaffolding that supported the weight of countless small dwellings, the trunk disappeared in a gray, dingy cloud high overhead. Pixies fluttered in the air, most of them averting their eyes and covering their mouths with their hands. Those that dared glanced nervously at Becky. Their fingers pointed as they chattered in bursts of broken syllables, unintelligible squeaks erupting from their tiny mouths. None of them had ever seen a Human before; Becky looked like a grotesque giant to them, with beady eyes and strange, misshapen ears. Some of them giggled nervously. Nick thought of his own Pixies, and it made his heart sore with longing.

Jardaine watched a single squat figure waddling down the length of the path, coming slowly toward her. "We must bow as well," she whispered to the others, "to show respect to the rulers of this place."

Awkwardly Jardaine got down on her knees, and with her gloved hands stretched before her, bowed her head low. She could almost feel the cold earth pulling her down; she resisted touching it with her forehead. Nick and Becky followed Jardaine's lead and knelt, too. "Come, pilgrims," came the warbling voice of the old monk. "Come with me. You must prepare to meet our Mage, and our Queen."

11

WHEN MORNING CAME the friends greedily ate the muffins and slightly withered-looking apples that Matt had bought the night before. None of them let a single crumb go to waste. Afterwards, dressed in their new outdoor gear, they filed into the hallway. Matt locked the door, led the way down the steps, and they headed toward Mary Suluk's place.

There were only a few distant figures dotting the harsh landscape; otherwise, the town seemed deserted. Matt had to squint to see through the glare. Tomtar and Tuava-Li plodded awkwardly with their mittens over their eyes, nearly blinded by the light. Everything, all the houses, fuel tanks, overturned boats and ATVs, as well as the gravel road, was blanketed by a salty white film. Matt could taste it on his lips. He quickened his pace. "Hold on!" Tomtar cried.

"We've gotta get some goggles," Matt said, as his friends stumbled behind. "We're not going anywhere if we can't see what's in front of us."

The old Inuit woman had suggested that they return in the morning, and Matt had many questions to ask. He'd been thinking about his parents, wondering if they'd managed to escape Helfratheim with the children who had fled into the forest there on the Canadian border. Perhaps he could contact the police or the fire department. Matt stuffed his mittens into his pockets, and drew in a deep breath of arctic air. It made him cough; his lungs felt brittle and fragile as glass. Unless he could find out some facts about his parents, something that would let him know whether or not they were back in the Human realm, then he was stuck on this path. He would still be obliged to help Tuava-Li and Tomtar find the Seed of the Adri and plant it at the hollow in the center of the earth. It still sounded crazy. Completely crazy, but here he was, traipsing around at the top of the world like it was the most natural thing to go on a quest for the sake of Faerie Folk. He felt a stab of something at the back of his mind and realized it was probably his conscience. He wasn't seeing things clearly. Tomtar and Tuava-Li were his friends, after all. Weren't they?

I'm helping them, he said to himself, *because that's what you do for friends, people you trust and care about, even if you don't agree with them one hundred percent on everything. And what—just what if they're right?* This had become something more than a trade-off, more than an agreement based on mutual need. Matt wasn't sure he'd ever felt anything quite like this before. He felt a little buoyant, somehow, as he trudged toward Mary Suluk's house. From one perspective, he had a purpose in life, something to really live for . . . if he lived long enough to see it all to its conclusion.

"Did you see the lights last night?" Mary chirped, when she answered Matt's knock on her door. "Come on in," she said, wiggling her fingers and smiling at Tomtar and Tuava-Li, who, by nature, needed to be invited to step foot into a Human dwelling. "They were incredible."

"What?"

"The northern lights, they were awesome last night. While you're here, you at least ought to see the lights."

"Nobody told me about it," Matt said. He remembered learning about the northern lights in school, but seeing some kind of light show in the sky wasn't top on his list of priorities.

"Well, if you go out tonight, you'll probably see them. It's cold, but it'll be worth it. Just pretend you're a tourist, here to see the sights."

"Okay."

The living room was full of children, sitting in front of the television as they had on the previous day. The place smelled damp and acrid, like diapers and sour milk. "Do you want some coffee?" Mary asked Matt. "I've got some muffins, too!"

She went to turn off her computer. Before the screen went blank, Matt thought he could make out the words *Shop Gems* at the top of the screen. There was a row of purple, blue, green, and gold stones, cut in geometric patterns, whose colors hung in a field of black. Then they disappeared.

"We already ate," Matt said, following Mary to the kitchen, as Tuava-Li trailed silently behind. "I hope you didn't go to any trouble for us."

On the table was a plate of corn muffins, looking suspiciously like the ones Matt had bought in the co-op. "I guess coffee would be okay, if you add a lot of milk and sugar."

"Have a seat," Mary said, filling a pot with water from the sink and turning on the burner on the propane stove. "What about you?" she asked Tuava-Li. "You wanna sit?"

"I believe I'll stand, thank you."

Mary shrugged and turned to Matt. "There's something I need to ask you. Do you know how to ski?"

Matt blinked in surprise. "Well, sort of. I used to go cross-country skiing with my family, but not so much since my baby sister was born. I've been downhill skiing a couple of times. Why do you ask?"

Mary smiled. "You remember my son-in-law, Joe, from last night? Remember I said he flew supply planes sometimes? I told him that you needed a lift after all, and that your dad left you some money for the fare. Joe checked with a friend about getting his hands on a Twin Otter, and if the friend can pull a few strings up at Alert, where he stops to refuel, Joe should be able to run you up there real soon! He'll have to grease a few wheels to make it happen, but it looks like you may be in luck, son!"

Matt furrowed his brow. "I don't have any money: cash, I mean. All I have are those jewels, like the ones I gave you last night. And what do skis have to do with anything?"

"I'll take care of the money," Mary said, sitting down at the table opposite Matt. "You're going to need supplies, and my daughter Joan will handle that. She's gonna pack you a sled, with cooking and camping equipment, food, a small kayak, and some skis for you. I told Joe that your dad was up at the Anderson camp, where the scientists were doing research this season. Joe knows how to get there, but it's still a ways from the North Pole. Without an ATV or a team of dogs you'll need skis to get the rest of the way. The pack is gonna weigh near two hundred pounds, and you can't drag it behind you if you've got nothin' on your feet but boots. Skis will do the job!"

"Sounds like it's going to cost a lot of money," Matt said suspiciously. He felt as if he were already in a little kayak, drifting helplessly off into deep, black water. "And what do I need a kayak for? Isn't everything frozen at the Pole?"

"Just a precaution."

"And what happens when we get to this campsite, and Joe sees that everybody's already gone? You think he'll just leave us?"

"There'll still be sheds and things up there," Mary said. "And the scientists are always out on the ice doing research during the day, anyway. Joe wouldn't give it a second thought if the place weren't crawling with people. Listen, Matt, I was thinkin' about how I greeted you yesterday when you came in, and I decided that I could stand to be a little more positive about things. You and your friends wouldn't have got this far unless you had somebody on your side, and far be it from me to quibble with the *Higher Powers*, if you know what I mean! If I can help you, son, I will."

Mary patted the back of Matt's hand and gave him a motherly smile. Matt smiled back, but wondered if he could trust her. She'd been looking at gemstones online, to try and find out what they might be worth. That could be perfectly innocent; she wanted to know what kind of exchange she might get for the jewels Matt had given her. He decided, for now, to put his doubts aside. "The one thing that worries me," he said, "is how we're going to get back home again after we plant the . . . well, after we finish what we came here to do. Is there a Cord, out there where your kids found us, that goes back to civilization?"

"This *is* civilization," Mary corrected him. "What you mean is *your* civilization. And yes, there's another Cord that runs along the same north-south route. You'll be able to make it back the direction you came from." She sat back. "As I said, there are powers working on your behalf. You gotta have faith in them."

Matt reached into his pocket and withdrew the sack with the

rest of his jewels in it. He placed it on the table. "Then I'll leave these with you. I don't know what they're worth, but I know it'll be more than the cost of renting a plane. Maybe way more."

At that moment Tomtar, who'd been hovering in the doorway, stepped into the room. "If it isn't enough," he said. "Tuava-Li and I still have pouches of our own in our —"

A fierce glance from Tuava-Li silenced the Troll, and embarrassed, he shot out a hand to grab a muffin from the plate on the edge of the table.

"I'm not gonna cheat you," Mary said. "I'll find some way to cash in these jewels, even if I have to go down to the city. When you come back this way, I'll give you whatever money is left over, beyond the cost of your trip and gear. I don't suppose you know how long you'll be up there, do you?" Mary glanced back and forth between Matt and Tuava-Li.

Tuava-Li shook her head. "We have no idea how long it will take. 'Tis a long journey to the center of the earth, and time in Elf Realm has never passed at the same rate that it does here in the Human world . . . though that's changed since the borders between our worlds have weakened. In times gone by, a Human who accidentally entered Elf Realm might spend a night or two with us, only to return home and discover that a hundred years had passed."

"I wouldn't expect Joe to wait a hundred years," Mary snorted.

"No," Tuava-Li said. "'Tis not like that, anymore. Several

times Matt has passed over the border with no perceptible lost time. But none has undertaken this quest in thousands of moons, so 'tis hard to say with certainty."

"Well, by the end of September, we won't have daylight again until March. You think you'll be done up on the Pole by then? Joe's not gonna want to take a plane up there once winter sets in."

"Aye," said Tuava-Li, looking nervously at Matt. "That should be long enough."

For his part, he felt a wave of shock pass through him, followed by despair. He berated himself for not pressing Tuava-Li harder about how long their adventure might take. If he was gone underground for too long, who knew what disasters might befall his parents? The possibility of rescuing them seemed ever more remote.

"We'll get you a two-way radio," Mary said, "and you can call Joe when you're ready to get picked up. We'll pack it with your things."

"I've never used one of those before," Matt said. Once again he was faced with his lack of survival skills. He could barely breathe.

"Look, everything will be all right. I know you're taking a lot of risks, and that you're bound to run into dangerous situations, but there are the three of you, after all, and I can't help but think that Faerie Folk know how to get by out in Mother Nature. You're on a quest, and the Goddess is working on your behalf, right?"

Matt looked at Tuava-Li. She nodded her head confidently.

Mary smiled and said, "I'll meet you at the co-op after I'm done with work, and Joan can show you how to set up a tent and tie it down on the ice, how to use a Coleman stove, how to pack and unpack gear. Most of it's easy stuff; you'll get the hang of it right away."

"Can I look on your computer?" Matt asked. "There are some things I really need to check out."

"Help yourself," Mary said.

Matt sat down in the battered old chair, got online, and searched for information about a fire in Sylvan Estates. There was nothing beyond an outdated Realtor's ad for luxury housing, and a small notice in a local Pennsylvania paper about the fire. He tried to open his mother's e-mail account, to see if there had been any activity, but none of the passwords he could think of would let him in. He was getting nowhere. He wrote his mom an e-mail from his own account. *Just in case she's somewhere she can see it,* he thought. In the first draft of his note he wrote that he was fine, and that he was going to do his best to help them, and that he was so sorry that all this had happened, that it was all his fault. He wrote the letter three or four different times, erasing the messages one after the other. They all sounded awkward and insincere. *Who am I kidding?* he thought. *She'll never see it, anyway.* He realized he'd have as much luck putting a message in a bottle and tossing it into the ocean. Then he looked up *arctic survival* and began scrolling through mountains of information, making notes on a pad at the side of the desk.

For Tuava-Li the afternoon crawled past. She watched Matt at the computer and Tomtar playing with the children, teaching them some games common to Trolls. He played his flute for them. There was much laughter and merriment, and Tomtar looked disappointed when the clock struck five, even though he'd spent nearly the entire day indoors. Mary shooed Tomtar, Tuava-Li, and Matt into one of the bedrooms and shut them in. She didn't want anyone to ask too many questions about the boy; they would have surely heard about him by now. She also didn't want to take the chance that Tomtar and Tuava-Li might be seen. They waited there in silence until all the children had been picked up by their mothers and fathers. "You can come on out now," Mary said, calling from the other side of the door. "It's time we head over to the co-op."

They all tugged on their cold-weather clothes and headed out into the chilly night. "You know," Matt said to Tomtar, "for somebody who doesn't like to be cooped up in human dwellings for long, you did okay today!"

"I did?" Tomtar answered with a shiver.

Later, after receiving some elementary camping lessons from Mary's daughter, Matt bought food for himself and his friends and hurried to his room at the back of the building. His mood was glum; he was pretty sure he didn't have what it took to brave the elements at the North Pole. With no experience and little training, the whole adventure left him feeling wary. Expert polar trekkers had died because of simple mistakes; how could he expect to do better? He wasn't very excited about seeing the northern lights, either. Mary had told him he'd get the best view of the light show around midnight, but Matt was exhausted and just wanted to eat and go to sleep. Tomtar and Tuava-Li, however, were curious about the lights. They'd both heard Faerie legends about the aurora borealis, and they were anxious to see if the display of solar lights would reveal anything about the bridge between the realms. Reluctantly Matt agreed to stay up with them.

As the hour grew late, the three sat in their room with the window cracked open. Tomtar was propped on the edge of the bed, breathing in the cold air. Tuava-Li sat with her eyes closed and legs crossed in meditation. Matt huddled by the heater in the corner, reading. In the laundry room, which scientists and travelers seemed to use as a lending library, Matt had found a book about the geological structure of the earth. "You know," he said, "it's four thousand miles from the surface of the earth to the core at the center. Do you guys know how far four thousand miles is?"

When he got no response, Matt continued. "Well, I'll tell you. It's nearly as far as going from New York to Los Angeles, and then coming back again. Do you have any idea how long it would take us to walk that distance, even if we didn't have to face rivers of molten magma and pressure that would crush our bodies flatter than a piece of paper?"

"What's New York?" Tomtar asked.

Matt grumbled and slammed the covers of his book. "The Human realm and the Elf realm are not the same," Tuava-Li said softly, rousing herself from her reverie. "One cannot expect to find the same things at the center of two different worlds."

"But we share the same world, don't we?" Matt said, getting up. Once again he was feeling hopeless. "How could things be so different? Tell me!"

Tomtar got out his flute, hoping some music might relieve the tension. "I think it's a good time for some tunes," he chirped. He lifted the flute to his lips and Matt shot him a look. "People are going to start banging on the walls, Tomtar. Remember, we don't want anybody to know you guys are here!"

"There's nobody else staying here," Tomtar replied. "You said so yourself, Matt. It's just us!"

"This quest has been undertaken before, Matthew," Tuava-Li said. "'Tis not impossible. We'll prevail."

Matt shrugged and got down on the carpet next to the heater. "Prevail," he repeated, as if he found the word itself absurd. He went back to reading his book on geology. Tomtar played a long, slow improvisation on his favorite song, "The Bonnie Banks of Loch Lomond." Matt felt tense; every time he heard the song, it reminded him of his dad, who used to sing it, and every time he thought of his dad, he was overwhelmed with sadness. Matt knew Tomtar meant well, but thought that the Troll ought to at least learn some new songs. He kept his mouth shut and tried to lose himself in the book.

Some time after eleven, Matt suggested to his friends that they'd waited long enough. They slipped into their coats, hats, and mittens, went out the side door, and looked up into the sky. Matt gasped. He spun around, taking in the vastness of the curtain of green that hung high across the night. It was strange, completely surreal. He could never have guessed. The wind roared, and the shapes overhead, like silk curtains lit from inside, twisted and turned in the air. "I've seen some crazy things," he said, "but nothing like this! These lights are the background on my tattoo!"

"'Tis a sign," Tomtar breathed, "clear as day!" His eyes were saucers; he blinked as if he could scarcely believe what he saw. "I knew it, I knew there would be a sign from the Goddess!"

Tuava-Li said nothing, but a tear rolled down her cheek and froze there. She wiped it away with the back of a mitten; the skin on her face hurt, burned with the cold. She shivered, realizing it wasn't just the frigid air that was shaking her but the presence of something magick. "It's like it's alive, like . . . like the underside of some giant green jellyfish, from the bottom of the sea," Matt cried. "I can't think of how to describe it!"

"You don't need to," Tomtar shouted into the wind. "We can all see what's happening. The Goddess is telling us everything will be all right!"

Matt walked down the steps and onto the gravel roadway, his boots crunching and his breath coming in frozen gulps. How many afternoons, he wondered, had he sat with Tomtar and Becky on the hill above his home and watched the clouds in the sky shift and change? It was nothing compared to this; nothing could compare with this. Misshapen neon faces thrust out of the darkness, then turned to ghosts, tendrils of chartreuse and jade swaying from their chins. Waves of moss and oceans of sap poured over the sky, sweeping away the faces and bringing in herds of spectral horses, stampeding across the heavens, throwing up clouds of teal and celadon. "The warring virgins, armed with helmets and swords," Tuava-Li cried, pointing, "just like in the legends. They're traveling through the realms, their shields shedding light!"

Matt shook his head; the Faeries were so full of superstition. "It's solar winds, Tuava-Li, we learned it in school. It's all particles from the sun, colliding with our atmosphere along the earth's magnetic field. That's all. It's still beautiful, though!"

No one could argue with those words. Tomtar and Tuava-Li shivered, watching the luminous shapes tumble over one another, fire and ice sweeping from one end of the sky to the other. Matt gasped; as he stood transfixed at the sight, he'd forgotten to breathe. The bitter cold made him cough, and he stumbled down the road past his friends. He saw the dark shapes of houses and sheds around him, rigid and still, and there was no sign of life anywhere. *Why isn't everybody out here to see this?* he wondered, then realized that such a display was probably nothing to the people who lived here, who got to see the northern lights whenever they wanted.

The parade of lights went on and on. Matt and his friends watched until their necks were sore. It was like being in a trance, watching the skies, watching the edge of the curtains of light fill, then spill back out in rivers of glowing green ink. "Let's go," Matt said finally. "We should get some sleep."

Tomtar was nearly dancing as they returned to the steps that led into the co-op. Later, as Matt fell asleep in the lumpy bed, he dreamt he was in an airplane that purred and thumped through a sky filled with sparks and flashes of green, and that he could hear the hooves of the spectral horses beating in his ears. "It's a sign," he mumbled in his sleep.

12

PRASHTA WAS COMPLETELY green with rage. With his body as stiff as the trunk of an old oak tree, he stood wheezing, puffing and working his jaw, his hands clenching and unclenching, as he tried to find the words to express his fury. "The unmitigated . . . , " he fumed, "how dare you, you little . . . you . . . have you no, no . . . *shame*?!"

Asra sat on the cold stone floor, glaring at the Council of Seven. They stood at a distance from the Princess, their arms folded; they looked profoundly uncomfortable in this place. Most of them had never actually stepped foot in the dungeon. Here, the art of coercion was practiced on uncooperative citizens, those unfortunate souls required to make their confessions at the point of a hot lance or a pair of sharp pincers. "I came back,"

Asra cried. "I didn't talk to anyone, I didn't tell anyone anything, I went out, and I came back. What's so wrong with that? If your guards hadn't caught me slipping back into the palace, you wouldn't even have known."

Prashta's jowls were shaking. "You left without permission, Elfmaid. *Anything* might have happened. Because of you and that Human girl, and Macta, too, as a matter of fact, the delicate balance of our leadership has been upset. You spoiled Brahja-Chi's Acquisition, you spoiled our plans for warfare with the Humans, and now, this disobedience. *Nothing* can be left to chance, Asra, we must keep tight rein over the smallest events to maintain control. You deliberately showed disrespect for those who have been your kind and generous hosts."

"Where's Macta?" Asra demanded.

"He's out looking for you! Do you think we could stop him? When he's got so much preparation to do before his big speech, he's racing up and down the streets of Helfratheim calling your name. Perhaps once you're married to him, all this nonsense will stop."

"You don't care about me marrying Macta any more than I do," Asra said venomously. "'Tis plain to see that you despise the King, and you welcomed his return as much as you'd welcome an infestation of bedbugs. You and your merry band of henchmen want all the power of this kingdom for yourselves, and Macta's return is a thorn in your side that you can't wait to have removed. Why else would you welcome this mission to the Arctic?"

Prashta raised an eyebrow ironically. "Oh? You think that planting the Seed of the Adri is ill advised, Princess? Oh dear, perhaps we haven't really thought the whole thing through." He turned to his cronies. "What do you say, gentle Elves, perhaps we should reconsider?"

Raucous laughter reverberated through the chamber. Prashta knelt so close to Asra that she could smell the onions on his breath. "If Macta returns having planted the Seed, he will be at *our* command, as we are united in our resolve to handle things here . . . properly. If he should fail in his mission, however, we will still stand united to rule Helfratheim as it should have always been run — a thriving business. Riches are the new Gods, Asra, untold riches. Royalty is dead, just like mythology, with its paper-thin heroes and villains. In our new world, dead heroes are the only kind really worth having. Don't you agree, Princess?"

Asra spit into Prashta's flabby face. She was shocked by her own impulsive behavior, but no more than Prashta was shocked by the sharp gust of air across the back of his neck, and the blow that sent him hurtling to the floor. The protective amulet that had hung around his neck bounced on the floor next to him; the string that held it close to his body had been cut. "Macta!" he whimpered, looking up, as his hand groped for the lost amulet.

Macta, dressed like a commoner, towered over Prashta. He kicked the amulet from the old Elf's grasp. Macta gazed in delight at the polished crystal blade affixed to the mechanical forefinger of his own right hand. He was learning to use the artificial arm and hand with finesse; he'd sent the mental signal to release the blade from its sheath alongside the finger, and stretched the arm forward to slice the cord from Prashta's neck without severing the old Elf's spine in the process. *What an improvement techmagick was over nature!* he thought. But his joyful expression quickly faded. "I heard a rumor that the Princess had returned; now I find you've brought her here, to this foul place!"

He reached out a hand to help her up. "Are you all right, my darling?" he murmured, as she stood.

"What are you—how did you . . . your arm?" Asra stammered, her eyes wide in disbelief. Staring at the mechanical limb, she got to her feet.

Macta lifted the arm, turning the hand this way and that and wriggling the fingers for the Princess to see. "I owe a debt of gratitude to the Techmagicians of Helfratheim," he said, "for my new, improved arm. But the Council owes *me* an explanation, and it had better be good! Why have you brought Princess Asra to the dungeon? Prashta, do your eyes long to look down upon the palace grounds from the top of a pike, where your severed head will hang?"

Prashta dragged his bulk across the floor and, with some effort, sat up. "'Tis her own fault, Macta. For her own safety, she must be kept under surveillance."

Macta's eyes turned to Asra. "He lies," the Princess said. "I went out into the market, 'tis true, but only to purchase cold-weather gear for myself. I returned of my own free will, and when I entered the palace, the guards snatched me up and treated me like a common criminal. The rest, you can see with your own eyes."

Macta approached Prashta, who held his amulet before him like a talisman. "You can't touch me," he cried. "I'm protected!"

"You're lucky I let you live at all," Macta sneered. "What do you think are the odds that I lose my temper and have you cut into tiny pieces and fed to the crows?"

"Not so fast, Macta," said Lehtinen in a steely voice. "If you think you are in charge here, you're sadly mistaken. Since your father's death, there's been a shift in power in Helfratheim. We have the military on our side, as well as the Techmagicians, and all those in cabinet positions in the government who wish to see our nation evolve and thrive. Though you may remain King, you're but a figurehead, here to do our bidding and follow our orders. That's all. Now step away from Prashta."

A pair of guards moved hesitantly toward Macta, their hands on the hilts of their swords. Macta pointed a mechanical finger at Lehtinen. His voice was a fearsome snarl. "You, my friend, are sadly mistaken if you think you can tell me what to do. I will have your head for treason. I will have the heads of the lot of you!"

Prashta was on his feet now, an imploring look on his face. "This is not the way we wish to do business," he said. "There should be no conflict among us; we must act as parts of one well-oiled machine, with the same goal, the same destination in sight. Lehtinen, you speak out of place when you say those things to your King. If there be a pecking order in our new regime, 'tis there only to see that each of us does our proper duty, showing fealty to the empire we love so well."

"You will show fealty to me alone!" Macta roared.

"No," said Lehtinen, "the rules of this game have changed, Macta, and you must change with them. That is why we've given you a new arm, and a quest to fulfill. You'll be a hero, thanks to us! Be grateful." The Elf scratched his chin and cast a glance at Asra. "Perhaps we *were* harsh with the Elfmaid. Take her with you if you wish, Macta; we don't need her kind of trouble. But return to your preparations for the speech tonight! There is much to be done before the Arvada comes to deliver you to your destiny."

"*The two of us,* you mean," Asra said to Lehtinen. "I'm going along, in search of Rebecca as well as the Seed." This *was* a time for new allegiances, she understood. If she needed to stay at Macta's side in order to get out of the dungeon, then so be it. It was her own choice, made of her own free will. Just because she chose to walk at his side, though, didn't mean she would be tied to him forever.

"Let us pass," Macta said, turning toward the guards who stood aghast in the doorway. He shook his fist at Prashta, Lehtinen, and the others. "This little discussion isn't over!" He took Asra by the arm and stormed into the corridor.

Asra stayed with Macta as he puffed and postured away the afternoon, plotting one revenge fantasy after another against his Council. All the while he stroked the fur of his new Goblin pup, feeding it treats, cooing and coaxing it to behave. Asra sat silently as tailors finished sewing Macta's gleaming satin suit, as the speechwriters coached him on how and where in the speech he should try to sound heartfelt, and where he should speak with righteous indignation. Later that night, smiling beatifically, Asra stood beside Macta on the balcony as he delivered his address to the Elves of Helfratheim. She wore a new gown, and she bowed and waved at the appropriate moments. She accepted, without quarrel, her introduction as Macta's fiancée. She dined with Macta and the Council members after the speech, as Powcca prowled beneath the table, begging for scraps. She listened to the royal mythmakers explain the legend of Fada and the heroes of the past who had planted the Sacred Seed of the Adri and saved Elf Realm. Asra smiled, and nodded, and held her feelings in check. She was making a bargain with herself, that she could rein in her emotions and play the role required of her, in exchange for the payoff—finding Rebecca, and winning her freedom.

Late that night, alone in her bed, Asra shivered. Though she willed the tears to come, to wash away her sadness, her loneliness, her contempt for this kingdom and everyone in it, her cheeks remained dry. Asra wondered how her heart was growing so cold. Then she felt something in her mind turn, just slightly. It was as if she were looking at her life through a crystal, and the light had shifted just enough for her to see it from another angle. In this strange and different light, Macta was no longer a vile, contemptible villain. He was simply another lost soul, trying to find a way to claim a few crumbs from life's vast, inequitable table. There was no longer a wall of hate between her and the King of Helfratheim, and she felt . . . what was it? Pity? She'd felt that, before. Sympathy? Compassion? Was it an understanding that they were on the same road, following the same path, moving inexorably toward the same end? When the history books were written, Asra's and Macta's names would be there, side by side. There was no way around it. Asra pulled the blankets close in around her neck. Her eyes and her lips were pressed tightly shut. She curled herself into a ball and for a moment, just before sleep overcame her, thought of herself as a seed, lying dormant inside a dark, hard shell, waiting to be born.

13

IN AN ISOLATED ROOM set aside by the monks of
Hunaland for their Human guest, Becky shivered. It was
not from inner turmoil, though; she was simply cold. Since
Jardaine's warming spell had worn off, she'd spent the night
tossing and turning on a lumpy pallet stuffed with tiny seed
husks. Her blanket had little more weight or substance than
dried brown leaves stitched together. As Hunaland was
situated at the top of the Elfin world, Becky had assumed that
the temperature there had always been frigid, like the North
Pole was to the humans. She learned that assumption had
been wrong. Not long ago, when the great tree, Yggdrasil, was
healthy and strong, its trunk and branches radiated warmth
that kept the citizens of Hunaland comfortable year-round.

But now, since the tree around which the city had been built was dying, its warmth was fading as well. Slowly the climate around Hunaland had begun to change, and cold was settling around it like a blanket of ice. Everyone in Hunaland shivered away the long nights; their dwellings were not as cold as the temperature outside the gates of the city, to be sure; none could survive *that* for long. The tree still had some feeble life left in it, so the citizens of Hunaland did not freeze. Few had clothing fit for extremely low temperatures, though, and the dwellings of the Elves of Hunaland had never been heated with fireplaces. The cold kept Becky at the edge of sleep, where she dreamed fitfully of summer waves crashing on a beach, and the eager ring of an ice-cream-truck bell. It rang and rang.

"Wake up!" a voice called from the darkness.

Becky sat up, rubbing her eyes, and saw three creatures standing in the shadows of the doorway, ringing a bell. She was startled, and it took her a moment to discern from their robes that they were Hunaland monks, wearing strange, carved masks. The noses of their masks were long, pointed things, almost like the beaks of aquatic birds. Each of them carried what looked like a wooden egg, and tendrils of smoke curled from little holes pierced in the wood. The air stank of incense. Vapor puffs came from the mouth holes of the masks as one of the creatures spoke again in a harsh whisper. "Get up! Get moving, Human! 'Tis time to stand before the Queen and the Holiest of Holies, the Mage of Hunaland!"

"Where are Astrid and Nick?" Becky asked warily.

Silence. Then one of the monks spoke. "Nearby. You will join them soon."

Becky was annoyed by the fierce expressions carved on the Elves' false faces, and embarrassed that she had been more than a little frightened when she first saw them in the corner of her dark room. "Why are you wearing those masks?"

Again, silence. The monks were reluctant to speak with a Human, even though she had come to be part of a ritual that would save all their lives. "To spare us from contagion," one of them finally said. "Your breath may be poison to us, so we take precautions."

The night before, when Becky and her companions were first ushered into the palace of Hunaland, the monks quickly separated Becky from the others and whisked her off to a distant room. Though they had long hoped and prayed for a trio of Human, Troll, and Elf to save them, they found themselves unprepared for the emotions they would feel when the Arvada arrived at the gates of Hunaland. With their fingers pressed ineffectually over their mouths and noses, they frantically rushed to lock the girl inside. Then they waved their little incense-filled eggs around until the air was thick with the scent of burning herbs. The Elves were overwrought at the sight of a Human girl, and terrified of the craft that had brought the three strangers into their midst. Like all Elves, they had been taught to hate Humans for all the wrong they had done, intentionally or not, to Faerie Folk. This girl, tall as a giant, was a fearsome sight. Though they all knew the legend of Fada and understood that the presence of a Human was necessary to the hero's quest, the presence of the girl filled their hearts with fear.

Becky, for her part, was full of questions and longing for answers. Astrid had warned her while they were still in the Arvada that upon their arrival at Hunaland, she should keep quiet, say nothing, ask nothing, and keep her eyes down. But Astrid was not around now, and Becky simply couldn't help herself. "But if there are germs," she argued, "Human germs that I'm breathing, you're just going to breathe them right into your bodies. Those masks won't help you at all. And I'm breathing air from your lungs, too, so don't you worry about me getting sick from you? I'm here to help, you know. Once I find my brother, and stop the bad Elves, you'll be a lot better off. Why won't you tell me when my brother got here? The monks last night wouldn't tell me anything, either. Why won't you?"

The monks did not reply, but gestured impatiently for Becky to follow, then turned and walked through the archway into the next room. She crawled out of bed and followed the three, ducking beneath the arch to avoid hitting her head. There was a large, varnished wooden tub in the next room, full of steaming water. Light from a high sconce fell like a shaft of sunlight on a lake. Becky looked up to see a Fire Sprite peering down at her. "You know I already had a bath," she said to the Elves, "last night, before bed."

"And you will have another bath now, because you must be clean and pure when you stand before the Queen and the Mage. Get in."

Becky sighed, but did as she was told. The three turned their backs as the girl slipped out of her thin, ill-fitting robe, and climbed into the tub. The water was very hot, and very deep, and Becky shuddered with relief at the sensation; she didn't realize how tense her body had grown after a long restless night in that cold bed. She watched the steam drift up from the water and disappear into the chilly air. One of the monks said, "Your wingless b-b-bird—"

"I told you last night," Becky interrupted, "it isn't a bird. It's some kind of . . . slug, or newt, or something. Just because it flies doesn't mean it's a bird."

All three Elves shuddered with revulsion; Becky could tell that they were frightened of birds. It had accounted, in part, for their reaction when the Arvada first arrived at Hunaland—an airborne creature, to them, must certainly be some kind of bird. Becky let herself sink up to her neck in the hot water. "What's the deal with you and birds?" she asked.

"The deal?"

"*The problem,*" Becky explained.

"They eat seeds," said the second of the monks.

"That's what birds are supposed to do! They eat fruit, and then they spread the seeds around in their poop so trees and plants will grow somewhere else. It's part of nature. I guess you don't see many birds this far north, though. Penguins live at the South Pole, and they don't fly. How do you even know about birds? From all the carvings on the walls around here?"

The third monk stole a glance at Becky over her shoulder. Becky thought she saw sadness in the monk's eyes. "We have not always been surrounded by ice and snow. Not long ago we had flying creatures, gentle birds and insects, and warm breezes that caressed fields of green. But as the veil between our world and the Human world came undone, Hunaland grew cold. The trees and flowering plants all died, except for the great tree, Yggdrasil, and the hungry birds stole the fruit from our one remaining tree. We thank the Goddess that the cold killed the awful creatures before they devoured the last of our fruit. 'Twas important that there remained one final Seed to give the saviors of our world."

"Oh," Becky said. The water in the tub was cooling. She thought of her brother, and the story the Elves had told him about planting a seed to save the world. It was a very odd story, she thought, though the Elves all seemed to put their faith in it. She couldn't imagine what Matt must have been thinking to go along with Tuava-Li and Tomtar. Now, unless she was able to stop them, the Faeries would kill Matt at the center of the earth in some kind of crazy, sacrificial ritual. And no one here in Hunaland would tell her anything about when Matt had arrived, or which path he had taken to go to the center of the Faerie world. She had no idea how far behind she was, or how long it would take for her to catch up. As far as she was concerned there was no time to lose, and the sooner they met the Queen of this place, the sooner they could get out of here and find Matt.

The monks produced a towel of thick green moss. Becky dried herself and slipped into a white undergarment, as thin and uncomfortably cut as the nightgown she'd been forced to wear. She put on a thicker white robe with sleeves that hung limply around her wrists, and a thick cowl around the neck. All the clothes had been quickly stitched together from smaller Elfin garb to fit her. Becky followed the monks along the dark corridors, her hair brushing against the ceiling, until they came to a place where two paths intersected. A number of monks waited there, each wearing one of the horrible carved masks. Each of them carried a *Kolli* with a glowing Fire Sprite inside. The air reeked of spices—myrrh, copal, and cedar. In the midst of the crowd Becky saw two familiar faces. Both of her friends were dressed from head to toe in white. "Astrid!" she called, reaching out to the Elf.

"The hour has arrived," Jardaine said, stepping back from Becky and smiling stiffly. She had chosen the name *Astrid* on a whim, and now she was regretting her choice. Every time the Human girl said it, she got chills up her spine. How much worse it would be, she thought, if the girl were to utter her *real* name! But then again, nearly everything the girl said made her quiver with disgust. She held out her hand and let the girl touch it. She was already very tense, and for the moment, that was all she could bear.

Becky was beginning to realize that despite Astrid's apparent good intentions, the Elf was far more wary of touching Humans than Asra had been. But, of course, in the beginning, Asra had been wary, too. It only made sense, Becky supposed, for creatures of a different species to be cautious. "Are we going to eat now?" she asked, hoping one of the monks would volunteer some information as they marched through a maze of corridors. Jardaine cast a harsh look at the girl. She put her finger to her lips, urging Becky to be silent. Becky's stomach was grumbling, though; in the preceding weeks she'd grown very thin. The feel of her ribs reminded her that it had been a long, long time since she'd eaten a proper meal.

"Food afterwards," said a monk. "You must be pure when you stand before the Holy Ones, not packed with *digesting matter.*" She said the last words as if the very thought of eating was vile and loathsome. "Likewise, you must wear white, to offset the darkness in your hearts."

"My heart isn't dark," Becky said.

The walls along the corridors were carved wood, rescued from ancient trees. Intricate lacy carvings of vines, leaves, and berries went from floor to ceiling. Nick ran his fingers along the carvings and one of the monks slapped his hand away. After a few minutes they came to a large open space with a wide set of stairs leading downward. There was a door, wreathed in carvings, at the foot of the stairs. Becky took one look at the door and realized she would never fit through the opening. She felt a flicker of hope that perhaps the Queen and Mage would come out to meet their guests in the larger room.

The door creaked open from within, and another monk in a carved mask gestured for the crowd to enter. The Elves formed a line and went through the door. As the door shut, Becky realized she was not going to meet the Queen and Mage. She heard a sound behind her and turned to see a pair of Elves in the dim light, near the top of the stairs. At the sight of the girl's face they backed away. "They said I was going to stand before the Queen and Mage," Becky said.

"The Holiest of Holies is just beyond, out of the reach of contamination. We all stand before her, even if we cannot see her."

"Okay," Becky said, her brow knitted in frustration. "Do you know anything about my brother? I know he was here. He came for the Seed."

The monks stood stiffly, alarm in their huge Elfin eyes, and said nothing.

Jardaine and Nick had the unmistakable feeling that they were walking downhill. The monks' *Kolli*, held before them, sizzled and snapped. The light threw eerie shadows on the walls, where sculpted figures, representing the earliest of the Elfin Gods and Goddesses, danced. Over their heads the wooden figures waved long, fat snakes. There were images of snakes everywhere in Hunaland, Nick suddenly realized.

He shuddered, glad that the snakes weren't real. Though he knew that snakes represented the Great Goddess, and the Cord that bound them all to her, he had always been frightened of them.

The reek of incense grew stronger as they descended another flight of stairs. Surrounded by a retinue of monks, Jardaine, with Nick close behind her, approached a raised platform. There an oaken throne stood, and on it sat Geror, the Queen of Hunaland.

Fire Sprites cast a spotlight glow on the Queen. She was very old, Nick thought to himself, as he looked over Jardaine's shoulder. She was older than old, more like a withered, parchment-skinned mummy than a living being. At first, Nick wasn't sure she was even alive. Her body was frail and hunched, and leaned against the side of the throne as if she herself might turn to ancient oak. Her head nearly sank inside the collar of her baggy white gown. Over her thinning white hair she wore a crystal crown, studded with diamonds. The monks had already dropped to their knees and bowed their heads. Jardaine and Nick followed their example. Then the Queen's eyes flickered open, and she gazed down upon her visitors. "You have come for the Seed," she said, her voice like wind whispering through trees. "We have been waiting long for your arrival, pilgrims. Elfmaid, tell me the name of your Human companion."

"My name is Jar—"

"Not you, not yet," the Queen interrupted. "Your Human companion, in the hallway—tell us her name, first."

"*Rebecca,* Your Highness. But why is that important? She doesn't even merit an audience with you!"

"The Mage chooses to keep her distance from Humans," the Queen said. "But she will not be able to make the appropriate psychic readings without having the girl nearby."

The Queen turned her head and stared at something lying next to her throne, something almost hidden in shadows. Jardaine peered into the gloom. She hadn't noticed before, but there was a figure—no, two figures lying on a mound of cushions. One hand reached up. The fingers were thin, brittle-looking claws with nails that curled around one another like the gnarled roots of a tree. Jardaine gulped when she realized that there was only one Elf lying on the mound, but that halfway up the body, the figure divided into two. It was impossible . . . two torsos, two heads, one set of legs and arms. Conjoined twins. One of the heads was smooth, like a charcoal drawing where the features have been rubbed away. The other was creased and wrinkled like an old apple. Neither of the heads appeared to have eyes: the creature was surely blind. Stranger still, the figure was dressed in the silver cloak of a Mage.

The old Queen smiled. "The Mage of Hunaland speaks from two opposing poles, one of them logic and reason, represented by Sacred Numbers, and the other the language of feelings, using words to communicate and interpret the Sacred Numbers, so that you may understand. The world we live in, you see, is dual. There is north and south, east and west, right and wrong, up and down, brave and cowardly, alone and together, life and death, Faerie and Human. In the next world, the world of spirit, there is one, where all duality is transcended in love."

On the smooth, featureless head, a tongue darted from the black gash of a mouth. It licked the lipless rim and slipped back inside, like a snake into a hole. Blind eyes stared. "Nine," said the thing. "Eighteen, nine. One and eight, nine. Not twenty-seven, not thirty-six, forty-five, fifty-four, sixty-three, seventy-two, eighty-one, ninety. Eighteen, nine, nine."

The head fell back on its pillow. After a moment the other head of the Mage began to speak. The voice was smooth and cultured. "The cornerstone reveals much. *R* is nine, the eighteenth letter of the alphabet. Nine knows how to find the heart in the world, and to share comfort and understanding."

The wrinkled head of the Mage looked through her sightless eyes as if into a land of wonder, as if she were seeing worlds of possibility unfold in the dark chamber of her own mind. Slowly her expression began to take a new shape. "*R* is nine, the number of satisfaction, of accomplishment, of ultimate attainment, of influence for the entire world. Nine is realization, the fruition of work and dreams. The shadow side of nine is selfishness, lack of compassion, and cruelty, but I see no shadows here." The face was beaming now. "Nine is also the number of completion, and it may bring with it loss, and death. Death, that leads to rebirth. Nine is immortality!"

"Very well," said the Queen. She turned her gaze on Nick. "Now what is your name, young Troll?"

"Nicholas," he answered. "I mean, Nicholas, Your Highness!"

"Is that the name you were given at birth?"

Nick's face froze. He hung his head. "Nooo. My given name is . . . Dalk."

Jardaine's eyes were wide with surprise as she stared at the Troll. She couldn't picture him as a *Dalk*. And who would have thought he had it in him to make up a new name? The first of the Mage's heads rose slightly from the pillow, and she opened her slit of a mouth. "Four," she croaked. "Not thirteen, twenty-two, thirty-one, forty, fifty-eight, sixty-seven, seventy-six, eighty-five, or ninety-four. Four, alone, thirteen equals four."

The head fell back and the other one craned its neck as if to stare at the Troll, as if she had eyes to see. "Four is the cornerstone, *D*, the fourth letter of the alphabet, the physical manifestation of the number four. Four is stable and grounded; four is the square. Four longs for order, reason, sense. Four must persist and endure."

Once again, the Mage paused. Her features rearranged themselves like shapes in clouds, drifting through a troubled sky. Nick pressed his hands together to stop their trembling, afraid of what the two-headed crone might next say about him. He hoped it would not be something too bad. "The shadow side of four is rigidity, conformity, stubbornness, imbalance. The shadow side of four is rageful and violent."

The Mage's face was quivering now, full of emotion. No longer did she sound charming and refined. Over her sightless eyes her black brows pushed together, like the wings of a bat. "Like *you*," she screamed, her face contorted, her head wobbling on her withered neck.

"Very well," the Queen said from her throne as the wrinkled head of the Mage sank back against its cushion.

"But I'm not rageful," Nick said. "I'm not—"

"Silence," said the Queen. "Now your name, Mage of Helfratheim."

Jardaine was shocked to hear that the Queen knew who she was, and she felt a thrill of pride at the same time she felt anxiety that the Queen might know too much of her true plans. "Your Highness," she said respectfully, "I am Jardaine. I have come here in hopes of fulfilling the quest of the ancients who planted the Seed of the Adri at the center of the earth, and saved Elf Realm. I am ready to offer my life in the service of the Goddess. I—"

"Enough," said the Queen.

"One," came a voice from the Mage's smooth head. "One from ten, never mind the zero, one on the second level, one."

The head lifted and its sightless eyes faced Jardaine. "The first letter of the name is *J*. This is the cornerstone. Your approach to life is more emotional than rational, as your name begins with the letter *J*, not *A*."

There was a long pause. "*J* is self-directing, original, a leader, not a follower. You do not enjoy taking orders. You find your best company is solitude. You believe that you are always right."

The features on the face were once again beginning to shift. "There are two sides to every number, the light side and the shadow side. The right side and the wrong side. The good side and the bad side. You, Jardaine, do not embody the light. You are motivated by self-interest. You cling to your desires, and you do not give up until you get what you want." The Mage was losing control again, it was plain to see. It was hard for Jardaine to imagine how a face so old and withered could express such ferocity. "You are selfish and greedy," the Mage frothed, "and though you possess a feral intelligence, you are an enemy of the truth!" She reached a gnarled hand toward Jardaine. "You are unworthy to save our Seed!"

Jardaine swallowed hard. "But I —"

"You are unworthy, because the relentless pursuit of your own ambition is the thing that brought you here to us, not love for the Goddess or your fellow Elves! Love for yourself! *Love for yourself!*"

The two-headed Mage bared her crooked teeth as she fell back against the pillow, her emotion spent. The Queen turned her gaze away and nodded to four strong servants at the back of the chamber. They approached their Master with a canopied pallet, knelt before the throne, and lowered the pallet as the old lame Queen was lifted into its seat. Then the servants hoisted the Queen up to shoulder height and began their march to the door. "Come along," ordered the Queen, gesturing to Jardaine with a crooked finger.

Outside in the waiting area, Becky and the remaining monks heard footsteps approaching. "You must go now," said one of the monks in a tremulous voice. "Back to your quarters!"

"I wanted to see the Queen," Becky said. "I wanted to ask her about my brother, I wanted to—"

The monk made pushing motions with her hands and ordered, "Hurry, hurry! The Queen must not breathe the vapors of a Human!"

Becky did as she was told and stomped back down the corridor toward her room. When she was out of sight, the door creaked open and the guards squeezed the pallet carefully through the frame. "Our Mage is very old," said the Queen, apologetically, to Jardaine.

Jardaine wondered which of them was older—the Queen or the Mage. Both of these doddering old Elves seemed far too feeble to lead. "We rely on our Mage for so much," said the Queen, "but perhaps her judgment can no longer be taken at face value. Time is passing, and the cold grows ever colder. You have arrived prepared to meet the challenge, Jardaine, and there is no one else but you who's seen fit to answer the call of the Goddess. We have prayed for many, many moons, and she has obviously sent you to us for a reason. Therefore, though you have failed the second test, the evaluation from our Mage, we shall allow you to face the third test. Are you ready?"

Jardaine's mind was swimming with possibilities, imagining all the dreadful, embarrassing, or deadly challenges that might still be in store. But what did the old Queen mean, the *second* test? "What was the first test, Your Highness?"

"The first test was your choice of entry into Hunaland."

"Did I pass that test?"

"Follow me," said the Queen.

They made their way through many long passages before they came to the great crystal windows at the entrance to the palace, which lay at the foot of Yggdrasil. Guards opened the doors and they all stepped into the smoky air of the courtyard. In wicker cages lining the perimeters of the entryway, crickets the size of cats rose to attention. They began to saw away with their jagged back legs, performing a song that let all the Elves know that the Queen was in their midst. The townspeople dropped to their knees and pressed their foreheads against the filthy paving stones. Jardaine and Nick grimaced as the smell of incense, wood smoke, and burnt offerings assaulted their noses. Their eyes began to water from the smoke, and their tears froze instantly to their cheeks. "Up there," said the Queen, pointing over the roof of her curtained pallet.

Jardaine and Nick peered heavenward. The sky was filled with smoke and ash, though dim sunlight filtered through the soot-flecked atmosphere and cast beams of gold through the high branches of the tree. "I don't see anything, Your Majesty," Jardaine said.

"The fruit is very small, and it hangs from a very high branch. Have faith when I say that it is directly above you. The Seed of Yggdrasil awaits the Savior, Jardaine. When the Savior stands beneath the branch, pure of heart and spirit, the fruit will release itself. Here you must stand, until the Holy Fruit that bears the Seed comes to you."

It was truly strange to stare up into the midst of the smoke and branches, for the branches went on as far as the eye could see, and the smoke gave the branches the appearance of disappearing and then appearing again. It was like watching a world born and then fading back into a void, over and over. It would have been hypnotic if the soot and the light didn't sting the eyes so badly. The Queen of Hunaland cocked her head and her servants turned her pallet back toward the palace. "Wait," cried Jardaine. "How long will I have to wait, Your Majesty?"

The Queen ignored Jardaine's pleas and disappeared in the smoke. "You will be brought before Her Majesty again, once the Seed is in your possession," said one of the monks. "Until then, you must pray and wait. The fruit will fall when it knows you are ready to receive it."

"I'm ready to receive the infernal thing now," Jardaine muttered under her breath. "Where is the entrance to the Underworld, when I have the Seed in my possession?"

"There," said the monk, pointing. "'Tis called the *Gate of*

Hujr. Between those two great roots is the passage that will lead you to your goal."

"I don't see any opening there," Jardaine said.

"The passage is sealed, like the skin of a Cord. It must be cut, to enter. Now, Mage of Helfratheim, shall we stay and chant with you?"

"No," said Jardaine. "You may go."

"What should we do, Jardaine?" Nick whispered, once the monks had gone.

"Pray and wait, are you deaf? And don't forget, my name is Astrid. We'll see the girl again soon enough, and I don't want you making any mistakes. If she knew that I was the one who abducted her parents near Alfheim, she'd never go along with our plans."

"Yes, Astrid," Nick said. "Pray and wait. What about magick?"

"No magick," said Jardaine, though when she stared up into the haze of smoke and branches, she was tempted to try something—a spell, perhaps, to make the fruit come down. "We don't really know what we're dealing with here." She thought and thought of what kind of spell might work, but her mind was blank. If there were a way to do it, it was beyond her. "Pray and wait," Jardaine said aloud, shivering from the cold. She wished she'd been able to wear some of the thick weatherproof clothing she'd brought from Helfratheim. In their white robes, she and Nick were vulnerable to every breath of winter wind.

The Elves of Hunaland returned to their sacrifices and offerings once the Queen and her monks disappeared into her palace. Some of the Elves were chanting, some reciting prayers, some openly weeping as they poured jugs of water over hot stones, coals, and blackened branches, gathered from the foot of the mighty tree. The Elves beat the fire with slick sheets of seaweed, sending smoke signals into the air, in an effort to communicate their desires to the Goddess and her kin in Heaven. Other Elves were lost in the ecstasy of trance, dancing and waving lengths of painted cord over their heads to represent both the Cord and the Holy Snake, the Mother of all things.

Creatures had been lured up from the ocean depths and pulled through the ice, then dragged to the exposed roots of Yggdrasil and sacrificed. A huge ocean mammal, bigger than a bus, lay on its back as a group of Elves worked away at the top of the beast, sawing open its belly and heaving out great mounds of blubber. Other creatures of a sickly pink hue, sporting suckered tentacles and bulging, bloated bodies, with preposterously large and glutinous eyes, lay stretched upon the ground. They, too, were being sawed apart for sacrifice to the Goddess. Monks encircled the sacrificial animals, working their magick to prevent contamination from Blood. "I'm cold," Nick complained.

"Pray and wait," Jardaine said.

Hours passed, and the day faded away. A circle of monks kept a silent vigil around the pair of strangers, waiting to see when the fruit of Yggdrasil fell. Jardaine finally drew Nick aside and whispered in his ear, "I'm going to ask the monks to pray with me. They'll go into a trance state, and that'll be your chance to slip away."

Nick's eyes widened. "Slip away?"

"I want you to climb the tree, and see if you can cut the fruit from the branch. You have your knife on you?"

"Aye, I do," Nick said, "but it's getting dark, and the smoke, and the branches, there are so many—how will I ever be able to find a little fruit on a branch?"

"Better you should ask what will happen if you don't find the fruit," Jardaine hissed. "These Elves will rip us to pieces if the fruit doesn't fall for us. They'll know we're not the Chosen Ones. They'll know we're imposters."

"They must already suspect," Nick said. "That horrible two-headed thing in the depths of the palace certainly didn't help our cause."

"But the Queen of this place doesn't trust her own Mage. That's why she's letting us have another chance—her hope is so great she'll take the risk. She's practically *begging* us to steal the Seed, Nick. Now when I get the monks where I want them, you find a way up the trunk of the tree and cut down the fruit."

What remained of the sunlight was fading fast when the monks circled around Jardaine and began their chant. Suitably distracted, they entered a trance where their pleas to the Goddess filled their hearts and minds, and Nick slipped away. He hurried toward the dwellings that rose along the trunk of Yggdrasil. He passed bulging roots that rose and twisted from the ground like the backs of giant leviathans, he passed the palace and towers of Hunaland, scaled winding stairways that led from one vertical apartment to another, and slowly ascended the gigantic tree. When he got to the highest point he could climb, he peered down through the smoke, his teeth chattering from the cold. The buildings fanned out below like distant children's blocks, and the Elves on the ground seemed no bigger than ants. But when he looked up, the lowest branches of Yggdrasil were still far, far above, and completely out of reach. As clouds of smoke drifted into the air, he thought he could see, far out on one of the high branches, a small cluster of greenish leaves. In the midst of the leaves nested a red, rough-skinned orb. He couldn't say for sure, but it appeared to be the last remaining fruit of the Adri. There was no way he could reach it. He had no choice but to return and tell his Master the bad news.

Jardaine was not happy when Nick made his way back down the tree and whispered his failure into her ear. There were no footholds on the branches that Nick could use to scale the tree any higher, so the cause was lost. The heady mix of fury, frustration, and helplessness seemed to trigger something in her mind, though, and a flash of inspiration lit up her thoughts like a golden sun bursting through clouds. *The Arvada,* she thought.

She had done it before; that fateful day when she stood in the kitchen of the boy, Matt, and called down a small fleet of Arvada to the dirty field of the construction site near Alfheim. It had taxed her powers to the limit, but perhaps she could command the single Arvada that was moored just outside the gates. If the fruit of the tree was hanging from a branch directly above her, and if she could guide the gigantic Air Sprite through the spaces between the branches, perhaps she could bring down the fruit. And if she couldn't manage to bring down the fruit in one piece, she would bring the entire branch down with it. "Are you sure it was the fruit?" she asked Nick. "It wasn't just some figment of your imagination?"

"No," he said, "I saw it with my own eyes."

"How big was it?"

"Hard to say, it was still so far away. Not big, not small."

"How much space is there between the branches up there where the fruit hangs? Enough for an Arvada to fly?"

Nick bit his lip. "Maybe, but the pilots can't navigate with that much control, Jardaine. They'd crash, for sure!"

"Get away from me, Nick," she whispered. "Hurry over there, by the far wall, and keep your eye on the low branches. I'll navigate the thing from here, and with you on the far side to signal me, we can make sure the Arvada makes it between the branches without getting punctured. If the fruit of the tree won't fall for us, we're going to take it."

Jardaine closed her eyes. With her teeth clenched, her

hands bunched into fists, and her eyebrows knotted in concentration, her willpower took form. It shot like a spark into the mind of the Air Sprite tethered on the far side of the wall. When the creature suddenly lumbered to attention, lifting its great translucent maw in the frigid air, the Aeronauts inside the vehicle clamored to their posts. Now it was down to a battle of will, and Jardaine had caught them all off guard. The Air Sprite was rising, yanking the ropes free from their icy mooring, and the frozen sea creaked and groaned in protest. Inside the Arvada the captain and his crew were tossed against the brass walls of the cab, banging limbs and cracking heads, and within minutes every Elf aboard was either unconscious or in no condition to offer any resistance to the great beast as it flexed and shot into the air.

Jardaine directed the Sprite over the wall, and with a mighty roar it spat flame from its mouth. At the sight of the fire and the brass cab the Elves of Hunaland ran screaming for shelter. The bloated, quivering shape of the Air Sprite could be seen moving through the smoke just above them. What appeared to them to be a giant, wingless bird was now moving among the branches of Yggdrasil. The Elves abandoned the courtyard and hid wherever they could, quickly followed by the chanting monks. Jardaine was left alone, keeping a close watch on the position of the Sprite, glancing now and again at Nick. He waved his arms around to let her know how close the Sprite was coming to the pointed tips of the branches. The smoldering fires that the Elves had abandoned, now fanned by winds from the Sprite, sent up columns of smoke.

Nick thought he saw that the blackened end of a branch, split at its tip into seven or more pointed fingers, was uncomfortably close to the Sprite. "Down!" he screamed, jumping on the cobblestones, waving his hands so that Jardaine would understand. Another moment, another thirty or forty feet, and the hide of the Sprite would be—*too late!*

The gigantic beast roared, and a burst of pain shot through Jardaine's skull. When she was in such close mental contact with the Sprite, its pleasures and pains were as real to her as her own. She fell back on the ground as it roared again. Impaled on the branch the enormous beast writhed, flames spitting from its mouth, its tail whipping against the high limbs. There was a splitting sound, like the crack of lightning, and the Arvada tumbled downward. The air was filled with the thick, greasy smell of the Sprite as the winds inside its body spewed out. Nick, in the shadow of the falling thing, ran to Jardaine. She was still sprawled on the ground. Above them the Sprite and its metal cab were striking branch after branch, breaking off chunks of bark in its terrible descent. "Get up!" Nick screamed. He tugged and tugged on Jardaine's arm. "Get up!"

Finally the Elf got up. She stumbled out of the shadow as dozens of tree limbs and the Arvada crashed behind her, the brass cab splitting into pieces. Razor-sharp splinters and chunks of metal flew past Nick and Jardaine. With a horrible, strangled roar, the Air Sprite lay heaving on the cobblestones. Parts of it lay across the sacrificial fires, and the body of the beast smoldered and cooked in dark patches. Nick retched at the awful odor, and now it was Jardaine's turn to haul him forward. "I see it," she cried, "I see the fruit!"

They dashed over the body of the Sprite, slipping again and again on its hide and tripping over folds of translucent flesh. There was a branch on the far side of the beast, with a cluster of green leaves, bigger than Jardaine and Nick together. At the center of the bunch of leaves lay the shattered fruit of the Adri. "Reach in and get the Seed," Jardaine hollered. "Get the Seed, quickly!"

The Troll reached into the gloppy pulp of the smashed fruit. His arms sank up to the elbows in the mess, and each time he drew them out, there was a terrible sucking sound. "Hurry!" Jardaine cried. "What's taking you so long?"

Nick pulled his hands free and then dug them in once again. Only after the third or fourth time did he notice the burning sensation, starting in his fingertips and then creeping up his arms. *"Owwww,"* he cried, yanking his hands free.

He held them up before his eyes in the frail light and saw that his skin was puckered and blackened everywhere the pulp of the fruit clung to his flesh. He screamed, wiping the mess on his clothing, trying to stop the burning. He saw a jug of water next to one of the fires and ran to pour it onto his seared hands. Jardaine, meanwhile, knelt to peer into the ruins of

NICK

the fruit. There was a lump at the center of the thing, a green lump, no bigger than an acorn. Taking the hem of her robe in her hand she reached into the spongy mass and withdrew the Sacred Seed of the Adri. She stood up, wiped the Seed clean, and dropped it into the pocket of her robe. "Let's go, Nick," she hollered, running for the palace. "We've got to get Becky, and then get out of here! They'll kill us for what we've done!"

14

THERE WAS A KNOCK at the door. Matt got up on one elbow, rubbing sleep from his eyes. The first thing he saw was Tuava-Li in the dim light, facing the window. Her arms were outstretched, her eyes closed. The knock at the door didn't seem to faze her. *She's doing one of her rituals*, Matt thought. *She's always up before anybody else, greeting the new day . . . no matter what kind of day it is, no matter what you need her to do.*

Then the knock came again, louder this time, and Matt threw his legs over the side of the bed. "I'm coming," he said.

Tomtar was on the floor in a heap of tangled blankets. He sat up, drawn back from the Gates of Vattar to the waking world. "What's going on?"

Matt peered through the tiny security hole in the door and

saw Mary's son-in-law, Joe, standing in the hallway. The light in the hall was a sickly greenish yellow. The fish-eye lens in the hole made Joe look like a seal, with his bristling whiskers and greasy black hair. When he knocked again, Matt jumped back. "What is it? What's wrong?"

"Nothin's wrong," Joe replied. His voice sounded hollow coming through the door. "Your ride's here. You ready to go, kid?"

"My ride?"

"We got the plane, and we've got clearance to take off, now. You comin' or not?"

"Give me . . . five minutes," Matt called, glancing frantically around the room. Clothes were strewn around, backpacks, books from the co-op laundry. *Earth calling Tuava-Li,* Matt said in his mind. He was getting better at thoughtspeak every day, and he enjoyed startling Tuava-Li with it the way she always seemed to startle him.

The Elf, roused abruptly from her trance, opened her eyes and stared. *We've got to go,* Matt said wordlessly. *The airplane's here! We're actually going to the North Pole!*

Minutes later, Matt opened the door, out of breath, and thrust a duffel bag into Joe's arms. "Can you carry this for me?"

The bag was meant to be a distraction. Even if Joe's mind didn't accept the possibility that Faerie Folk were real, and he wasn't able to see Tomtar and Tuava-Li, he might well see the Human coats they were wearing, and one thing might lead to another. It wasn't worth risking it, at any rate. Joe clomped down the corridor as Matt followed, dressed in his cold-weather gear, and Tomtar and Tuava-Li hung back, out of sight. "Looks like a good day for flyin'," Joe said. "I got some muffins and a coffee, start the trip right!"

"Great," Matt said.

Tuava-Li's mind was still in an altered state from the exercise she'd been doing, *the Cross of Gold*. Her fingers were still tingling, and there was something wrong—she could feel it. Here they were, so close to their goal; certainly by day's end they would reach the North Pole, and there they would pluck the Sacred Seed from the fruit of the Adri at Hunaland. *Is it something about Matt that's bothering me?* she wondered. She'd been plagued by the thought that when the time came for him to die, she had no idea what would happen, how it would happen, or who would do the deed. She trusted that the momentum of the myth would take over, when the time came. There was no point telling the boy about the sacrifice he would be making; in all likelihood, he would die willingly, heroically. She knew the story could not be changed, even though there was a part of her that wanted to forget their quest and just let Matt go home. But no . . . it wasn't Matt that bothered her; it was something about Joe.

The sun was coming up on the horizon as Joe threw open the door of the building and stepped out onto the splintered deck. The wind howled, and the temperature was easily ten degrees below freezing. The wind stung Matt's eyes as he hurried down the steps and followed his guide across the gravel road. He imagined that Tomtar and Tuava-Li, with their large, sensitive eyes, would feel the sting even more than he did. "You picked up snow goggles, didn't you?" Joe asked.

"Yeah, I got three pair yester—"

"What?"

"I mean I picked up a pair at the co-op. I've got them in one of my pockets, somewhere. Maybe in my backpack."

"You better know! You're gonna need 'em."

They came to a blue pickup truck. The motor was running, and a cloud of exhaust sputtered from the tailpipe. Matt saw the big sled in the back, packed with gear and wrapped in a khaki tarp. "That's for me?"

"Yeah," said Joe, pitching the duffel bag. "Mary said your old man needed some supplies. Toss your stuff in the back, then get in. We're runnin' late."

Joe climbed in through the driver's side door. *Lift us in next to the sled,* Tuava-Li said in thoughtspeak. *'Twill be easier to keep our presence hidden from the Human if we stay out of his sight.*

"Come on, Tomtar," Matt said quietly. "I'm going to lift the two of you into the back."

"I don't mind being outside," said Tomtar, lifting his arms to be picked up. "We'd better be getting used to the cold, where we're goin'!"

Matt left his friends to hunker down next to the sled, hurried to the passenger's side door, and opened it. "What were you doin' back there?" asked Joe.

"I—well, I never saw a pack like that before, with the kayak, and the skis and all, put together like that, so I was just getting a look." Matt searched for a convincing explanation as he climbed in beside Joe and latched his seat belt. "I just wanted to make sure it was all fastened down in case we stop too fast or something."

Joe scowled and shifted the vehicle into gear. The heat coming from the dashboard vent blasted Matt in the face. Though he tried to ask Tuava-Li in thoughtspeak if she and Tomtar were okay, he couldn't concentrate. With the flick of a knob Joe had turned on the CD player. Music blared out of the speakers, rattling the seats. In the thick polyfoam coat with the hood and hat pulled low over his forehead, and all the layers of clothes he had on, Matt felt ill. "Can I turn the heat down a little?" he asked.

"Whatever floats your boat, Captain!" Joe said, flashing a toothy smile.

"And the music, too?"

"What, you don't like music?"

"Sure, but . . ."

Minutes later they pulled up at the airstrip. There was one small building on stilts, jutting out of the snow. There was another flat-roofed structure with a short viewing tower, and a freshly shoveled gravel strip for takeoffs and landings. The Twin Otter was waiting in front of the building, its fat rubber tires shining like black balloons in the sun. As soon as

Joe put his truck into parking gear, Matt hopped out of his seat and ran around behind to unhook the flap on the back of the cab. Tomtar and Tuava-Li hurried out of sight before Joe appeared. "A man with a mission," he said, coming around to undo the knots that secured the supply-laden sled. He shook his head. "I could have sworn that duffel bag was red. Did you see something red back here? My eyes must be playing tricks on me. I just saw it out of the corner of my eye. Now it's gone!"

Matt thought of Tomtar's winter coat: it was bright red. Tuava-Li's was orange. "No. I didn't see anything red. Should I help you pull the sled out on this side?"

"Might as well get used to haulin' it yourself," Joe said, scratching his chin and smiling that fierce smile. "Go ahead, kid, pull it out!"

Matt tugged and heaved at the sled, trying to get its awkward weight angled so it would slide out of the back of the truck. Finally it landed with a plop on the gravel, and Matt dragged it slowly toward the Twin Otter. "Bend your knees," Joe instructed, walking alongside Matt. "Keep your weight forward. You won't have to drag it like that once you're out on the ice. Your dad'll show you, for sure."

"Yeah," Matt said, baring his teeth with the strain. "My dad's an expert on all this stuff."

Another man, tall and heavyset, came out of the control tower and hurried toward the plane. He grabbed the ropes

Matt was using to haul the sled and said, "What are you doing, dragging this over gravel? You're gonna damage the skis!"

"It's a little bit heavy to carry," Joe grumbled, "and we're almost there, anyway." Then he said to Matt, "Kid, this is my buddy Charlie. He's the one who flies the plane."

Matt shook the man's gloved hand. "Okay, Charlie," Joe said, "let's get behind this thing and hoist it into the hold."

While the two men were bent over, lifting the heavy sled up through the freight door, Matt helped Tomtar and Tuava-Li into the single door at the front of the plane. From inside, the Twin Otter looked like something out of an old war movie. The paneling and most of the seats had been removed in back to make room for freight, though there was still a partial wall between the seats for the pilot and copilot and the rest of the cabin. Multicolored cables dangled from the ceiling, and a pair of old fans hung from the corners, their blades turning slowly in the breeze. Light spilled in through tiny windows on either side of the plane. "Kid," Joe called in an annoyed voice from the back door, "get over here and help guide this sled inside!"

"Sure thing," said Matt. He nodded his head toward a stack of boxes and blankets behind the single passenger seat, and Tomtar and Tuava-Li took the opportunity to hide behind them. Then he hurried to the rear of the plane.

Soon the sled was secured with nylon ropes to hooks in the cabin walls. Matt strapped himself into his seat behind the pilot. When the tower gave Joe and Charlie the signal, the plane took off. Matt jammed his fingers into his ears; the roar of the engines and the screech of the tires over the gravel runway were deafening. His stomach did flip-flops as the plane lurched forward, moving faster and faster. Once the Otter was airborne, the roar diminished, but it never let up. Tuava-Li and Tomtar sat huddled behind boxes. Both of them were holding on tightly to the nylon ropes stretched around the sled. Both of them chewed furiously on *Trans* they'd taken from the *Huldu* in their backpacks. Nearly everything around them was metal, and the *Trans* barely offset the weakness and nausea they were feeling. "How's it goin', kid?" Joe shouted from the front.

"I'm okay," Matt hollered back.

"You got the landing coordinates?"

"The what?"

"The coordinates, the latitude and longitude where we're supposed to touch down. We're gonna stop in Alert to refuel. They're about eighty-two degrees north, and sixty-two degrees west. You understand? We've got to know exactly where your dad's camped, so we can get you as close as possible."

Matt swallowed. "He's . . . at the North Pole!"

Joe looked at Charlie and smiled faintly. Matt could see Joe's expression from where he was sitting, and there was something in it that he didn't like. "Isn't *the North Pole* enough directions?" Matt asked. "You said you'd been there before!"

"Oh, we've been there," Joe shouted. "But there are

three North Poles, kid. The North Magnetic Pole, the North Geographic Pole, and the Pole of . . . what's that called, Charlie?"

"There are four North Poles," the pilot said. "There are the two you said, then there's the Geomagnetic Pole, and then the Pole of Relative Inaccessibility."

Joe snorted. "What's that one?"

"That's where you're up a creek without a paddle." Charlie laughed. "It's the spot on the Arctic Ocean where you're the farthest from land."

Matt desperately tried to remember where Mary had said she'd told Joe they'd be landing. "My dad—he's at the Anderson camp. That's the place Mary said you'd been!"

Charlie bent close to Joe and whispered in his ear. "What did he say?" Matt asked.

"He said, take it easy, and we'll talk again when we stop to refuel at the CFS in Alert."

Matt didn't know what the CFS was, or where Alert was, but he assumed that Joe and the pilot knew what they were doing. He tried to settle back and relax, but the roar of the engines and the constant shifts in altitude kept him nauseated, tense, and distracted for the entire flight. When they finally made a bumpy stop on another gravel runway, outside another handful of dreary buildings on stilts, Joe climbed out of his seat. He told Matt to get down on the floor of the cabin and not get up again until he said it was okay. From his new vantage point on the floor Matt had a better view of Tomtar and

Tuava-Li. They looked as ill as Matt felt, if that was possible. Once the motor was cut, and Joe and Charlie had climbed out of the plane to head for the nearest building, Matt peeked out the window to get a look at his surroundings. Why would Joe want to keep his presence a secret? "'Tis not good," Tuava-Li said aloud, her voice still shaky with the wobble of the plane. "There's something wrong."

"Well, I've been lying to them from the beginning," Matt said. "They don't know about you guys, for one, and then they think I'm going to see my dad. Maybe you're picking up on the bull I'm passing off, and it's giving you bad feelings. So far, everything seems aboveboard with these guys. I felt like we could trust Mary, basically, and Joe is related to her, so he's probably okay."

"Probably," said Tomtar. "Basically."

"Yeah? What's wrong with that?"

Joe and Charlie were coming back with another man. Matt ducked down, but now he could hear their muffled voices outside the plane. There was a rattling at the side of the hull, then a swooshing sound and the smell of gasoline. Tomtar and Tuava-Li were green with nausea, and they each popped another fresh *Trans* into their mouths. "How long you gonna be up here this year?" they heard Joe ask.

"Another couple of weeks and I'll be headed for Ottawa, thanks to you."

"Hey, you set the price," Joe said. "Off-the-books gas is a

lot more expensive than the regular kind. I know the Air Force likes to keep its records nice and clean!"

"I'll keep this little ole pile of jewels you gave me clean, Joe," the man laughed.

Now it was Charlie speaking. "This is just another run, no more, no less. Nothin' special."

"Well, you'd better get your *nothin' special* business done and hurry back. Good luck finding any solid ice to land on up there! Every year it's worse. Another couple of years and there won't be anything left of the North Pole but water."

Minutes later the plane was back in the air. Matt was in his seat, with his backpack safely in his lap. The roar of the engine was just as loud as before, though Matt's ears were numb with fatigue. He could see the two men talking up ahead. Their mood no longer seemed so casual; their faces looked different somehow. *What are they saying to each other, Tuava-Li?* Matt reached out in thoughtspeak. *Can't you read their minds? I think I overheard Joe say he'd paid that other man with jewels. That can only mean one thing — he got them from Mary!*

Be patient, Tuava-Li replied. She was not inclined to read minds, though she felt the same anxiety as Matt.

It wasn't long before Joe unfastened his seat belt and stood up, hunched over in the cramped space. He turned to face Matt. "It's time we do a little business, son."

"Business?"

"It's a little matter of payment for the trip. Now we know

211

you don't have a father up at the Pole. Our friend back in Alert told me that the last of the scientists cleared out a week ago. There's nobody up there but seals and polar bears now. So I don't know what your game is, but you're gonna have to pay more than you gave Mary back in town. That's if you want to go to the North Pole. Otherwise, we can leave you right here, son. It's a long drop to the water, though!"

"But I don't have any—"

Joe was standing over Matt now. "You're wastin' time, son. I know you have more of them jewels in your backpack, so why don't we make this simple. Just take it easy and hand me the pack."

"I don't know what you're talking about," Matt cried. "I don't know what Mary told you, but I gave her all my money!"

"Mary didn't have to tell me anything! She has a hard time keeping her trap shut with Joan, though, and she showed her a couple of the jewels you gave her. I'm sure you weren't foolish enough to give her all you had."

"But—"

"Mary didn't want to fess up to the truth, but in the end, she gave me the jewels." Joe pulled a knife from his pocket and drew it from its sheath as he grinned at Matt. "Now hand the rest over."

Matt felt helpless. But instead of handing Joe the backpack, something made him toss it onto the floor. When Joe bent over to get it, Tuava-Li crept from her hiding place behind the seat and stood up. She looked Joe straight in the eye. "Wha—?" he said, stumbling back.

Matt could feel the force radiating from behind the seat. *The Belt of Power,* he thought, recognizing the sensation. Joe's head hit the wall between the cabin and the pilot's seat and he fell, groaning. Matt tore open his safety belt buckle and turned to see Tuava-Li, with Tomtar behind her. Waves of energy came spiraling off them as they stood unsteadily before Joe. "Who— who are you?" he cried from the cabin floor. "What are you?"

Charlie jerked his head around to see what was going on. He and Joe had planned to take the jewels, and then leave the kid and the sled on the nearest chunk of ice big enough to land a plane. *It's more or less what the kid wants, after all,* he'd said the night before. *And what's he doing with a fortune in jewels stuffed in his backpack, anyway? It's not fair that a kid like that, an American kid with no more sense than a bucket of ice water, should be rich.*

"Joe!" Charlie shouted. "What's going on back there?"

Joe moaned. He couldn't believe what he was seeing. Two figures stood over him, two children, judging from their size, but they *weren't* children. Their eyes, their ears, their skin: they weren't even Human. They weren't real, they just couldn't be! The image of them shimmered, flickering like bad reception on a TV. Joe pressed a hand to his head, where he'd bumped it. *Where's my knife?* he thought helplessly. *I've got to get up, I've got to—*

Stay where you are. Tuava-Li's voice appeared in his head.

Then she spoke to Matt and Tomtar. *Both of you go and make sure the other Human isn't going to cause any trouble.*

"Don't try anything stupid," Matt said to Charlie as he slipped into the copilot's seat.

Tomtar stood beside him, glaring at the frightened man. "You're going to take us to the North Pole, just like you agreed."

Matt's heart was pounding. Tuava-Li had been right not to trust Joe and Charlie, and now they were in more trouble than ever. Charlie's hands, white-knuckled and trembling, gripped the controls of the plane. A strange whining sound came out of his mouth, like air escaping from a tire. His eyes were wide with terror. The airplane began listing heavily to one side. The wings groaned. "Tomtar," Matt said, "get back there with Tuava-Li. Maybe if this guy isn't looking right at you, he'll come around before we crash into the ocean."

"Charlie!" Matt shouted at the pilot. "Get it together, dude, get ahold of yourself! Pay attention! You're in control here; do what you're *supposed* to do! You're going to get us all killed!"

Charlie, his hands on the pilot's controls, was trying unsuccessfully to fend off his fear. "What was that?" he choked. "What have you brought onto my plane?"

"He's a troll. Deal with it, Charlie, it isn't the end of the world."

But Charlie wouldn't listen. "I'm not g-g-gonna have that on board! No way, no how!"

Charlie shifted the controls and the nose of the Otter began to dip. Tuava-Li stepped up from behind. *Matthew, balance your own energy*, she said in thoughtspeak. *Breathe into your belly, soften your belly; everything that will ever be is already done. There's no need to fear. Be at peace, and breathe your peace into this Human. Together we'll bring him back.*

It seemed to Matt like a bad time to do relaxation exercises; they were headed right for the water. He grabbed Charlie's hand on the lever and pulled, like he'd seen the man do when he was bringing the airplane up from the fueling station in Alert. "Noooooooo!" Charlie cried. But his grip was softening, his frozen, terrified expression was melting away. Tuava-Li was enfolding Charlie in an envelope of peace and calm, and the very atoms of his being were changing, slowing, allowing tranquility to come into him.

Matt beamed at Tuava-Li. "We make a pretty good team, you and me! I do the physical labor, and you take care of—whatever it is that you do."

Tomtar, in the cabin, stood over Joe. He was holding the man's knife in his hand, comparing the weight of it to the knife that had killed his uncle, back in Argant. Joe didn't dare make a move. The plane was leveling off again, in no danger of crashing into the frigid arctic waters. "How far are we from the North Pole?" Matt demanded.

"Not far," Charlie said, his voice still quivering. "As soon as I see enough pack ice to land on, we'll bring 'er down!"

The sea below was choppy, with broken planes of ice as big

as football fields floating in the water. Some of the ice was thin, pack ice no more than a few years old, so thin that it might not withstand the weight of a child walking on the surface. Joe called from the cabin, "It would be better for you if I was up front with Charlie. Can I have my seat back?"

Matt looked to Tuava-Li for an answer. She was apprehensive but gave a nod. "Okay, Joe, you can come up. But no tricks. Tomtar, use the knife if you have to."

"Aye, I will," Tomtar said, glad to play a role in this battle for control.

Matt withdrew his own knife from his pocket and held it within Charlie's sight. "You're gonna behave, right?" Then he got up from the seat and let Joe slip behind the control panel.

Matt, Tuava-Li, and Tomtar stood, clinging to the backs of the seats, and keeping an eye on the view from the front window. Joe and Charlie sat in silence, their expressions grim. Whatever they were thinking, they kept it to themselves. The engines roared on. As they headed north, the black gaps and lines in the ice slowly faded away. "How about there?" Joe said, finally.

"Not yet," Charlie answered. "Too blue. We've got to look for the thick pack ice. Just a little farther."

Matt glanced at the compass on the handle of his knife. The needle was spinning from side to side; it could only mean that the North Magnetic Pole was near.

"What about there?" Joe asked, pointing at a stretch of ice ahead of them.

Charlie worked the controls. "Kid, you and your . . . your friends are gonna have to sit down, or you'll get tossed around the cabin like Ping-Pong balls when we land. It's gonna be rough."

"I don't think so," Matt said. "I'll stay where I am."

"Look, I just want you off my airplane in one piece, okay? That's all I'm asking. Sit down, and I'll land the plane. You'll get what you want. No tricks."

The Belt of Power, Tuava-Li said in thoughtspeak. *We can still use it to hold them off if they try to attack us.*

What if they just turn the plane around and head back? How would we stop them?

They don't want us in here any more than we want to be here. They'll land, believe me.

Matt got into his seat and fastened himself in, while Tomtar and Tuava-Li strapped utility belts around their waists and clipped them to the wall. "Here we go," hollered Charlie, and they descended toward the ice. Matt's teeth banged together as the tires careened off the rough surface, striking again and again. Finally, with a sharp twist to the right, the plane came to a stop. Joe and Charlie leapt from their seats. "Not so fast," Matt shouted, holding his knife out in front of him. He could see the blade quiver with the tension in his arm.

"We're just gonna open up the hatch and get your sled out of here," Joe said.

The two men crept around the massive wedge of equipment that had been stored under the tarp and quickly untied the ropes. Then they slipped on their gloves and lifted the hatch. The wind blew into the plane like a battering ram. Tuava-Li's hair flew into her face, and she hurriedly brushed it away, thinking that the men might still be planning some kind of mischief. But they were already outside the plane, tugging the sled out of the hold and onto the ice. "I guess this is it," Matt said. He strapped on his snow goggles, then fought the wind to gather up the rest of his belongings in the plane and pushed open the door at the front. Tomtar and Tuava-Li followed, and Matt helped them down onto the ice. The wind was so strong that he had to guide his friends over to the sled, where there was a little shelter. "How about those jewels, now?" shouted Joe, approaching Matt for the last time. He knew he wouldn't get them, but it wouldn't hurt to ask. "You won't need 'em out here!"

"Not on your life," Matt replied, standing tall.

"Well, I guess I'd better tell you, then," he said, turning back toward the plane. "It's near five hundred miles from Alert to the North Pole, and you've still got a long way to go. The three of you have a hell of a hike ahead of you, all of it straight into the wind. Good luck!"

Matt felt rooted to the spot as he watched the two men climb into the Otter and start the engine. They turned the plane around to face their makeshift runway, roared along the bumpy strip of ice, and lifted into the air. A moment later the plane was nothing more than a speck on the horizon. "How long do you think we were in the airplane before those guys tried to rob us?" Matt asked.

"I don't know," said Tuava-Li.

"We could still be hundreds of miles from the North Pole. How are we going to hike *hundreds of miles*?"

"It can't be that far," Tomtar cried. "Let's get going. I'm cold!"

Matt looked at his friends. There was no way they'd survive a trek of hundreds of miles across the snow. They didn't even know which way to go, with the compass needle spinning around. Joe had said something about moving into the wind. Maybe he was telling the truth, maybe not. There were skis on the sled for one adult; that would be Matt. But as for Tomtar and Tuava-Li, it would be best for them to climb under the tarp and ride inside while Matt dragged the sled behind. "Okay," he said, lifting up one corner of the tarp. "It's my turn to be the leader of this expedition. I want you guys to ride in here."

Tomtar shook his head. "But, Matt—"

"I'll make better speed than you. Just climb in, and think positive thoughts. That might be the only thing left that will help us. It's gonna be a long day!"

Matt strapped on the skis and the harness, like Joe's wife had shown him back at the co-op. Had she been in on this deal, too? Or was it Joe and Charlie, all by themselves? It didn't matter now. He'd never see any of them again, anyway. Whether he and his friends made it to the Pole or not, the past was the past, and it was gone. There was no turning back, so Matt bent his head low and pushed off across the ice. His thigh muscles already felt sore. His lips were chapped. He put one foot in front of the other, right foot first, like the Mage had taught him. It would bring him good luck, he was sure. *We can do this, Matt,* Tuava-Li said in thoughtspeak, from inside the tarp.

Whatever you say, Tuava-Li, Matt replied. The wind was roaring in his ears. *Whatever you say.*

15

So I WIN AGAIN," Asra said in a flat voice, sweeping the playing cards into a pile. She took a deep breath as she concentrated on tapping the edge of the deck and straightening the cards in her right hand. "Why must you always let me win?"

"*Let* you win?" Macta said, wide-eyed, feigning surprise. His long, ringed fingers stroked Powcca, who sat grumbling in his lap. "Why ever would I do something like that? You're just lucky, Asra, that's all. Let's play again! And maybe this time you'd care to place a little wager on the outcome?"

The air outside the Arvada was getting cold. Since leaving Helfratheim, they'd been traveling at a steady rate for the North Pole, but the winds had been against them, and the pilots all lacked experience as well as nerve . . . so the going was slow.

Asra and Macta sat at opposite ends of a gaming table in the captain's quarters. "You know," said Asra, "this *quest* business is far less interesting than it's made out to be. I'd imagine soldiers going into battle must experience this same kind of thing, with long periods of boredom, endless hours where it's impossible to do anything, think anything, where one feels like screaming, but knowing that even screaming would be a complete waste of energy."

She thumped the deck of cards onto the table and got to her feet. "You can't fool me with your *cheerful and friendly* act, by the way. I know you're only on this mission because you want to catch Jardaine and kill her. Your heart has room for nothing but revenge. The rest is all playacting."

"There's nothing wrong with being playful," Macta said, lowering Powcca to the floor. The Goblin limped to the corner and sat down with a grunt.

Asra scowled. "I believe you're playing with my mind!"

A moment later the ship made a sudden lurch and the Princess lost her footing and fell. Macta leapt up from his seat and expertly caught her in his arms. "Owwww," she complained, pulling away, and glaring disapprovingly at Macta's mechanical arm. "You ought to be more careful with that thing."

"I apologize if I hurt you," Macta said. "Perhaps some more padding in the sleeve would do the trick."

"That wouldn't even begin to make a difference!" Asra brushed herself off and paced to the portholes on the side of the vessel. She peered out into the clouds. There was nothing but bland, seething whiteness beyond the crystal panes, and the ground below was shrouded in mist. "We might as well not even exist, floating out here in the midst of nowhere."

"Oh, you are a Princess," Macta said with a wry smile, "seldom pleased, and easily bored. I recognize the type, because a Prince is like that, too."

Asra sighed, vexed that Macta's every utterance seemed designed to draw her to him, like a fisherman slowly pulls in the string on his catch. "You and I are nothing alike, Macta. Throughout time there have been dark Elves and light Elves. I needn't remind you of which type you represent. Shall I rattle off a list of attributes for you? My kind is fair, yours is cruel. Mine is generous, yours is greedy. Mine seeks equality, yours seeks power. Mine is brave, yours is—"

"Come, Asra," Macta said, drawing close to his beloved. "I hope you weren't planning on saying *cowardly*. Perhaps your friends are besotted with this mythic business of planting a Sacred Seed, but let us be reasonable. Light Elves, dark Elves, each of us has light and darkness inside us. Each of us has the choice, at any moment, to exemplify the best qualities or the worst qualities. 'Tis only bad habits that tie us so firmly to bad behavior."

"Speak for yourself."

Macta smiled gently. "I always do! And I promise you that I shall not undertake any other task before you are reunited with your beloved Rebecca."

223

"Light Elves tell the truth," Asra said, "dark Elves lie."

Macta shrugged. "More generalizations. At least I know what the truth *is*!"

There was a rapping on the door and an Aeronaut stepped through the doorway, followed by Macta's trainer, a battle-scarred Elf named Petar. "Your Highness," he said, "'tis time for your lesson."

Powcca got up from his blanket and growled. "Lucky me," Macta said, "more practice with my new arm, flexing my shoulder muscles until the aching makes me want to die. Asra, do you care to come and watch?"

Asra stood with her arms folded, gazing out the porthole. She shook her head just a little; Macta ought to know by now that she wasn't interested in his business. "Very well, then," Macta said. "There's no rest for the weary!"

"There's no rest for the *wicked*," Asra said.

"Powcca and I will be back before long! I don't believe I'll ever top your skills at playing cards, my dear, but perhaps a little knucklebones might suit your fancy?"

"Don't count on it."

"Sir," Petar said, "the Goblin should stay with the Princess during our exercises."

"But Powcca can't bear to be away from me for that long," Macta whined, picking up his pet and burying his face in its fur.

"Must I look after that thing?" Asra cried. "It's wild and ill behaved."

"Just like me," Macta said. "I love Powcca for those qualities. And I love his cute little limp; it reminds me how none of us is perfect."

"You need to be reminded of that?" Asra said drily. "All right, leave him. But don't expect me to play with him."

"Very well," Macta said, placing his Goblin back on the floor, and patting the creature's rump. He pulled a well-chewed ball from his pocket and tossed it to the Princess. "If you don't distract him, Asra, he'll never let me leave!"

Asra caught the ball with awkward hands and made a face. "Come, Powcca," she said in resignation, "I suppose we'd best be getting to know each other!" Then she flicked the ball into the corner of the room and wiped her fingers on her dress. "Fetch!"

An area had been cleared out in the upper cabin of the ship for Macta to go through his range of motion exercises. Without several hours of grueling and tedious practice every day, the mechanical arm would never live up to its potential, and its potential was, indeed, great. Not only could the arm duplicate all the movements of a real arm, but the hand, too, could grasp and point. With proper nerve stimulus, the fingers could be moved independently. All Macta had to do was make sure his control of the various muscles in his shoulder was adequate to send the proper messages to the gears and motors in the arm. The King stood with his feet wide, his shoulders flexed. That way the motions of the airship were less likely to throw him

off balance. "Let's get this over with, Petar. I find it all quite boring."

"Swing the arm to the left," said his teacher. "Ninety degrees."

"My left, or yours?"

"Yours!"

Macta felt anger trickling into his veins. "Once again you fail to show me the proper respect, Petar. You should know I expect you to address me as *Your Highness*. I can still have your head—don't forget the blades sheathed in the fingers of this contraption. I could probably decapitate you myself."

Petar returned his pupil's stare. "Shall we continue, Your Highness, or try again another day?"

Macta swung the arm left. "*Fine*. Is that high enough for you?"

"Now to the right, *Your Highness*!"

Macta swung the arm to the right. He continued the exercises for the better part of an hour, performing finer, ever more articulated movements of the wrist, elbow, and digits, following his instructor's commands. "Very good, sire," Petar said. "Now I think you're ready for something a little more . . . challenging."

He turned and knelt with his back to Macta, and withdrew a pair of daggers from a pouch on the floor. When he got up he tossed one of them to the King. Macta caught the dagger in his mechanical hand, and turned it this way and that, so the light from the windows danced on the obsidian blade. "This is more

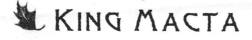

KING MACTA

like it," Macta said, his eyes gleaming. "Care to make a little wager on who's the victor of this mock battle?" He lunged at Petar with his mechanical arm.

The trainer stepped aside and thrust his own dagger toward Macta's abdomen. Macta easily dodged the blade and spun around, out of Petar's reach. The floor of the Arvada shifted slightly; the Air Sprite was moving through clouds, and the ride continued to be bumpy. Macta bent his knees and kept his center of gravity low as he locked eyes with his trainer. "Do you think this practice is wise? You might fall and hurt yourself!"

Petar shrugged and moved sideways, twitching the blade in his own right hand. "The motion of the ship adds an element of uncertainty . . . perhaps you're not ready for it, sire. Perhaps we should wait until the clouds have cleared, or suggest to the Aeronauts that we climb to a higher altitude, where the ride might be smoother. 'Tis your call."

Macta chuckled, then thrust again. "Then I call you *loser*!"

The King of Helfratheim would risk much to avoid the appearance of weakness, and he thought that perhaps he could use the erratic motions of the ship to his advantage. Though his arm was new and untested, he had much experience in the art of the knife fight. Petar leapt back from Macta's thrust and swung his blade back and forth in front of him, holding Macta at bay. "The trick, Your Highness," he said, "is to be so confident about the movement of the arm, for its motions to be such second nature to you, that you never fail to pay attention to what is truly important. . . ."

Macta lunged. Petar felt the blade crease his jerkin as he twisted to the side, narrowly avoiding injury. He raised both arms and brought them down hard on Macta's mechanical arm. The blade fell from the hand as the fingers sprung open. "You fool," Macta yelled, his surprise making him careless. "You could have broken—"

Petar was behind Macta in a second. With his left hand he grabbed Macta by the hair and wrenched him backwards. With his right hand, he pressed his blade to Macta's throat. "You mustn't care about the arm, you must care about your own skin. The arm is far more durable than you are, my King."

Petar planted his foot on Macta's posterior and gave him a shove. Macta stumbled forward, catching himself against the wall, as the ship lurched again. The King's eyes scanned the floor, looking for the missing knife. When his eyes caught the gleam of the blade in the corner, perhaps ten feet away, he glanced up at his instructor. He hesitated; he wasn't sure if he'd make himself too vulnerable by reaching for the knife, or if he could trust Petar not to take advantage.

"Pick it up, sire," said Petar. "We'll start again."

"I don't need a knife," Macta said as the realization dawned on him that his mechanical hand had its own built-in weapons. He held up his fingers and wiggled them. "I've got these!"

For a moment Petar could see in Macta's expression that he

was searching for the right muscle in his shoulder to work the release mechanism of the blades along his mechanical fingertips. "We're working together on your skill set," Petar said, "not fighting to the death. Pick up the knife, and we'll begin again."

Macta's shoulder jerked as he held his hand before him. "You must call me—"

Petar dropped to the floor as the massive Air Sprite above them twitched its tail in the turbulent air. The ship lurched to the right and Macta fell backwards. As he hit the floor with a loud *oomph*, the clips on his fingers released their spring-loaded blades. The blade on his ring finger, though, shot like a flechette from its sheath, rocketed through the air, and lodged more than halfway through the brass ceiling. "What?" Macta cried out and climbed to his feet.

"I'm glad you didn't have that thing pointed at me," Petar said.

"It wasn't supposed to do that, was it?"

Petar shook his head. "I don't think so, sire, no. The blades were meant to stay attached to your fingers, out of harm's way, until you exert the muscles that release them. But I don't imagine—"

An earsplitting roar filled the cabin. Macta and Petar dropped to their knees, their hands pressed over their ears. There was a hissing sound coming from above, and the air suddenly reeked with sulfurous fumes. "The blade must have ripped open the belly of the Air Sprite!" Petar yelled.

"Impossible," Macta cried. "They're bred stronger now, after what happened to my father!"

Petar climbed to the bank of windows and peered out into the clouds. He saw snatches of the ground rushing up to meet them. "Impossible or not, we're going down!"

The Air Sprite had not been damaged badly enough for a disastrous crash, but as the air came squeezing out, it dropped precipitously to the ground. The once-mighty Arvada bumped along, knocking over stumpy trees and dragging itself over boulders and foliage. There was a screech of metal at the base of the great cab as it tore open like a can of sardines, and stopped. "'Tis your fault, Petar," Macta cried accusingly as he climbed shakily to his feet and pointed a mechanical finger at his teacher.

"Don't you point that thing at me," Petar said, creeping toward the door. "Get ahold of yourself, Macta, and let's find out what the damages are!"

"What the damages are, *Your Highness,*" Macta reminded his tutor.

There was a grumble above the cab, as the Air Sprite convulsed and writhed, unable to lift off the ground. Then Macta heard a familiar squeal from somewhere outside. "Powcca!" he cried. Suddenly it occurred to him that Asra, too, might have been injured in the crash. The captain's quarters, where he'd left her, was at the fore of the craft, just beneath the command deck. That would have been the first part of the cab to hit the rocks and rip open. Macta raced down a flight of steps. Aeronauts were crowded in the corridors, rushing to find the air leak in the Sprite and fix it before all the air escaped. "Let me past, you fools!" Macta yelled as he shoved the Aeronauts away.

When he reached the captain's quarters he saw that the bottom of the deck had been completely peeled away. His eyes scanned the crumpled metal for any signs of Asra or Powcca, but there were none. There were no bloody smears, or scattered body parts, like there had been when the first Powcca had been run over by a truck on the highway in the Human realm. All Macta saw was a gaping hole in the side of the cab, and a rugged snowy landscape stretching into the distance. "Asra," he cried, "where are you?"

Macta's words were whipped away in the wind. He could feel the fetid air of the Sprite still gushing out of the knife wound in its belly, and the shadow of the thing blanketed the land. It was astonishing how delicate and vulnerable Air Sprites were, and how much faith was required in order to place one's life at the mercy of such a beast. As Macta hurried through the opening he saw that a crew of Aeronauts was already at work on the roof, trying to cauterize the wound in the Sprite with a gleaming silver object, its tip aglow with red. The Air Sprite twitched, and a puff of smoke drifted from its gigantic maw. A distant bark drew Macta back to focus. "Powcca! Asra! Where are you?"

"I think the sound was coming from over there, by the jagged rocks," an Aeronaut hollered.

Macta stiffened at the familiarity in the stranger's tone. "I am your King," he said, "and you must address me with proper respect."

"Your Highness," said the Aeronaut, bowing. "I saw the Princess right after the crash, sire; she was following your pet Goblin."

"Very well, then." Macta nodded, feeling a stir of happiness that his beloved would try to stop Powcca from escaping. "Lead the way!"

They raced across the rough terrain, where heaps of rocks and boulders lay strewn like cannonballs on a deserted white battlefield. There was precious little flat ground to traverse, and the Aeronaut took advantage of what little he could find so that their pursuit might be the quicker. "This way, sire!" he yelled.

Macta struggled to keep up. His shoes were not meant for such treacherous ground, and he cursed when he lost his balance and scratched his good hand on the prickly, stinging bushes that grew amid the black gaps in the rocks. "Asra!" he cried. "Say something! Tell me where you are!"

The Aeronaut and the King struggled on. The wind whistled in their ears, and the only other sound was that of their feet scrabbling on the craggy path. No more than a few minutes ahead Macta saw a wall of basalt spikes, jutting from the ground like cathedral spires. "She must be up there," the Aeronaut huffed. "I think I heard the Goblin, sire."

The path disappeared in a vast heap of rock ascending to the ridge above. "I'm coming," Macta hollered and began climbing. As he clambered up the mass, with the Aeronaut at his side, his hands and feet knocked loose a cascade of snow and rock. For every three feet he scaled, he slid back down a foot. When Macta finally reached the top of the heap, the Aeronaut cried, "Lend me a hand, sire; I can't make it!"

Instinctively Macta held out his right hand and the Aeronaut gripped the mechanical fingers and pulled. The straps on Macta's shoulder rubbed against his flesh and his nerves screamed as if they'd been doused with fire. He yanked his hand away from the Aeronaut and growled, "Climb on your own!"

He scurried ahead through a break in the wall of rock. "Asra! Powcca!"

Macta lurched forward and nearly tumbled into a deep ravine. He windmilled his arms and fell back against the rocky outcropping, his heart pounding and his brain swirling with terror. Pebbles fell into the abyss and bounced, tumbling down, and down, and down. He heard the sound of barking, somewhere far to his left. Then the Aeronaut appeared at his side, and cried out in surprise at the chasm that loomed below. "They're not here," Macta gasped. "They're not anywhere near here."

The Aeronaut was panting. "I tell you I heard them, otherwise I wouldn't have come all this way!"

Fury overcame the King as he stood on the precipice, and he swung his arm at the Aeronaut. "You do not address your King like you're an equal! Fool, you can't even tell which direction the sound of a barking Goblin is coming from!"

The mechanical hand struck a blow to the Aeronaut's face. The ferocity of Macta's emotions had sent the sheathed blades into their weapon position, extended several inches from the tips of the fingers. When Macta withdrew his hand, flexing his shoulder to send the signal to withdraw the Bloody blades, the Aeronaut toppled from the ledge and fell. Macta watched in surprise as the figure struck first one icy outcropping and then another, bouncing like a discarded toy. *What a waste*, Macta thought, *though the fool deserved to die for his insolence*. The King had never taken the life of another Elf, though there had been many he had wished to kill. *This is really nothing more than an accident*, he thought, *just lashing out in anger. If I'd done it on purpose, there'd be something to be proud of. But as it is* . . . Then he heard Powcca bark.

"I'm here," Macta shouted into the wind. He worked his way along the ridge, scraping his face and hand repeatedly on the sharp rocks, and cursing the Aeronaut for leading him astray. Finally he saw Asra in the distance, kneeling at the foot of a crevice in the rock. When he reached the Princess's side he was dirty and bleeding. Asra looked at him, horrified. "What happened?"

"I might ask the same of you," he panted. "Are you all right? Where's Powcca?"

"We're both fine," Asra said, pointing into the crevice. "What happened to the Arvada? Why did we crash?"

"I have no idea whatsoever. But the Aeronauts are repairing it now."

"When the Arvada fell, I thought I was done for. But by the time we'd ground to a halt, the side of the cabin was torn open. Your darling pet didn't waste any time escaping. I couldn't stop him; I think he smelled an animal hiding among the rocks, and took off in pursuit. I decided I'd better catch him before he got away, or you'd never let me hear the end of it. I know how attached you are to the little monster. Now he's down there, tormenting whatever creature he's managed to corner. What happened to you? I thought you'd be all right, in the upper cabin. You look dreadful."

"I appreciate your asking," Macta said. "I've had a rather difficult time looking for you." He crept to the edge of the crevice and called down inside. "Oh, Powcca, come out! I have a treat for you!"

Asra raised an eyebrow. "You have a treat for the little mongrel? What on earth is it?"

Macta reached his mechanical hand into the crevice. The Blood of the Aeronaut was still damp upon the leather. Powcca came up from the darkness, his muzzle quivering with excitement at the scent. Just then a call came from beyond the ridge; Macta recognized Petar's voice. "We're over here," he replied. "I've rescued Asra and Powcca!"

Petar appeared over the crest of the horizon. "I've been looking for you, sire! The Air Sprite's wound has been closed. The crew's reinflated the cavity of the beast, and sealed up the damaged lower deck—we're ready to resume our flight!"

"Very well," Macta hollered. He snatched up his pet in his arms and turned to stalk back to the ship. "Come, Asra, we've got to make up for lost time!"

16

JARDAINE WAS BURSTING with the thrill of
success, and the terror of being caught, as she and Nick stole
into the palace. First they raced to their own rooms, to change
out of their white robes into clothing better suited for a journey
to the center of the earth. The Seed of the Adri was in the pocket
of Jardaine's white robe. She could feel the energy from the
Seed making her skin tingle all the way down into her toes and
up into her belly. She yanked on her boots, trousers, and jerkin.
She couldn't imagine she'd be needing her mittens, fur coat, or
goggles anymore, so she left them behind. But she still had a
sheaf of spells, curses, and incidental magick that she'd brought
from Helfratheim. She stuffed the papers into her *Huldu* and
strapped it on. Then she carefully tucked the Seed of the Adri,

wrapped in a strip of cloth torn from her discarded robe, into the pouch as well.

In his room, Nick was miserable; his hands felt as if they were on fire. The acid flesh of the fruit had burned his skin, and the pain was excruciating. He wondered, for the hundredth time, why he hadn't stayed outside Argant with his Pixies, stealing pizza from dumpsters. Life had been so good, then; why hadn't he been able to see it? He couldn't manage to get changed by himself, as his hands were too swollen to be of any use. He went to find Jardaine and begged her to help him. As soon as he was dressed, the pair bolted along the shadowy corridors to Becky's room. They found, to their dismay, that it was locked. Jardaine focused her energy into the delicate mechanisms of the lock and opened it: just a simple Mage's trick. Nick stood in the shadows, moaning pitifully. His hands were green and swollen, like ripe fruit. They were beginning to take on an unpleasant odor. "Hush," Jardaine hissed.

Flinging the door open, she stalked in and pointed a finger at Becky. "Get dressed in your own clothes," she said, "quickly."

The three of them fled for the outdoors. Chaos reigned in the courtyard as Becky, Nick, and Jardaine hurried toward the great tree, Yggdrasil. Fires were roaring out of control. The wind blew clouds of smoke and ash across the square. Elves were racing through the sooty darkness, coughing and crying and covering their eyes to shield them from the horror of the burning Arvada. Old Queen Geror, no doubt, would be in shock when she heard what had happened. But it might not take her long to round up her guards, and when she did, they would be after Jardaine's head. As they forged onward Jardaine explained to Becky that the source of all this madness was, in part, her very own brother. She claimed that Matt had just arrived in Hunaland along with Tuava-Li and Tomtar. She said that the Elf and the Troll had stolen the Seed of the Adri, and that they and Matt were now on their way to plant it. She reminded Becky that it was imperative that they hurry and catch them, before Matt's sacrifice could take place. Becky swallowed Jardaine's lies like a glass of lemonade on a sunny afternoon.

In a matter of minutes they reached the Cord that bulged up through the Gate of Hujr. Jardaine tore through the sealed membrane with her dagger, and the three of them peered inside. There was a faint, blue-green glow and the sound of rushing wind. Bits of leaves and charred debris were drawn through the opening and sucked downward. Jardaine told Becky and Nick to stay calm, that this descent into the Underworld would be like traveling in any other Cord, that they should stay close together and hold their arms in front of them to navigate the passage. She warned Becky in particular to stay alert and focused, to avoid getting hurt or separated from her companions.

Becky was glad that there appeared to be some kind of platform and perhaps even a flight of steps built just inside the

Cord. Perhaps they could begin their descent gradually, and not just leap into the unknown depths beneath the mighty tree, Yggdrasil. But when they slipped through the opening in the membrane they realized too late that Jardaine couldn't have made the cut in a more inconvenient place. Becky cried out as she slid helplessly down, scratching and clawing for some sort of handhold. Nick and Jardaine shrieked as well, as head over heels they tumbled down the slope. The three of them were not flying, as in the Cords they had traveled in before; they were falling. A combination of gravity and the inexorable pull of the wind in the Cord drew them downward, hurtling faster than they could have ever imagined.

There was little in Becky's experience to gauge what was happening. She'd traveled in a Cord before, but it wasn't anything like this. She was in a giddy freefall, and it didn't take her long to realize she had no hope of any control. She couldn't breathe; it was as if there was a lock on her chest. When she finally managed to gulp a mouthful of air she had the sensation that the wind was rushing right through her, like she was dissolving, like she was nothing more substantial than a sugar cube in a glass of water. She was coming undone. Her body was telling her, *This is the end. You are falling from a great height, falling fast and free. This is the end.*

She tumbled down and down, for hours, days, even, it seemed, and her thoughts were swept away to a safer place. In her mind she was in a rowboat on a lake, feeling the coolness of the breeze on her cheeks and the gentle rocking of the boat. *It's so pretty out here,* she thought, and gazed across the water.

Her body continued to fall in the milky haze of the Cord, her hair whipping across her face, her limbs twisted and limp. Her mind and her body were coming unmoored, drifting apart, and it was happening so easily, almost like it was meant to be. Astrid had told her to stay present. Astrid . . . *who was Astrid, again?* She was falling so fast and so far that her mind couldn't comprehend it. Her body was tumbling over and over; she couldn't recognize her own hands and feet anymore, or Nick, or the monk she knew as Astrid; she couldn't even remember having ever known them. She couldn't remember what she was doing here, in this void, this nothing, this nowhere and everywhere, all at once.

Finally there was a noise . . . a buzzing, or maybe a yelp. No . . . someone was calling someone else's name. *What was it?* But there was no anxiety, no fear anymore, just watching, as if from above, and waiting. Who could know how much time had elapsed? It was nearly four thousand miles to the center of the Human earth; who knew how far it was to the center of Elf Realm? *Becky!* a voice cried out, somewhere.

Becky, wake up!

Wake up!

Becky's mouth hung slack, her eyes drifted in their sockets, lids half closed. Her arms and legs flailed aimlessly as she hurtled downward. She was like a rag doll, tossed from a window. *Becky, wake up! Now!*

She saw a shape pass before her eyes; she realized it was her own hand, attached to her own arm. She gasped at the sight. It was transparent, at first. She really was beginning to dissolve into air. But reality came rushing back. Beyond her own hand was another shape, dark and blurry, and when she blinked she realized it was Astrid, her clothing billowing around her like storm clouds on the horizon. Becky turned her head. There was Nick, right above her, floating on the ceiling. But wait, there wasn't any ceiling; Becky remembered she was falling, and if she was falling, then her head was facing downward, and Nick was below her. That had to be right; that was the only thing that made sense. "Astrid," she cried, and the name flew from her mouth and was whipped away in the wind.

Suddenly there were roots protruding from the wall of the Cord. Little ones at first, then bigger ones, all grayish brown and smooth as river stones; the roots began to block the passage forward. "Owww," Becky cried, as her head struck a small dry tendril and snapped it off with a *crack*.

Then a larger root struck her foot, and another smacked her in the ribs. The branches were arms, clutching and grasping, breaking her fall at the same time they lashed at her flesh and threatened to rip her to pieces. She looked down and saw a limb hurtling toward her. This time, she reached out and grabbed it. She swung around, nearly pulling her arms out of their sockets. She realized she was howling in pain. Or was it Astrid, or Nick making the sound? Becky was so disoriented, so lost. Her fingers were losing their grip. She swung her feet to the side and felt something strange; it was as if she'd kicked them into a vat of marshmallow, moist and soft. *It's got to be the wall of the Cord*, she thought. Out of the corner of her eye she saw a figure moving toward her, hand over hand, gripping fistfuls of the sticky white membrane. It was Astrid! Her movements were painstakingly slow; her legs were knee-deep in the lumpy mass. Her right hand drew back and she drove a dagger deep into the Cord. With the muscles in her arm trembling from the strain, she drew the blade down, cutting a long slit. "Come, Becky," she cried, and gestured with a hand covered in milky muck. "Hurry!"

Becky reached out, but she was too far away. The Elf turned and slipped through the opening. "Astrid!" Becky cried. The length of root she was holding was smooth and hard, but the wind moving against her was strong. With her hands above, gripping the limb, and her feet barely reaching another, smaller root, she edged toward the side wall of the Cord. Then something stretched out of the opening. It was Astrid, with a branch in her hand. She had snapped it off the tangle of roots that lay on the other side of the wall. "Take hold of this," she said, "and pull yourself closer!"

Nick was creeping toward the slit. Every handhold was agony for him; he clenched his teeth, gripping the pulpy membrane with his still-swollen hands, and drew himself slowly toward the cut Jardaine had made. His hair whipped across his eyes as he stared up at the girl, still balanced precariously on the root. "You can do it, Becky," he cried. He reached his blistered fingers into the slit and pulled it back, so that it looked like a grinning black mouth. "Jump, it's the only way!"

Becky leapt, tumbling into darkness. Nick heaved himself in after her, as the flap of Cord shuddered in the wind. Now all three of them were inside. Becky felt as if she'd landed in a tangle of bones, and the thought if it filled her mind with terror; but it was too dark to see where she was. Jardaine reached into one of her robe pockets and withdrew her *Kolli*. She flipped open the lid and the Fire Sprite peeked out. Then she held it up before her, a torch in the darkness, and gazed around in the flickering light. They were crouching in the midst of a tangle of black tendrils that had burst through a bulwark of stone and grown out through the wall of the Cord. Roots were everywhere. "Are we there yet?" Becky asked tentatively.

"Does it look like the center of the world to you?" Jardaine snapped.

"I d-don't know what the center of the world looks like!"

Jardaine sighed and climbed away from the outer wall of the Cord. "Follow me," she said.

"I don't like it," Nick piped in. The blisters on his fingers had popped, and he looked down at them sorrowfully. "We should have stayed in the Cord, Jar — I mean, Astrid. Once we were past those roots, everything would have been fine. Who knows how much farther we had to travel?"

"We went as far as we could," Jardaine said. "We'll work

our way around these roots, and see if we can't get in again. I have a feeling we're very close."

She came to the end of the root mass and stepped onto a stone floor. The light from the Fire Sprite leapt up the wall, illuminating the dusty carvings there. In the dim light Becky peered at the intricate stonework and her mouth dropped open in disbelief. "Look! Those three figures, there in the rock, are they the ones? Look what that one is holding in his hand—it looks like a seed. Are they the ones who saved the world?"

"That's not the Sacred Seed," Jardaine said. "'Tis far too large. The real Seed is no larger than a grape. Look closer, girl."

Becky crept to the edge of the roots and jumped. A cloud of dust blew into the still air when her feet hit the floor. She coughed. "Careful," Jardaine said, covering her face with her hand.

"I'm sorry," Becky said. "I forgot to cover my mouth."

She looked up at the carvings and saw that what she had thought was a seed was in reality a skull, with the eye sockets turned down into the hand that held it. She looked further and saw that the carvings represented some kind of battle. Great stone figures of Faerie Folk wielded swords and shields, and in frozen motion they hacked and hewed their way through their enemies, dressed in feathers and primitive armor. Skeletal figures danced through the battle scene. There were snakes carved everywhere: wrapped around columns, forming decorative circles on the low ceiling, marking borders. "I don't think we're at the center of the world, yet," Becky said, realizing that the scenes on the walls didn't really seem appropriate for a holy, sacred place. In reality she didn't know what to expect, but she knew that it wasn't fighting, and battles, and death. "I wonder how the Elves got down here to carve these things? We must be awfully far down into the ground. How long do you think we were in the Cord, Astrid?"

"A very long time, child," the Elf said. She herself couldn't say how long they had been traveling; there was a kind of stupor, a sedative daze that had come over them all as they descended in the passage beneath Yggdrasil. She knew that long travel in a Cord could bring on a paralyzing mental fog, and that even the most experienced Faerie Folk needed to be on guard, or risk a fatal accident. They'd narrowly avoided such an accident themselves. "I don't know who carved these, but the snakes are a good sign," she said. "The Goddess loves snakes. Snakes, and lizards, of course. Chameleons, especially."

"Astrid," Becky said, "you told me that Matt and Tuava-Li and Tomtar stole the Seed and started down into the earth, but you had to cut open the Cord at the gates when we fell—when we went down inside. I didn't think that the skin of the Cord healed itself that quickly after it was cut."

"There is surely more than one entrance to the center of the earth, child," Jardaine answered. "They must have come in through another place."

"Then how will we ever find them?"

Jardaine knew that she had to think fast to come up with a plausible answer; the Human girl wasn't completely gullible. "Legend says that the paths converge as we reach the center of the world. We're probably not far from them now."

"Those roots slowed us down," Nick said. "But if the others traveled in another Cord, what's to say they're not already at the center of the earth?"

Jardaine threw the Troll an irritated glance. "We must keep our voices low, and talk as little as possible. If Tuava-Li and the others are near, we don't want to give away our position."

Jardaine was feeling angry at herself for not looking a little harder for a suitable Troll to accompany her on the journey. Nick, she thought, hardly inspired confidence. He'd ruin the entire charade if he said just one wrong thing. It was crucial that Becky remain in the dark about what was going on. But it was also crucial that there be a Human, an Elf, and a Troll to accomplish the planting of the Sacred Seed. What choice did she have? "Tuava-Li is a powerful witch," she whispered, "and Tomtar is no better. The Goddess will help us, though, as long as we're smart and take no chances. Do you understand me, Nick?"

"Aye!"

Jardaine led the way as they followed a trail around the mass of roots. In the flickering light of the Fire Sprite they saw that huge chunks of stone had fallen from the wall, and the path was littered with rubble. Roots jutted through gaps in the stone wall. "We've got to get back to the Cord," Nick said, dodging tendrils.

"I think somebody's been here," Becky murmured. "Look!"

On the ground, thick with filth and debris, there were places where all the dust had been swept clear. "It's not footprints, exactly," Becky said, peering down. She ran a finger through the powdery grime. "It's like somebody swept it with a broom!"

"These marks must have been made by Tuava-Li's robe," Jardaine said as she knelt to examine the tunnel floor. "They've been here, my dear, they've been on this very path!"

Becky's heart beat a little faster. "Then we've got to follow the trail in the dust, and that will lead us right to them!"

"The Cord must be over this way," Nick said, gesturing in the opposite direction with his swollen hands. "There's a path that runs parallel to the Cord; that must be what these tunnels were made for—maintenance, or something, maybe."

Jardaine was frustrated that she didn't know more. The myths she had been taught as a youth revealed only so much, and left many questions unanswered. The details of the quest to plant the Seed were largely unknown. Of course, if the fruit of the Adri had fallen for them in the conventional manner, and they'd received the blessings of the Queen and the Mage, perhaps then they would have been provided with help and answers to their questions. As it was, they were somewhere between the surface of the earth and its center, without food or water, and it seemed to Jardaine that they were quite lost. Nick was right; they had to find a place to get back into the Cord, past the section blocked by roots.

Suddenly Jardaine had an idea. She placed her *Kolli* on the top of a boulder. With both hands free, she reached into her *Huldu* and removed the folded papers. She remembered one of the spells — *methods for using mental energy to conquer an enemy with the power of the mind*. Surely there must be a similar spell to break up the tangled roots that blocked the Cord. She went through the papers, one by one. There was barely enough light to see, but she finally came upon a spell that she thought would do the trick: *methods for using mental energy to move inanimate objects with the power of the mind*.

"Astrid," Becky called. "Shouldn't we hurry? If we want to catch up with Matt, we'd better get going."

"*Shush*, child," Jardaine answered. "Just as soon as I can make out how to pronounce the spell on this paper, I'm going to use it to break up the roots that stopped us from going any farther."

"But Matt and the others are *here*, Astrid, you said so yourself! We don't need to go back into the Cord!"

Nick was wondering how long it would take for his hands to heal, when he heard a strange, swooshing sound behind him. He spun around. Was it bats? Those animals were fond of underground places, like caves and dungeons. But he saw nothing in the air. Then he saw movement behind one of the fallen boulders. "Jard—" was all he could manage to say.

"What is it?" Jardaine cried, annoyed to be distracted yet again from the spell she was trying to learn.

Nick pointed. His face was twisted in fear; he was trembling all over. Jardaine had never seen him like this before. "I saw a s-s-snake," he whimpered. "Or an Elf and a—a s-s-snake, together." Even in the near darkness, the whites of Nick's eyes were enormous. "Why would an Elf and a snake be together?"

"You saw the carvings, and your eyes deceived you," Jardaine answered. "There's nothing alive down here. Now just pull yourself together and—"

"There it is again!" Nick screamed this time.

Becky ran to his side. She clung to a faint hope that what Nick had seen was a glimpse of Tomtar or Tuava-Li behind the rocks and roots, and that her brother was nearby. "Matt," she called. "Matt, is that you?"

There was a strange smell in the air. Becky wasn't sure if it was Nick's burned and swollen hands or something else. Then she remembered where she'd smelled something like this before. The odor was like the lion and tiger cages at the zoo. It was dark, and meaty, and almost sweet in a sickening kind of way. It was a smell that crept up close to you, an invasive, dangerous smell.

Out of the darkness the creature lunged! Nick and Becky sprang back. Its snake tail whipped past them. It disappeared in shadows before spinning around to reveal its head. The eyes were huge and yellow and glittering in the dim light. The pupils were black slits. But what stood out the most, as Becky and Nick cowered and tried to hide behind a mass of roots, were

the teeth. The creature had a snake body and a head not unlike an Elf, with pointed ears and a fine, delicate nose. But when it drew back its lips and hissed, its teeth gleamed. They were long and sharp, more lethal than a Goblin's teeth, or the Lamia's teeth, or anything else Jardaine, Becky, and Nick had ever seen. They were transfixed by the hideous, leering face.

Jardaine dropped behind a boulder. She heard a *swoosh* and spun around to see another of the creatures, sidewinding toward her through the dust. This one didn't seem to be in much of a hurry; its face, a mask of predatory glee, came slowly closer. Jardaine saw its tiny, misshapen arms. A cloud of dust rose where it paddled along the floor. The monster's tongue flicked delicately. Then, all at once, it sprang at her. Jardaine grabbed her *Kolli* and ducked, and the monster shot over her head. She smelled the dank underbelly of the thing and nearly retched. She grabbed a thick root and swung her body underneath.

Becky screamed in terror as one of the monsters snapped its jaws and ripped her shirt. There were at least five or six of them now, closing in on all sides. There was only so much dodging, so much running she could do. She felt fingers on the leg of her jeans and cried out. But when she looked down, she saw that it was Jardaine. "This way!" she whispered.

Nick turned and saw his two companions backing toward a narrow corridor. He spun around, but lost his balance and fell. The dust swirled around him. "Wait for me!" he cried, holding up his injured hands. The creatures were on him in

 BECKY

an instant. Becky managed to turn and run down the corridor. Jardaine was chanting the spell she'd memorized for using mental energy to move inanimate objects: *Kan De Gudind tilladen de ønskeri af hendes ydmyg tjener tol at kompte rigtigt, og medfoere de sten onur Uhyrer til simmenbrod og knuge dim!*

There was a sound like thunder, and a black jagged line split the roof of the tunnel behind them. Jardaine and Becky raced ahead as boulders began to fall. The Fire Sprite blew out like a candle as the blast struck them full force, a barrage of debris and granite dust. They stumbled and fell in the darkness. A high-pitched keening filled the air, muffled only when the cascade of rock sealed off the passage. When the dust settled, and Jardaine's Fire Sprite flickered back to life, they could see that the way back up the passage was closed to them forever. "We've got to get to Nick." Becky coughed. "We've got to save him from those—those monsters!"

Jardaine almost felt pity for Becky. The girl was so very, very stupid, so clueless, so . . . *hopeful*. How, Jardaine wondered, could she even ask such a question? Of course, Nick was dead. If he hadn't been dead before the rocks fell, then certainly he and the monsters were crushed now, buried beneath tons of debris. "Too late," she said.

"If you made the rocks fall with magick," Becky pleaded, "you can use magick to move them, and maybe we can save Nick!"

Jardaine shook her head. "He died trying to save the two of us!"

Becky wiped the tears from her blackened cheeks. "He did?"

"Why, certainly, my child," Jardaine lied. "He drew the creatures away from us so we could escape. He was brave and true, and now he lives among the immortals, as the Goddess teaches us. Feel glad that he died bravely, in service to the Great Ones. Weep no tears for Nick!"

Becky was confused. "But how could the Goddess have let him die, when we needed him to help us stop Tuava-Li and Tomtar? What are we going to do now?"

Jardaine clenched her jaw. How, indeed, were they going to plant the Seed of the Adri, without a Troll to complete the trio required to do the job? How were they going to find a Troll now? Return to the surface, somehow, and grab one from Hunaland? Impossible. Her only hope was to wait for Tomtar to arrive, and then use her magick to force him to join *her* team. He and the others would surely be thrown off course by those infernal roots in the Cord. It was imperative that she get back to the Cord and wait. *But how?* "I need time to think, dear one," she said, feeling suddenly exhausted. "We must sit here a while, and think."

"Do you think it's safe?" Becky asked, casting a glance into the dark corridor. "There could be more of those . . . those snake things down here. We won't be able to get away!"

"Faith, girl, have faith," Jardaine said.

Becky knelt by the Elf and looked into her eyes. "Do you pray to your Goddess? I mean, do you pray for help, and guidance, and stuff like that? Because sometimes I . . . we . . . I mean, *people,* pray for help. Do the Faerie gods and goddesses that you believe in, do they ever, like, do things for you, when you pray really, really hard?"

"Aye, my dear," Jardaine replied. "Prayer is communion with the Great Ones, and there's a part of me that's always with them, no matter what else I might be doing or thinking. The Goddess who watches over this earth is with me all the time. There's not a thought or a feeling that passes through me that the Goddess doesn't hear."

"Do you think she could hear me, too? Because . . ."

Becky lowered her face. Her tears fell in the dust. "Because I'm really, really scared. I'm scared of the dark, and how quiet it is, and how alone I am. I'm scared about Matt, and my mom and dad and baby sister, but right now I'm just afraid. I'm afraid of everything, Astrid, except . . . for you."

"Hush, child," Jardaine said. "Fear is not your friend. Fear will not help us find the way to our goal. Now have faith, and let me think. Let me pray. If you want to pray to your Human gods, go ahead. But all will be well. All will be well!"

Jardaine felt the falseness in her words, and hoped that Becky didn't feel it, too. She wasn't remotely certain that *all would be well.* And if there were any Goddess out there that cared about her well-being, she'd never seen any evidence of it. The world was full of creatures and spirits and forces that were beyond her ken; but from all appearances, every living soul in the world was out for itself, greedily trying to take what it could from every other soul. That was the way of the world. And all would *never* be well.

17

THE HORIZON WAS A GRAY LINE, trapped between a fractured sheet of ice and a fading sky. The sun hung low on the horizon, though it must have only been late afternoon. Autumn was quickly giving way to arctic winter. The temperature was dropping, too. Matt had been pulling the sled for hours, and he was finally getting the hang of it. The motions of the skis had to be perfectly coordinated as he leaned into the wind; he couldn't go too fast or too slowly, without risk of losing his balance and momentum. The neoprene face mask protected his cheeks from the bitter cold. His goggles, though, were a nuisance. They had the tendency to fog up, making it impossible to see where he was going, and he'd have to stop and wipe them clean. Once in a while he'd turn his head and, for a moment, he was convinced that he'd seen a glimpse of trees behind him. But then the illusion would quickly fade. The thin, cold air was undoubtedly playing tricks with his mind; there were no trees anywhere within hundreds of miles.

Though his face still felt cold, Matt's body was uncomfortably warm inside his insulated pants, coat, and gloves. His back was sore where the sled harness rubbed. There were muscles in his legs and hips and arms he never knew existed; every one of them cried out in fatigue. There were blisters on his heels, too. He could feel the pain with every step, though his fear of falling through the ice made it hard to concentrate on anything but the ground beneath his feet. He had to be vigilant, avoiding as many of the cracks and fissures as he could, staying clear of patches of thin blue ice. Beneath the surface were two miles of ocean, straight down. The thought of slipping into the frigid depths was terrifying. Every time he had to drag the sled over a gap in the ice, sometimes a crack no wider than a pencil, other times a foot or more, he imagined what it would be like to fall in and drown.

Crouching beneath the tarp at the back of the sled, Tuava-Li and Tomtar stayed warm and out of the wind. Matt was glad they were covered up; their cold-weather gear wasn't as good as his own, and their tiny fingers, toes, and ears wouldn't have stood up to the biting cold. Their eyes weren't equipped to take the glare of the sun, and the kid-sized goggles Matt had bought for them in the co-op didn't really fit. The three traveled in silence. Matt was listening for polar bears, and the breaking up and grinding of nearby ice into pressure ridges, and he didn't need any distractions.

He had read online about pressure ridges, places where broken ice floes were forced together by the waves and ocean currents. Some of the ridges were twice Matt's height, and he had to glide over miles of terrain looking for a way across. Blocks of ice bigger than houses were scattered around, and the journey was slow and deliberate. Still, he was managing it better than he would have imagined possible, and he figured he'd made good time as he headed into the wind. He'd been worried about polar bears, but he'd seen no sign of any living creatures, and heard nothing but the endless creaking, groaning, and popping of the ice sheets, and the howl of the wind. He'd been pessimistic about his chances in the Arctic. Yet he'd managed to make it through a day without any setbacks or surprises he couldn't handle. Though he'd never been good at sports, his brief experience with cross-country skiing had come in very, very handy. He was feeling cheerful and positive when he came abruptly to open water.

There'd been no warning sign. Suddenly the ice just stopped, and the ocean began. The water was black and choppy, and angular slabs bobbed on the surface. Matt thought he could see a field of unbroken ice in the distance, but it was impossible to judge just how far away it was. His depth perception was worthless in this environment. There were no regular markers to help him judge distances, and things that looked like they might be a hundred feet away could just as well be miles.

At the edge of the ice, with the sun going down and the temperature dropping, Matt felt his optimism fading and the weight of despair creep over him. He knew he'd have to tell his friends about the ice; they'd wonder why he'd stopped so suddenly. He turned around and began to ski back the way he'd come. Maybe it was a good time to stop for the night; he'd think more clearly in the morning. Tuava-Li's voice appeared in his head. *What's happening?*

I'm looking for someplace to set up the tent, Matt answered in thoughtspeak, *with ice that isn't blue and covered in cracks. I can't go any farther without some rest and something to eat. It's getting dark, anyhow.*

As soon as Matt decided to stop, fatigue caught up with him. His legs felt like they were made of lead, and the thought of curling up in a sleeping bag was the only thing that kept him going. Matt had been relying on the wind from the north to guide him, and that was, of course, an unreliable tool. Tuava-Li and Tomtar had said that once darkness fell and the stars were out, they could tell which direction was north. Then they'd have a better sense of how to navigate the next day. Matt knew it wasn't going to be so easy for them to find a way around the open water and get back on solid ice. Maybe they could kayak across. Still, it would be good . . . unbelievably good, to stop and rest. He skied for a quarter of a mile, just to put some distance between himself and the ocean. It was nearly dark. He had to blink to make the image of several jagged trees on the distant horizon fade away. Why, he wondered, did he keep imagining that he was seeing trees? Was it because the terrain here was so bleak and unfamiliar? He studied the ice beneath his boots. It looked white, as far as he could tell. That meant it would be thick enough to sink in six long screws and set up the tent. "Okay, guys," he said, "come on out. We've got work to do."

Once it was dark, a fog of ice crystals settled over the terrain. Everything looked like it was blanketed in glistening, silver cobwebs. Tomtar and Tuava-Li crept stiffly out from under the tarp and stretched. It didn't seem as if they'd been any more comfortable on the sled than Matt had been pulling it. The three of them worked fast to unpack and set up the tent. Matt had remembered most of what he'd heard at the co-op about how to sink the big screws. He knew where to place the three support poles for the double-thick nylon tent. He knew how to organize and arrange the things they'd need inside—the lantern, cookstove, and food on the right, and the clothing and bedding on the left. There was an extra pot, and a portable toilet, which they left in the tent vestibule. There were hooks and a nylon cord at the roof where they could hang up their hats and mittens, and any other clothing that needed drying out.

Matt tied the kayak, sled, and skis to one of the ice screws and crawled in. Tomtar and Tuava-Li were busily flattening the foam sleep mats, and getting ready to unroll the sleeping bags. Matt felt too weary to talk. He pulled off his mittens, leaving just the thick liner gloves on his hands. He found a pack of matches and lit the lamp. Then he unpacked the stove. He ran the tube at the top into the gasket in the fuel bottle, and lit it, too. Matt had filled one of the cooking pans with snow and ice before he came into the tent. He put the pan on the burner and melted the ice, just enough to pour it into his thermos bottles. The arctic air was as dry as a desert, and it would be easy to get terribly dehydrated without taking in enough water. Finally, as the inside of the tent began to warm, he pulled the soggy neoprene mask from his face. If he tugged too fast, it might take a layer of skin with it. "Careful, Matt!" Tomtar said.

"Tell me about it!" Matt answered, as he clipped the mask to the cord at the top of the tent. Then he peeled off the gloves and wiped away the grit crusted around his eyes. "This isn't too hard, is it? Well, not too hard for the two of you, anyway, sitting back there in the lap of luxury, while I drag you to the North Pole."

"Faerie Folk travel like Kings!" Tomtar said, grinning. He'd unzipped his coat but not taken it off. The temperature was still cold enough that every breath was a cloud of vapor.

"Matt," Tuava-Li said, "may we look at your tattoos? I want to see if anything has changed."

"Hang on," Matt said. "Let me finish getting set up, we can have a bite to eat, and then you can look all you want." He thought about his tattoos; when they changed, he always seemed to get an itchy feeling. He hadn't noticed anything during the day, and he was glad for that. The fact that the inky marks under his skin had a will of their own always gave him the creeps, even though he understood that they provided valuable information . . . if he could only figure out a way to interpret them. He took a long draft from his canteen. "I'm glad you guys are saving your energy for finding that seed when we get to the city at the top of the world. What's it called again?"

"The fruit, or the city?" Tuava-Li asked.

"Both, I guess."

"The Sacred Fruit of the Adri hangs from one of the boughs of Yggdrasil, the great tree that grows inside the walls of Hunaland."

"No wonder I couldn't remember," Matt said. "That's a few too many faerie words in one sentence for me."

"They say that magick hides the realm from the eyes of outsiders," Tuava-Li said. "Yet if we're the Chosen Ones, perhaps the Goddess means us to know when we're near. Have you seen any sign of the mighty tree?"

"No." Matt shook his head. He began sorting through the packs of food stacked against the wall of the tent. "Nothing out there but ice and sky. Oh, and the ocean. We came to a pretty big crack in the ice, and we're gonna have to find a way around it when we get going in the morning."

"I'm a little concerned about the direction we've been traveling," Tuava-Li said.

Matt shrugged. "Well, we made good time today. If those creeps who flew us up here had an ounce of decency left in them, and what they told us was true, we're a little closer to the Pole."

"What do you think, Matt," Tomtar asked. "Were those men telling us the truth?"

"If they'd wanted to kill us, I suppose they could have done it right away. They *did* leave us the sled. We'd be lost without it. Maybe they were feeling guilty, since they were dropping us so far from the place we were headed."

"It was Mary and the other woman who packed the sled," Tomtar said. "They *couldn't* have known what the men had in mind. I trusted Mary! I thought she liked us, too. She was supposed to be our spirit guide, remember? To help us on our way?"

Tuava-Li shook her head. "Joe and Charlie believed they were sending us to our deaths. They'll lose no sleep over our fate. But they don't know about Hunaland, and they don't know about the veil between the worlds. Once we pass into Elf Realm, 'twill be far easier for us to find our way—I know it. I have a feeling we're very, very near."

"I do, too!" Tomtar said with a hopeful smile.

Matt shook a packet of dried potato flakes into a small pan, then added some water and powdered milk. He set it on the stove. Soon the three of them dined on instant mashed potatoes, with walnuts and cashews on the side. They washed down their meager meal with mugs of warm tea, and opened up a handful of small peanut butter cups for dessert. The inside of the tent was now above freezing. The clothes they'd hung from the roof of the tent seemed to be drying nicely. "Okay, tattoo time," Matt said, as he peeled off his fleece jacket and the top of his long johns. "You'd better look fast; I'm not in the mood to freeze."

In the golden lamplight Tuava-Li and Tomtar stared at Matt's tattooed torso. They were so close that Matt could feel their breath on his skin. "Sorry, guys," he said. "I know I must smell like a bear. It's been a long day."

"How do you know what a bear smells like, Matt?" Tomtar asked. "Have you ever seen one?"

"In the zoo, I guess."

Tomtar shuddered. "Bears, they're pretty dangerous, right?"

"It's just an expression," Matt said, looking down at his chest and arms. "Wait, is that another green man? Like the one I had back in Pittsburgh?"

"Aye," Tuava-Li said. "'Tis Khidr, like before. But there's not just *one*. This time there are three!"

"It's weird," Matt said. "When I was skiing today, sometimes I'd look back and get the feeling I saw trees in the distance."

"Trees, or Khidr?"

"Trees, I guess," Matt said, "but I never thought about them being green men. I thought it was an illusion, like a mirage or something. I wish your goddess could just write her messages in the sky. I'm no good at interpreting things."

"The Goddess *does* speak to us with signs in the sky," Tuava-Li said as Matt pulled his undershirt back on. "Don't you remember the way the lights in the heavens change at night? Telling us stories, guiding our way with parables and the legends of our heroes? You can't have forgotten the colored lights we saw just last night. The Goddess is at work in every aspect of our lives, every moment. She's in the food we eat, the air we breathe. She's in the ice, and the snow, and in the dark waters below us."

"Don't remind me about the dark waters," Matt said. "You didn't have to look down into those ice crevasses like I did today, and see the water underneath. If there's anything good about that, I can't imagine what it could be."

Tuava-Li nodded. "'Tis not up to us to decide what the Goddess considers good or bad. The value we place on things is our own, and the wisdom of the Great Ones is not for us to understand."

"Do you think there are Green Men in the tattoos because of the quest we're on?" Tomtar asked. "Are they a symbol, because we're going to save the tree?"

"Green Men used to roam the world," Tuava-Li said. "'Tis hard to imagine they could survive up here, though, in all the ice and cold. So maybe the images *are* a symbol; maybe we're not meant to think of them literally."

"Whatever," Matt groused, reaching for his sleeping bag. "We'll be on the lookout for green men, while we're thinking about the quest to plant the seed. Maybe we'll figure out what it all means, clear as day! Or maybe the tattoos will change again before I can wrap my mind around what it means. Look, will you guys be able to stay awake long enough for the stars and lights to come out tonight, so you can see if there are any messages we need to know about? I have to get some sleep. I can hardly keep my eyes open."

Tuava-Li shook her head. "You must stay awake, Matt. We need you to help, to give us your interpretation of the signs. We can't afford to miss anything."

"Great," Matt grumbled. He sat up cross-legged on one of the pads. "In that case, why don't we pretend we're sitting around a campfire, just like back in Cub Scouts. Anybody know any songs we can sing?"

"I do!" Tomtar said brightly. He didn't realize that Matt was trying to make a joke. He reached into his pack and found his wooden flute. "I can play Becky's song!"

"Just what I've been waiting for," Matt said with a sigh.

Tomtar played "The Bonnie Banks of Loch Lomond" a few times, as Tuava-Li hummed along to the music and Matt tried desperately to keep his eyelids from closing. He was so tired of the song that when the chorus came around for the fourth time he said, "Guys, I just remembered, I read somewhere that music attracts polar bears. Maybe you shouldn't play the flute out here. They say that bears have pretty good hearing."

Tomtar dropped the flute. "Oh," he said and stared at his lap.

Matt felt guilty as the Troll pressed his lips together and fidgeted with his fingers. He was obviously frightened of the idea of bears. The walls of the tent flapped in the wind, as if someone were outside, drumming restless fingers. "I'm sorry, Tomtar,"

Matt said softly. "Maybe we can play a game or something. If only we had some cards."

"A game of words?" Tuava-Li asked.

"I know a game," Tomtar said cheerfully. "'Tis called *Aebler*!" His eyes glittered in the lamplight. "Usually we play with crab apples, but since we don't have any of those, we can use . . ."

The Troll glanced around for a substitute. "Peanut butter cups!" he exclaimed. "Here's how it's done. First each of us puts one of the snacks in front of us, then we clap our hands together, like this."

All three clapped their hands, and Matt was reminded of the preschoolers sitting around and playing games in Mary Suluk's living room. "Now," Tomtar explained, "after we clap our own hands two times, each of us reaches out with our left hand to grab the apple—or the peanut butter cup—of the person on your right. Then you quickly place it in front of the person on your left, like that!"

"What?" Matt said.

"We'll start slowly," Tomtar said with a smile. "You'll get the hang of it."

Within a few minutes the three of them were clapping and laughing and moving peanut butter cups back and forth, and keeping up a simple rhythm that let the game continue until Matt said, "Let me teach you one. It's called *Rock, Paper, Scissors*."

Tuava-Li knew a few children's games, as well, and they took turns thinking of clapping and rhythm games and giving each of them a try. Matt forgot about his sore muscles and felt some of his strength returning as the games went on. But a loud popping sound outside the tent made them all sit up. "Bears?" Tomtar whispered.

Matt shook his head. "No. I'll take a look. I think it was just the ice."

He pulled on his coat and mittens, and tugged the zipper down from the side of the vestibule. He crept out onto the ice on his hands and knees and saw what had made the popping sound: the ice had cracked, twenty feet beyond the tent, and there was a fissure as wide as his little finger. It was close, though, too close for comfort. It zigzagged into the distance, like someone had drawn a lightning bolt on the ice with a fat black pen. Matt wondered if it made sense to move the tent. It would be hard work, and it was dark, and windy, and what would the chances be that another crack might open up right beneath their tent? If he moved the tent, a crack might just as easily open up in the new place. Better, he thought, to stay put.

When he glanced up at the sky, Matt saw the northern lights swirling and pulsing, putting on their nightly show. It might as well have been an enormous green rainbow, stretching from one end of the sky to the other, dancing in the darkness. The way the light flicked and turned he could almost imagine the great green smears and blobs were waltzing to some celestial music that only they could hear. Stars flickered in the distance, knowing they couldn't hold a candle to the northern lights. "It's time to look at the sky, you guys," Matt called. "Put on your coats and boots and get out here. We've got to decide which way is north!"

A few moments later Tuava-Li and Tomtar stood next to Matt, shivering in the frigid arctic air. Their eyes turned toward the heavens, and just like the night before, their faces beamed with an almost religious awe. "North is that way," Tuava-Li said, pointing. "The green ribbon of light points directly there. You see, Matt, the Goddess is speaking as clearly to us as if she'd chosen to use words!"

"Okay," Matt said. "That's one good thing that happened to us today—those jerks pointed us in the right direction, after all. I wish there were some landmarks out there that I could use for reference. The wind led us this far, but it's too risky to depend on that, and nothing else. Maybe we can just imagine a line running through the opposite corners of the tent, and that'll be pointing, let's see, northeast. As long as we're not on an ice floe that's drifting south, in the morning we'll be able to tell which way's north."

"Look," Tomtar shouted. "Khidr! There, behind the green ribbon!"

Matt almost thought he could make out the shape of one of the Tree Faeries there in the sky; the stars had arranged themselves to resemble a figure made of a dotted white line, its great arms extended into the heavens. "What do you think it's trying to tell us, Tuava-Li?" he asked.

Tomtar squinted into the sky, his eyes burning from the cold, dry wind. He waited, too, for Tuava-Li's response. "'Tis hard to interpret," she said, after studying the constellations. "The green ribbons of light resemble snakes to me, and snakes can be a good sign or a bad one. Khidr has many foes and much work to do before the night is through. The stars confirm we've been traveling north, and we've made good progress, so we should be content with that knowledge. Perhaps more wisdom will come to us beyond the Gates of Vattar tonight."

The three climbed back into the tent and peeled off their outer garments. Matt turned off the lamp, and each of them crawled into a sleeping bag and pulled the zipper tight. Still dressed in hats, mittens, and several layers of clothing, they would stay warm throughout the long night . . . if the flapping of the tent, the popping ice, and groaning wind didn't keep them awake. "I've been thinking," Matt said in the darkness, "about this business of planting the seed, and all."

He was feeling uneasy, and he couldn't put his finger on the source of his discomfort. "I know you told me the story before, Tuava-Li, about the three people—I mean, the elf and the troll and the human, but there are things that don't make much sense to me about what we're supposed to do."

"Perhaps the story would be better told in the morning, when we're all refreshed," Tuava-Li said. She wondered if Matt had been trying to think the whole thing through, and found a hole in the story that a lie wouldn't fill.

"I just want to get it clear in my mind," Matt said. "Maybe *now* would be a good time."

Tuava-Li turned over in her sleeping bag and propped her chin on her mittens. "All right, Matthew. The old tales are meant to be told, and retold. This is the legend, the way I learned it." She chose her words carefully. "Long, long ago, when the Human and Faerie realms were undivided, there was much strife in the world."

Tomtar lay on his back and stared into the darkness. He held Mary's carving in his hand, turning it over and over. He didn't object to hearing the old story again, either, for, in a way, it was a story about him, and Matt, and Tuava-Li. Tuava-Li said, "There was an Elfin Prince named Fada, who lived in a land that no longer exists; 'twas called *Gvikud*. All the Faerie Folk were suffering when the Adri at the top of the world began to wither and die. Since the legendary tree was bound to all the Cords that encircle the earth, the Cords, like the Adri, were dying, too. None could travel anymore without walking on the Human roads, and those were no longer safe for Faerie Folk."

"Like now," Tomtar said.

"Indeed," answered Tuava-Li, "like now. The Goddess spoke to Fada and told him that all the Great Ones were terribly disappointed that the beings of Earth couldn't find a way to live in peace. That's why they were allowing the world to die. No longer were they breathing life into the world, and without the breath of the Gods and Goddesses, all life would soon perish. Fada spoke boldly. He told the Goddess that all the strife in the world was the fault of Humans, and that Faeries weren't to blame. The Goddess took pity on him. She told Fada that the earth was the responsibility of all living creatures—Faerie or Human. If he wished to see his world survive, he must find two companions, a Human and a Troll, who also wished to save the earth. They must travel to the hidden land at the North Pole, where the great tree grew. There they must pluck a Sacred Fruit from the Adri, and journey to the center of the earth to plant the Seed. Fada found his companions and set off for Hunaland, and the tree, Yggdrasil. The three travelers did as the Goddess instructed them and saved our world. Afterwards, the Human realm and the Elf realm were divided by an impenetrable veil, a border only Mages are able to cross."

"All right," Matt said. He sat up, and pulled the sleeping bag around his shoulders. "I remember all that. But what doesn't make sense is how we're going to save the world by doing what those guys did, way back in time. Especially since there's no goddess or anybody telling us exactly what to do, or how to do it. This is like a big puzzle, as far as I can see, and we don't really know what the whole picture looks like, or if we have all the pieces, or anything. I know I'm tired, and maybe I'm not thinking straight, but I just don't get it."

"The Mage and I had a vision," Tuava-Li said. "The Goddess *spoke* to both of us, and told us what had to be done. I'm sure there've been times in your life, Matt, when you did something a certain way because you'd done it before in the same way, and you achieved certain results."

"Like when you find a place where there's good fungus growing," Tomtar volunteered, "and you go back there again to look for more!"

"'Tis very simple," Tuava-Li said. "Life is a circle. The seasons of the year, the seasons of a life, go around and around. There is birth, and there is death, in an endless cycle. What happens once happens again and again; though the faces may change, the pattern remains the same. That is why the legend of Fada must be lived anew. There's a key for opening every lock, and when you wish to open a particular door, you always use the same key."

"Whoa," Matt said. "If I answer a bunch of questions on a math quiz one way, I don't put the same answers down on the next quiz, because it's not the same quiz the second time around, and the old answers will be wrong if I try to use them again. Life is more like a road than a circle, Tuava-Li. We're born, and we walk down the road, and things happen that have never happened before. We meet people, we do stuff, and then we die, and we're gone. We don't start over again. Our world isn't the same as it used to be. It's the twenty-first century. People aren't fighting with elves anymore, and if gods and goddesses ever spoke to people, they're sure not doing it now."

Tuava-Li shook her head. "Matt, you're not listening to me! I told you, I had a *vision*. The Goddess speaks to us, whispers of her love, she breathes life into us every minute of every day. She wants us to be happy, and whole, and to love her like she

275

loves us. She speaks to us in the movement of the lights in the sky, in the passage of seasons, in the scent of the flowers, and the hum of the bees, in the song of birds, in everything that exists."

"And what about the bad stuff?" Matt asked. "What does the goddess have to say about winter, and hunger, and when things get old and die, or when accidents happen and there's pain and suffering?"

Tuava-Li sighed. "The Goddess knows better than we do, Matt, why things happen the way they do. We're like children, you know, and we just have to have faith in her."

"I don't have faith in anyone," Matt said. "I only believe in what I can see."

"Then you must not believe in very much," Tuava-Li said, "because you intentionally close your eyes to almost everything!"

She was glad Matt couldn't read her thoughts. If he knew what the legend foretold about his fate at the center of the earth, perhaps he'd be more inclined to believe, or at least to fear, what the Goddess had in store. But that truth, as far as Tuava-Li understood it, could never be shared. "We told you that we'd rescue your parents from Jardaine, once the Seed was planted. You have faith that we'll live up to our word. We have faith that you'll stand by us on this journey, and we'll all honor the trust we have in one another. That's enough, isn't it?"

"I don't know," Matt said skeptically. "Tell me more about what happened when they got to the city at the North Pole.

What does this fruit look like? How did they get down inside the earth? What's it like there? How did they know where to plant the seed? One of the things that bothers me most is how they got back out of the earth when they were done. If there are Cords running down there, do Cords run back out, too? If we end up back in the ice and snow and cold, once we plant that seed, how are we going to get back to civilization? We can't really call Joe and Charlie to come get us. How are we ever going to find Helfratheim and get in there?"

Matt's questions had been piling up all day, as he skied across the frozen ocean. They'd been piling up since he got tattooed outside the Elfin kingdom of Ljosalfar, back when he'd first heard of the quest. And no matter how much Tuava-Li explained, it still didn't make any sense. He didn't want to face up to it, but with so many unanswered questions, there wasn't much room in his mind for faith or hope that it would all come out okay in the end. He was just about to say something else when a loud crack, like a rifle shot, split the air. One side of the tent lurched downward. "Out!" Matt yelled. "Out of the tent, now!"

They all grabbed their boots, mittens, and coats, and Matt yanked down the vestibule zipper. He knew his worst fear had come true as soon as he exited the tent. A crevice had opened up beneath them, like the mouth of some hungry beast. Tomtar lunged at the corner of the tent, to try to drag it away from the abyss, but the corners were anchored to the ice. No matter how hard he pulled, it wasn't going to budge.

Matt hollered, "Get the skis!"

Too late, Matt saw them slip into the void as the ice groaned and split. Then the crack sent inky fingers across the surface of the entire ice sheet. Matt felt the ground lurch, and he landed hard on his back. He managed to flip over and get up on his hands and knees. A gulf was opening between him and his friends. He was trapped on a small floe, quickly slipping away. *"Nooooo!"* he screamed and dashed to the edge of the ice. Tomtar and Tuava-Li reached for him helplessly.

Matt leapt, as the corner of the floe dipped into the frigid water. He landed with a thud on the other side of the ice where Tomtar and Tuava-Li were waiting. He grabbed for the kayak, which was still tethered to the corner of the tent. Everything they had was either on the sled or in the tent—food, clothes, everything they'd need to survive. If it all went into the water they wouldn't last the night. The three of them crouched at the corner of the tent, pulling and pulling on the tether to the last aluminum screw as the ice gave way. The far side of the tent was in the water, and the weight of the stove, lamp, and other gear still inside was pulling it down. Suddenly the long screw came loose, and the kayak shot into the dark water, out of their reach. The submerged side of the tent flew up, caught by the wind, and landed on the ice. "Grab it!" Matt yelled. The three of them tugged the tent away from the crevice, but there was nowhere safe to haul it. "Get onto the back of the sled," he commanded.

Matt grabbed the padded strap and tugged. His feet slipped on the ice as the crack suddenly yawned open, and the back of the sled dropped into the churning water. Tomtar shimmied up the top of the sled as it lifted into the air like a flagpole, but Tuava-Li, behind him, lost her grip. With a cry of surprise she tumbled backwards and splashed into the black arctic waters. "Noooo!" Tomtar yelled. He leapt from the top of the sled and landed safely on his feet, as the sled disappeared in the waves. He spun around and raced to the place where Tuava-Li had vanished. The groaning, splintering ice was so loud that Tomtar barely heard the Elf's cries for help.

"There she is," Matt hollered and pointed into the void between two jagged floes. If the wind and the water washed the ice floes back against each other, Tuava-Li would be crushed. If the space between the floes widened, she'd drown. Tomtar was reaching out a hand, hollering, "Here, Tuava-Li, I'm right here," but there was no way that she could reach him.

Matt didn't hesitate. He tore off his boots and coat and plunged into the water. He disappeared beneath the crashing waves. Then with a splash he sprang up, his face white as a ghost. His ears heard nothing. His eyes saw nothing. The shock of the freezing water was too much; he was senseless, numb, unable to tell if his churning feet and hands were going to keep him afloat, even for a minute. As he sank into blackness he saw Tuava-Li paddling helplessly toward him. Tomtar was reaching for them both, his hoarse cries carried away in the wind. Tuava-

Li stretched out her arm and touched Tomtar's fingertips, but her own hand was too cold and numb to grip. She sank back into the water.

As he slipped into unconsciousness Matt felt something moving below him. It wasn't just ice, or the shifting waves; his feet touched something solid. Awareness came hurtling back as he realized, with shock and wonder, that something was scooping him out of the water. It was a tree branch. He turned to see a wooden face, with a massive, knobby nose; thin, hard lips; and two deeply set eyes, like black pits carved into the trunk. The creature was kneeling on the ice, drawing its boughs from the frigid water. Matt's teeth chattered so hard he thought they would break. His fingers and toes felt like they were on fire. A groan escaped from his mouth, part panic, part fear, part exhilaration that he'd been saved. Another bough dipped into the black sea and came up clutching the limp figure of Tuava-Li.

It was one of the Green Men. It hadn't been just a trick of the eye, earlier that day! He'd really seen them. The Green Men had been following them, keeping their distance, watching out for trouble. Tomtar stood on the ice, his mouth open, his eyes agleam. Matt looked out toward the dark horizon. There were two more of the Green Men coming toward them, scuttling over the ice. Their legs were short and bowed, like tree roots, and their arms were stretched out, their smallest limbs resting on the ice before them, so that their massive weight was distributed over all

of their branches. "More Green Men," Tomtar said, jumping up and down. "Khidr has come to save us!"

"Stop it, Tomtar," Matt cried. "You'll break the ice!"

The Green Man lowered his branches so that Matt and Tomtar could move Tuava-Li to safety. Tomtar lifted her face in his hands. "She's alive!"

Matt moved tendrils of limp, half-frozen hair from Tuava-Li's forehead. "Tuava-Li!" he shouted. "Can you hear me?"

The Elf turned her head and began coughing up water. She hacked and choked, but managed to get enough water out of her lungs that she could suck in a gasp of frigid air. Matt heard a voice in his head. *Place her in the hollow of my trunk—there is moss, soft and warm, to blanket her until we reach Hunaland.*

The other two Green Men approached and stood facing Matt. *You must climb inside, where you can rest. You will be safe and warm.*

"The G-G-Green Men," Tuava-Li gasped. "In the name of the Mother and her Cord, you're here! The Goddess wants us to reach our g-g-goal, 'tis plain to see." Tuava-Li was crying. Matt had never seen the Elf so overcome with emotion. "Thank you, thank you, with all of our hearts and souls! In the name of the Mother and her Cord, praise be! Praise be!"

The three Green Men nodded and bent low, so that Matt and Tomtar could lift their shivering friend into a thick gray bed of moss in the hollow of the tree. Matt, too, was soaked to the skin with ice water, and the cold wind whipped away his strength and resolve with every step. Tomtar took his hand and guided Matt toward the open belly of the next tree. With his arms and legs shaking uncontrollably, he managed to creep into the mossy cocoon that awaited him. He let himself fall into the soft warmth, and a moment later, in a space so secure, so sheltered it might as well have been his own mother's womb, he fell into a deep sleep.

18

MATT AWOKE TO FIND himself faceup on a sagging tarp, hauled across a courtyard by a group of scared-looking Elves. His eyes fluttered open to see massive tree limbs hovering overhead in the gray, smoky air. *What's going on?* he thought, lifting his head.

The courtyard of Hunaland was in chaos. Some Faerie Folk pushed through the crowd with their belongings strapped to their backs, as if they were planning to leave. Some scurried aimlessly about, with misery on their faces. By the high walls ahead Matt saw a pair of gilded cages. Inside, immense black crickets were hunched over and rubbing their serrated legs. The music they made was forlorn and sorrowful. *This is too weird,* Matt thought. *My whole life is weird. At least I'm still alive, I think!*

He fell back against the tarp, pressing his hands over his ears. To make matters worse, his eyes were burning from the smoke and incense. There was a rank smell in the air. It reminded him of scorched meat at a barbecue and the tang of vinegar. He tried to sit up a little more but only succeeded in straining his neck. A dozen Elves hauled Matt's tarp toward the fortress; each had a large withered leaf tied around his or her mouth and nose. *So we're still doing this,* he thought, realizing that the Elves were afraid of contamination. He tried to let his resentment go. It didn't really matter anymore. All that mattered now was that the Green Men had saved him and his friends. *Where are you?* Matt called out to Tuava-Li in thoughtspeak.

We're here, came the reply. *They're taking us into their palace, to meet the Queen and the Mage.*

Matt tried to sit up once again. He recognized Tomtar's cap and realized that his friends were being carried ahead of him, surrounded by crowds who wanted to get close to the new Faerie visitors. Black-robed monks formed a wall in front of the palace. Each of them wore a mask with a long, beaked nose. Tomtar and Tuava-Li disappeared inside the building as the Elves carrying Matt drew closer. The eldest of the monks stepped from the line and pointed a bony finger. "Do not try any of your Human tricks!"

The Elves lowered the boy to the ground, then dropped the corners of the tarp and hurried away. On unsteady feet Matt got up and faced the monks. His hair, still damp with salt water, hung over his eyes. He flicked it away and glared down at them. "Tricks?" he said. "Human tricks? I'm here to help you save your magic tree. You think I came all the way here just so you could insult me?"

Stone-faced, the monk turned toward her subordinates. "Show him to his room."

A group of monks surrounded Matt. At a safe distance they led him into the palace. Becky's head had just brushed the ceilings, which were high for Elves, but they forced Matt to walk hunched over. Somewhere along the line he'd lost his boots. His wet socks squished on the polished wooden floors. He barely registered the intricate carvings and fine woodwork that decorated the corridors; his eyes were on the monks, and their eyes were on him. In their hands they clutched ceramic eggs, smoldering with foul-smelling incense. "I didn't do anything," Matt said, coughing. "I'm not *going* to do anything. Can't you just show me where you took Tomtar and Tuava-Li? I want to be with my friends."

They rounded a corner and one of them flung open a small, oblong door. Matt crouched to enter the room and gazed quickly around. There was a thin mattress in the corner, made up with a pillow and flimsy blankets. A dim light filtered in from smoky glass windows. Matt had no idea that this was the same room where his sister Becky had slept the night before. "What am I —"

"Get undressed," ordered one of the monks, stepping past Matt and entering an adjoining room. "There is a bath waiting.

You must be cleansed of contamination, as much as possible, before you see the Queen."

Matt climbed into the big ceramic tub without complaint. The dried salt water in his clothing had been rubbing against his chapped skin, and the hot, steaming bath soothed his nerves. But when he gazed down at his chest, he saw that his tattoos had changed once again, and it made him flinch. There was an image of a face embedded there; even from upside down he recognized the likeness. *Becky?* Matt's mind was racing. *Why is she here, on my skin? Is she in danger, back in Ljosalfar? Does she need my help?*

Matt realized that no matter what was going on, he was in no position to come to his sister's aid. Wherever she was, whatever was going on, there was nothing he could do. She would have to solve her problems on her own. That wouldn't stop him, though, from asking Tomtar and Tuava-Li what they thought of the change. He couldn't wait to see them again. After being in close quarters for so long, it felt strange to be separated.

Matt bathed and scrubbed his hair, and dabbed himself with the scented oils provided by the monks. Then he picked up the pants and robe they'd left for him to wear. Like Becky's had been, the clothes were cut from several smaller garments and hastily stitched together to fit someone much larger than an Elf. They were clean, though, so Matt tugged them on. He looked at the wooden shoes they'd left for him and couldn't help but smile ruefully. There was no way they'd ever fit; though they were large by Elfin standards, they were still far too small. Matt met the monks in the hallway and plodded along barefoot behind them. He met Tuava-Li and Tomtar at an intersection of two narrow corridors. They were similarly clad in white, and reeked of oil and incense. "You smell good, Matt," Tomtar said, sniffing the air.

"Yeah, like a rose in swamp water. Listen, how did we get here? Did those green men bring us all the way?"

"They did," Tomtar said. "They brought us through some gates at the back wall of the city. As soon as they dropped us off here, they went back out into the ice and snow. All the Elves are saying it's a very good sign, that the Goddess is protecting us from harm, that it shows we're the Chosen Ones!"

"Maybe you and Tuava-Li," Matt said, "but they're not making me feel so special."

Tomtar shook his head. "It's crazy here. You were still sound asleep when the Elves pulled you out of the tree. You should have seen what was going on in the courtyard! They were cleaning up the biggest mess you've ever—"

"*Shhhhh,*" whispered Tuava-Li. "We must show reverence for our hosts!"

"Got it," Matt said with a sigh. "I'd better tell you about my tattoos, though. They've changed again."

She gazed up at Matt, and thought of how he had leapt into the ocean to save her life. He'd done it so readily, without a thought for his own safety. She would have drowned, she knew it. That would have been the end of the quest, the end of them all.

Of course it was the Green Men who had saved them, but what was most important was that Matt had risked his life to save her. He was preparing to make the ultimate sacrifice, to be the hero he would need to be when they reached the Underworld. *How did the tattoos change?* she asked in thoughtspeak.

There's a picture of my sister Becky on my chest!

Tuava-Li looked up at Matt, perplexed. *We'll talk about it when we're finished here.*

The monks led the trio down the hallway, holding their *Kollis* before them to light the way. They filed along shadowy passages until they came to a peaked wooden door. When the monks inside the room opened it, Matt could see dusty blue light spilling from tall, stained glass windows. They illuminated an altar along the far wall. Since Jardaine's theft of the Sacred Seed, the Queen had moved her chambers to the chapel facing the great tree, Yggdrasil. Here she prayed, and fasted, and listened as the Mage of Hunaland recited passages from the Scriptures. "Finally," said Queen Geror, as a pair of monks helped her from her knees. She was wearing one of the hook-nosed masks, and Matt thought it made her look like an old bird in a velvet robe and crown.

"Stay outside the door," one of the monks said to Matt. "The others, come in."

"You may leave the door open," called the Queen. "The masks will protect us from contagion, and the Mage will be better able to sense that one's intentions."

The Mage lay propped up on a flax-husk mattress, resting

her two masked heads on soft pillows. She had been carried from her quarters deep in the palace to the chapel, where she had better access to the Queen. The monks surrounding their Mage drew back in disgust at the sight of the Human boy standing in the open doorway. The old blind Mage sniffed the air. "Who's there?" one of her heads called. Matt gazed in disbelief.

"Tell us your name," said the Queen.

Matt's mouth moved, but no sound came out.

"I said, tell us your name!"

"I—I'm Matt," he stammered. He couldn't believe that the strange, two-headed thing was real, until it lifted one hideous clawed hand and gestured at him. "I'm M-Matthew McCormack. I come from—"

"Silence," the Mage commanded in a muffled voice.

One of the heads, straining on a frail neck, rose from its pillow. "Thirteen, four," it said. "One and three, four. Not a pure four, or a twenty-two four, or a thirty-one four. Not a forty, forty-nine, fifty-eight, sixty-seven, seventy-six, eighty-five, or ninety-four four. Thirteen, four, that is all."

When the head dropped back against the pillow, the beaked mask fell slightly away from the face. Matt was shocked to discover that she seemed to have no features at all, except for a slit mouth. He was dumbstruck. He'd seen many strange things since his journey began, but nothing like this. He stood transfixed as the other head began to speak. "The cornerstone is four, the letter *M*, not the physical *D*, or the spiritual *V*."

This head's voice was stronger, purer, clearer, but what was she talking about? Was it some kind of code? Nothing made any sense. The monstrous Mage seemed to be making some kind of analysis, or some evaluation of Matt's character, based on nothing more than the first letter of his name. It was preposterous, ludicrous. "This four is the emotional four," she continued. "It longs for order and stability. It lays foundations that are purposeful and contained. This four has limitations, but within those limitations is great strength, great sense of purpose. The shadow side is rigidity and inflexibility. It is the inability to express itself, the unwillingness to accept change. This four will apply itself tirelessly for what it desires and believes in, but I regret that I do not see greatness in its future."

"It?" Matt said aloud. "You're calling *me* an it?" He felt stung by the Mage's words, even as he sensed that they were nonsense. "You're telling my fortune, like some kind of birthday party gag. You can't be serious."

Matt, be still! Tuava-Li said in thoughtspeak. *If we expect any help from these Elves, we must show respect.*

"Hush," the Queen said to Matt, and turned toward Tuava-Li. "We are running out of time. What is your name?"

"I am Tuava-Li."

"Very well." The Queen turned her anxious gaze toward the Mage, sprawled on her mattress.

"Two," came the voice from the head with indistinct features.

291

"Two, from twenty. Not nineteen, thirty-eight, forty-seven, fifty-six, sixty-five, seventy-four, eighty-three, or ninety-two. Two."

The head fell back on its pillow as the other one lifted slightly and turned toward Tuava-Li. "Two as the cornerstone, from the letter *T*, reveals one who is gentle, receptive, tactful, and sensitive. Two is not a leader but a follower. Two is there to aid, to assist, to support. Two represents the law of opposites, of duality. The two can blend opposing views into a single vision. Two from twenty shows spiritual subservience, patience, and devotion."

"Very good," the Queen said, barely hiding her impatience. "And you, Troll, what is your name?"

"I'm Tomtar!"

"Another two," said the masked head, nodding. "Very interesting, very interesting!"

The Queen let out a weary sigh. Though she wanted to make sure her Mage approved of these three strangers, and gave her blessing, she was doubtful that in the end it would make any difference. "Please, my Mage, if these three are the ones we've been waiting for, we must send them on their way as soon as possible."

"I know that," the Mage snapped. "And if they are *not* the ones, then we must stop them here, before this goes any further. The damage done by the last three was incalculable."

"The last three?" Matt asked.

"Silence," hissed the Mage. She turned her sightless eyes on the Queen and whispered, "I told you it was wrong to bring the Human into my presence. He is vulgar and shows no respect. The purity of my reading is polluted with his every breath!"

The Queen blanched. "But you said—"

"I'm standing right here," Matt said. "I can hear you!"

"Silence!" repeated the Mage and Queen.

The featureless head, obviously stressed by Matt's intrusion, began reciting a seemingly meaningless sequence of numbers. "Nine is one and eight, or eight and one, not seventy-two, or twenty-seven, not sixty-three or thirty-six, not fifty-four or forty-five. Eight is one and seven, two and six, three and five, four and four . . ."

The other head cleared its throat and continued, shouting over the din. "Two is helpful, considerate, and understanding. Two likes companionship, and is a lover of music."

"That's me," Tomtar interrupted cheerfully. "I love music!"

"Quiet!" shouted the Queen.

The other head continued its barrage of numbers. "Seven is one and six, or six and one, or four and three, or two and five, not sixteen, twenty-five, thirty-four, forty-three, fifty-two, or sixty-one. Not—"

"This two is sensitive and strives to be honest," the more lucid head shouted. Then she turned her head to the Queen. "I see no reason to fear these young ones who stand before us. The Human is coarse and unruly, but the other two are innocent of guile, as far as I can tell. The Troll, in fact, is a bit simple. And the

Elf is weak and indecisive. Still, they are here, and perhaps they will surprise us when all is said and done."

"Very well," the Queen said icily. "Thank you, my Mage." She bowed low, then turned toward Matt, Tomtar, and Tuava-Li. "Follow me."

Guards helped the frail Queen onto her pallet and carried her out past Matt toward a room at the end of another long corridor. It was a library, its shelves full of ancient manuscripts. Woven baskets stuffed with papyrus rolls stood alongside the broad desk. The guards helped the Queen into a high-backed chair, then stood away. Matt stood crouched uncomfortably in the corner. "Ma'am, I mean Your Highness," he said, "I don't want to be rude, but the three of us came here to get your sacred seed and plant it at the center of the earth. I don't know why you let your mage treat us like this, but you should know we're here to help you, and we're going to need your help to do it."

"Then let us speak freely," said the Queen. "There's no longer any need for pretending; we're all in great jeopardy. We'll provide you with anything you require to make your descent into the Underworld. The only thing we cannot give you is the Sacred Seed."

"Your Majesty," Tuava-Li said in surprise, "you must entrust us with the Seed!"

"Let me explain," the Queen replied. "Three pilgrims arrived here before you, in a flying ship called . . . I believe it was called . . ."

One of the monks whispered in the Queen's ear. "Ah, yes, 'twas called an *Arvada*. We're still cleaning up the wreckage in our courtyard. The craft damaged Yggdrasil; it nearly set our great tree aflame when it crashed there!"

"An Arvada crashed, here?"

The Queen nodded. "There were many on board who died. But the three who stole the Seed of the Adri were already among us, when the ship came hurtling down."

Tuava-Li swallowed. "The three who stole the Seed?"

"Aye. They were an Elf, a Troll, and a Human, just like the three of you. Upon their arrival the Elf, a female, told us that they had come to take the Seed and plant it at the center of the earth—that they planned to re-create the journey of Prince Fada, and save the Adri from extinction. But when the fruit of the Adri did not fall for them, they drove their craft into the branches of the tree in order to steal the Seed. The flying ship plummeted to the courtyard and burst into flames! Now Hunaland is cursed, contaminated with Blood. Our Mage and her monks are doing what they can, but our Sacred City has been poisoned."

Matt tried to make sense of what the Queen was saying. "Are you saying that the elf and the troll and the human, they already started down into the underworld with the seed?"

The Queen hung her head. "Aye."

Tuava-Li took a deep breath. "How long ago did they leave?"

"Yesterday morning."

"Did you send anyone after them, to try and stop them?"

"We have no soldiers. We were unprepared for anything like this. Our Mage and her monks work ceaselessly to make sure Hunaland is hidden from view, and the Goddess has never allowed anyone to approach who means us harm. The will of the Great Ones is beyond our understanding. But perhaps the Goddess sent the Khidr to rescue you and bring you here, so that if you proved to be the three who are meant to save our world, you could stop the imposters."

"Who were they, Your Highness?" Tuava-Li asked. "The imposters? What were their names?"

"The Elf said her name was . . ."

Once again the monks whispered in their Queen's ear. "She called herself Jardaine, and she claimed to be the Mage of a place called Helfratheim. The Troll was Dalk, also called Nicholas. We do not remember the Human girl's name; she waited outside while we spoke to the Elf and the Troll. The point is, our Mage told me the three were not fit to save the Seed, and I did not listen. Because I didn't trust the greatest spiritual authority in the realm, the likelihood is that something will go terribly wrong, and if it does, 'twill be my fault. Why would anyone want to steal our Seed, unless they desired to plant it, to see it grow? The Goddess would surely not allow those three to enter the deepest recesses of the world if they're not worthy! If they took the Seed in order to serve their own vanity, they'll never succeed in planting it."

"I know the monk named Jardaine," said Tuava-Li. "But *Mage of Helfratheim*? How could that be?"

Tomtar addressed the Queen. "Your Highness, may I ask, what did the Human look like?"

She thought a moment before responding. "'Tis hard to say; all Humans look alike. 'Twas a female." She threw a glance at Matt. "A number of moons younger than this one, most likely. She was somewhat tall and gangly. She had tiny brown spots over her nose, thin lips, and longish, sand-colored hair. Her eyes were beady, of course, and her ears small and misshapen, not like Elfin ears at all. Wait . . . her name was something like, *beckoning* . . . I remember because it struck me as absurd that anyone would ever be drawn to a face like hers, a *beckoning* expression. . . ."

Matt felt his stomach turn. "Becky?" he said. The name felt hard, coming out of his mouth. He dreaded saying it again, just in case his suspicion was right. "Was the girl's name Becky?"

The Queen's eyes lit up. "Indeed it was! Becky, or . . . Rebecca. How on earth did you guess? Do you know this Human?"

Matt banged his fist on the wall. Then he took a step toward the Queen and yanked open the top of his robe, so that the tattoo on his chest would be visible. The monks gasped in horror and rushed to stand between Matt and their Queen. She craned her neck to see past them. "Aye, that's the one!"

"The girl Rebecca is Matt's sister," Tuava-Li said to the Queen.

Then she turned to Matt and Tomtar. "Jardaine knew that this quest would require the presence of a Human; that has to be the reason she got Becky to come along with her. But how did she ever find her? Becky's supposed to be in the forest, outside Ljosalfar! And why would Jardaine want to plant the Seed of the Adri?"

"Jardaine was always jealous of you, Tuava-Li," Tomtar said. "If she found out that you were coming to find the Seed and plant it, maybe she wanted to *beat you to it*! Maybe she wanted the glory, to have her name go down in history. I don't know how she'd convince Becky and Nick to go with her, but I know her, and she's a good liar."

Matt shook his head. "Jardaine already kidnapped our parents, so why didn't she bring one of them along with her, or my baby sister? Why Becky?"

Tomtar scratched his head. "I don't know!"

"I know what Jardaine looks like," Matt said. "I saw her, when our house burned outside Alfheim. Becky's heard me talking about Jardaine, but I don't think she ever *saw* her."

"Maybe Becky doesn't know it *is* Jardaine!"

"Is she calling herself by another name?" Tuava-Li asked.

Matt frowned. "Becky might trust whatever story Jardaine told her."

"Your sister's in grave danger."

"What kind of danger, Tuava-Li?" Matt asked. "Why would Jardaine bring my sister all the way to the North Pole just to threaten her? Do you think my parents are up here, too? Are they involved in this somehow?"

"I—I'm not sure," Tuava-Li said. She had to be more careful about what she revealed to Matt. He would not be happy if he knew the truth: that the quest was meant to end with a Human sacrifice.

"What do you need to find these villains and take the Seed from them?" the Queen asked.

"My sister's not a villain," Matt said. "She's been tricked into this, somehow. We're going after them. *As soon as possible!* We need decent clothes, boots, food, I don't know what we need— you tell us! What's it like down there? How long will it take to get to the center of your world?"

"There's a Cord beneath Yggdrasil," the Queen explained. "'Tis a long journey, to be sure, though the distance cannot be measured in miles. Time and space have their own laws in the Underworld, different from ours. Your rivals have a head start, but if the Goddess is as outraged as I am by the theft of the Seed, and I'm sure she is, they will find obstacles in their path."

"What kind of obstacles?"

The Queen hesitated. "You must stay in the Cord until you reach the center of the earth. Danger awaits those who traverse the labyrinth!"

"What do you mean, labyrinth?" Matt asked. "What are you talking about?"

"A labyrinth is a maze," the Queen said. "There was once a tribe of Elves who lived near the center of the earth. They were of the Ouroboros Clan and meant as a second defense if we failed here. The maze they built there was meant to represent the journey of the spirit through life, learning and moving forward, forgetting, and losing the way . . . back and forth, forward and back, from birth to death, to birth again at the heart of the world. Pilgrims once journeyed down to visit the labyrinth to worship with the Mage of that place. But over time the pilgrims failed to return to the surface, and we've not heard anything from that tribe in many, many lifetimes. None in my own time have ventured down there to see what has become of the Ouroboros."

"So what are you saying?" Matt asked.

"If you stay in the Cord until you've reached the center of the world," the Queen said, "you'll bypass the labyrinth entirely. But you may face dangers there, as well. Now, my Mage says that the three of you are weak, that you do not have the skills to save the Seed. Do you think you are capable of proving her wrong?"

Tuava-Li glanced at Matt and Tomtar. She knew herself all too well. She knew her indecisiveness, her timidity, her fear of leadership. Too many times, when she thought her own Mage was dead, she had failed to take the reins of power and authority in Alfheim. She knew Tomtar, and Matt, too. Each of them had limitations and weaknesses; she couldn't deny it. But they'd managed to come this far; that had to count for something. "Show us the way," Tuava-Li said. "If we can have clothing, and food, and Fire Sprites to light the path, we shall continue our journey. We shall save the Seed. We will not let you down."

Matt put his hand on Tomtar's shoulder and gave him a squeeze. "We've got to find Becky! Come on — we're wasting time talking about it!"

"Then we shall assemble your provisions," the Queen said. She nodded to her monks, who hurried from the room. "Follow my subordinates and they'll provide for you. May the Goddess smile upon us all! I'll meet you again, when you're ready to descend in the Cord."

The Elves of Hunaland redirected their efforts from cleaning up the wreck of the Arvada to preparing for Matt, Tomtar, and Tuava-Li's journey into the Underworld. The trio was fed and clothed, and provided with packs of supplies for their journey. When they were led back to the courtyard, a ceremony was in progress. Hundreds of Elves chanted and sang, banging drums, blowing long horns, and shaking gourd rattles. "I know this music," Tuava-Li said. "It accompanies the Great Snake dance."

"Snakes?" Matt asked. He adjusted the collar of his new woven jacket. The Elves had made it especially for him, and it fit him far better that the robe and pants he'd been forced to wear when he went to see the Mage. Beneath the jacket he wore his old T-shirt, in addition to jeans and boots, which had been cleaned and repaired.

"Snakes?" Tomtar repeated with a shiver. He and Tuava-Li had also been given new garments, more befitting an Elf and Troll than their Human castoffs had been. The crowd of Faerie Folk parted to let them through.

They made their way to a smoking pyre, which seemed to be at the heart of the festivities. Matt towered over the Elves. On the far side of the pyre he saw a huge painted snake head, like a costume made for a Chinese New Year's celebration, coming toward him. The jaws flapped up and down. A long strip of cloth trailed out from the back, symbolizing the snake's body, and at least a hundred monks followed, single file, waving the cloth over their heads. They moved through the crowd in a large spiral and slowly made their way toward the center. "Ouroboros," the Elves chanted, "Ouroboros, Ouroboros."

"What are they saying?" Matt asked Tuava-Li.

"*Ouroboros.* It means 'tail-devourer.' The creature's also called *Jormungandr.* The snake stands for the union of all things, the cycle of life that never ends. Watch what happens!"

The snake circled around the pyre, as the drumming and chanting grew frenzied. Matt no longer felt the cold in the air that had burned his cheeks and ears when he stepped out of the palace. In fact, he felt hot. He wiped sweat from his brow with the sleeve of his jacket, as the giant snake head opened its jaws wide and clamped down on its own tail. "It bit itself!" Tomtar cried.

The drumming stopped. The Elves crept out from beneath the head and tail of the painted serpent, laying their costume on the cobblestones. Along the back wall was a two-story structure, like a bandstand, built on a platform with a roof and walls on three sides. Golden carvings of snakes decorated the roof.

Colorful garlands hung, serpentlike, from each corner. Monks stood guard around the platform, and on the second level, on a golden throne, sat the aged Queen. All Matt could see of her was her head and shoulders and the elaborate headdress she wore. "In the name of the Mother and her Cord," she said to the crowd, "may we be as one." A thousand voices joined in repeating the blessing.

Then the Queen began her speech, in a voice that was surprisingly strong. "When there is no longer two, but one, when all that was outside is inside, when nothing comes in that is not already in, and nothing goes out because *in* and *out* are no longer opposites, there is no need for eyes to see. There is no need for ears to hear, or lips to speak, because all is known, all is now, all *is*. Lacking nothing, the Ouroboros is freed from time and conflict. The most perfect form in this world is the circle, complete in itself, needing nothing. The crown of the tree is round, the earth itself is round, as is the dome of Heaven. The Goddess gives us the Cord, which encircles our world like the veins and arteries in our bodies, like the umbilicus that feeds us in the womb. Because in the circle all things are one, there is no final birth or death, but an eternal return, a coming back, again and again. That is why these three heroes are here with us today, Tuava-Li, Tomtar, and Matt, to undertake the quest once fulfilled by Fada, and Desir, and Volsung. In reliving the journey, we return once again to wholeness, and completion that is never complete but begins anew in every age."

Matt whispered, "It's like Jardaine, Becky, and Nick were never here! They're acting like *we* have their seed, and everything's going according to plan!"

Tuava-Li's voice appeared in Matt's head. *Perhaps this is the plan, Matt; you do not know. We cannot know. Now if you feel you must talk, use thoughtspeak.*

Matt sighed. *I just wanted you to understand that these elves are seriously confused if they think we're their saviors now. If we're lucky, we'll be able to stop Jardaine and get Becky out of there. But why does she talk like we have the seed? She's delusional.*

Tuava-Li hesitated before answering. *She believes, or wants to believe, that we were the Chosen Ones, the three who were meant to undertake the quest. She prefers to ignore Jardaine and the others.*

Matt glanced down at her. *Yeah, well, I'm not going to ignore them, because one of them is my sister.*

Tuava-Li nodded. *You know there's great risk ahead.*

Big surprise!

None of us knows what the Goddess has in store for us. None can predict the future.

Matt shook his head. *Except that it'll be bad.*

Tuava-Li's eyes grew dark. She realized that there must be something inside Matt that already knew what was coming. Even if they were able to get the Seed back from Jardaine and plant it, even if they rescued Becky, Matt was still going to die.

Relax, Matt said in thoughtspeak. *You look like you're going to cry. If I didn't think we could do this, do you think I'd be standing here?*

When Queen Geror's speech was finished, the Elves banged their drums and blew their horns again. The crickets in their golden cages scratched out a merry tune. The monks led Matt, Tomtar, and Tuava-Li to the Gate of Hujr, the place where the Cord bulged up from between the roots of Yggdrasil. Along the way the Elves tossed fistfuls of dried leaves onto the path. "I guess they didn't have any rose petals saved for us," Matt said, as the leaves crunched underfoot.

The Cord's surface was shiny and stretched. The cut Jardaine had made the previous day was healing; the only trace of it was a thin brown streak. The Queen uttered a silent prayer. The drummers worked themselves into a frenzy; then all at once they stopped playing. The Queen took a gold-handled obsidian blade from one of her monks, and with trembling hands, slit open the Cord. Matt could feel his pulse in his temples. At Tuava-Li's urging, he stepped closer to the Queen. He peered into the milky-white haze of the Cord and saw a narrow flight of steps, built in along the ledge. "Do I go down the steps," he whispered, "or do I just jump in?"

The monks shuddered, and the Queen shook her head gravely.

"You take the steps, Matt," Tuava-Li instructed. "Tomtar and I will follow. There's a platform just inside where we'll leap into the void. We must say a prayer to the Goddess, first, and make an offering. 'Tis part of the ceremony."

"You know more about this than I thought," Matt said. "What are we supposed to offer?"

"I've got the offering," said Tomtar. He held out his hand and showed Matt three enormous, glittering emeralds.

"Wow, I thought we lost all of those when the tent went into the ice water!"

"You ought to know me better than that," Tomtar said with a grin. "We've still got a good supply. . . . Never know when you might need 'em!"

Tuava-Li gave Matt a gentle shove from behind. "Please," she said, "we must hurry."

19

BECKY LAY NAPPING on a bed of dust, with nothing between her rumpled, dirty clothing and the cold stone floor. She would have given anything for a blanket, or a pillow, but her exhaustion was so complete that she fell asleep as soon as she laid her head back and closed her eyes. Jardaine sat in the flickering light of the *Kolli,* hunched over a sheaf of spells, curses, and incantations. She had told the girl that she'd stay awake and keep guard against any of the creatures that had devoured their companion. And indeed, she gave only half a mind to the words printed on the pages, the words that might help save them both from Nick's fate. She'd memorized the spell that brought down the ceiling of the cave and crushed the nightmarish creatures. She could use it again, and she would, too, at the slightest provocation. But the monsters were fast. They might be upon her before she had the chance to utter the spell, and then what? She would never forget their smell; she'd carry the memory of it as long as she lived. It was . . . indescribable. She could almost see the monsters' awful segmented bodies, their rippling, misshapen arms, their gleaming yellow eyes. Then her mind wandered over to the image of her own advising snake, Sarette, who had led her astray so many times with his ridiculous prattle. *What a foolish trend that had been,* she thought, *when Elves wore trained snakes like necklaces and listened to their illogical nonsense.* Jardaine was glad she had thrown him from the top of the wedding tower in Alfheim. One should never listen to a snake.

She considered her options once again. She knew that the Elves of Hunaland would be furious at her theft of the Seed; she wouldn't dare go back there to find another Troll to accompany her on the journey. She'd seen a variety of Faerie Folk aboveground, but it was too risky. She wasn't yet sure how she was going to get back, anyway. She'd been praying for some kind of revelation, but nothing had come to her. No . . . she had no choice, now, but to wait for Tomtar. Tomtar . . . what a clueless, ignorant Troll he was. As a matter of fact, Tuava-Li was no smarter, and the boy, Matt, was just a Human. What chance did *he* stand of reaching the North Pole? Jardaine had a disturbing thought, and it made her shiver. Perhaps the others would *never* get here. Perhaps she'd remain underground, waiting, until she starved or was eaten by monsters. *All will be well*, she breathed, and chanted the words until she felt a little calmer. There was no point in panicking, not yet.

Jardaine imagined that she had succeeded in planting the Seed. She pictured the lovely ceremony, given in her honor. She would be so gracious, so warm, so humble; she would be the very picture of a hero. She imagined that there was a new Sacred Tree growing over Hunaland, and that Elf Realm once again flourished in integrity and health. All of the world would be in balance, and all thanks would be due to Jardaine. She wondered what Queen Geror and her monks would say, then. Would they spoil the story and tell all of Elf Realm that Jardaine had stolen the Seed? Not likely. There was no such thing as a true story, after all. Good stories were all the better for the lies built into them, to make the foolish masses do their Masters' bidding. No, once the world was back in balance, Queen Geror would support Jardaine's story that the Goddess had *presented her* with the Sacred Seed.

Becky groaned softly. She rolled over, sending a cloud of dust into the air. Then she got up on one elbow. "What are they?" she asked sleepily.

"What are *what?*" Jardaine asked, fixing her eyes on the words to a spell, annoyed that the girl had awakened so soon.

"What are the . . . the monsters called? Do they have a name?"

Jardaine folded her papers with a sigh and slipped them

back into her *Huldu*. "I don't know. Honestly, I didn't know that things like that were real."

Becky rubbed her eyes with the back of her hand, leaving her face dirtier than before. "We've got to get back in the Cord, right? That way we'll reach Matt and save him before Tuava-Li and Tomtar . . . well, before they—"

"Hush," Jardaine hissed. "Did you hear something?"

Becky froze. She drew in a deep breath, testing for the telltale odor of the snakelike creatures. Then she shook her head slowly. "I don't smell anything! If those things were close, I think we'd smell them. Maybe it's Matt, and Tomtar, and Tuava-Li!"

"Follow me, and be still," Jardaine whispered. "We should proceed along this path and see if we can't find another way to reach the Cord. If we find your brother and his captors, we must take them by surprise."

Jardaine and Becky worked their way down one narrow corridor after another, relying on Jardaine's judgment to lead them back toward the Cord. But the tunnels were a tangled maze, not unlike the roots of a tree, stretching endlessly ahead, then turning back on themselves. The carvings in these small passages were much the same, and many times Jardaine had a sneaking feeling they were going around in circles. She carefully watched the floors for footprints, and she began notching the crumbling stone with her knife. That way, when she'd come to a turnoff, she would know for certain that she was making progress.

It occurred to Jardaine after a while that she'd made a terrible mistake. It might have been best to use her magick to collapse a larger part of the first great tunnel, after they'd met the awful monsters. Doing so might have opened up a path that led back to the Cord. But on the other hand, it might have crushed them, like the first collapse crushed Nick and the monsters. Jardaine stumbled over something and swore. More roots had burst through the walls of the corridor, and a lacy mesh of young vines covered the ground ahead. It was going to make further passage slow going. "I'm starving," Becky said.

Jardaine stopped and glared at her. Becky cried, "I can't help it! Won't you please check your *Huldu* again, just in case there's something left in there?"

Jardaine shook her head. "I've already looked, child. We can't eat paper, and the *Trans* I've saved aren't nutritious."

Then she glanced at the network of vines stretching along the floor. "I've got an idea," she grumbled.

She bent down and felt among the roots for something small and pliant. Most of them were tough and leathery, but the youngest roots were still soft. Jardaine pulled out her knife and cut a handful of them from the dusty mass. She carefully peeled away the bark from one of the black strips and pressed it to her lips. She sucked at the moisture, then drew back her lips in a grimace. "It tastes a little bitter, but it's not poisonous. 'Tis the milk of the Cord—very good for you! You can chew it. Here, have a piece."

Becky took the root and let her tongue run along the length of it, tasting the beads of liquid on the surface. The flavor wasn't unlike water from a dirty cup, but she had to admit that it was better than nothing. She shivered when she swallowed. Reluctantly she nibbled at the tip of the root, as more moisture bubbled from the spongy mass. An ironic smile formed on Jardaine's lips as she watched Becky chew. "The Goddess provides, eh?"

Becky didn't dare recall what her reaction would have been, just a few short weeks ago, to the thought of sucking on a dirty plant root. She was doing it to survive, she knew, and thanks to Astrid, she might not starve. She wondered if her brother was hungry and thirsty, too. "Matt could be anywhere around," she said, realizing how hard it was going to be to find a path back to the Cord. "These tunnels go on forever. He could be anywhere. I don't know how we're ever going to find him! And if those snake things attack, it could be . . ." Becky's eyes were rimmed with red.

"Don't cry," Jardaine said. "Once we find our way back toward the Cord, then I'm sure your brother will be near. Tuava-Li will undoubtedly take the same approach I'm taking—stay close to the Cord, and listen to the voice of the spirit inside. The Goddess will provide!"

"I know you always tell me the Goddess will provide," Becky said thoughtfully. "But the Goddess can't be on your side and Tuava-Li's, too, can she? Doesn't the Goddess want a new Cord, and a new Sacred Tree, and a new wall between our worlds, so that people and Elves don't have to fight? If the Goddess were nice, it seems to me that she wouldn't want somebody to have to die, just so she could have a new tree. Sometimes I wonder if we're on the right side. All I know is, I don't want them to kill my brother!"

Jardaine shook her head. "That's not the way it is, my child! Beliefs are odd things. You can spend all your energy, waste endless moons, in the service of an idea that isn't true. You can devote your every breath to the cause of a being that never existed. Aye, there is a Seed, and there is a tree, and the Gods and Goddesses are real. But the Goddess Tuava-Li believes in is just a fabrication, something to justify her existence to herself. Sacrifice is a noble ideal, but a real, literal sacrifice of a living being, so that some chain of events can be set into motion?" Jardaine chuckled. "You're right, 'tis preposterous . . . a monstrous idea."

Becky chewed on the root until there was no liquid left inside. "May I have another?" she asked.

"Of course," Jardaine said, and peeled back the bark of another strip. "You may have *one* more piece! But we must be on our way again, as soon as you're finished."

A voice drifted past, like a faint breeze from a faraway place. *Soon, you will be finished.*

"What was that?" Jardaine cried, her skin crawling.

Becky shivered. "I don't know. Don't *you* know?"

"Hush, child."

The pair of them waited, barely able to breathe. "Do those snake things talk?" Becky whispered.

"Didn't I tell you to be quiet?" Jardaine hissed. "I just read of a spell to take your voice away, child, don't make me use it!"

The sound of laughter echoed down the corridor. Jardaine wasn't fooled, though. There was a distinct note of menace in it. With trembling hands she held her *Kolli* aloft, turning her head from side to side, peering into the blackness. Then she happened to glance up and saw that the ceiling was riddled with holes, passages that might hold a thousand unknown horrors. Something flashed in the corner of her vision; she wasn't sure if it was real, or just a figment of her imagination, and she almost screamed. She gestured for Becky to follow her; the two of them hurried into the darkness. "What's wrong?" Becky cried.

They came to a fork in the tunnel and Jardaine saw a dark streak on the wall, about head level. As she drew closer she saw it was a notch in the stone. "So we *have* been here before!" she murmured, glad to have marked her path. If the creatures noticed the marks in the stone, it would make it easier for them to follow them; but she was about to make sure they were not followed again. "The Cord is near," she whispered to Becky. "I can feel it! I want you to walk ahead of me, dear one."

"But it's black," Becky protested. "I can't see anything! I'm going to stay right here with you!"

"Just go ahead," Jardaine ordered. "I have to bring the tunnel down behind us! I don't want you to get hurt. Now go!"

The Elf began chanting the words to the spell that would collapse the roof of the tunnel. Becky headed into the blackness, tripping over rocks and roots and trying not to shriek in terror, when she heard the rumble of stone from above. Suddenly everything was shaking, and she was lying on her face, choking on dust. Her nose stung; she lifted a hand and touched something hot and wet. "Astrid," she called out. "Astrid, are you there?"

The violent, wracking cough that followed let her know the Elf was still alive. A moment later the Fire Sprite flickered on once again. Becky saw Astrid on her hands and knees, covered in stone dust, looking more like a statue than an Elf. When she glanced up at Becky, she drew back her mouth in disgust. "Blood!" she said.

Becky touched her nose again; there was a sharp pain, and she tasted the salty, metallic taste on her upper lip. "I—I think I broke my nose!"

"It doesn't look broken. Just wipe that off your face. I don't want it anywhere near. It might carry contagion, child, and if anything should happen to me, you'd be left down here by yourself. You wouldn't want that, would you?"

Becky got up and wiped her hands on her jeans. "No, I wouldn't. Were they following us?"

Jardaine shrugged. "There's no chance of that now!"

"But what if they're in front of us? What are we going to do then?"

"The Cord is nearby," Jardaine lied. "I can feel my fingers tingling, the closer we get. If we keep going this way, I know we'll reach it soon. Have faith, my child. We're almost there!"

20

T HE ARVADA PILOTS SAW the plume of smoke on the horizon and steered toward it. The monks of Hunaland, distraught over what had happened to the Seed of the Adri, had let down their guard. Hunaland was no longer shielded from view as it had been throughout history; the smoke that trailed into the heavens let everyone know just where they were.

Techmagicians had been working ceaselessly to keep the tear in the Air Sprite from growing larger. Their spells, along with the constant application of healing balm, kept them afloat. Princess Asra stood inside the captain's deck and peered out from one of the upper windows as the Elves worked. "I'm amazed they can manage to stand out there on the top of the cab, in the wind and cold. They're tied to the rigging, but still you'd think they'd be blown away!"

Macta sat in a plush chair, stroking the Goblin on his lap. His mechanical arm was in fine form; he'd nearly forgotten that it wasn't real. "'Tis always a wonder what one can accomplish, when one's mind is fixed upon the goal." Though his words were meant to refer to the Elves standing outside, rubbing greasy fistfuls of ointment onto the Air Sprite's tender flesh, Macta was thinking of himself. The part of him that wasn't full of hate . . . was full of *love*. He considered his good fortune to be traveling with Asra, and the easy way she'd learned to converse with him now, as if all the errors of the past had been forgotten. For they *were* just errors, after all. Macta hadn't meant to shoot Asra's father. It had been nothing more than an accident; it could have happened to anyone! And the battle following the wedding in Alfheim, that had been Jardaine's idea from the start, not Macta's. Jardaine, and her stupid snake, Sarette. The only thing Macta ever really wanted, well . . . *one* of the only things, was Asra's heart. He wanted her to love him, to respect him, to honor and cherish him, as much as he honored and cherished her.

Macta knew that Asra didn't understand the depths of his feelings for her. He knew that he was, in part, to blame for his inability to express his love in the appropriate way. But he had saved her life now, several times. That ought to count for *something*, he thought. But being grateful was no more like being in love than a grape was like a pebble; they were both roundish in shape, but one would taste deliciously sweet and the other would break your teeth. "What do you make of the smoke?" he asked the captain. "It concerns me. Do you suppose Hunaland has been burned to the ground? I wouldn't have thought Jardaine could destroy something so quickly. Can't we go any faster?"

"Your Highness," said the captain, "at this altitude, and with the damage to the Sprite, we're making remarkably good time. As for the smoke, 'tis not necessarily a bad thing. There are many possible reasons for it: burnt offerings to the Gods and Goddesses, clearing away the detritus of the old Sacred Tree to make room for the new one . . ."

"Or the complete and utter destruction of the city," Macta said, "because a violent and criminally insane Mage has laid waste to the most sacred place in Elf Realm."

"She wants to plant the Sacred Seed," Asra said, turning from the windows, "not ruin the chance for Elf Realm to be restored. Jardaine is after recognition, she wants power and glory, and all that will come with being the Savior of her people. Why would she throw all of that away? It would make no sense."

Macta got up, Powcca in his arms, and stalked to the front window. Before him an icy plain extended in either direction. There were fissures and broad puddles of salt water along the ice; but the sky, at least, was an unbroken slab of gray. In the middle of it all a black cloud billowed up into the heavens. High above, it spread out and disappeared in the upper atmosphere.

But at the base of the plume Macta could see an irregular shape reaching into the clouds and smoke. "Could that be *the tree*?" he mused aloud. "I'm curious, Captain; perhaps you'd be willing to make a little wager on what we find when we get to Hunaland?"

"No more gambling," Asra scolded. "You promised."

"Indeed I did," he replied. "But some promises are meant to keep, like my love for you, and some promises are meant to be broken."

Asra snorted. "That's nonsense, and you know it. Conditional morality isn't morality at all. How could I expect you to be true to me if you can't be true to yourself?"

"Ah," Macta cried in delight. "So you want me to be true to you? If that's the case, I'll follow you to the ends of the earth to prove it."

Asra took a deep breath. Macta was once again trying to steer her into waters too deep for comfort. "I've spoken to you about the conditions of this expedition a hundred times, Macta. You're not following me, like a young Goblin follows its Master. We're going as a team to save my friend Becky and try and stop Jardaine. How can we hope to accomplish our goals if you keep changing them?"

"My love for you will never change," he answered.

Asra threw up her hands. "You're impossible! You won't stop until you've completely worn me down!"

"How I will spoil you," Macta said with a voice as smooth as the barrel of a Dragon Thunderbus, "once my affections have rendered you helpless."

Asra bit her lip. There was something about Macta's relentless flattery, the flirting that found its way into every shuttered part of her heart and mind. How could she keep it out? She wanted to stomp on it, to crush it so that she would remember only the bad things he had done. At the same time, though, she thought she could feel Macta changing, changing because of her, because of the way he felt about her. There was a certain power in that; the taming of a wild animal, the reining in of a force so strong it could knock someone off her feet. "Promise me you'll stop this nonsense when we get to Hunaland, Macta. We have important work, dangerous work ahead of us. We must stay focused."

"I'm always focused," he said, "you can count on that. And be careful what you ask for, Asra. It may come true!"

The Arvada skirted the branches of Yggdrasil and came down, at Macta's command, outside the main gates. As soon as the cab's shadow cast its inky smear over the ice, the Aeronauts spun out of the windows on braided ropes and rushed to tether the Arvada. The ice was far less stable than it had appeared from the air. The heavy ice screws, taller than an Elf and thicker than the trunk of a sapling, bit into the ice and released geysers of slushy water. Every footstep left a wet print on the ground, and the entire sheet of ice groaned in rebellion at the weight of the enormous craft. As soon as the stairway was in position, and the doors were flung open, Macta emerged into the frozen world.

Powcca huddled, whimpering, in his arms. "Ah," he breathed, sniffing the air. "I love the smell of burning wood! I see the spires of the palace, and if I'm not mistaken, the smoke looks like it's coming from the courtyard. I suppose that means I was wrong about Jardaine burning the entire place to the ground. It was generous of me to think her capable of such a thing!"

"Indeed," said the captain, shivering behind him.

"Look at those limbs," Asra gasped, pointing to the immense tree that rose from within the walls, spreading toward the heavens. The trunk was gnarled and gray and pitted with age, and the branches, though nearly barren, twisted in and out with a busy vitality. "'Tis impossibly large. How can something grow that big?"

"Well," Macta cried into the roaring wind, "now we shall see if a King of Helfratheim is considered a King in Hunaland!" He turned to the captain. "Do they even *have* a King in this place?"

"Sire, there are stories that speak of a Queen who rules the land, in cooperation with a Mage and her monks. Still, there's much secrecy surrounding this place, and we know very little."

Macta adjusted his goggles and stared down his nose at the great stone gates. "Do you know why there is no welcoming committee to greet me? Shouldn't a Queen come out to meet a King?"

"A better question," Asra asked, "is if the ice is stable enough to support our weight. Does it extend all the way up to the walls of this place?"

The captain pressed his lips together. Already there was ice forming in his goatee, and crystals dangled from his nostrils. He wiped his face with the back of his sleeve. "There was once land, not water, surrounding Hunaland. Yggdrasil didn't grow in water, you know. I fear the contamination of the Human world has now spread all the way to the North Pole. Once solid has become liquid, anything is possible. Good can become bad, right can become—"

"Enough," Macta said sternly. "You don't know what you're talking about! Now you have more work to do, Captain—I want you to see about getting those gates opened for us. Then hurry back to your ship and make ready for departure; we won't be terribly long. Asra and I are about to see what the Elves up here are made of!"

"Sire, 'tis not right that you enter this kingdom alone," the captain said. "Won't you let me gather the Aeronauts to accompany you?"

Macta shook his head. "I fight my own battles. I always have, and I always will. You and your Aeronauts would only slow me down!"

A terrible, earth-shaking groan suddenly arose from the ground. It was the great tree, Yggdrasil, slowly drawing its roots from the depths of the earth. The branches of the tree shook as the Elves covered their ears with their hands. "If that's the tree," Macta shouted, "then its roots are still grounded in soil. We don't have much time, though. That was the same sound the oaks of

Alfheim made when they began pulling up their roots. They do it bit by bit. It may take days, but before you know it, that tree will come crashing down!"

When the creaking sound faded away, the small group of visitors descended the Arvada stairs. With measured steps they headed across the fractured ice toward the gates of Hunaland. It was obvious to them that the gates had not been opened in a long, long time; drifts of ice and snow piled high along the thick, dark wood. There were other footprints, however, all along the edge of the gate and leading off to the side of the fortress walls. Macta studied them as he passed, stroking the Goblin pup that shivered in his arms. "Male and female boot prints. And look, look at these enormous, grotesque prints, they can only have been made by a Human!"

"Becky," Asra said, kneeling by one of the prints. "She's here."

"She's here, and we'll be meeting up with her before long, as soon as these rude, arrogant Elves open up and let us in!"

The Arvada captain raised one gloved fist and pounded on the gates. The sound was nearly swallowed up in the wind. "Hellllllloooooo," Macta cried, "in the name of the Mother and her Cord, let us in! Please!"

He turned and grinned at Asra, delighted that they were finally closing in on Jardaine. He glowed with the certainty that it was only a matter of time until he held her beating heart in his hands. "You see," he said to the Princess, "I can be the picture of grace and formality when it's required of me!"

"Am I supposed to be impressed?" Asra stepped back and gazed up at the top of the walls. "I don't think we'll be getting in this way. Perhaps we should follow around the side of the fortress and see where the others entered. Look, their footprints all go in that direction, but there are none coming back."

"There's a bit of sleuth in you, Asra," Macta said, "but we're staying here. Believe me, they'll come. They must know that a King doesn't go around to the side door."

"I seem to recall that going in a side door is exactly what we were forced to do when we entered Helfratheim, on the night of the last full moon!"

Macta shook his head. "That was different." He held a hand to his mouth and hollered again. "Helllllloooooo! In the name of the Mother and—"

A Pixie fluttered up from inside the fortress and came to rest, clinging to a high balustrade. She stared down disapprovingly at Macta and Asra. "You're not welcome here," she said, fighting the wind from her stony perch. "You must leave at once, by order of Queen Geror of Hunaland."

"What?" Macta gasped. "Of all the . . ."

Asra said, "Please tell Her Royal Highness that the King and Queen of Helfratheim have arrived, at great risk to their lives, and that they request an audience. They are in possession of important facts the Queen needs to know, concerning the Sacred Seed of the Adri."

The Pixie looked dubious, but fluttered out of sight behind

the fortress walls. "The right words are like a key to unlock many doors," Asra said.

Macta grumbled. "Well, we're not in yet. And what are you doing telling that Faerie that my mother and father, the King and Queen, have arrived? They're quite dead, you know."

"Fool," Asra said. "'Tis but a tiny lie; I meant *you and me.* I could have said, 'Please allow entrance to the King, accompanied by the female who hates him,' or 'Please let in the King, and the Princess who'd rather be anywhere else in the world than here, if it wasn't for her endangered Human friend who recently passed this way.' For a notorious liar, you're quite naive at times."

"Well, look where it's gotten me," Macta said. "And by the way, I thought you claimed to have never lied?"

Asra frowned. "Perhaps I'm picking up some of your bad traits."

A minute later a bright blue-and-pink cloud of Pixies descended over the wall and hovered around the visitors. The glittering Faeries steered them along the wall, away from the gates. "I am a King," Macta complained, scuffing his boots. "I go through *front* doors!"

"No one comes or goes from Hunaland without permission of the Queen, and these gates have been sealed for quite some time," one of the Pixies said. "The entryway chosen by a visitor to Hunaland reveals much, however; 'tis one of the tests used to prove a guest's intentions."

"And did we pass the test?" Asra asked.

"You'll see!"

They rounded the corner and found the empty niche, where the hidden door swung wide to allow them entry. "Are you absolutely certain you do not want some of the Aeronauts to come along and protect you?" asked the captain.

"When you see us next we will be basking in the glory of our success," Macta said, "and the glory will belong to me alone. Me and Asra, of course!"

The captain saluted, then turned and walked away, shaking his head. Macta and Asra followed the Pixies through the opening in the thick stone wall. Asra's gloved hands traced the mazelike patterns carved into the door frame. She thought momentarily of younger, happier days, when she'd played in the mazes of her homeland, running carefree, and hoping to get a kiss from a handsome Elflad. Then she thought of her departed friends and relatives. She pictured her father and her mother, and all her thoughts were a blur of loneliness and loss. But then she turned her gaze to the courtyard of Hunaland, and her memories were swept away.

Asra gasped as she stumbled after Macta across the littered and broken cobblestones. Hunaland was in shambles. The ground was strewn with a thick layer of grain husks that crunched beneath their boots. A rank, fishy smell permeated the air. The carcasses of earth and sea animals lay dismembered on makeshift altars. There were altars everywhere; many were nothing more than heaps of blackened twigs and scorched bones. Groups of monks wandered from place to place, chanting sorrowfully, waving incense burners. Charred bundles of rosemary, sage, Rose of Jericho, and rue smoldered in fire pits. Asra recognized the scents from cleansing rituals she'd witnessed in her youth; the Mage of Alfheim had always been fixated on cleanliness.

Elves knelt before the smoking pyres with their heads cast down in helpless resignation. Through a haze of smoke Asra saw the great tree, Yggdrasil, looming in the distance. At first the scale of it seemed impossible; an illusion caused by the swirling gray ash. But she lifted her eyes and saw the branches reaching upward into the heavens, even larger than they had seemed from outside the gates. "This way," cried one of the Pixies, as the cloud of fluttering wings suddenly banked left.

An enormous tree limb, a hundred feet long, lay on the shattered cobblestones ahead. Macta and Asra stepped around the workers who busily sawed the branch into pieces. Amid the splinters, there were also rubbery chunks of some translucent material heaped on the ground, and Asra's boot sank to the ankle in one of the quivering globs. Her nostrils curled at the smell. "'Tis exactly like the odor of the punctured Air Sprite."

Macta shook his head and snorted. "How could that be, unless the Arvada that brought Jardaine here was destroyed?"

"My thoughts exactly," Asra said.

The Pixies led them to the doors of the palace, where they were met by a small group of black-robed monks. One of them stepped from the group and blocked Macta's path inside. "The

Pixies say you have information regarding the Sacred Seed. What is it?"

"Facts I'm prepared to share with the Queen alone," Macta blustered. "Enough of your nonsense. Take me—I mean us, to her at once!"

"We've sailed from Helfratheim," Asra interjected, "in pursuit of the Mage of that kingdom. She's wanted in her homeland for crimes against the crown, and we know that she's come here with the intention of taking the Seed of the Adri. Whatever her motives may be, she's dangerous, and we've come to apprehend her and return her to Helfratheim. There she'll be punished for her infractions."

"Her depravity, you mean," Macta said.

The monk narrowed her eyes at Macta. "If the two of you are who you claim to be, then why did you not send soldiers on your behalf? A King and a Queen are meant to lead their people, and soldiers are meant to risk their lives for the good of the realm. Elves with royal Bloodlines would not take such reckless chances with their personal well-being."

"Are you calling us liars?" Macta scowled. "I see no reason why a common monk should be permitted to question a King. Take us to your Queen, immediately!"

The monk shook her head. "Three saviors have already come to rescue the Seed from the thieves and see that justice is done. They have descended in the Cord beneath the roots of Yggdrasil and are already on their way to bring honor and blessings upon our people. You're not needed here," she pronounced with a smile, showing her teeth, "Your Highness!"

An elegantly robed and ancient Elf appeared behind the monks. She wore a crown of braided golden snakes around her wizened forehead and leaned heavily on a staff with a two-headed snake on its shaft. "I am Geror, Queen of Hunaland," she said.

The monks spun around. Shocked to see their Queen walking unaided, they immediately dropped to their knees and bowed. Asra, too, knelt on the stone-tiled floor. But Macta stood and spoke with casual familiarity to her. "Finally," he said. "There's no time to waste, Geror. I'm King Macta of Helfratheim, and I'm here to save your—your kingdom, or whatever you call a place without a proper King! I want to meet with your generals, so that I may familiarize myself with the underground passages I'll be traveling. Asra and I will need provisions for the journey, as well as appropriate gear for trekking underground, and anything else your experts deem necessary. Tell me now, when did Jardaine arrive here? Is the Seed in her possession?"

Asra tugged on Macta's sleeve. "And Becky," she whispered. "Ask about Becky."

"Asra, you're a Queen," Macta admonished her. "You may address another Queen directly!"

Geror nodded at Asra and said, "The Human girl Becky was fine, when last I saw her. The Elf whom I believe you call Jardaine, and the Troll called Nick, left here two nights ago, after they stole the Seed from the fruit of the Sacred Adri."

Macta swore, and the Queen turned to him. "I had my doubts that you were who you claimed to be, but only a King would be so naturally inclined to insolence as you have been with me. Most Elves cower in their boots at the very sight of their Queen. I welcome you and your consort. I don't believe for a moment that she's a Queen, though, or that she has any inclination to become one. Now . . . before you meet with the Mage of Hunaland, you must undergo ritual preparations. She'll tell us what we need to know about your worthiness."

"I think things have gone a little too far for you to be concerned over my *worthiness*," Macta said. "You need me!"

The Queen pursed her thin lips and turned, gesturing for Macta and Asra to accompany her into the palace. "Come out of the cold and shut the doors behind you. I cannot bear the sight of this destruction in my land. I've been pacing about, knowing there's nothing I can do."

"You can show us the entrance to the Cord," Macta said.

"As my monks undoubtedly told you," she said, ignoring Macta, "another three self-proclaimed heroes arrived in Hunaland yesterday, with the intention of taking the Seed to the Underworld and planting it there. They arrived too late, however, and our prayers are with them as they attempt to catch up with the thieves. They remain our greatest hope that the Seed will be planted, that the appropriate sacrifice will be made. Their names were Tuava-Li and Tomtar—an Elf and a Troll. I cannot recall the Human's—"

"Matt!" Asra interrupted. "The Human's name is Matt. He's Becky's older brother. Those three, their quest, began before any of the rest of us even thought of coming here. You see, the Goddess spoke to Tuava-Li in a vision and told her she'd been chosen to relive the quest of Fada in the Underworld!"

"So I heard," said Queen Geror.

"Did you send soldiers after the thieves?" Macta asked, hoping that the answer would be no. His greatest passion lay in the thought that Jardaine's punishment for everything that had happened would be his responsibility and his alone.

"As for armies and generals and soldiers," Geror said, "we have none. Our monks have always shielded our whereabouts with protective spells that render Hunaland invisible to the naked eye. In that way we've protected the Seed from harm . . . at least, up until now. Perhaps it's our Mage's fault that you arrived here so easily. Our monks have obviously let down their guard. Perhaps it pleases the Great Goddess to see us brought low. Who knows?"

The Queen turned and shuffled slowly away, mumbling to herself as the monks directed Macta and Asra down one of the corridors. "Now what?" Macta demanded.

"The ritual bath, and then the audience with the Mage."

Monks were filling the single porcelain tub with buckets of steaming water when Macta and Asra entered the elegant royal suite. Unlike the room where Matt and Becky had bathed, this part of the palace was well appointed, elegant, and warm. Macta waited in a room with a stone fireplace while Asra undressed, bathed, and anointed herself with the proper oils and lotions. Then, dressed in a simple white robe tied at the waist with a golden braid, and her hair still damp and hanging down her back, she went to find Macta. His thoughts of vengeance against Jardaine disappeared when he saw his beloved approach him, her face shining, her eyes bright with expectation.

"Come," she said, "let me help you take off the mechanical arm. You've got to be quick, so that we can meet their Mage and go after Becky."

Macta drew back. He knew that after their journey he wouldn't smell his freshest when he took off his shirt, and the healing skin on his shoulder would still stink of ointment and sweat. And yet, Asra was the one who had sawn off what remained of his rotten arm when she could have watched him die. For once he was at a loss for what to say; he couldn't think of anything clever or witty, and there was no flattery that would do justice to Asra's beauty. So he leaned forward and kissed her. For a brief moment the Princess was too stunned to respond. Macta had made his intentions clear for so long that it should have come as no surprise. But despite his inappropriate remarks and his bold tongue, he had always shown restraint. Asra felt the warmth of his skin like a fever and she pulled away. "That should never have happened," she stammered.

"It was meant to be," Macta said and tried to draw her close again.

"I said no!"

"What do you expect of me?" Macta pleaded. "Did you expect me to go to my grave without the pleasure of tasting your lips?"

Asra turned and hurried from the room. Macta struggled to undo the harness on his mechanical arm, undressed, and slipped into the water where Asra had bathed, just minutes before. *This might be as close as I ever get to you,* he thought, *sitting alone in your tepid bathwater.* Then, somehow, he thought of Jardaine. Here he was, joined forever to these two Elfmaids . . . one of whom he loved and the other he hated. With his good hand he pinched his nose and quickly doused his head.

Soon Macta was following Asra and a group of monks along a darkened corridor. Walking with a purposeful stride they soon came to the chapel, where the Queen knelt before the altar and recited poetry she had memorized from ancient Holy Scrolls. The Queen's monks helped her get up from the altar when she heard footsteps approaching. She was weary of strangers, and she realized her disappointment in her Mage's pronouncements had made her careless when the last group of three showed up. The Human boy should never have been allowed near the chapel; he should never have been allowed to address the Mage. Despite all that had happened, the Queen knew that she was still responsible for Yggdrasil and the heritage and promise of Hunaland. She stood in the doorway and said, "'Tis best if the pair of you stay out in the hall. The Mage doesn't like to be stared at."

 MACTA AND ASRA

"I'm not the staring type," Macta said. "Neither is Asra. We couldn't care less about your Mage. We don't need to meet her, anyway. Just get us provisions for our trip, and we'll be on our way."

"Who is it now?" came a croaking voice from inside.

"I told you," the Queen said. "Have you forgotten already? 'Tis the King of Helfratheim, and a . . . friend of his. The two of them want to enter the Cord to the Underworld and help the others stop Jardaine from planting the Seed."

"*Someone* must plant the Seed," came the voice from the withered, sightless head.

"Aye," said the Queen, "*someone* must. But not a thief, not someone who shows such disrespect, such contempt for the will of the Goddess. That's not the way to begin a new era!"

The Mage's wrinkled head seemed to shrink in concentration. "How did this *Jardaine* enter the Gate of Hujr? Why did you not bring her to me first? Surely I would not have given my permission to take the Seed!"

The Queen recalled how the Mage had responded to the presence of Jardaine in her chambers. She'd been filled with contempt, and rage, and anger after her revelations about the stranger's heart. Now, apparently, she'd forgotten the entire episode. The Queen felt strangely relieved to know that the Mage wouldn't blame her for failing to keep a closer eye on Jardaine when she had the chance. "In any event," she said, "the

Goddess will not allow Jardaine to plant the Seed; you can be sure of that."

"I can be sure of nothing," said the Mage, "until I've tested this King and his consort to see the contents of their hearts and souls. I can sense them from here. But where is their Human? They cannot hope to plant the Seed without a Human to accompany them!"

The Queen got down on her knees before the Mage and whispered, "I told you, they're not going to plant the Seed, they don't *have* the Seed. They're going to help those who wish to *save* the Seed from Jardaine, and see that it is planted correctly. Don't you remember what I told you?"

"Bring them to me," said the Mage, "and I will discover if they're worthy!"

A pair of monks helped the Queen get up, and she hobbled to the door. "The Mage says you may enter now."

Both Macta and Asra stood in stunned disbelief to see the misshapen creature reclining on her bed of pillows. "What is your name, Elfmaid?" the withered head demanded.

"I—I'm Asra, formerly the Princess of Alfheim. But Alfheim was burned to the ground when the—"

"Enough," said the withered head, dropping heavily back onto the pillow. Her clawed hands felt the air as if molding some unseen mass.

The other head lifted jerkily, like a marionette on a string.

The smooth and featureless face waved back and forth as the gash of a mouth opened to speak. "*A* is one, nothing more. Not nineteen, twenty-eight, thirty-seven, forty-six, fifty-five, sixty-four, seventy-three, eighty-two, or ninety-one. One, just one. That is all."

Macta and Asra stood in bewilderment as the other head lifted from the pillow and began to speak. "The letter *A* in the cornerstone reveals one who is self-motivated, self-directed, and at times self-absorbed. It is the beginning; it is ambition and intention. Its element is fire. Letter *A* is the number one; it seeks attainment and success. The letter *A* in the capstone position reinforces the notion that this soul finds herself not only at the beginning, but also at the end. This soul will meet many, but will always be alone; she will seek ways of finding attainment through the self, wishing to take on the role of a leader, but will find her greatest satisfaction walking a solitary path."

"That's not true at all," Asra said, indignant. "I came all the way here to help my friend. I'm not selfish or self-indulgent. All I ever think about is other Faerie Folk, my obligations to my family, my homeland! How can you say—"

"Enough, child," said the Queen. "This is but a formality, the Mage does not want to hear your protests."

"What is your name, King?" asked the Mage.

"Macta."

"Aha," the Mage said. "To be a King is an interesting thing; what is a King, but the servant of his people, the scapegoat for their sins, the one who bears the weight of his crown and must sometimes risk his own life for the good of the many?"

"The numbers?" interrupted the Queen.

"So we shall hear the numbers," answered the withered head.

"Four," croaked the other head. Its slick, glossy face bobbed on the pillow. "Four is one and three, not four, but one-three-four. Not twenty-two, thirty-one, forty, fifty-eight, sixty-seven, seventy-six, eighty-five, or ninety-four; four, simply, four."

"The cornerstone is *M*, or four," said the withered head. "*M* represents the limits of Elfinkind. *M* seeks to pit spirit, mind, body, and soul against the elements air, earth, fire, and water, in order to persevere, to endure, to achieve by hard work and effort. *M* is emotionally limited, unable to attain the heights of feeling. *M* must sacrifice in order to reach his potential, to grow, to understand. The dark side of this soul is rigidity, inflexibility and . . . violence."

The Mage's body began to shake. Her face contorted, her shoulders hunched. "What is the date of your birth?" she cried.

Macta was taken aback, but he managed to blurt out the answer. The featureless head translated it into her strange numerological code. "One, one, eight, seven, two, zero."

"As I thought," said the other, managing to calm herself. "Nine."

"What does that mean?" Macta cried.

"Completion."

"Completion of what? I stand here and listen to this drivel, and you don't give me the courtesy of even explaining what you mean?"

The heads dropped simultaneously onto their pillows; they were exhausted from their efforts. The Queen stepped forward. "Very well. Let's see if the monks have prepared your packs for travel. Be forewarned—you must stay alert in the Cord, and do not get out for any reason until you reach the center of the world. Now hurry, if you wish to catch up with the others who preceded you!"

"That's what I've been trying to tell you since we got here," Macta said, his hands balled into fists. The mechanical hand let out a low buzz as the fingers began clenching and unclenching.

"Ignore what they said," Asra murmured. "They know nothing, obviously. The Mage is just guessing, trying to throw us off balance, for some reason. No one knows the future, no one knows what the Goddess has planned for each of us. You've seen Fortune-tellers before, I'm sure. They're all bizarre, absurd, laughable!"

"She said *completion*," Macta said. "That means that I shall finish what I started, that I shall reap the rewards of my efforts. I know! And yet she said I was limited, and I'm just the *opposite* of that. I always go farther, take more chances, indulge in more risk for its own sake, than anyone else I've ever known."

"Then ignore it," Asra said, understanding Macta's injured pride. Soothsayers and Sagas had had the same effect on her; she couldn't help but picture the card, The Hanged One, that an old Saga had shown her back in Ljosalfar. To show her sympathy she reached out, and her fingers brushed Macta's chest.

He forgot all about the Mage's pronouncements. She was standing so close to him that he could draw in the sweet smell of her hair, and he found it completely intoxicating. It was all he could do not to take her in his arms. But at that precise moment, the palace shook. The air was filled with that same hideous screeching sound they'd heard outside. All the Elves pressed their hands to their ears. The screeching could only mean that the Sacred Tree was once again struggling to pull its deepest roots from their prison of rocks and soil.

21

MATT WOKE WITH A START. He blinked, and
his eyes felt like they were on fire. He squeezed his lids shut
against the wind in the Cord and opened his mouth to scream.
The rumble in the air penetrated his body and he felt as if a giant
were shaking him. No, it was worse; it was as if the atoms of his
body might come undone, like a bag of marbles dropped on the
floor. "What's—"

He had to concentrate on drawing breath into his lungs.
He was still falling, still dropping down inside the Cord and
plummeting to the very heart of the Underworld. His ears had
gotten used to the high, keening whistle of the wind; the skin on
his face, neck, and arms knew the slow burn of the constant blast
of air as he hurtled downward. But the feeling of the rumble in

the ground was like nothing he'd ever known. *The tree is wrenching its roots from the earth.*

It was Tuava-Li's voice in his brain. Matt opened his eyes to look for her, but the burning sensation was so bad that he squeezed them shut again. He moaned and felt the salty tears gathering beneath his lids. *I'm here,* she said in thoughtspeak, *just behind you. You must have fallen asleep.*

Yeah, I fell asleep. I was in a playground, my dad was pushing me on the swing, and I could feel the sun and the breeze and there was laughter everywhere.

Tuava-Li said, *You can't fall asleep here; you might never wake up again.*

My eyes are burning so bad! It's killing me!

'Tis hard to hold on to consciousness in the Cord, Tuava-Li reprimanded. *Your mind and body were drifting apart. You must have floated away with your lids open, and the wind dried out your eyes.*

I can't see!

Just keep blinking, Matt. Be glad that the sound of the tree roused us. We've got to get to Tomtar and wake him, too!

What? Even you fell asleep? How long were we out?

The rumbling was beginning to subside. Matt stretched out his arms, gazing ahead, squinting, eyes nearly shut. He blinked again and again to see what lay before him in the dim, milky glow. The tunnel was wide; a river of rushing air and little more. Then his burning eyes recognized a dark, ragged ball weaving in the wind below.

"Tomtar," he cried hoarsely, "Tomtar, wake up!"

Then something else began to come clear in the vast white distance. Growing larger, coming closer, closer still, a zigzag of black, scribbled lines; dark, brittle fingers reaching across the void; tree roots piercing the Cord and grasping in the moist air ahead. "Tomtar!"

Tuava-Li stretched her body like a cat, and with less resistance to slow her down, shot forward. She ricocheted off Tomtar and he bounced to the side, narrowly avoiding a long black root. But there were many more obstacles ahead. As he opened his eyes and cried out, his shoulder banged against another root. He spun around helplessly in the air, spinning like a top. "Tomtar, get ahold of yourself. Watch out!"

The tendrils were thicker now, and the passage narrowed where the roots had pierced the walls of the Cord and drawn them inward. Matt grabbed on to one of the roots as he swept past, slowing his descent just a little as he swung back into the airstream. Tuava-Li bumped Tomtar once again and forced him against the glutinous wall. She managed to pin him there, though she was much smaller than the Troll. Grabbing fistfuls of Cord and squeezing hard, she called out to Matt. "The Cord is too thick to penetrate with my fingernails—do you have your knife?"

The wind roared in Matt's ears. "Yeah, I do," he cried, fishing one hand into his pocket. He arched his back to avoid another massive root and headed toward the wall where Tuava-Li and Tomtar were clinging.

Matt grabbed the Cord directly ahead of his friends and jammed his knife through the wall. There was a loud *POP,* and air hissed through the opening as he ripped back the Cord and pushed a foot through. "It's not dirt or rock behind here—there's at least a pocket of space on the other side. Come on!" he yelled and gestured to Tuava-Li and Tomtar. They crept along the wall, straining for handholds among the tangled roots, and worked their way toward Matt and the dark gash ahead.

"Tuava-Li," Matt called, "wrap your arms around Tomtar's waist and hold on tight—I'm going to pull you both in!"

Matt grabbed Tomtar's wrist and yanked hard. At the same time he leaned into the opening he'd made, and the trio tumbled out of the Cord and into the darkness. Wind poured through the hole and threw up a thick cloud of dust and gravel. Coughing, Matt reached out and tried to smooth the ripped wall of the Cord back into place. "Give me a hand," he cried, and Tomtar and Tuava-Li leapt up to join the effort to seal the Cord.

A moment later the spongy mass began to heal itself. The three could hear the whistle of the wind on the other side of the wall. They were left in blackness at the edge of a maze of tangled roots, their hearts pounding. Tuava-Li was the first to pull off her pack and dig for her *Kolli.* She flicked open the lid and the Fire Sprite peered out, sending an orange glow into the dusty cave. "I must have drifted off, out there," Tomtar said. "I'm sorry!"

"We all did," said Matt. "If Tuava-Li hadn't woken me up, you and I'd have dashed out our brains on those roots. What's going on, Tuava-Li? Do you know why roots would grow out through the Cord like that?"

"Pressure, perhaps," she said. "Roots grow, and if their path is blocked, they find another, easier way. 'Twas simpler for them to grow back through the Cord than into solid rock. Or maybe the roots are an obstacle put there by the Goddess to thwart infidels. It may be hard for us to get past this; with the winds so strong, 'tis dangerous to try and navigate around the roots. Perhaps we should try to find our way alongside the Cord for a while, and see if we can't slip back in, once we've passed the worst of it."

"The Queen told us not to get out of the Cord until we reached the center of the earth," Tomtar said.

Matt shrugged. "What choice did we have? I wonder if Becky and Jardaine hit the same roadblock with these roots. The Cord couldn't have gotten choked up like that in a day. If they had to bail, like we did, they might be out here, too, looking for a way back in. We should keep our eyes open for any signs of life, footprints, stuff like that!"

Tuava-Li nodded. Matt might be right; but none of them knew how many decayed passageways might snake through the Underworld, how long they could walk alongside the Cord before the path veered away, or what unknown dangers might lie in wait. "Very well."

"I was dreaming," Tomtar said. "I was just a young Troll, standing on the roof of my home in Argant. The sun was shining, and the breeze felt cool on my cheeks. It was a nice dream, clear as day!"

"I was dreaming about the sun, too," Matt said. "Since we're so far from it here, our bodies must be craving sunlight."

Tuava-Li kept silent. When she'd awakened inside the Cord, she'd also been dreaming that she was standing in the warmth of the sun. There had been a lake, or a pool of some kind, and she'd come out of the pool to find herself in the midst of a crowd; it included Matt, Becky, Tomtar, Macta, Asra, and Jardaine, and someone else, a monk, perhaps, who she didn't know. In her dream, a struggle broke out. She couldn't quite remember who was fighting, but suddenly a long black root, like an enormous snake, slipped up from behind Matt and thrust its pointed head straight through his body. The root pierced his heart and came out through the front of his chest, twisting and flicking its Bloody tip. It was that horrible image that had awakened her, just in time to save them all from being battered on the subterranean roots. What had the dream meant? Was it a warning, an omen, a message, or a clue of some kind about the sacrifice that was to come? "May we see your tattoos?" she asked Matt.

Without protest Matt pulled up his shirt. Peering down, it was easy for him to see that the tattoos had changed. The old image of Becky was gone. In her place there were three black strips. He yanked off the shirt and leaned in closer to Tuava-Li's Fire Sprite. "What do you see?"

Tomtar pointed a finger at the tattoo on Matt's chest. "It looks like doorways! Portals, entryways of some kind."

"Indeed," Tuava-Li said. "But portals to what?"

"I think one of the three is a different color," Matt said in a trembling voice. The changes in the tattoos always made him feel helpless and vulnerable, like his life was truly out of his control. "Look, it's subtle, but that one, the one on the end, I think it's kind of a dark red color. The other two look black."

"Does it mean we should look for the third portal, somewhere down here?"

Matt frowned. "Or does it mean we should avoid the third portal, and the red is supposed to be blood? I guess we'd better get moving, then, whatever it means." He pulled his shirt back over his head. "We're looking for three portals."

"And we're looking to see if we can't get back into the Cord," Tuava-Li said, "once these roots no longer block the way. If the great tree is pulling all of its roots out of the ground, the ones that block the Cord may be drawn out, eventually."

"Or they might get broken off in the rock," Matt said. "Let's get going, okay?"

They strapped on their packs, stepped over a clump of roots, and found a smooth, stone floor beneath their feet. "The cavern's ceiling is higher here than the ceiling in the palace at Hunaland," Matt said, flexing his shoulders and standing tall. "I was getting pretty tired of having to bend over all the time."

They followed a sloping path, creeping through gaps in

massive roots that punctured the wall of the Cord. Some of the crumbling stone walls were carved with images of battles and military conquest. At first they tried to make sense of the scenes, looking for clues as to their whereabouts, and Tuava-Li explained what she could of the ancient Elfin culture and history revealed there. Tomtar, though, was feeling anxious. "Do you think we're in the labyrinth, the one the Queen told us about?"

Tuava-Li shook her head. "The passages here are so badly damaged, 'tis hard to tell."

Matt said, "I guess there could be portals, like the ones we're looking for, in a maze!"

Tomtar tried to ignore the sensation of being trapped in the subterranean depths; he longed for open spaces and fresh air. "Why are there sweeping marks in the dust?" he asked.

"Probably just the movement of air over the floor," Tuava-Li answered.

"But there's no air down here; it's completely still!"

"Maybe it's gravity," Matt offered. "Maybe the dust rolls downhill and leaves traces. What else could it be?"

The darkness and isolation underground were beginning to set all of their nerves on edge. Distant rumbling, like muffled thunder, let them know that the roots of the Adri were still working their way loose from the depths of stone and soil. The sound filled each of them with dark foreboding. If the tunnels should collapse, they'd all be crushed. Matt and Tuava-Li kept quiet, watching the paths for crevices and footprints and the walls for mysterious portals. Tomtar chattered on, despite his friends coaxing him to be quiet and listen for unusual sounds. At times they were able to keep the Cord within view, and at other times they were forced to veer away from it into dank and winding corridors.

Eventually, after endless hours of hiking ever downward, the path they were on dropped away into blackness. They stood at the edge of a large, cavernous hollow. The Fire Sprite cast flickering shadows over the walls, giving the distinct impression that there were figures moving among the fallen rocks. "What's that?" whispered Tomtar, pointing to a dark pile of boulders. "I see something out there!"

"'Tis a trick of the eye," Tuava-Li said, as her voice echoed off the walls. "'Tis a trick of the eye, a trick of the eye, a trick of the eye," came the echo, again and again.

Tomtar's eyes brightened. "That's fun!" he cried aloud. The echo came back, "That's fun, that's fun, that's fun, that's fun . . ."

He unstrapped his pack and rooted around until he found his flute. Matt said, "What are you doing? I figured you lost that thing when our tent went into the ocean!"

"I tucked it into my belt, just in time. I'm only going to play a little—it'll cheer us up!"

Tomtar raised the instrument to his lips and blew a quick string of notes. As the echo swelled, racing circles around the cavern, they all heard a low rumbling sound beneath the flute's shrill whistle. Tomtar held his breath as gray flakes fell like

TOMTAR

rain from the ceiling. The three of them leaned back against the wall and waited for the sound to stop. Soon the rumbling faded away. Matt glanced upward, then leaned toward his friend and whispered, "There aren't any tree roots right around here, Tomtar. That groaning came from the rocks right over our heads. You can't play your flute here. These old tunnels are ready to collapse. If we're not careful, the sound vibrations might be enough to bring the whole roof down on us!"

"I guess there's no place I can play my flute anymore," the Troll grumbled.

They backtracked away from the chasm, following twists and turns in the dark corridors, as Tuava-Li tried to determine where the Cord might be. She often felt a tingling sensation in her fingertips when a Cord was near, but here in the Underworld she just wasn't sure. It had been the same with Matt's compass — it was a useful tool that no longer worked the way it should. It seemed to Tuava-Li that they hadn't wandered too far from the Cord, but they were surrounded on all sides by walls of earth and stone. Without a doubt they had entered the labyrinth, and in the end, there was no real way to tell how to get back out. "I think I need to rest," Tomtar finally said. His legs and arms felt like lead weights hanging from his body, and his anxiety about being underground was wearing him down. "Can't we stop and sleep somewhere, just for a little while? I keep imagining I'm seeing things out of the corner of my eye."

"We've got to find our way back into the Cord, Tomtar,"

Matt said. "Becky's in danger. We don't know what Jardaine has in store for her, down in this hole. If we stop to rest now, we might be too late to help her. We have to keep going!"

"Aye," Tuava-Li said. "We have to keep going. Jardaine has the Seed of the Adri, and we've got to get it back, so that we can plant it the way the Goddess intends. Otherwise this entire quest will have been for nothing."

Even as she said the words, Tuava-Li knew that she was trying to convince herself that they were true. Nothing, so far, had gone according to plan. Setbacks and unpleasant surprises all along the way made her wonder if it was nothing but her own stubbornness that made her carry on, when the Goddess might be making another path clear. When the time came for Matt to die for the Seed, she wondered, would she try to stop it? Would she try to save him, like she'd done so many times before?

"Nothing?" Matt said. "This will all be for nothing if we don't plant that seed? I'm going to find my sister."

Tomtar sighed. He hitched his pack a little higher on his back and shuffled his feet. A cloud of dust wafted up around his ankles. "I wonder what happened to the Elves who built these passages down here. It looks like no one's been down here in a really long time. I wonder why they don't keep these tunnels in good repair, if they really care about that Seed. You'd think they'd want it to look nice for us when we came down here. It's the least they could do, really!"

Matt took a deep breath. If it helped Tomtar stay awake and

alert, he could tolerate the Troll's useless chatter. But he was beginning to think he was seeing things out of the corners of his eyes, too.

Deep in a crevice in the thick rock wall, not far from where Matt, Tuava-Li, and Tomtar kept up their weary trek, Becky lay sleeping. Hunger and fatigue had taken a toll on her. When she'd collapsed in the dust, crying pitifully, Jardaine had no choice but to stop and let the girl rest. At the back of the crevice the girl would be safe from a surprise attack by the creatures; and if Jardaine heard their slithering, shifting movements, or smelled their foul, meaty odor, there were several spells she could try that might stop them in their tracks. For one, there was that spell she had used to create the image of a monster in the minds of the palace guards who'd tried to arrest her in Helfratheim. Jardaine was good at projecting thoughts into the minds of others, especially fearful minds. The monsters didn't seem like the fearful type, though.

Then there was the spell that brought down the roof of the passageway when Nick was being devoured. She would use that spell if she had to, though it might be dangerous for her and the girl at such close quarters. Beyond that, there was the spell she'd learned in the palace of Helfratheim—the one she'd used to knock out the guards outside Prashta's sleeping quarters. It had worked on Nick, too, when she'd tried it on him in the Techmagicians' labs.

Of course, if it came down to survival, Jardaine knew she could change herself into a chameleon and scurry away while the monsters ate Becky. She yawned. She was so terribly tired! A few hours beyond the Gates of Vattar and she'd be refreshed and ready to proceed; if only she dared to risk falling asleep. She felt the throb of the Seed from within her *Huldu*. The thing had great power, to be sure. And then, somehow, the thought occurred to her that the Seed was what was making her so tired, that it was tapping her strength.

Suddenly the image of Nick appeared in her mind. *Poor Nick,* she thought for a brief moment. She'd treated him so unkindly, and all he had ever wanted was to be close to her. Jardaine quickly got ahold of herself. Of course, what Nick had really wanted was some of her power and prestige, such as it was. His death had been his own fault. If he hadn't been so clumsy and weak, he never would have been eaten by the monsters, and Jardaine would now be that much closer to real glory, timeless adoration, and, dare she say it, *worship. Aye,* she thought, *generations will worship me for what I'm about to do.*

There was a sound, not far away. Someone talking. It wasn't the smooth, mocking sound of the creatures; it was the sound of . . . a Troll. Was she dreaming? Imagining things? Jardaine held her breath, every muscle in her body tingling in attention. The sound became clearer as it got closer. *Praise the Goddess!* She peered carefully over the edge of the stone and upward along the wide corridor. There was a dim light, growing brighter and brighter. She thought she could make out three voices. Then she saw, in the distance, a Human boy, an Elf, and a Troll.

Jardaine's mind raced: what to do, what to do? *Praise the Goddess.* She had to get Tomtar away from the others. He was already trailing up the rear. Before the three got any closer, she thought, she'd plant the image of the monsters in Tomtar's mind. Or, maybe, first she would cast the spell that would make the Troll mute, in case he called for help and alerted the other two to stop and turn around. Yes, that was it! *Praise the Goddess.* Steal the Troll's voice, make him think one of the hideous snake things was between him and his friends, so he would fall back. Then, once the Human and the Elf were past the crevice where she hid, Jardaine would bring down the roof of the tunnel on them and crush them to a pulp. Tomtar would belong to her, and she would have her Troll to complete the journey and plant the Seed. *Praise the Goddess.* It was a lot to do, in very little time.

Tomtar paused to adjust his pack again. He had a blister on his shoulder where the strap rubbed. "You know, I think those packs we had back in Argant were the best of all. They had canvas straps, and the zippers on the side pockets were —"

He felt something odd, like a breeze brushing across his face. Tomtar realized his lips were moving, but no sound came out. He tried to cough; maybe it was all the dust down here that had blocked his throat. But no, he could breathe just fine. He took a step forward, hoping to catch up with Matt and Tuava-Li and tell them something was wrong. Then his eyes caught movement in the shadows to his left. When he spun his head around to see what it was, a hideous snake thing was there, grinning at him. Tomtar froze in his tracks. He tried to cry out, but it was as if his voice had been stolen. He couldn't utter a sound, not even a gasp. He dashed a few paces to the right, but the thing with the grotesque head of an Elf and the body of an enormous snake was there, right in front of him. He turned to the left, but there it was again! He blinked, thinking his mind was playing tricks on him. But everywhere he looked, the awful thing was there.

Matt and Tuava-Li didn't notice that Tomtar had fallen behind. They trudged ahead, moving ever downhill in the glow of the Fire Sprite, when there was an eerie rumbling sound from above. Matt cringed. "Is it more of those roots pulling out of the rock?" he asked.

"Nooo," said Tuava-Li, "'tis too close! I don't like it; the rumbling worries me. We've got to keep moving!"

Now there was a distinct grinding sound, like jaws of stone. Broken shards of rock began falling from above. *"Owwww,"* Matt cried, as something struck his forehead. He brushed at his hair and felt Blood, and dust and stone began raining down.

A crack opened up above them. Bigger rocks began to tumble from the aperture. A boulder crashed, and then another. "Tomtar, come on!" Matt spun around and was surprised to see that his friend wasn't keeping up. "Hurry up, we've got to get ahead of this thing, we've got to—"

As a cloud of dirt and debris struck him in the face Matt

thought he saw a grinning figure staring at him from a crack in the rock wall. It wasn't Tomtar; it was an Elf. And as he charged ahead, stumbling over Tuava-Li and pushing her to safety at the intersection of another corridor, just as the roof of the tunnel collapsed, he realized whom he'd seen. It was the monk, Jardaine.

Before the dust had even settled Jardaine leapt from the crevice, her *Kolli* held high. She was operating on sheer willpower now; the use of so much magick, so quickly, had cost her terribly. She was also beginning to think that the Seed was dangerous, and that she should try to keep it away from her body. Heart pounding, she made her way over heaps of fallen rocks and boulders to where Tomtar lay. He was facedown in the dirt, immobile, when she grabbed his shoulders and tried to turn him over. *I'm so weak,* she thought, unable to budge him. She looked helplessly at her own hands and wondered where she'd find the strength to go on.

A cough came from the crevice. "What happened, Astrid?" Becky cried, covering her mouth, and coughing again. "Are you all right?"

Becky was still more asleep than awake when she saw the figure sprawled amid the refuse on the dirty floor. There was dust in her eyes, sharp and stinging. She blinked, realizing they weren't alone. Could it be—no, the figure was too little to be Matt. She leapt from the crevice and crossed the corridor. "Look who we've caught," Jardaine said wearily. "Part of the ceiling collapsed, and he got trapped here. Quickly, child, help me tear a strip of cloth from his jacket. We must tie his hands with it, so he won't be able to hurt us when he awakens!"

Becky helped Jardaine bind Tomtar's wrists. He lay stunned in the dust, unable to speak, and senseless from the barrage of rocks that had fallen on him. Jardaine was certain that Matt and Tuava-Li had been crushed in the collapse of the passageway. Now all she had to do was find her way back to the Cord, proceed to the end, and plant the Seed. A sound brought Jardaine out of her thoughts. She realized Becky was whimpering. "What's wrong, child? Aren't you glad that we've caught one of your enemies?"

"But where's Matt?" she asked. "Where's Tuava-Li? Do you think anything happened to them? They should be with Tomtar! Maybe they got smashed by all these boulders! Maybe they . . . the snakes . . ."

Becky was choking on dust and her own sobs. Tomtar was coming around; he managed to sit up, despite the fact that his hands were bound. His eyes went wide when he saw Becky with Jardaine. But he couldn't say a word, he couldn't utter a syllable. He was terrified, too, that the hideous snake creatures were still nearby. His eyes darted around, looking for any sign of movement among the fallen rocks. Becky stared him in the face. "Where's my brother?" she cried accusingly. "Talk to me! You think you and your Elf friend can kill Matt, so you can plant your Seed and get famous? You won't get away with it, Tomtar. Astrid and I came halfway around the world to stop you!"

Tomtar's eyes bulged. *Who was Astrid?* He shook his head and mouthed the word no, but it was no use. It was clear that Becky hated him, and somehow she thought he was in on a plot to kill her brother. Tuava-Li had never told him about the real plan, so he was completely befuddled. He knew that Jardaine was up to no good, but why? Tomtar's gaze went from Jardaine to Becky and back again, pleading, imploring, but he could not make a sound. He wanted to tell them about the monsters, too, so they could all escape before the creatures came back. "Why don't you talk?" Becky cried. "Why don't you tell me what you're doing? Aren't you ashamed of what you've done, after you pretended to be our friend?" Becky grabbed Tomtar by the collar of his jacket. "Tell me! Tell me!"

There was a low groan from the rocks in the ceiling. Little pieces of stone fell like drops of dirty rain. Something rumbled, deep, yet not so far away. "Enough, dear one," Jardaine said in a soothing voice, as her eyes anxiously scanned the ceiling. She brushed some of the dirt and broken pebbles from Becky's hair as they stood beside the bewildered Troll. "Now that this tunnel's collapsed, we must find another way back to the Cord. Let's grab our things. We'll take the Troll along with us."

"But—but shouldn't we look for Matt?" Becky asked. "Since Tomtar was here, Matt and Tuava-Li have to be nearby!"

Jardaine put on a pained smile. "The Troll could tell us, if he wanted. But it appears he's not interested in cooperating! Come, we really ought to leave."

Once again Becky grabbed Tomtar by the shoulders. "Where are they?" she pleaded. "You have to tell us where they are!"

Tomtar turned his head toward the wall of fallen rock. He would have gestured with his hands; he would have pantomimed what had happened. He wanted to tell Becky that she was wrong. He wanted to tell his friend that Jardaine was her real enemy, and this was all part of some bizarre plot to—to what? It made no sense. Tomtar struggled to his feet. Jardaine struck him with the back of her hand, and he fell back against a boulder.

Jardaine steadied herself against the wall; fatigue came over her like a fog. She knew that the spell she'd placed on Tomtar was going to wear off before long, and he'd be able to talk again. It was imperative to get to the heart of the Underworld before the Troll was able to tell Becky the truth. She had to get back to the Cord, and soon it would be too late. "This is getting us nowhere," she said. "He refuses to talk because he knows whatever lies he tells will only get him into more trouble. We'll go back the way we came and listen for sounds. Perhaps the other two went down another passage. We'll find them, don't worry!"

22

FLYING, FALLING, it didn't matter to Macta. The little Goblin in the crook of his arm whimpered and whined in the winds of the Cord. Macta held him tightly, whispering quiet reassurances, while he held his mechanical arm before him as if it were the prow of a ship. If there was one skill at which Macta excelled, it was riding the Cord. Even in this strange underground passage, where the sensation was less like a bird in flight and more like plunging into an abyss, Macta negotiated the twists and turns as if it were his birthright. What was terror or monotony for others was to him boundless pleasure. He loved the subtle flexing of his muscles to swoop and soar, navigating the air, becoming one with its power. He was a born Aeronaut in the Cord; but it was not this way for everyone.

"Asra," Macta cried, but it was obvious to him that the Princess didn't hear.

He saw her falling next to him, not twenty feet away. She was curled into a ball, her eyes shut, hair streaming back, dropping like a rock through space. Macta knew that if she lost consciousness her spirit could slip out of her body and be lost forever. She'd never been fond of travel in the Cord; when she'd been forced to ride, it had almost always been in the royal Gondola. She wasn't weak, or spoiled, not really. This just wasn't her element. And when her friend Skara had been killed in the Cord accident outside Storehoj, her opinion had been sealed. "Asra, are you awake?" Macta called again.

When they went to enter the Cord at the Gate of Hujr, it had been difficult for him to convince Asra that she really needed to relax, have faith in him as well as the winds to take them safely to the heart of the Underworld. The Goddess had given them the Cord for this purpose, after all. He coaxed her, told her that she'd come this far; it would be foolish to give up now. In the end Asra leapt into the void as if it would be the last thing she ever did. Now, many hours had passed. Fear for herself had given way to worry over Becky's fate, boredom, fatigue, and finally a kind of numb distraction, a wide-eyed daydreaming that was perilously close to sleep. Macta had to be vigilant to make sure Asra stayed awake and alert. He'd been rubbing Powcca's knobby head for some time, too, preventing the Goblin from drifting off.

Macta twitched one shoulder, shifted his weight, and arced

across the width of the Cord toward her. As he drew closer he called her name again. "Asra!" Each time he said her name, he found it sweet beyond measure. His capacity for love and gentleness surprised him; he knew the passion in anger, contempt, and the desire for vengeance. He knew how bitter, how cold his heart could be. It was only this time with Asra that let him know how much tenderness there was inside of him. With his mechanical arm outstretched he reached for Asra and drew her close.

Her eyes fluttered open. "What?"

"Don't be afraid," Macta soothed, whispering in her ear. "You mustn't go to sleep. Stay with me. Watch the way I ride. Try to copy my motions. Let me try again to teach you, now that you're not afraid anymore. It's exciting! You'll like it, I know."

He let go of Asra and maneuvered back into the open air. Then he turned and met her gaze. She was looking into his eyes, and he smiled at her. "Arms out," he cried into the wind, "like this!"

For Asra, the following hours seemed like an eternity of reaching, stretching, paying undue attention to the position of her hands, and how the hands and arms either met with wind resistance or cut through the air like a hot knife in butter. It was deadly dull. It was also a lot of work. For Macta it was an exercise in sharing something that was important to him, something that he was good at, something that would help his beloved grow and help her get to know him. This time together, just the two of them and little Powcca, was challenging her to succeed at a skill that Macta loved. Perhaps, he thought, they would do this together, riding in the Cord, when they were both old and gray. Maybe their children would join them. That is, if any of the Cords were still around by then. If the tree died, and all of the Cords withered away, life would certainly change. But for now, Macta was in paradise. All thoughts of Jardaine and her betrayal were set aside as he flew toward the heart of the Underworld, next to his beloved.

Like most good things in Macta's life, though, the feeling didn't last long. Perhaps it was the pressure in his ears. Perhaps it was a subtle shift of the wind. It was a sensation honed through years of experience, and Macta was the first to notice a change in the air. He had an odd sense that the passage was narrowing up ahead. They'd come so far, they'd dropped down into the earth for . . . *how long?* Time, in the Cord, was meaningless. But so far, Macta had felt nothing particularly unusual on this trip, even though their travel was vertical, not horizontal. As his apprehension grew Macta drew close to Asra, so that they were flying side by side. "I've got a strange feeling," he cried.

Asra blinked at him, trying to stay focused. She brushed the hair from her face and stared. "What?"

"I haven't felt this way since my old friend Druga broke his neck, when a Cord we were riding in took a sharp turn."

"What are you saying?"

"Just that something's about to change, Asra, something . . . *big.* I don't know what, a change in direction, I'm not sure. We may be reaching the center of the world, and the Cord may be winding around the core, getting ready to continue on to the other side of the earth. Listen: when the time comes, I'm going to take you in my arms and hold on to you. Powcca will be between us. You must make sure he doesn't slip out. His leash is tied around my waist, but it may not be enough to hold him if anything drastic happens. You'll need to wrap your arms and legs around me and hold on, tight. No matter what happens, you mustn't let go!"

Asra frowned. With her arms extended overhead, and the wind coursing over every inch of her body, she already felt exposed and vulnerable. "It sounds like another one of your tricks to make me get close to you."

At that moment a large black root came into view; it jutted into the Cord like a hand tipped with daggers. Startled, Asra threw her arms around Macta's chest, and they sailed past it. "That's just what I meant!" he hollered, as they swept past another root, and then another.

Macta bobbed and weaved through the sprouting underground branches like a fish hurtling through rapids. He dodged the barbs and clots of black wood, narrowly avoiding every barricade and blockage, until the Cord veered sharply to the right. Asra clung to him, squeezing so hard that Macta could barely breathe; and then he grabbed for the side of the Cord with his mechanical hand. The razors at the ends of his robotic fingers shot from their hiding places and tore an opening in the Cord.

He swung his body back around, so that the soft membrane absorbed the impact of the hit. Asra's face was pressed against his own rough cheek, and Powcca squealed in alarm. "Now," he ordered, "reach for it! We're going inside!"

They tumbled into darkness. They rolled over and over, until Macta let go of the Princess and they lay sprawled on a dusty floor. Asra got to her knees and coughed convulsively. Powcca trotted away from her, shaking his coat and grunting. A creaking sound came from above. Then, seconds later, a pitter-pat of tiny rocks and stone dust sprinkled around them. *"Shhhhh,"* Macta said, helping Asra to her feet. "You must try to be quiet."

He pulled off the soft pack he wore on his back and reached inside. The Queen of Hunaland had provided them *Kollis*, like those she'd given Tuava-Li, Matt, and Tomtar. Macta opened the lid of one and held it aloft. The Fire Sprite raised its head and lit up like a torch. Macta opened another and handed it to Asra. They looked at the place where they'd come out of the Cord: a layer of stone had crumbled to coarse powder, and the wall of the Cord bulged against the rock that remained. Asra went to smooth the cut Macta had made. Then the two travelers lifted their *Kollis* high and surveyed the scene before them. They were at the top of a huge, round amphitheater. Concentric circles of stadium seating surrounded a gnarled, black column that rose all the way from the floor to the ceiling, hundreds of feet above. Macta eyed it up and down. He observed how it thickened, split, and braided itself back in a convoluted knot, and disappeared into a high crevice. Thousands of little branches, tendrils, fingers of wood broke from the main stalk and grew around the dome of the ceiling. The stone itself was a lattice of cracks and fissures. Macta was certain the place was structurally unsound; too much noise, too much vibration might well bring the entire cavern down on their heads. "Where are we?" Asra whispered. "Is this the center of the world? Is that gnarly stalk where the Adri begins? Does it start like this?"

Macta shook his head and trod lightly toward the ancient column. "Who knows?"

The bottom of the stalk, surprisingly, descended straight into a pool of black water. The form of the pool was strange; it took Macta a minute to realize that it was the shape of an Elfin figure, with arms, legs, and a head. It was enormous, though, perhaps thirty feet long. The black column rose up like an umbilical cord from the abdomen of the figure. Macta held up his Fire Sprite as he approached the pool, and saw his reflection there. He wondered absently how deep the pool might be. Powcca limped to his Master's side. He sniffed the air, let out a low growl, and backed away from the water. "It's strange," Macta said to Asra. "Do you feel it? Do you feel the energy here? I think we must be getting close!"

"I know what you mean," Asra agreed. She shivered, flush with an energy that might have been excitement or anxiety; it was impossible to tell. "But I don't think we're close, Macta. I think we're *here*. I think we've reached the center of the earth . . .

thanks to you! It was amazing, the way you got us through that jungle of roots in the Cord."

Macta tried not to smile. If he let Asra know that she'd given him a compliment, she might be inclined to take it back. "'Tis odd how we were the last to leave Hunaland, and yet we've beaten everyone else to this place . . . if, of course, this *is* the place. There's no sign of anybody else having been here in thousands of moons. No footprints, nothing. Just some swishing marks in the dust."

"I know why we're the first to arrive," Asra said. "Those roots would have stopped anybody with lesser skills than you. I think the others must have cut their way out of the Cord a little higher than we did, just to avoid being battered to pieces."

"Or perhaps they *were* all battered to pieces?"

Asra shuddered. "That's impossible. We'd have seen . . . signs."

Macta sat down on a piece of a broken column and rooted in his pack for a treat for Powcca. When he held up a chunk of dried biscuit, the Goblin barked, prancing on his hind legs and begging. "Quiet, my boy, quiet," Macta cooed, "this entire place could collapse at any moment!"

Powcca gulped down the biscuit, and then greedily licked the crumbs from Macta's fingers. "Well," Asra said, "if it's too dangerous for us to wait here, perhaps we'd be better off trying to find Becky and the others!" She wandered toward an archway at the side of the chamber and raised her *Kolli* into the darkness.

371

"This looks like a way out of here, a corridor!" Light flickered on the carvings along the narrow passage. "Harvest scenes. Our ancestors were peaceful folk!"

"There's only one way to find out where it goes," Macta said, joining her.

Asra turned and looked again at the vast ceiling, the pool, and the tree that grew out of the black water. "There must have been Elves who came down to this amphitheater, long ago. Perhaps they sat on these stone seats, watching something in that pool. Perhaps they watched the birth of the Adri, the last time the tree grew from the Sacred Seed! Where do you suppose the Seed must be planted? There, in the pool?"

Macta shrugged. "It doesn't matter. All that matters is that we find Jardaine — I mean, Becky, and save her from that witch. Let's see what lies along these corridors. If we have a sense of where the others may be coming from, the greater our chances of surprising them. We must play the *offense*, now."

"The offense?"

"As opposed to the *defense*, my dear. Sporting terminology. I shall have to explain it to you."

"Perhaps another time," Asra said.

They wandered together into the dark passage at the side of the amphitheater, with Powcca trailing behind. The Goblin kept up his low growl. He was obviously concerned about some subtle odor in the stale air, something that escaped Macta's and Asra's notice. The corridor slowly arched to the left. When they came to a place where another corridor branched from the main path, Asra lifted her *Kolli* high, peered into the darkness, and said, "I have a feeling we ought to turn here."

Macta shook his head. "Why would you say that? If these passages keep splitting off, and we keep following them, we'll be lost in no time. We should keep going on the main path. The others will surely come this way."

"Not necessarily," Asra said. "If I'm right about this, there'll be another junction not far ahead. Then . . . we'll go to the left."

"How could you possibly know what's ahead?"

"Just . . . a funny feeling, that's all."

Macta grinned. "Then perhaps you'd care to make a little wager? If you're right, I'll—"

"Don't start," Asra said.

"Very well," Macta said with a sigh. He picked up a chunk of stone from the path and scraped it against the wall. "Whether you're right or wrong, we can at least mark the trail, so we'll be able to find our way back to the amphitheater, when the time comes."

Though the grinding of rock against rock left a mark, it was still hard to see the gouge Macta made amid all the ancient carvings. "Wait," he said. "I've got an idea." He placed his Fire Sprite on the ground. Then he stood up straight, took a deep breath, and flexed a muscle in his shoulder. A moment later the blades along the fingers of his mechanical arm shot out with a satisfying *click*. He pressed the point of his metal pinkie against the stone and dragged his finger downward. After the first scratch, he deepened the notch by chiseling away at it, pushing down on the mechanical hand with his good arm. "That's better! Now we'll see the marks, for sure!"

"You're wasting time," Asra said. "If you want, you can wait for me here, and I'll go on ahead. I'm sure there'll be another juncture this way, and then to the left."

"I'm not letting you out of my sight," Macta said, and they proceeded down the branching path.

Not more than a hundred yards ahead there was yet another opening on the left, just as Asra had predicted. She looked at Macta and said, "Now this way!"

As Macta notched the stone in the arch, Powcca began growling more fiercely. "What is it, boy?" the King said. "I wish you could talk to us." He knelt to give the Goblin a reassuring pet.

"Perhaps there's someone near," Asra said hopefully. "Goblins must have acute senses; you'd know more about that than I do!"

"Of course they do. In Helfratheim we use them for hunting."

"In Ljosalfar," Asra said, "hunting is considered a crime against the Goddess."

Macta chuckled. "Where I'm from, nearly all of our behavior would be considered a crime against your Goddess."

"Let's keep moving," Asra said, ignoring his remark. When they found another corridor on the right, and then a fork to the left, Asra turned to Macta. "We're inside a maze, you know."

"I didn't know. But now that you say it, I can see what you

mean! If that amphitheater is the midpoint of the earth, we must be moving now toward the outside of the maze. Maybe Jardaine, and Becky, too, are already in the maze, trying to find their way toward the center!"

Asra nodded. "That's right."

"How did you recognize it? What gave it away? Even with all these carvings, and all the broken rock and rubble to distract you, there must have been something that let you know."

"When I lived in Ljosalfar, young Elves often played in a labyrinth made of hedges. Elflads entered the maze from the north, and Elfmaids from the south. There was a race to the center of the maze, and if the lads and maids happened to meet at any of the places where the corridors were joined, they were expected to . . ."

"Expected to what?"

Asra blushed. "Expected to kiss, but that's entirely beside the point. The important thing is, we're inside a maze, and it's remarkably like the one I know from Ljosalfar. Perhaps ours was based on this one. It was an ancient maze, an ancient tradition."

"There were such mazes in Helfratheim, too," Macta said. "My father would sometimes place a convicted criminal at the entrance to a maze, and then loose a wild beast to chase him through the passages. We'd watch the chase from our viewing stands. Whether the criminal managed to reach the center of the maze or not, he was still torn apart and eaten. That was all part of the—" Macta stopped himself from saying the word *fun*. He didn't want to give the Princess the impression that he was as much of a brute as his father had been. "Well, it certainly wasn't entertaining to me!"

"Honestly," Asra said, "I don't know how you managed to come out as well as you did, given the horrors you had to endure in that place."

Powcca stopped in his tracks. He bent low to the ground and let out a growl from the back of his throat that made the hair on Macta's neck stand up. A swishing sound came from above, and Macta thrust his *Kolli* overhead. Above him he saw a jagged black tunnel carved into the rock. The ceiling was, in fact, laced with tunnels. In the dark distance he thought he could see something moving. Something was gleaming—eyes, or teeth. Snakelike, the thing was moving too fast for Macta to recognize it. All he had time to do before the creature opened its slavering jaws was shove Asra out of the way. Squealing with delight, the monster dropped from the hole and reached for Macta. There was no time to think. Macta thrust out his mechanical arm, and with the razored fingers jutting into the air, he punctured the monster's soft underbelly.

Macta flung the creature to the floor. He watched it writhe there, throwing up clouds of choking dust, as emerald-colored fluid gushed from its wounds. It took Macta a moment to realize that Asra was behind him, with her own arms wrapped tightly around his waist. The Princess still clutched her *Kolli*; Macta felt the heat singe his belly. Reluctantly he pried away Asra's hand.

"Careful, darling," he said, and stepped backwards. The creature was still thrashing. Powcca rushed at the monster, growling and snapping, snatching bites from its hide. In a strange, soft voice, the monster moved its lips and cried, *"Noooo, intruders, intruders must die, intruders — must —"*

"Disgusting," Macta said. "The thing talks!"

"'Tis like the story of the beast in your father's labyrinth," Asra choked.

"A different kind of creature," Macta said, "but aye, I'm reminded of the same thing. Perhaps someone is toying with us, watching all this from afar! Your Great Goddess, perhaps?"

The creature twitched as Powcca lunged again and again, tearing at its body. Then it shivered and died. It lay stretched across the corridor as Powcca chomped hungrily away at the monster's abdomen. The odor was repulsive. Asra gagged. "Can't you make your Goblin stop that?" she choked. "The monster spoke to us!"

"It was a monster, all the same," Macta said. "And I'd wager there'll be more where that one came from."

Other sounds began to come from the darkness. Asra thought she could make out words in the distant, ominous buzz. "They're coming," she whispered. "They're coming to get us!"

"Then we have to be fast," said Macta. He held up his *Kolli* as his eyes scoured the ceiling for more of the holes, and more of the hideous creatures in the holes. "We've got to get out of here; we've got to find a place where the ceiling isn't pockmarked like this."

"Follow me," Asra said, holding her own *Kolli* aloft. "Let's try this way. If the labyrinth in Ljosalfar is exactly like this one, there's a place ahead where we'll have access to the entrance of three different tunnels. Come on!"

Macta snatched Powcca from the monster's carcass and raced after Asra. When they came to a juncture in the corridor Macta turned to look back one last time. For one terrified moment he thought the monster was alive and moving, until he realized that a horde of other snake creatures had descended upon the fallen one and were gorging themselves on its succulent flesh.

23

TOMTAR!" MATT CRIED. With one hand holding the
Kolli, and the other waving away clouds of dust from his face,
he stumbled toward the place where the ceiling had collapsed.
"Tomtar, can you hear me?" he hollered, yanking a jagged
chunk of rock from the wall of rubble.

"'Tis no use," Tuava-Li said from behind.

"What do you mean, no use? We've got to do something!
Help me move the rocks, Tuava-Li. Don't just stand there!
You're not helpless; can't you do something? You must know
some trick, some spell, to move the rocks?"

Tuava-Li felt as if her spirit had been crushed in the tunnel
collapse. This was the end of her dreams, the end of her hope
that the Goddess meant for her to plant the Seed of the Adri

and save Elf Realm. Without Tomtar, there was no Troll to complete the trio, no way to form the perfectly shaped key that would unlock the door of myth, and legend, and please the Great Ones in Heaven. It was over, and she knew it. Matt grunted with exertion as he moved away the small, jagged rocks and heaved them onto the floor. "Come on," he cried again. "You can make dolls move, you can create balls of fire to melt stuff, you told me about it, Tuava-Li! You can open locks, you have powers in your mind, you almost brought down the green man in Pittsburgh with those energy bursts of yours. You have to be able to get this tunnel open again!"

The Elf shook her head helplessly. She'd always believed that life had a purpose, and meaning, and a direction. But now, it all seemed hollow and empty. "I can't believe it, we've come so far, and now it's all ended by . . . *an accident*?"

"This wasn't any accident," Matt said. "Just before the ceiling fell, I saw Jardaine's face staring at me out of a crevice. She's down here, we both knew it, but why would she do this? She's already got the seed, and she's already got her own troll, Nick. Why hurt Tomtar?"

Tuava-Li was taken aback; Jardaine was a more dangerous opponent than she'd ever realized. "She's hateful and malicious. Perhaps it's her appetite for destruction. But I don't think she intended to kill Tomtar alone—maybe she's hedging her bets, and trying to kill us all, so there'll be no chance we can interfere with her plans!"

"Look," Matt said, "there's no reason to assume Tomtar's dead. He might be trapped on the other side of that wall, wondering if we're okay!"

"I — I have an idea. All these passages seem to be connected in some way, Matt. If we can find the right tunnel, we should be able to come back around again, and see if Tomtar's all right."

"He's got to be," Matt said. "We didn't come this far just to lose him!"

The pair hurried along the corridor, trying not to stumble on the endless mounds of rubble. It wasn't long before they came to a series of three arches carved in the wall. Each of the arches was a portal into another stone corridor, cold and black as night. "Tuava-Li, these are the arches on my tattoo," Matt said breathlessly.

"Let me look at your tattoos again!"

Matt pulled up his shirt, though he didn't need to see the inky arches on his skin to remember that the third one had been colored bloodred. "Okay," he said, "we've got to think. Tomtar's blood isn't red, it's green, like yours. I thought the arches were supposed to be giving us a clue about how to find Becky. But now I don't know. Maybe red means stop, don't go that way. Maybe we're supposed to take one of the other two tunnels. But which one? Why do my tattoos change if we can't understand what they mean?"

"We should have looked at this more carefully," Tuava-Li said, peering closely at Matt's chest. She felt a sudden thrill of hope. "Or maybe the tattoo has just changed again. There's a tiny spot of green, like a teardrop, running from the third portal. We'll go that way, and if the Goddess smiles on us, Tomtar will be alive when we find him."

Matt yanked his shirt down, turned without a word, and headed into the third corridor.

Tomtar stumbled along another passage, not far away. Becky walked in front of him, and Jardaine behind. Though she was exhausted, Jardaine wasn't going to take a chance on the Troll attempting to get away. Tomtar struggled to speak. He kept trying to say something, to say anything, but Jardaine's spell kept him mute. They came to the end of one corridor and had to decide whether to turn left or right. Jardaine leaned heavily against the wall; she felt as if she might pass out. Where her *Huldu* rested, her chest was throbbing. *It has to be that infernal Seed,* she said to herself. *The Seed is drawing all my strength into itself.*

"Are you all right, Astrid?" Becky asked.

The monk's face was ashen. "I have to stop and rest. Just for a few minutes, that's all. Becky, you keep an eye on the Troll and rouse me if he tries anything. He doesn't dare run away without a Fire Sprite; 'twould be too dark without one. Make sure you keep your *Kolli* out of his reach."

"But we tied his wrists," Becky said. "He won't be able to do anything!"

"Don't trust him," Jardaine ordered, and then she plopped down onto the floor with her back propped against the wall.

"You can't go to sleep now," Becky cried. "What if those snakes come back? I can't fight them, and Tomtar's tied up, so he couldn't help even if he wanted to!"

Jardaine's eyelids fell. Her head drooped to one side, and her jaw dropped open. With a sigh, Becky sat down in the dust across from Jardaine. She stared at Tomtar in the flickering light. He looked back at her pleadingly. Becky glanced at Jardaine, then scowled at the Troll. "Go on," she whispered. "Just tell me what you want. Do you have to go to the bathroom? Are you hungry? Thirsty? I'm not going to do anything for you unless you talk to me and tell me where Matt is."

Tomtar lifted his hands and pointed his fingers at his throat. He shook his head mournfully. Becky narrowed her eyes. "What are you trying to tell me? You can't talk? Something's wrong with your voice?"

Tomtar nodded vigorously. Becky looked at Astrid, deep asleep in the shadows, and then back at Tomtar. Her instinct was to take the chance and see if she could find out what the Troll wanted to say. If he could make any sound at all, there was a possibility she could figure it out. Maybe it would be just more lies. But if there was something else, if Tomtar was prepared to tell her anything about Matt . . . Nervously Becky crept toward him. "So you can't talk. Can you whisper? Can you mouth the words you want to say? Maybe I'll be able to understand."

Becky's face was just inches from Tomtar. He exaggerated the movements of his lips as he formed the words. He found that if he forced air through his lips, he could actually make a tiny, croaking sound that was too faint to be a real whisper. But with some effort, it might be enough to communicate. "H—her name is Jar—daine."

"What?" Becky said.

Tomtar tried again, thrusting his head in the direction of the sleeping Elf, so that Becky would get the point. "Jar—daine, not As—trid."

"Jardaine? Is that what you said? Wait, I've heard that name. Jardaine is the Elf who took my mom and dad and baby sister to Helfratheim!"

Tomtar nodded; Becky sat back, stunned. "You're telling me she's not who she says she is? If Astrid's not her real name, if she's the one who kidnapped my parents . . . then—then what's going on? Why would she bring me here? Why would she lie to me, and make up some complicated story? Has she been lying to me from the beginning? Lying about everything?"

Tomtar nodded again.

Becky gave Tomtar a dubious look. "How do I know you're not lying?"

Tomtar shrugged helplessly, though his face was wreathed in misery. There was nothing he could do to convince the girl he was on her side. Becky whispered, "Is Jardaine the one who stole your voice?"

Tomtar nodded.

"And what do you know about Matt—is he all right?"

Another nod.

"Is he with Tuava-Li, now?"

Tomtar mouthed the word *aye*.

"Did you know Matt is supposed to die when the Seed gets planted? Astrid, or Jardaine, whatever her name is, told me that you and Tuava-Li were planning to sacrifice his life when you got to the center of the earth."

Tomtar's eyes grew wide with horror at the thought. He shook his head and shuddered. Becky sat back and tried to put the pieces of the puzzle together. "I know you and Tuava-Li and Matt came here to plant the Seed. Does Tuava-Li have the Seed, now?"

Tomtar shook his head again.

"Then who has the Seed?" Becky asked. "Does anybody have it?"

Tomtar had a pretty good idea where the Seed might be. Though his wrists were tied, he tapped his thumbs against his own chest, and cast a glance at Jardaine.

"She has the Seed?" Becky asked. "On her chest? You mean, in her *Huldu*?"

Tomtar pressed his lips together and nodded.

"I don't know what to do," Becky said. "I can't wait until she wakes up and ask her if she's been lying to me, and demand that she shows me what's inside her *Huldu*. But I don't know if

I can peek in there, either, without waking her up. I guess I'm just going to have to try. If she's got the Seed, it'll prove that you're telling me the truth, Tomtar. And if she's got the Seed, I'm going to have to get it away from her."

Becky crept over to Jardaine. As delicately as she could, she undid the tie at the top flap of the *Huldu,* and then taking a deep breath, slipped her fingers inside. If the Elf woke up and found Becky digging around in her private pouch, she'd be very, very angry with her. But Jardaine didn't even stir. There was a scrap of cloth at the back of the pouch. Becky felt the contours of the little bulge hidden inside, and she closed her fist around it. A jolt of electricity leapt up her arm like she'd put her fingers into an electric socket. *"Oooooowwww!"* she whimpered.

She yanked her hand back. Clutching her fingers, she looked at Tomtar. He nodded vehemently and glanced back at the *Huldu.* Jardaine hadn't moved. Becky reached into the pouch again. This time, she took the cloth scrap by the corner and gave a far more gentle tug. When she'd extracted the scrap she could still feel its energy pulsing. She placed it on the boulder in the light of the *Kolli* and gingerly pulled the cloth away.

The Seed was glowing. A tiny shoot grew from its smooth surface, and two pale leaves sprouted from the top of the shoot. For a moment all Becky could do was stare in awe. She'd never seen anything so beautiful, or so strange. The sprout with the tiny leaves seemed to be swaying gently from side to side, like

an underwater creature moving in the waves. Becky wrapped up the Seed, carefully avoiding touching it. *It needs water*, she thought. *It needs water to grow.*

Then she hurried to Tomtar's side and dropped it into his pack. "I'm sorry," she whispered, "I don't know why I doubted you. Let's get away from Jardaine, before she wakes up. Once we've put some distance between us and her, we'll stop to cut you loose!"

24

DISTANT RUMBLES SHOOK the earth to its core, reverberating in every stone passage of the Underworld. Yggdrasil was pulling itself up by the roots, tendril after tendril. The shriek of wood against rock was an assault on Matt's and Tuava-Li's ears. They followed a long, curving passageway, staying alert for any sign of life. The slope of the floor seemed less pronounced, now; they both had the feeling that they weren't descending anymore, that they were on a flat plane. The wall carvings that lined the rubble-strewn passages looked impossibly old, and every surface was thick with dust. They couldn't help but notice, though, that the nature of the carvings was changing. The friezes they'd seen earlier, depicting war and battle between Elfin Clans, had given way to images of strong, gentle figures tilling the soil; lush fields of grain; birds, rabbits, and deer. There were places where deep burrows were gouged into the walls and ceiling. At first, Matt, whose energies were so focused on finding Tomtar, failed to notice the rough tunnels. They might have just been places where roots of the tree had pulled away, or where parts of the stonework had crumbled with age and neglect. But a strange odor was causing a nearly imperceptible dread to creep into his mind. "Tuava-Li, do you smell something?"

"I do," the Elf whispered, her eyes scanning for danger. "I noticed it as soon as we left the Cord. But we had more urgent things to think about, and I assumed the odor must be mold, or possibly the residue of some kind of insect."

"Insect? How could anything live down here, without food or water?"

"You'd be surprised, Matt," Tuava-Li said, "how life adapts. But the smell has grown stronger, *too* strong. We might be approaching a burrow, or a nest of some kind. We should be care—"

There was a scuttling sound above their heads. Then a squeal, like a door opening on rusty hinges. Matt gasped when he saw the face of the thing appear from the darkness, its huge, yellow eyes glittering with menace. In alarm he dropped his *Kolli*. The lid snapped shut when it hit the floor. Now in semidarkness he grabbed Tuava-Li by the shoulder and yanked her toward him. She dropped her *Kolli*, too, and the Fire Sprite leapt from its box and dashed out of harm's way, a rolling figure of smoke and orange flame. The awful creature was slipping down from a passage in the ceiling right above them. Matt could see its long, segmented body. Its gnarled claws had Tuava-Li by the hair and she was too shocked, too horrified, to do anything but collapse on the floor.

Matt reached instinctively for the knife in his pocket. He opened the blade, then grabbed for the monster and sunk the knife up to the hilt in its abdomen. When it let go of Tuava-Li she lurched forward, then spun around and faced the creature. Matt was backing up, keeping the wounded beast in sight, though there was something hypnotic about its gaze; he felt his mind freezing up, his body stiffening. Then he tripped over a rock and fell backwards. The monster was on him in a second, its foul breath like a poisonous fog. In the dim light of the Fire Sprite Matt could see its gleaming teeth descending toward his face; he managed to lash out again with his knife. Tuava-Li was shouting, though Matt couldn't make out the words. He felt his arm working, slashing at the thing; he felt its hot Blood splattering on his skin, and he felt a blow from behind that swept past his head like a cannonball. The monster flew off him and struck the stone wall with a sharp crack. Its limp form collapsed on the floor.

Matt met Tuava-Li's gaze; he knew she'd saved him with a bolt of energy that had stopped the monster's terrible heart. He didn't have time to thank her, though. There were more scuttling sounds from behind and from above. Hunched and ready to fight, Matt dashed toward Tuava-Li. One pair of glittering eyes appeared from the ceiling, then another. *Intruders*, a voice screeched. *Intruders must die*, said another, and suddenly all the creatures were chattering in their strange, shrieking voices. They were behind Matt and Tuava-Li, they were in front, and they were above. There was no way to know how many there were, but it was obvious to Matt that they couldn't fight them all. This was the end.

Then, oddly, exhilaration came over Matt that he'd never felt before. Free from all fear, all panic, all obligation to his family and friends, he lunged at one of the monsters with his knife outstretched. The blade struck one of its fearsome teeth and snapped in two. Now he was without a weapon; but still he threw himself at the monster and grabbed both its jaws in his hands. With his fingers wedged in between the beast's teeth he pushed the jaws apart. He heard screaming and realized it was his own voice, roaring, full of terror and fierce abandon. Tuava-Li's Fire Sprite leapt up and down on a boulder, its fiery arms and legs sparkling in excitement.

Tuava-Li turned to face the monsters gathering at their rear. She focused her energy and sent it hurtling into the closest creature's body. Then she struck again, and the monsters reared back, snapping their jaws, and dropping, one by one, to the floor. "All right," Matt yelled. "Way to go!"

A crack split the pockmarked ceiling and a shower of dust fell on them. "Get back!" Tuava-Li cried, and she and Matt turned and ran.

Chunks of rock dropped from above. In a deafening crash the roof of the tunnel collapsed, sealing the passage behind them. Matt and Tuava-Li were left on one side of the wall of rubble, in complete and total darkness. Matt's ears were ringing, drowning out his ragged breath. "Tuava-Li," he cried, "are you there?"

"I'm here," she said, coughing. "I'm right here."

Matt began to feel panic in his veins once again; his lungs were full of dust, and he coughed and coughed until he thought he'd pass out. When he was finally able to breathe again, he said, "Where are you? Can you come closer?"

Tuava-Li put her hand out before her and moved it back and forth in the darkness until she felt Matt's shirt. Matt reached up and took her hand in his. He held it tightly, and then he began to cry. He drew the Elf close to him and took her in his arms, rocking her back and forth. Tuava-Li was almost too stunned to know how to respond; Matt's tears wet her hair and fell on her bare arms. In the darkness she felt her body so close to his that she reacted with instinctive panic. An Elf and a Human were not meant to be friends, after all. This alliance between the two of them had been born of necessity. A part of her wanted to pull away from Matt. But another part of her felt his warmth, and the beating of his Human heart, and she was strangely consoled by it.

Tuava-Li knew that they would die here, in the darkness. Even if the hideous snake monsters didn't attack them, she was certain they'd never find their way out of here. Not without a Fire Sprite to light the way. Tomtar was gone, and Jardaine had the Seed. It had all been for nothing. She knew she'd been wrong to think that she could lure Matt to his death, at the center of the world, for the sake of the Adri. Even if the Goddess seemed to have called her to fulfill the quest of the Ancients, it was wrong to have misled the boy. It was wrong to have lied to him, to have made him think he had a chance. "I brought you down here to die," she choked.

"It's not your fault," Matt said, and squeezed her close. "You couldn't have known about this. You just wanted to do the right thing. You were trying, that's all anybody can ever do." Matt ran his hand over Tuava-Li's shoulder and realized it was sticky and wet. Then he felt the puncture wounds and pulled away. "You're hurt! The thing bit you! Are you okay?"

"I—I don't know," she answered, and touched her own shoulder. There were deep wounds in her flesh and a stab of pain went through her. She got up from Matt's lap and stood in the darkness, moving her arm cautiously. "I'm bleeding, and it hurts, but nothing's broken. I can still move my arm!"

"You might get an infection," Matt said, "like I got in my foot, when I stepped on that wedding shoe that belonged to the Princess. It's the whole different species thing, you know?"

When Matt thought of the shoe he could hardly believe how little time had actually elapsed since this whole fiasco began; his world had been completely turned upside down since then. "You must have medicine for that, right? In your pack? I know they put a lot of first-aid stuff in there."

Tuava-Li wanted to tell Matt that it didn't matter now if she had an infection. She was certain neither of them would live long enough to see the consequences of the snake creature's bite. But instead she said, "I lost my pack when the monsters attacked!"

"I lost mine, too," Matt confided. "Well, I didn't really lose it. I just threw it off because it was in my way when I was fighting those things. Now I know what the tattoo was all about, with the three portals, and the green streak. It was saying that you'd be injured, maybe killed, if we went down that third passage. It was a warning, and I didn't get it."

"I had my suspicions," Tuava-Li said, "and I tried to be cautious, because of it. 'Tis our job to listen more closely to the signs, but this environment doesn't encourage quiet reflection. Sometimes one must go *through* danger, to come out safely on the other side."

"What are those things?" Matt asked.

"I fear they may be the remnants of the lost Clan of Ouroborus."

The two of them sat in silence for a long moment. Then Tuava-Li heard the sound of ripping fabric. Matt had pulled off his shirt and was tearing long strips from it. "Come here," he said. "I'll try to wrap up your wound so at least it won't get dirty."

"Your shirt is probably the dirtiest thing in the Underworld!"

Matt let out a chuckle. The Elf had a sense of humor after all, and he was pleased when Tuava-Li came closer. He could smell her strange Elfin scent, an odor of fresh-picked herbs, mixed with sweat and dust. As best he could in the darkness he wrapped her shoulder and tied the ends of the fabric in a knot. He was glad that he didn't have to actually see her injuries; he could imagine how bad the bites really were. He'd seen the monster's teeth; he'd felt them. He knew at the very least that Tuava-Li would bear the scars of those wounds for the rest of her life.

"Thank you," Tuava-Li said, when Matt was finished bandaging her.

"Thank *you*," replied Matt. "You saved my life again."

"And you saved mine, too. Many times."

Feeling awkward and vulnerable, Matt didn't know what to say. So he sat in silence, feeling his skin tingle as his tattoos rearranged themselves once again, and listened to his belly's faint rumble. "The tattoos are up to something," he said finally. "But we can't see a thing. Worse than that, I'm starved. I wish I still had some of the food that was in my backpack. Even if it was elf food. I'm kind of getting used to the taste of it."

"You're really hungry?"

"Of course! Aren't you?"

"I'd be too tense to eat, even if we hadn't lost our packs."

"Looks like we're running low on luck," Matt said. "No food, no light, no weapons. We're still alive, though, and you've still got your magick! Things aren't completely hopeless, are they?"

"If changing into a hawk would help us, I'd be glad to do it.

But I'm afraid there's not much my magick can do for us anymore, Matt."

Matt shook his head. "You killed those monsters, all right! And you brought down the roof on them, too!"

"Matt—" Tuava-Li started.

"What, don't tell me the roof collapse was an accident?"

Tuava-Li was about to say, "*There are no accidents*." But she wasn't quite sure she still believed in fate. The entire enterprise now seemed to have been scarred with botched, hapless accidents.

"Well?"

"The bursts of mental energy that killed the monsters wouldn't have been enough to bring down tons of rock. At least, not unless it was already weakened. I'd be more inclined to guess that it was going to happen anyway. With all those holes the monsters clawed away, the rock might have been very unstable."

"It *was* very unstable," Matt said. "But how about if you try again, just to see? If you shot some more of your magick beams at the rock, maybe we could at least get our packs and find our fire sprites. That's assuming they're still on the other side of the wall and not completely crushed."

"Aye, and it's assuming the snake creatures are all dead," she replied. "I pray that they are. But if I were to succeed at moving the rock, it might make it worse. More of the ceiling could collapse on top of us."

"I'm not ready to lie down and die, Tuava-Li," Matt said. "You've got to do something! If you're gonna pray that the snakes are dead, how about you pray to your goddess for guidance, or help, or whatever, and see if that does anything? Pray that we find a fire sprite, pray that we find the Cord again."

"Pray?" she said. "Don't you remember, you told me we're supposed to figure things out for ourselves. You said the Goddess doesn't even exist!"

Matt sighed. "I don't know what exists and what doesn't exist anymore, Tuava-Li. I've given up trying to figure it all out. What you believe seems to be about as good as what I believe. So go ahead and pray. Who knows, maybe it'll help. We've got to do something, anyway. My sister's life's still at stake, not just ours."

Tuava-Li reached out in the darkness and found the boy's arm. "You know, Matthew, I have to tell you, you've risked your life many times on this journey, you've taken many chances, you've been brave in a way I didn't know Humans could be. But I haven't been brave, or honest. There's something I haven't had the courage to tell you. What would you think of me, Matthew, if I told you that—that you wouldn't survive this adventure?"

"Survive?" Matt scoffed. "*Nobody* survives the adventure. That's the rule of the game. Everybody dies, sometime! I know the score, Tuava-Li."

"Noooo, that's not what I meant. 'Tis said that the Human who first journeyed to the center of the earth, King Volsung, didn't—"

"*Shhhhh!*" Matt interrupted. He tried to focus on the faint sound that was growing ever louder, echoing down the black corridor. *I hear something,* he said in thoughtspeak. *Is it more of those snake monsters?*

No, answered Tuava-Li. *Someone's coming toward us, someone with a Fire Sprite.*

The glow grew brighter. Soon they could recognize voices — a male and a female. *They're Elves,* Tuava-Li said. *It's not Jardaine. But I think . . .*

Matt didn't recognize either of the figures when they came into view. But Tuava-Li gasped when she saw the pair in the flickering light of their *Kolli.* A small Goblin tromped behind them and growled when Tuava-Li stepped into the corridor. "In the name of the Mother and her Cord," she said, "what are you two doing here?"

Princess Asra's mouth dropped open in amazement. "Tuava-Li, it's you!"

Macta bent to pick up the Goblin, then stepped up from behind the Princess and smirked. "One never knows where one might bump into an old friend!"

"Indeed," said Tuava-Li. "What's going on, Asra? You're supposed to be in Ljosalfar! And why are you with this . . . this *Elf*?"

"He's all right," Asra said, stepping over rubble to greet Tuava-Li. "He's promised to help me save Becky from Jardaine. We're the last to arrive in Hunaland, but we were the first to reach the center of the world. We've been following the passageways out of there, hoping to find you or Becky. She's traveling with that witch Jardaine and a Troll named Nick." She looked Matt up and down. "Is this Becky's brother?"

"You bet I am," Matt exclaimed. "What do you know about Becky?"

"Oh," Tuava-Li said, "Matthew, this is Princess Asra of Alfheim and Prince Macta of Helfratheim."

Macta smiled drily. "No longer just a Prince, my young monk. They made me King, upon my return home." Then he turned to Matt. "And I know who the Human is. I know very well. My father died in an unfortunate accident where his Arvada was shot down by a weapon fired from the floor of a burning forest. I believe you know something about that, Matthew?"

Asra said, "And my father died in an unfortunate accident as well, Macta. I believe the time has come to put all that behind us and continue with our search for Becky."

"Tell me what you know," Matt said impatiently. "Why is Becky with Jardaine? And Macta, you're the King of Helfratheim, that's supposed to be where Jardaine took my parents and baby sister. What do you know about that?"

"Absolutely nothing. But I make it a habit to avoid speaking with those who do not show proper deference to my position. You must address me as *Your Highness*."

"All right, Your Highness," Matt said scornfully, "tell me if my parents are all right."

Macta smiled. "You'll just have to ask Jardaine about your

family members when we see her in person. It will undoubtedly be any time now."

"We believe Jardaine has our Troll friend Tomtar with her," Tuava-Li said, "as well as Becky and Nick. She worked some kind of magick, and brought down a wall of boulders to split our group apart. She nearly killed us all."

"Why would she do that?"

"We have no idea. But we have so much to talk about, Asra, so many questions! How is it that you know Matt's sister? How did you find your way here? And do you have any idea what Jardaine is planning?"

"We came down the Cord through the Gate of Hujr, just like you," Asra said, "though when we found the passage blocked by a mass of roots, Macta got us past the barrier. Tuava-Li, we'll have plenty of time for talk, now that we're together. We can wend our way back toward the amphitheater and wait for Jardaine to arrive. She has the Seed of the Adri, we've been told! I think that's what this is all about."

"Aye," said Tuava-Li. "She stole the Seed from the tree, at the cost of many lives. Are we close to the center of the earth now?"

Asra nodded. "Macta and I came out of the Cord there, and then ventured into the labyrinth to look for you, not more than an hour ago."

"And the Princess knows a thing or two about mazes," Macta said.

"The Queen of Hunaland told us to stay out of the maze," Matt said. "We got trapped here, anyway."

"Tuava-Li," Asra said, "'tis exactly like the one I used to run through when we lived in Ljosalfar. That's why I know the twists and turns so well! It consists of a series of concentric circles, arranged around a central core."

"Do we have any reason to believe Jardaine's close?" Tuava-Li asked.

"She left Hunaland before any of the rest of us. She should be here already. Unless the snakes ate her, or she got out of the Cord too early and got lost in this maze!"

"Well, which is it?" Matt asked, stricken at the thought that his sister might not have survived the journey.

Macta took a step toward Matt and held the Fire Sprite high, to get a better look at the boy's face. "Do not question the Princess, Human. Know your place!"

"This is stupid," Matt said to Tuava-Li. "This guy, I don't care who he is—why do we have to listen to him?"

"Macta's our friend," Asra said again, "as much as it surprises me to say it. He's saved my life more times that I can count, and he's going to help me get to Becky. Listen—I know the way back. There's a chasm that's opened up along one of the paths we'll have to take. I think the roots of the Adri have been pulling themselves out of the stone and leaving places where the floors collapse. It's a bit of a challenge, creeping along the edge, but with some caution it can be done. We did it on the way here, didn't we, Macta?"

Macta nodded. "Of course we did. I also made some scratches along the top of each passage where we turned, so there'd be no chance of us losing our way!"

Tuava-Li turned to see if Matt was prepared to leave. He stood shirtless in the flickering light, and Tuava-Li's jaw dropped at the sight of him. "What now?" she cried.

Matt glanced down at his chest and saw—bare skin. His shoulders, too, were bare. The tattoos had begun moving over his body like worms crossing a sidewalk, and the black lines and blurs of color were all headed for his right wrist. Even as he watched they seemed to be in motion, and the sensation filled him with revulsion. "This is just great," he said. "What's happening to me now?"

"I'm not certain," Tuava-Li said. "I must meditate on it."

"Perhaps it's like rats deserting a sinking ship," Macta volunteered. "If the tattoos have a mind of their own, they're probably planning to escape before the Human's life is sacrificed!"

Suddenly all eyes were riveted on Macta. Realizing what he'd said, he attempted to rephrase his remark. "That's just a little joke, you understand, I'm referring to . . ."

"Sacrificed?" Matt said, as Blood pulsed in his temples. "Sacrificed? What do you mean by that?"

Tuava-Li was horrified that Macta had revealed the secret before she'd had the chance to do it herself. She drew close to him and looked pleadingly into his eyes. "Matthew, that's what I've been trying to tell you! In the legend, the Human King Volsung sacrificed his life so that the Seed could grow. That's why I've decided to abandon our mission. Our quest is finished. I finally realized, I won't have you give your life for the sake of the Seed, or the tree, or all of Elf Realm. 'Tis wrong for the Goddess to ask us to make that sacrifice!"

"Us?" Matt said, backing away. "What do you mean, *us*? I'm supposed to get sacrificed, and you say it isn't right for *us*? What was supposed to happen, anyway? Were you planning on killing me when we got to the middle of the maze? Rip my heart out, or drink my blood, like the Aztecs did when they made human sacrifices to the sun?"

"Nooo," said Tuava-Li. "It isn't like that. There's a world of difference between someone sacrificing his life and someone *being sacrificed*. You risked death rescuing me half a dozen times, Matthew, and you would have given your life gladly! The legend of Fada doesn't tell us how Volsung died. It only says that his Blood nourished the Seed. Perhaps you'd have given your life voluntarily, trying to help someone, doing what you've already done, again and again. But it all means nothing, now, because we're not going through with it. The quest is finished. I've decided!"

Matt was so furious that he could barely find the words to speak. "Well, I'm glad you've decided, Tuava-Li. I'm glad because it would be *my* choice, not yours, if I wanted to give my life for your cause. I can't believe you knew this and didn't tell me. I guess you realized what I'd say about it, so you just decided to rope me into this adventure and have me be the pawn in your little game. What were you thinking? And what about my mom and dad, and my sister? Were you really planning on going on to Helfratheim to rescue them after I was dead?"

"I—I just—"

Matt stomped away from Tuava-Li. As he passed Asra, he reached out and grabbed the *Kolli* from her hand. He said nothing, just stalked down the corridor and out of sight. "The only thing bigger than my mouth," Macta said with a shrug, "is my regret for speaking out of line. I believe I must be harboring a bit of resentment toward the lad for murdering my father." He hoped that his loose talk hadn't changed Asra's opinion of him for the worse, but if it had, it was too late to do anything about it. "I don't suppose it matters what's been said, Tuava-Li, if you weren't planning to go through with the sacrifice after all!"

"Better that he knows the truth," said Tuava-Li. "He can't survive down here by himself, though. I must go after him. There may be more of the snake monsters, there may be—"

"You saw those beasts, too?" Asra said with a shudder.

"Aye, why do you suppose these bandages are on my shoulder? The creatures nearly tore me apart. Matt bound my wounds. I've got to go to him and convince him that it's over, that I'm not lying."

"He won't get far," Macta said. "The floor of the corridor collapsed, just a short distance ahead. He may well be too big to make the crossing on the narrow ridge; Asra and I were barely able to do it. There's really no room for any of those snake monsters along the path. You needn't worry about your friend."

"Then come with me," Tuava-Li said.

"Certainly not," Macta said. "You mustn't go after him. Don't let him control you like that. No, the Human must come back to *us*. Give him a few minutes to think it over. He'll come skulking back like a Goblin with his tail between his legs, I'm sure!"

25

AFTER PASSING THROUGH several portals in the vast maze, Becky and Tomtar paused to rest. Becky placed her *Kolli* on a rock while she looked in Tomtar's pack for something sharp. When she found a large obsidian blade tucked into a pocket in the side, Becky carefully pulled it out and cut the rope that bound Tomtar's wrists. "There's a lot of useful stuff in this pack, Tomtar," she said. "Did they give this to you in Hunaland?" The Troll nodded and managed a feeble grunt. It was more sound than he'd been able to make in many long hours, and it made him hopeful. He grunted again, and again. After the third time, Becky urged him to be quiet. "When Astrid—I mean, Jardaine, comes after us, we don't want to give ourselves away. She's going to be ready to kill us for the Seed!"

Tomtar nodded. He rubbed his wrists and then took off his pack. He found two small portions of food inside and handed one to Becky. They opened them and hungrily ate the dried fungus, nuts, and seeds. When they were finished, Tomtar pointed the way down another passage. "I wish we would have thought to take Jardaine's Fire Sprite," Becky whispered. "Then there wouldn't even be a chance of her following us. I just wasn't thinking clearly. It was stupid of us to have left her like that. We could have tied her up; we could have taken her *Huldu*!"

She glanced at Tomtar. "I know what you're thinking, we didn't want to *kill* her. I know. If we'd tied her up, or left her completely defenseless, she'd end up starving down here, or those monsters would gobble her up. Maybe they'll do that, anyway. But if we don't manage to get far away from her, she'll make sure we don't ever cross her again, I'm sure of that!"

Suddenly there was a faint tapping along the stone wall. Becky stopped in her tracks, all of her senses on alert. She put her finger to her lips and looked at Tomtar, who shrugged helplessly. He wouldn't be able to talk even if he wanted to. Becky's mind raced. If it was Jardaine who had heard her talking, why would she have tapped on the wall? She would have been stealthy; she would have been sly. She wouldn't try to get Becky's attention and let her know that someone was very near. Becky lifted her knuckles, and very, very cautiously, returned the knock. Immediately there was a response. It sounded a little farther away, so Becky, still holding the knife, raced ahead and knocked again. Another response, just a short distance ahead.

Becky hurried onward, with Tomtar right behind her. She listened for a knock, then rushed ahead and returned each knock, each time a little louder, a little stronger. Becky wondered who it could be on the other side of the wall. Was it Tuava-Li and Matt? Who else would be down here? Who else would be capable of knocking like that? Surely not the monsters. If they were close, they'd be sneaky, like Jardaine. But still . . . as Becky held the *Kolli* before her and saw a black portal opening just ahead, she hesitated. She clutched the handle of the obsidian knife. If it were one of the monsters, she'd be ready to strike. She glanced back at Tomtar and gave him a look that meant he should be prepared to fight.

It was then that Matt, like an apparition in the flickering gloom, appeared in the portal. He stood, shirtless and panting, before his sister. His hair was longer than when she'd last seen him; he was leaner, stronger, older looking, somehow. But the look on his face was sheer joy. Becky dropped the knife and ran into Matt's arms. "Becky," he cried, "what are you doing here? What's going on? They said you'd come down here with that monk Jardaine and her troll, Nick. I couldn't believe it. I thought you were safe and sound, back where I left you in the woods!"

"I came to rescue you," she said. "Nick is dead, but I got away from Jardaine. I'm pretty sure that Mom and Dad and

Emily are safe, too. They escaped from Helfratheim before I even left to come here!"

"What?" Matt said. "If I'd known Mom and Dad were okay, I'm not too sure I would have agreed to go through with this! We'd both be back at home, where we belong."

Becky noticed her brother's pale and glistening skin; the last time she'd seen him, he'd been covered in tattoos. "What happened to all those tattoos the Elves put on you?"

"They've been moving around, like they're up to something," Matt said, holding out his right hand. It was completely covered in a jumble of inky black lines. "Not a pretty sight, is it?"

Becky gently touched his skin. "Does it hurt?"

"No, it just creeps me out. And it makes me feel dumb. Some kind of faerie goddess is trying to give me messages, clues about things, but I usually can't figure out what they're trying to say. Tuava-Li understands more than I do."

"What about Tuava-Li? Where is she? Is she all right?"

Matt snorted derisively and turned his gaze toward Tomtar.

The Troll had been watching the reunion of his good friends with delight, but his warm feeling disappeared when he saw the look in Matt's eyes. "And what are you doing with *him*, Becky?" Matt demanded. He pulled away from his sister and took a step forward.

"Matt, it's Tomtar, he's our friend! We escaped from Jardaine with the Seed of the Adri! It's in Tomtar's pack! What's wrong with you; why are you acting like this? You and Tomtar came all this way together, didn't you?"

"He and Tuava-Li were planning to kill me, Becky," Matt said. "I hate to be the one to break it to you, but they knew all along that when we got to the center of the earth, I was supposed to die, so that the seed could grow into a new tree."

Tomtar shook his head and gave a pitiful moan. He held his hands before him, begging to be understood.

"Matt," Becky said, "I know that story, but you've got it wrong. Jardaine told me that Tomtar and Tuava-Li were luring you down to the middle of the earth to die for the Seed, that's why I came here to begin with! But Tomtar didn't know anything about it. Otherwise would he have shown me where the Seed was? He wouldn't have let me take it, if he wanted everything to go according to Tuava-Li's plan!"

"Yeah, well, I got the whole story out of Macta, as in, Macta, king of Helfratheim. And Tuava-Li confessed it. She didn't even try to lie."

"But did she say Tomtar was in on the plan?"

"Not exactly, no."

"And where did you talk to Macta?" asked Becky. "Is he here?"

"Yeah, he's here, and he's not alone. He's with Tuava-Li, now, and that princess from Ljosalfar, Princess Asra. She said they'd come looking for you, to save you from Jardaine! It seems like everybody came here to save somebody from something. But these guys were going to take the seed to the center of the earth and *sacrifice me.* Isn't that right, Tomtar?"

Tomtar pulled off his pack and with trembling hands he reached into it. "What's he doing?" Matt cried. "Get away, Becky. He might have a weapon!"

"No, Matt," Becky said. "Tomtar's not dangerous. Besides, the knife from the pack they gave him in Hunaland is right here." She picked up the knife from the dusty floor and held it aloft for her brother to see. "Something's wrong with Tomtar's voice."

"Here!" Tomtar managed to whisper.

Jardaine's spell had finally begun to wear off. He was thrilled that he could speak, even though his voice was still little more than a feeble croak. "Here it is, Matt, the—the Seed. I'll give it to you. You have to believe me, I don't know anything about any kind of sacrifice. If Tuava-Li had something like that in mind, she kept it from me." Tomtar stopped to cough. "We were going to do this together, the three of us! We were going to save the world, and then rescue your parents! That's what I thought, that's what I always believed. Here, Matt, it's the Seed. Take it, by the corner. But watch out, don't touch the package in the middle, it's—"

"*Ooooowwww!*" Matt cried and dropped it on the ground. "It shocked me!"

"He warned you," Becky said. "I got shocked, too!"

The Sacred Seed of the Adri fell from its little cloth pouch. Matt saw the tiny roots growing from the bottom of the thing, and the shoot at the top with its three leaves, swaying gently. It glowed as if lit from inside, as if there were enormous power in it.

"So this is what I was going to die for," Matt said. "Well, I'm sorry if I misjudged you, Tomtar. It's gotten really hard to tell who's supposed to be your friend around here. I don't know anymore who knows what."

"You shouldn't judge Tuava-Li, either," Tomtar said. "I'm certain you must have misunderstood. She wouldn't betray you like that. She wouldn't keep something like that to herself. The three of us have been friends since this all began! We came all this way, we watched one another's backs, we've been a team, Matt!"

Matt shook his head. "Yeah, what a team. After Macta blew her cover, Tuava-Li told me that it had been a mistake, that she'd changed her mind, that she wasn't planning on going through with it. But what am I supposed to do with that? All along, she led me to believe one thing, and then when the truth comes out she expects me to trust her? Not a chance, Tomtar, not a chance."

Matt nudged the Seed back into the piece of cloth and gingerly picked it up by the corner. "This thing has been the source of all our problems. I'm going to get rid of it, once and for all."

Tomtar blanched. "But, Matt, if the Seed doesn't get planted, the Cord will die! There'll be chaos in the world. The borders between our world and yours will dissolve, and Faerie Folk all over the world will be exposed to the Humans! 'Twill be a slaughter, Matt, it will be the end of Elf Realm and the end for the Faerie Folk! Thousands—millions will perish, both your kind and mine!"

"I don't know that, Tomtar; all I know is what Tuava-Li told me, and all I know about her is that she's a liar! I've seen enough, done enough, now, to know I'd die for my friends if I had to. I'd die for what I believe in. But I don't believe in Tuava-Li or her stories."

Matt turned and stalked through the dark portal. Becky followed, holding her *Kolli* so Matt could see where he was going. "Becky," he warned, staying close to the wall, "stop where you are. There's not much floor over here; it just drops off into the darkness. There's a ledge, but only a narrow, little ledge. It's the path Asra and Macta took back from the center of the earth. Macta made notches in the walls every time they took a turn, so they could get back after they'd found us. I don't think we're gonna follow that path, though. I'll toss the seed, and then we'll have to figure out if there's a Cord we can use to finally get out of here."

Matt raised his arm to pitch the seed into the black void, but his arm suddenly froze in place. "Step back," came a voice from the darkness.

"It's Jardaine," Becky cried. "She's found us!"

Matt had the corner of the seed packet gripped between his thumb and forefinger. He felt his fingers pried back, as if by an invisible hand, and there was nothing he could do to stop them. The Seed lifted slowly into the air. The cloth dropped away and the Seed hung in the blackness, glowing like an emerald-colored star. Then Matt felt a blow to his chest. It was as if an enormous fist, a giant's fist, had struck him, and he toppled from the ledge.

"Matt, no!" Tomtar yelled and reached for his friend.

Matt grabbed Tomtar's extended hand and braced his feet against the wall of the chasm. Becky gripped Tomtar's legs as Matt's weight dragged them both to the edge of the precipice. "I can't hold on!" Matt cried.

"Don't let go!" Becky screamed. Her knees scraped over the stone; her body tensed and stiffened as she kicked up clouds of dust, trying to stop the relentless drag toward the abyss.

Becky and Tomtar lodged themselves against a boulder at the edge of the chasm. Becky clung to Tomtar, and Tomtar shrieked in pain as his arm was nearly yanked from its socket. Matt struggled to hold on, but he knew that he would pull all three of them down unless he let go. So he did. "Nooooooo!" cried Tomtar and Becky.

Suddenly a single black line, etched into the flesh of Matt's hand, leapt from his skin and wrapped itself like a vine around Tomtar's hand, and then his wrist. Again and again it spun around, strengthening its grip. And as Matt fell, it held him like a rope. The black line that tied the two friends together slowed Matt's fall as it unraveled. And when he reached the bottom of the pit, he landed with a thud on his back, shocked but unharmed. The last black line on his hand snapped away.

As Tomtar tumbled away from the boulder, he saw the glowing Seed still moving through the air. Jardaine stood in the darkness with her *Huldu* open before her like a trap. The Seed moved slowly into the pouch and Jardaine slammed it shut. Then Becky cried out. She fell to the ground in a faint. Jardaine uttered a spell and Tomtar watched in horror as a great blue bubble began to form around the girl. The bubble lifted from the ground with Becky, still unconscious, trapped inside. "Ha! It worked!" Jardaine cackled. "Now I have the Seed, and I have your friend Becky. Come along quietly, Tomtar, if you care about her. We're a Troll, an Elf, and a Human, once again, as it was in ancient times. We have a mission to fulfill."

"But you're only going to kill her when you get to the center of the earth!" Tomtar cried.

"Perhaps you'd rather I kill her now! Or perhaps you'd like me to send a blast of psychic energy at *you,* and see what it does to your heart. Or perhaps you'd like me to use my magick to push you off the edge of this precipice, and you can join your friend Matt at the bottom of the pit! Or," she cackled, playing to his heroic instinct, "you can help me save the world!"

Tomtar felt weak at the knees, and his shoulder burned with pain from supporting Matt's weight as he had fallen into the chasm. His arm tingled all the way to his fingertips, and his wrist was black where the lines of the tattoo had buried themselves in his flesh. Futility washed over him. "All right," he moaned. "I'll come with you."

Tuava-Li heard shouts echoing through the stone corridors and jumped to her feet. "Something's happening," she cried. "I've got to get to Matt, now!"

She grabbed the *Kolli* from Macta's hand and ran headlong into the dark passage. Macta and Asra, with nothing to light their way, hurried after her. Tuava-Li was horrified when she reached the end of the long corridor and found that the floor had completely dropped away. "There's no one here," she called to Macta and Asra. "I hope that he —"

"I'm here," Matt called from the bottom of the pit. "I'm down here! Can you guys help get me up?"

"If I'm not mistaken," Macta said to Tuava-Li, "the Human abandoned us already. And now that he's in need, he cries for us to forgive him and waste our time with a rescue attempt? Bah!"

"No," said Asra. "He's Becky's brother. We'll help him if we can."

Tuava-Li put down her Fire Sprite. She closed her eyes and concentrated her energy on a spot between her eyes. She willed her arms to change to wings, her skin to feathers, and her arms to feet with hooked talons. Her eyes spread apart on her head, and the front of her face swelled and changed to a beak. Then she flapped her kestrel wings and dropped into the pit. She couldn't see where she was, but she could feel the flow of air around her and she knew when she was close to the bottom. She fluttered to a stop at the top of a chunk of basalt, and gripped the rock with her claws. She called to Matt, *Are you all right?*

"Yeah, I'm okay." His voice rose from the darkness. There was no need for him to respond in thoughtspeak. He hadn't forgotten why he'd been so furious at her, but he was overjoyed that she'd found him. "Well, my arm is killing me. I think my wrist is sprained. And I'm going to have a pretty bad bruise on my tailbone. I'll have to tell you later about my tattoos—they saved my life!" There was an uncomfortable pause. "Is that why you're here, Tuava-Li? To save my life, too? You haven't changed your mind again about sacrificing me for the seed, have you?"

I just want to help you, Tuava-Li said. *I want to get you out of here, and I want all of us to go home. I want you to go back to your world, and be happy, and I'll stay and be happy in mine. That's what I want.*

Asra and Macta peered down into the darkness. "Is he hurt?" the Princess called.

"No," shouted Matt, "I'm fine! Can't you think of some way to get me out of here?" Then he said to Tuava-Li, "You just missed out on something pretty big. I found Becky and Tomtar, and they had the seed. They'd stolen it from Jardaine. But she came to get it, and she knocked me off that cliff, and then, from what I could hear, took Becky away in one of those blue orbs, like the one that you and your mage used to protect me from the fire in Alfheim. She's also got Tomtar and the seed again. Now she's on her way to the middle of the earth. She'll probably kill Becky, like you were going to kill me, unless we stop her!"

Tuava-Li felt stung but ignored Matt's accusation. It was more or less true, after all. *But Jardaine doesn't know how to get there . . . does she?*

"Well . . ." Matt hung his head. "I told Becky what Asra and Macta told me, and I think Jardaine must have been listening. They're going back that way, past the ledge. A few last twists and turns, and they'll be there, unless the snakes get to them first."

Then there's no time to waste, Tuava-Li said. *I'll take my cue from Jardaine.*

Tuava-Li focused her thoughts around the image of a blue sphere. Matt felt air swirling around his feet and looked down. A blue fog was forming in the blackness. As it rose up around his body, and lifted from the floor of the cavern, he fell back against the rubbery wall. He felt himself swaying back and forth. A moment later he saw a pair of golden, gleaming lights — Macta's and Asra's *Kollis*. Matt realized he was hovering over the edge of the precipice again and the Elves stood back to make room for him. He leaned forward and pressed gently on the inside of the sphere. *Anytime,* he called to Tuava-Li in thoughtspeak. With a tiny popping sound, the bubble burst. Matt fell to his knees on the dusty ledge. Then he turned and called into the abyss. "You did it, Tuava-Li! You can come up now."

Soon they heard the rustling of a bird in flight.

419

26

BECKY LAY UNCONSCIOUS within Jardaine's blue orb. It hovered in the air as the Elf stepped from the corridor into the amphitheater, using all her strength, all her magickal reserves, to keep it aloft. "Finally," she said through gritted teeth. "Finally I'll get what I deserve!"

She lowered the orb to the rubble-strewn floor, where it bounced gently, flattening like a balloon with a slow leak. Tomtar slogged down one of the aisles of the amphitheater, barely able to keep his head up. "Give me my *Huldu*," Jardaine ordered.

She'd placed it in the Troll's pack because she knew that having it close to her own body had sapped her strength. Inside the *Huldu,* the Seed of the Adri pulsed and throbbed. Drawing energy from everything around it, the Seed was now draining

Tomtar's vital energy. Wearily he sat down on one of the raised stone rings around the pool and the black, ascending root. He took off his backpack and let it drop to the floor. The high, domed ceiling groaned, and a shower of dust and pebbles fell. Jardaine spun around and glared. "Fool," she whispered. "Can't you see you have to be careful in this place? Look at the walls, they're crumbling!"

"I can't see anything," Tomtar said in a hushed voice. "You're the one with the Fire Sprite, not me!"

Jardaine grabbed her *Huldu* from Tomtar's pack and walked toward the center of the chamber. Tomtar struggled to think of something to do that would stop her. Time was running out, but he hardly had the strength to get up. Jardaine raised the orb again and guided it over the pool surrounding the massive root. "Perfect," she said.

She closed her eyes, recalling the spell that her Mage had uttered, so many moons ago, when a Human girl named Anna was entranced and placed at the bottom of a stream at the outskirts of Alfheim. Jardaine uttered the words to the spell and withdrew her energy from the orb. It disappeared with a faint pop, and Becky slipped beneath the surface of the water.

"What have you done?" Tomtar cried. Once again the ceiling responded with groans and rumbles and a rain of dust.

"Be quiet," Jardaine whispered, glancing nervously at the dome. "She'll be safe under the water, safer than we are out here. . . . It looks deep. And I can't concentrate when I have to keep that orb afloat. She'll be fine, there, until I figure out what to do. I can't risk having her wake up and cause a commotion in here! It would spoil everything."

Tomtar remembered watching over Anna, the daughter of the hunter who killed Prince Udos. He'd stayed by her side as she lay in the stream, neither dead or truly alive, for countless seasons. He also remembered how Anna had lost her mind beneath the water, and how when she walked on dry land again, she was no longer truly Human. "You can't keep Becky in there for long," he said to Jardaine, forgetting that her plan was to sacrifice the girl.

Jardaine held her *Kolli* high and peered into the flickering shadows. "If only I could get a sense of everything in this chamber. I don't know where the Seed should be planted; there are no signs, no clues! Why doesn't the Goddess guide me, why doesn't she tell me what to do? 'Tis her bidding I want to perform, 'tis her will I want to carry out!"

She went to examine the walls, and realized that the chamber was ringed with dusty light sconces. Carefully she lifted one of the lids and saw an ancient Fire Sprite curled inside. "Wake up," she hissed.

Roused from endless centuries of sleep, the Fire Sprite took only a moment before it burst into flames and stood on its porcelain platform, burning with abandon. Jardaine went to each sconce and opened the lid. Soon the entire chamber was brightly lit. "That's better," she said with satisfaction, and gazed up at the dome overhead. What she saw there was so awful, so frightening, that for a moment she didn't dare to breathe. The walls and ceiling of the chamber were riddled with holes. Inside the holes were creatures, blinking down, squinting in the glare of the Fire Sprites. "Noooo," Jardaine whispered, when she saw their horrible, luminous eyes.

"Not them," Tomtar cried in fear, "not again, not here!"

Footsteps echoed in the corridor, just outside. Matt appeared at the entrance to the amphitheater. Tuava-Li, Macta, and Asra were right behind him. "Where's my sister?" Matt demanded, when he saw Jardaine standing by the pool. "What have you done with her?"

The ceiling groaned, and the creatures darted back into their holes. The sound was louder now, and it stretched from one end of the dome to the other. Bits of stone and dust fell in a torrent. Tomtar met Matt's gaze and with exaggerated motions he gestured to the pool. "She's in the water," he whispered. "Jardaine put a spell on her, and she's in the water!"

Matt ran for the pool. Tuava-Li watched in horror; in the dream she'd had, traveling down through the Cord, she had been standing with this same group by a body of water. Now she knew that the dream foreshadowed this dreadful moment. Matt dove into the pool and disappeared beneath the surface. He saw something bright, far below him. He swam with all his might, keeping his eyes open for any sign of Becky, and the light at the bottom of the pool grew brighter and more vivid. When he felt his lungs would burst, and that he couldn't dive any deeper, he kept on, cutting through the water, paddling ever deeper. His limbs grew weary as the distant light filled his field of vision. It came over him like the light of the sun on a summer afternoon, like the glorious balmy days he had sat on the hillside with Becky and Tomtar, telling stories, and looking for animal shapes in the clouds. And then it all faded to black.

"I can stop your hearts," Jardaine said in a harsh whisper. "I can stop all of you!"

Macta took a step forward. Powcca raced ahead, baring his teeth and growling. "How I've longed to see you again, Jardaine! How I've longed to rip out your heart with my bare hands, after what you did to me and my kingdom. You traitorous flea, I'll show you what it means to suffer!"

"Macta," Asra cried, surprised to hear such venom coming from the King's mouth. He'd shown her a gentler, kinder side since they left Helfratheim. Now she wondered — had it all been an act?

"I'll kill you, Macta," Jardaine said. "I swear I will!"

"If you're going to kill anybody," Asra cried, "it had better be these monsters, Jardaine, because they're going to eat us all alive if you don't!"

"We can stop them together," Tuava-Li pleaded. "Jardaine, you and I can try to stop them, and then we can think this all through. It doesn't have to be this way. We can plant the Seed together, we can —"

The creatures were wriggling from their holes again, jaws slavering as they whispered together, *"The intruders must die! The intruders must not be allowed to live in the Chamber of the Seed!"*

They came from every direction, gliding through the dust, their bodies leaving trails on the floor. Powcca leapt up and down and began to bark as Macta pressed his mechanical hand over his pet's frothing mouth and gazed in panic at the crumbling dome. Then Tomtar had an idea. He reached into his pack and found his wooden flute. He raised it to his lips and blew a single high note. The ceiling responded with an ominous rumble and a shower of debris. Tomtar paused to look around. Many of the creatures, gripped in fear, crept back toward their holes. Others opened their mouths and let out a sharp *hisssss.*

"Go away," Tomtar said in a quiet but steady voice, "go away, all of you, and leave us alone. I can bring down the roof of this place on top of us; it won't take much! I'd rather die like that, than have you gobble me up. It's up to you! Do you want to risk it?"

He raised the flute to his lips again. The song started low, and quiet, but quickly gathered force. The roof of the cave rumbled ominously. As Tomtar's fingers played over the little holes along the shaft of the flute, a chunk of the ceiling, as big as a house, came loose. It landed with a crash on the amphitheater seating, crushing rows of carved stone to powder. There was a moment of terrible silence. Then the entire ceiling seemed to cry out in protest, as a thunderous roar shook the air. "Nooooo," the creatures hissed. Though they warily eyed the ceiling of the dome, only a few turned to wriggle away. They were far, far too hungry.

Suddenly Tuava-Li was overcome with a feeling she hadn't experienced since she'd received her vision from the Goddess, back in Alfheim. The sensation was so strong that she nearly fell to her knees. Her body seemed to open up, as if her molecules were expanding, as if she were dissolving in thin air. A shimmering image of a monk appeared in her mind. *Approach the water,* the mysterious figure said in thoughtspeak. *Do not be afraid. You must dive to the bottom of the pool, to reach the true center of the earth.*

Who are you?

You will meet me, soon! Hurry, now. The creatures will not follow you.

As the vision began to fade, Tuava-Li called to her companions. "Come with me! We're going into the pool."

Asra cried, "But we can't breathe underwater—we'll drown!"

"No, we won't. Trust me, this is the only way. We must dive to the very bottom. We have no choice!"

"I'm certainly not going into that pool," Macta said. But when Jardaine grabbed her *Huldu* and leapt into the water, Macta snatched up his Goblin and ran forward. At the edge of the pool he turned, his eyes burning with excitement, and looked back at Asra. "Come, my darling," he said, holding out his good arm. "I won't leave you here!"

"Now, Asra," said Tuava-Li, "come now, before it's too late!"

The Bloodthirsty monsters scuttled ever closer, their lips drawn back and ready to strike. Their shiny white teeth gleamed in the light from the sconces. Tomtar raised his flute and began to play again. This time he was completely drowned out by the awful grinding of stone against stone, and the shriek of the creatures as rubble began to fall from above. As the dome collapsed, there was only one place for the Faerie Folk to go. "Now!" Tuava-Li cried, and she, Macta, Asra, and Tomtar dove into the pool.

Matt lay on his back, his hair hanging in wet rivulets across his forehead. He woke up, coughing fluid from his lungs. He got up on one elbow and coughed some more. *Where am I?* he wondered. The air was sweet, and sticky, and hot, like a greenhouse on an August afternoon. Becky lay beside him. He brushed her wet hair out of her face and saw that her eyes were open, blank, and staring. "Becky," he cried, fearing the worst, "Becky, wake up! Wake up!"

He grabbed her by the shoulders and turned her over on her belly. Water spouted like a fountain from her mouth. With his hands on her chest he could feel her heart beating; she wasn't dead, just entranced, like Tomtar had said. He lay her gently down on her side just as he saw a shadow creeping over Becky's face. He turned his head around and stared in wonder. A light flickered dimly in an emerald sky, and set against the green Matt could see a distant figure approaching. "Where am I?" he cried aloud. "Who are you?"

The figure coming toward him was a Troll, a female Troll, dressed all in white. She stood over Matt and smiled beatifically.

The pupils of her eyes were tiny points of black in a field of blue. There was suddenly a strange sensation in Matt's chest, a vulnerable, defenseless feeling, unlike anything he'd even remotely experienced before. It was as if an invisible force was reaching into every fiber of his being, probing, cleansing, healing. He opened his mouth to speak. "Where am I? How did I get here?"

The Troll gestured, and Matt turned to see where she was pointing. Behind him appeared to be a wall of trees, shimmering in a milky haze. "You passed through the membrane, as all must do who wish to participate in the birth of the new Seed! I am Desir. You've arrived at the heart of the world. Are you the King?"

"King?" Matt repeated. "No, I'm not the king. I'm—Matt. And you—how can you be *Desir*? Desir came here thousands of years ago, to plant the seed. You can't be the same—"

There was a sound from behind, a burbling, sucking sound, and when Matt spun around he saw the wall of trees bulge, as if the forest itself was an apparition. A foot appeared, and an elbow, and water gushed out as Jardaine stepped through the shimmering membrane. She stumbled to her knees, dripping wet, beside him. She got up, coughing water, and shaking her dark hair. "And you," Desir asked, "are you the Mage?"

"Her name's Jardaine," Matt volunteered, "and she's not supposed to be here. She was never supposed to be here! It's Tuava-Li who had the vision, not Jardaine!"

"But I have the Seed," Jardaine croaked.

She reached into her *Huldu* and withdrew the pouch by its corner. But the cloth fell away, and the Seed slowly drifted overhead, out of Jardaine's reach. The Seed was glowing so brightly now, so radiant with energy that it literally buzzed, and the air around it popped and crackled. "Now," Jardaine said, "we're an Elf, a Troll, and a Human, just as in ancient days. Let the ritual begin!"

Desir narrowed her eyes at Jardaine. "You're mistaken if you think that it's we three who will deliver the Seed to its proper home! I'm here to supervise the ritual, not to take part in it. And where is the King?"

At that moment the wall of the emerald-colored womb bulged inward again, and one after the other, Macta, Tuava-Li, Tomtar, and Asra tumbled through the illusion of trees and forest. All four of them lay stunned as the wall behind them sealed itself like a cut in the Cord. Powcca leapt from Macta's grasp, shaking water from his coat, as the King of Helfratheim slowly got to his feet. Jardaine cried out, "Not you again, not here, not now!"

She focused all her strength in generating a burst of energy to stop Macta's heart. *Nothing.* Again she concentrated, trying to shape a ball of fiery light behind her eyes, and again she willed it to grow, she willed it to blossom into a fierce, destructive force. *Nothing.* Feverishly she recited the words to half a dozen incantations, curses, and spells, trying again and again to hurl a devastating blast at her adversary. But nothing happened. "'Tis the end for you, Jardaine," Macta jeered. "Your power's gone!"

Desir frowned at Jardaine. "Did you truly expect to work such dark magick in this place? Your spells and incantations have no power here!"

Macta laughed. He flexed his mechanical arm, and he contracted the muscles in his shoulder so that the blades along his fingers would spring into action. "Finally," he said, "after all this time, I shall have my vengeance!" But he found that his commands had no more effect than Jardaine's spells; the blades stayed tightly sheathed, and the metal fingers remained limp.

"How dare you," Desir thundered, "how dare you bring your petty squabbles to the very heart of this world!"

As she glared at them all, the light behind her seemed to dim, and the air felt oddly cold. The Seed of the Adri, still hanging in the air, snapped and flared. "What's happening?" cried Matt. "What's happening to the sun?"

"The light behind me is not the sun," Desir said. "'Tis the last vestige of the life of the old Seed! When the power of the new Seed joins with it, it will burn with a radiance that will blind you, should you look directly into its fire. And now . . ."

Matt felt a terrible anxiety flood his senses; he knew instinctively that the time for the sacrifice had come. "Wait!" he cried, panicking.

"Enough," Desir intoned. "'Tis too late for any of us to change our minds or alter our destinies! All that must be will come to pass, whether we choose it or not."

Desir's eyes focused on Tuava-Li. "It seems that *you* are the

Mage who has come to replace me. *You* are the One whom the Goddess called."

"But *I* brought the Seed!" Jardaine cried.

"The time has come!" Desir turned her gaze upon Macta. "And you—are you the King?"

"I'm the King of Helfratheim," Macta said proudly, "and I'm here to deliver justice to this so-called Mage, Jardaine. I've come all this way, I've sacrificed my throne, my honor, even my arm, to get the revenge I'm due. If I have to take her life with my one good hand, I will!"

Desir quivered in righteous indignation; her eyes burned into his. "Do you not understand what your proper role is here, King Macta? Have you not been told?"

"No one tells me anything," he snarled. "*I tell others.* That's what a King does!"

With that, Macta sprung at Jardaine. But instead of closing his grip around Jardaine's throat, he grabbed the Seed that hung glittering in the air. As a searing river of current raced up his arm, he pushed the Seed into Jardaine's open mouth. She fell back, gagging, as Macta jammed it deeper down her throat. "So you wanted to plant the Seed, did you?" he cried. "I think I know where to plant the Seed, Jardaine; what do you think about that? What, you can't talk?" He turned his head to Desir. "Tell me, O wise one, where the Sacred Seed belongs!"

Matt leapt for Macta. Despite all that Jardaine had done, he didn't want to see her choked to death before his eyes. As he

431

grabbed Macta's good arm and began to pull, the King yanked away and swung his mechanical arm at Matt's head. Even with the slashing blades withdrawn into the fingertips, the fist struck Matt like a mallet. He dropped, unconscious, to the ground.

Tuava-Li rushed to Matt's side. Was this how it was meant to be, had the boy given his life like this, for the sake of the Seed? Blood ran from a deep cut on his forehead. But his eyes sprang open, and he turned his head to see Jardaine struggling with Macta. He rolled onto his side, then struggled to his knees. He was in no condition to fight, but he pushed Tuava-Li away and tried to get up. *Wait,* Tuava-Li said in thoughtspeak. *Things are happening as they must. You must bear witness; 'tis not our place to interfere with fate!*

Tomtar pummeled Macta with his fists. He grabbed his flute and used it like a bludgeon, but it only seemed to strengthen the King's terrible resolve. Asra pulled helplessly on Macta's good arm. She tugged at his sleeve, she yanked at his hair, but it was no use. "If you love me," she cried, "stop this, now! Macta! I'll do whatever you want, I'll be whoever you want me to be, just stop it! Stop!"

In the back of his mind, Macta heard Asra's pleas, and he couldn't believe his great good fortune. He had won her; he had the heart of his beloved, and all he had to do was let go of Jardaine. All he had to do was let go of his plan for revenge, of his crushing desire for murder. *And he could not do it.* While his fingers forced the Seed so deeply into Jardaine's throat that she gulped the scorching, incandescent mass, he wondered for a moment what his life would have been like if he had been like any other Elflad—if he had been born with a kinder disposition, if he'd been thoughtful, and gentle, and free of artifice and duplicity. He wondered how his life would have fared if he'd stayed to rule his father's kingdom with reason and justice, instead of stubbornly traversing the planet to get even with someone who had wronged him. *What were the odds of that?* he wondered ruefully. But Macta knew; none of it had ever been even a remote possibility. If he'd placed a wager on the odds that he was free to be whatever he chose, he would have lost. He was simply who he was, and there was nothing he could have done to change. Or . . . *was there?*

He took a step back from Jardaine as she choked and gasped for breath. He turned to the Princess, who had collapsed, sobbing, to the floor. "Asra," he said, "I don't know what came over me. I'll do whatever you ask. I—"

But there was a flash of light and he spun back to see a blazing white tendril burst through Jardaine's belly. It was followed by another twisting, coiling tendril, like the head of a snake, pausing to taste the damp, sweet air. Then, moving as fast as lightning, the thing shot toward Macta's chest. It burrowed through him and exploded from his back. A thousand new shoots sprouted from the tendril and began pushing their way into every cavity of Macta's body. As the final vestiges of consciousness left him, he managed to say two words to Asra that he had never uttered to another living soul before. *"I'm sorry!"* he whispered, and then he died.

Fresh white tendrils were sprouting by the score from Jardaine's and Macta's arms, legs, and torsos, weaving through their bodies and binding them together more tightly than if they'd died in each other's embrace. As the force of the growing Seed consumed them, their bodies disappeared in a white ball of incandescence. For a moment there seemed to be two suns hovering in the air; the flickering energy of the old Seed and the radiant power of the new Seed were moving inexorably toward each other. And then there was *one*. Tendrils of light shot forth.

"It is finished," Desir cried, stepping back. "The legend is fulfilled. The two are now one! The King has given his life, so that the Mother may live."

Roaring and scraping sounds filled the air. Yggdrasil, far, far above, was pulling irrevocably on its deepest roots and drawing them from the earth. "What do you mean, the *king*?" Matt cried. He tugged at his sister Becky, who was waking from Jardaine's spell, now broken as the Mage died. Matt helped his sister to her feet. Yawning black holes began to appear in the pale green walls all around them. The illusion of a field and a forest was fading fast. "I thought that a human had to die!" Matt said. "I thought *I* had to die!"

"Noooo," Desir said. "A *King* had to die. That is what the sacrifice demands. The King, in my time, was a Human. This time, the King was an Elf—and he sacrificed his life that all may live!"

Tuava-Li nodded. "I misunderstood. We all misunderstood.

 JARDAINE AND MACTA

Our ancestors had such arrogance and disrespect for Humanity, that they failed to even *consider* the possibility that a Faerie might be sacrificed. We never needed an Elf, a Troll, *and* a Human to complete the quest. We just needed a *King*!"

"I've much to explain," Desir said, "and not much time. Close your eyes, all of you."

Tuava-Li trembled. With her eyes squeezed shut, she found herself far from the sounds of groaning, tearing, and burning that were transforming the Underworld. *Tuava-Li,* Desir said in thoughtspeak, *'tis your turn, now, to keep watch over the life of the new Seed, as it grows into a Sacred Tree. 'Tis your turn to stay here at the heart of the world, to express and radiate the love of the Goddess to all things.*

I—I'm to stay here, all by myself? Tuava-Li asked, shivering.

Indeed you are.

But I'm not a Mage, I'm just a monk!

You underestimate yourself. You are indeed a Mage, and a very special one, at that.

Tuava-Li thought about the prospect of this imprisonment, this isolation, of being condemned to an eternity of solitary confinement. "It isn't fair," she cried. "Even if I were a Mage, what evil did I do to deserve this fate?"

'Tis not punishment! The endless hours at the heart of the world will be as mere heartbeats to you; I have lived here, watching over the Seed, and the womb, for countless moons, and to me the entire time has passed like a quiet afternoon. So it will be for you, Tuava-Li. Someday the old Seed will grow tired, and the cycle will need to be started once again. Then, when the

Goddess wills it, another hero will come to replace you, as you are about to do for me.

Tuava-Li was stunned. She'd had no inkling that this was to be her fate. *But—where will you go now, what will you do? What will I do, when—*

I will return to the surface of the earth, and live out the rest of my life traveling and exploring this great world, as you will do when your service has ended. Do not be sad or afraid! You are blessed to remain here. You will be as close to the world of the Gods as an Elf may ever come!

Tuava-Li found herself crying. She'd spent so much time, so much of her energy, striving to reach this place; she felt as if her life's purpose had been fulfilled. But here she was, with a new purpose, and a new role to fulfill. And she knew that when she was finished with the next chapter of her life, everyone she'd ever known and loved would be long, long dead. Desir's voice was soothing, healing, and strong. *I must go now. Your friends must go, too. They will know your love, and your sacrifice, all the days of their lives, and they will thank you for it. You will also feel the love of all the Faerie Folk, yet unborn, who will learn of your quest, and cherish the gift you will make of your life, Tuava-Li. Good-bye! In the name of the Mother and her undying Cord, good-bye!*

Tuava-Li opened her eyes. She was standing on a plain of soft green grass, and the sun shone down, sending warmth to every cell in her body. Far away, standing by the edge of the woods, were Matt and Becky, Tomtar and Asra, and Desir, too. A gentle breeze caressed her hair as she waved good-bye to her friends. Birds were singing, and distant clouds moved in a stately procession across the skies.

"Where am I?" Becky cried, still coming to her senses. "What's going on? What happened to your head, Matt? You're bleeding!"

"I'm not sure," Matt said. "Maybe somebody hit me, but it feels like . . . like a dream. Did Desir talk to you?"

"Of course! She thanked me for what I did, and she said it couldn't have happened without me. Didn't you hear, Matt?"

"I heard what she said to *me*! I think she must have spoken to each of us, somehow. She told me that I'd shown real courage, and that everything I did was for a good purpose. Not bad, huh?"

"Why is Tuava-Li out there in the field, Matt?"

"She's going to stay here," Matt said. He waved to Tuava-Li, standing alone in the blazing sunlight. "But it's time for us to go!"

He heard the screech of wood and stone and felt something slip around his waist. He panicked for a second, thinking of the snakelike creatures, but when he looked down he realized that tendrils of wood, the last roots of the Adri, were enfolding him, and Becky, as well. Matt looked to his side and blinked at the flickering image of Tomtar and Asra, standing with Desir. The limbs of trees seemed to reach out like arms, gently taking the Faerie Folk in their embrace. The world was a womb, the earth and sky warm and sheltering. Matt and Tuava-Li waved a final good-bye. The monk's voice appeared in his mind as Matt looked back. *You taught me so much,* Tuava-Li said. *You were braver,*

438

stronger, wiser than I could have known. I am glad this turned out to be our destiny. The world is not done with you, Matt. I feel honored, blessed that we met, when our realms touched.

Matt smiled, and spoke one last time in thoughtspeak. *Remember when the tunnel collapsed, Tuava-Li, and we were trapped together in the darkness? Just you and me? I think I would have given up hope if it weren't for you. You never gave up, never!*

And neither did you, Matthew!

Matt tapped his chest with his fist. *You're in here, Tuava-Li. Forever. I won't forget.*

Tuava-Li's smile was tender but brave. *May the Goddess guide you!*

The light in the sky seemed to flare, an all-enveloping orb of power and love. "Is it real?" Becky cried. "Is it all *real*?" Then the world slipped into darkness once again.

27

WHEN MATT AWOKE, Becky and Tomtar were
kneeling over him. He held up his hand to block the brilliance of
the sun. The air was warm and humid, and his throat felt parched
when he tried to speak. "Where—where are we?"

"We're back in Hunaland," Becky said with a grin.

"And look," said Tomtar, holding his arms out at his sides,
"it's summer!"

"We were underground for almost a year," Becky said. "Do
I look ten?"

"Whoa," Matt cried, struggling to get up on one elbow. He'd
heard repeatedly about how time passed differently in the Faerie
world. But nearly *a year*? And how could there be green fields,

and mountains covered in forests, just beyond the walls? This was the North Pole, after all.

"Careful, friend," Tomtar said. "There's no hurry to get up! Macta gave you quite a knock on the noggin, down in the Underworld!"

Matt touched his forehead and found it was covered with a poultice of leaves and salve.

"The monks put that on," Becky said. "It was pretty bad. They think you'll probably have a scar."

"How long have we been out here?"

"Not long! They wanted to take us right into the palace, but since we'd been underground for so long, and the sun is shining . . ."

"We decided the sunlight would be good for you," Tomtar said. Then he added, "And for me, too!"

"But what happened to the ice and snow? We were sitting on a frozen ocean before!"

Tomtar furrowed his brow. "Once the new Seed took root at the center of the earth, it changed things. The Mage always said that would happen! The veil between our worlds closed, and Elf Realm went back to the way it had always been, before the things that the Humans did . . . well, the things that *some* Humans did, messed up everything for us. Human world and Faerie world, they're not the same, Matt!"

"And they'll never be again," he answered.

Becky touched Matt's wrist, where the tattoos had pulled away from his skin. "Does it hurt?"

"Not much," Matt said.

"Look at my wrist," Tomtar said. "Your tattoos are mine, now! I think they must be fading, though. I guess there's no need for them anymore."

"Wow," Matt said, looking at the Troll's forearm. "They're not fading, Tomtar. They're changing. Look, the black lines are starting to spell something!"

Becky traced the elegant letterforms with her finger. "It says . . . *Matt and Becky*! Now we'll always be a part of you, Tomtar!"

Tomtar grinned as he gently stroked his forearm. "I like it!"

"I'm just thinking," Matt said. "We sort of did what we set out to do, didn't we? Elf realm's safe from humans!"

Becky laughed. "Now if only the *Human world* was safe from Humans!"

"Looks like you've got your work cut out for you," Tomtar said, "once you get home. But don't worry, you two are heroes! You can do anything."

"Oh, yeah," Matt said, pressing a hand to his forehead. "I'm a hero who can't even stand up!"

He lay on his back and squinted into the sun. Then he remembered that the last time he'd seen Hunaland, everything had been shrouded in smoke and shadows from the branches of the great tree. "Where is it?" he asked. "Yggdrasil, where did it go?"

Becky pointed. "Over there! We came up out of the earth with the ends of some roots twisted all around us, to protect us. Once we were back on top, they let us go, safe and sound. Well, mostly safe and sound, except for your head!"

"Then . . . the tree's still alive?"

"Noooo," said Tomtar. "Not anymore. It pulled out its own roots, don't you remember?"

"I guess I remember," Matt said, thinking of Tuava-Li standing alone in the field and waving. "But I'm not really sure what happened!"

Tomtar and Becky laughed. "You *are* confused," the Troll said. "'Twas a rough ride, and we tore through some nasty patches of dirt and rock. But everything came out all right. If you can turn your head, take a gander at the old tree! It's right there!"

Matt looked over in amazement. A massive, black ball of roots reached nearly to the clouds. Like gnarled, knobby fingers caked in dirt, the roots stretched to the left and right, almost as far as the eye could see. Elves and Trolls clung to high scaffolds, ladders, and rope nets. They worked away at the roots with obsidian-bladed saws. Chunks fell to the ground below, where they were quickly piled onto carts and hauled away. Matt saw that one of the walls of Hunaland had been utterly crushed when the gigantic tree pulled up its roots and toppled over. Stonemasons worked around the massive root-ball to rebuild the wall. "Wow!" Matt exclaimed. "So . . . the trunk must be out there on the other side. And the branches, too, I guess. That tree must reach for miles!"

"So they tell us," Tomtar said. "They plan to saw up all the wood and put it to good use. Elf Realm will be full of furniture and dwellings made from the Sacred Tree!"

"And check that out over there," Becky said.

Matt forced himself to sit up. He saw a circle of monks standing around the edge of an enormous pit, their arms raised before them. Matt could hear them chanting, and he shook his head. "They have a long wait ahead of them if they want to see the new tree. Four thousand miles to the center of the earth? It'll be years before that seed grows into something that sticks out of that hole—centuries, maybe!"

"No," Becky said, "it's growing already. It's magick, Matt! When the old roots pulled out, all the monks were waiting. They chanted, and did all kinds of Faerie stuff, and the dirt and rocks tumbled back into the hole and nearly filled it up. Grass grew over it right away. So far, the new Yggdrasil just looks like any other little tree, poking up out of a valley. But it's not any other tree! It's special, and it's growing like crazy. If you stand up, you can see it!"

Matt slowly got to his feet. His head was killing him, but he could indeed see that there was a small, fragile-looking tree rising from the hole. "What about the Cords that were down there? All the tunnels, the maze? What about Tuava-Li? Did we really leave her down there?"

"Aye," said Tomtar sadly. "They told us that they're going to start all over, build the tunnels again, once the trunk of the tree gets as big as it's going to grow. The Cords will grow back, too, all over the world! And down at the center of it all, Tuava-Li's restin' in that magickal field, keepin' watch. She'll still be there, a long, long time after all of us are gone and forgotten."

"You won't be forgotten, Tomtar," Asra said, as she approached with a group of monks, and Powcca trotting at her side. "None of us will be forgotten, you don't have to worry about that. Now come on, all of you—we've got to get changed! They have fresh clothes for all of us. Then we must say our good-byes to Queen Geror and her Mage, because the Arvada have arrived to take us back to Alfheim!"

"What?" Matt cried. "But how—"

"Macta's Arvada ran low on supplies while waiting for us to return from the center of the earth. The captain took the ship back to home port. But the Queen of Ljosalfar, at my mother's insistence, bought more Arvada from the council in Helfratheim. She sent them here to wait for us! Apparently my mother's feeling much better now, and she's planned a celebration for us in Alfheim to celebrate our success."

"But there *isn't* any Alfheim," Matt said. "You were there, Asra, you saw the forest burn!"

Asra shook her head. "They're rebuilding it, now that the Sacred Trees are growing again. Everything is growing again, now that the veil between the worlds has been restored. Life is a circle, Matt, not a straight line. *What once was, will be again!* Now come, we must pay our respects to the Queen, as she wants to pay her respects to us."

Asra took Becky's hand, and together they led the way to the palace of Hunaland. The square was now a makeshift camp for hundreds of Elves whose homes were destroyed when the great tree fell. But there was no more smoke, and no more crying or running around in confusion. Everyone seemed to be busy at some task or other, and it was obvious to Matt and his friends that there was an overwhelming amount of work to be done. But the work didn't stop the Faerie Folk from putting down all their baskets and tools, and bowing low before the heroes as they passed. "I guess we *are* a big deal around here," Matt whispered to his sister.

Soon they were airborne, sailing through the clouds of Elf Realm back to the place where the adventure had begun. Tomtar rode with Matt in the cab of one Arvada, and Asra rode with Becky. "I never thought I'd have to get into one of these things again," Becky said, lying flat on her back and looking up at her friend, sitting beside her.

Asra stroked Powcca's Goblin head and nodded. "The last time I flew in an Arvada, I was hurrying to Hunaland, hoping I'd find you alive, Becky. I sat up in the front with—" Her words caught in her throat and she turned her head away, gazing from the window.

"With Macta," Becky said, grimacing. "Was it awful?"

"Ah," Asra said with a wistful smile. She wasn't sure Becky would understand; she wasn't sure she understood it herself. "Well, yes and no."

"What do you mean?"

Asra sighed. "I never had an adventure like this in my life. Never. And if it weren't for Macta, I wouldn't be sitting here with you now. He saved my life more than once. Don't you think that means something?"

Becky eyed her friend warily. "I suppose."

"You know," Asra said. "If there was anyone in Macta's life that he really hated, it was Jardaine. But if there was anyone whom he truly loved, it was me. I pushed him away for so long, and for many good reasons, too! But toward the end I realized I'd been doing it out of habit. Toward the end I realized that the fact that he loved me might well be enough, that it would suffice when I became his Queen. I truly considered ignoring everything else."

"You were going to *marry* him?" Becky asked incredulously.

Asra scratched Powcca under the chin. The Goblin lifted his head and grumbled contentedly. "We'll never know, will we? Despite everything that happened, there was a time, not long ago, when I might have said yes. I never met anyone else like him, Becky. He wanted to help me find *you;* he cared more than anything about my wishes, my desires, my safety . . ." Asra paused, collecting her thoughts. "I suppose I should feel honored that the one who inspired such conflicted emotions in me is the one whose name will live in legend, for sacrificing his life for the sake of the new tree, for the sake of Elf Realm."

"What was it like when he . . . when he died?" Becky asked.

Being under Jardaine's spell at the center of the world, she remembered very little.

Asra tried to block the image that immediately appeared in her mind: Macta and Jardaine joined in a fiery white ball of energy, and an emerald spray of Blood. "It was strange, and very, very sad, too. I keep thinking there was something I could have done to stop it, if I had it to do all over again . . . but I suppose everything happened the way it was meant to be! What about you, Becky? Is there anything you'd have chosen to do differently?"

Becky furrowed her brow. "Well, I didn't trust Tomtar, for one. I should have, but I didn't. I listened to Jardaine's lies and believed them, because . . ." Becky frowned. "I don't know!"

"Because Jardaine was a good liar?" Asra suggested. "Because you're young, and young people always prefer to believe what older people tell them is true? It makes the world seem like a safer, more predictable place. That's what we all want, isn't it?"

"I don't know," Becky said slowly. "I like feeling safe. But that's not why I went to Helfratheim with you, or why I went to Hunaland with Jardaine. I wanted to help the people I care about. That's all. Even if I didn't really help them, I tried. I just wanted what I did to matter."

Asra beamed. "You did more than *try*! That's why you mean so much to me, Becky. I never knew a Human before I met you. When we met, I never thought that I'd see something in you that I admired, something that I wanted to be. You should be proud of yourself, because what you do *does* matter. It will always matter to me."

Becky bit her lip. "Are we going to be able to be friends, once we get back to Alfheim? Once this is all over?"

Asra took the girl's hand and squeezed it.

Matt lay in the second Arvada, with his knees pressed up against the roof of the craft. The brass ceiling yielded to the pressure of his knees, and every time he pushed, the Air Sprite above responded with a rumble of irritation. "I'll make him cry for mercy," Matt said.

"Better not," Tomtar replied, sitting beside his friend with his flute on his lap. "That's my job!" He picked up his flute and played the first part of "The Bonnie Banks of Loch Lomond." The cab rocked as the Sprite let out a roar.

Matt and Tomtar laughed. "He really doesn't like music," Tomtar said.

"At least, not *your* music," Matt said. "That was some risk you took playing your flute down in the cave, when those snakes were after us!"

Tomtar shuddered. "Horrible. I assume they all got crushed when the rocks came crashing down and the tree roots pulled out . . . but there are probably a couple of little baby monsters left, and they'll find a way to survive until the next time a Seed needs to get planted!"

Matt nodded. "That was a weird way to plant a seed, wasn't

it? I thought that somebody would have to dig a little hole in the dirt and tuck it into the ground. Once we got the seed down into the middle of the earth, though, it didn't seem to need much help—the way it floated, burning like the sun, and shot out its little roots like they were snakes! Amazing."

"Snakes, snakes, snakes!" Tomtar said. "If I never see another thing that reminds me of a snake, I'll be happy!"

"Well, I don't suppose we needed to see any snakes to begin with, since you and I weren't really needed down there, anyway. Tuava-Li got it messed up from the beginning. Everybody did, thinking that the whole quest thing needed an elf, a troll, and a human. When that turned out to be wrong, it was pretty clear that you and I went down there for nothing."

Tomtar shook his head. "As far as the Goddess was concerned, it seems like a Princess stood in perfectly well for a Prince, to go with the King and the Mage! And as for you and me, Matt, I think we played a pretty important role."

"Oh, yeah?"

"You might never have agreed to go on the quest if it weren't for me comin' along, 'cause you weren't sure you could trust Tuava-Li."

"And now I know why!" Matt exclaimed.

"Jardaine never would have come after the Seed without havin' Becky to help," the Troll continued, "'cause she thought she needed a Human to go with her."

"You're right about that."

"And think about it, Asra and Macta never would have come, if it hadn't been for the fact that Macta wanted to kill Jardaine and Asra wanted to save Becky! The Seed would never have gotten planted at the center of the earth without the help of each and every one of us!"

"Seems like you've thought the whole thing through pretty carefully."

Tomtar shrugged. "It's all clear as day."

"Yeah." Matt laughed. "We were all there to do our job. Like Tuava-Li used to say, *the goddess always provides*!"

When the Arvada sailed within view of Alfheim, the crowds of Faerie Folk cheered. Snake-tailed kites flapped in the breeze as Elfmaids in ceremonial garb danced joyfully, and bonfires sent clouds of colored smoke into the air. The Air Sprites roared and shot pillars of flame. "You'd have thought they'd have had enough of fires around here," Tomtar said, gazing out the window. "I'm surprised they're even tryin' to rebuild, after all the destruction that took place. You'd think the Mage would be afraid to come home, but they say that the fires cleared the land of contamination!"

"What does it look like?" Matt asked. "Alfheim, I mean." He'd strained his neck to peer from the Arvada portals, but from his angle, all he could see were clouds.

"'Tis green," Tomtar said. "Things are definitely growin' back. There are tents, hundreds of 'em. Some big ones, too. And lots of Faerie Folk!"

"All hail the returning heroes," Matt said, shifting uncomfortably. He thought of Kalevala Van Frier, the Mage of Alfheim. He knew he'd be seeing her soon. She'd sent him on the quest with Tuava-Li expecting that his life would be sacrificed at the end of the journey. Though Tuava-Li had time to regret her decision, there was no reason to think that the Mage ever felt guilty about it. He couldn't wait to tell her what he thought of her.

The Mage of Alfheim stood on a viewing stand facing the field, watching the Arvada descend. Beside her stood her friend and fellow Mage Neaca, Queen Shorya of Alfheim, Queen Metis and King Adon of Ljosalfar, as well as Tacita, the Secretary of the Synod of Ljosalfar. Behind them, representing the kingdom of Helfratheim, were Prashta, the Most Reverent Official Agent of Dockalfar Security Operations, and Lehtinen, Director of Operations. Hundreds of other dignitaries, religious figures, and royal families from neighboring kingdoms were gathered nearby, waiting to see who had survived the ordeal at the North Pole and the center of the earth. The crowd would have been far bigger, but for the fact that the Cord was now in a transitional phase. As the roots of Yggdrasil grew anew, overground travel was still the only real possibility. Many others from more remote outposts were still en route and hoped to arrive in time to get a glimpse of the heroes, fresh from their adventure. At the back of the crowd, a contingent of Green Men stood proudly, their leafy branches held high.

Prashta and Lehtinen sweated profusely as they watched the Arvada land. As of yet, they had no idea whether or not King Macta was alive. Both had substantial bets riding on their leader's fate. War planners, meanwhile, had worked out strategies for every possible scenario. The Council of Seven had provided not only the Arvada, but resources for setting up tents and providing food and entertainment for the guests at the celebration. They were prepared to pay quite substantial funds for the rebuilding of Alfheim, as well, as long as certain requirements were met. They had promised to reveal their terms at a meeting with the Mage of Alfheim and those who returned in the Arvada.

All eyes were on the hatch door as clouds of dust blew up around the great brass cabs. Aeronauts climbed down ropes drawn from the riggings, and anchored the craft to the soil. The Air Sprites twitched in discomfort in being lashed to the ground, for they were born to fly. The first Elf to emerge from the cab was Princess Asra. Her mother, Queen Shorya, cried out in relief to see her daughter smile and wave. Asra grinned at the cheering crowd and descended the steps to her homeland. Royal guards escorted her to a large gray tent. Members of the flight crew were the last to exit the craft. Aeronauts at the back of the cab turned the enormous screws to release Becky, for the final time, from her flying prison. There was substantially less applause when the girl crept into the sunlight, wiping the dirt from her hands onto her jeans, and hurried to follow her friend Asra.

Then the hatch door opened on the second Arvada. Tomtar stepped out, ducking his head and squinting. Raucous applause erupted in the crowd as Tomtar's cousins, Megala, Mitelle, and Delfina, cheered and clapped their hands. Tomtar waved and smiled broadly, wondering how they'd managed to get invited to the ceremony at Alfheim. Guards hurried him toward the tent before he had the chance to greet them personally. When it was clear that the captain and his crew of Aeronauts were the last Faerie Folk to leave the Arvada, Prashta and Lehtinen exchanged glances of enormous relief. Macta, they rightly assumed, was dead. "Let us meet the others in the octagonal tent," Prashta said to the Mage. "We have much to discuss with you as well as Princess Asra and the Troll."

Having seen Asra and Tomtar get out of the Arvada, but not Jardaine, Macta, Nick, or Tuava-Li, the crowd dispersed. Until the evening, when they would gather again to hear the story of the quest revealed for the first time, they were content to gossip, and speculate on what had happened, and enjoy the refreshments provided for their comfort and pleasure by the good folk of Helfratheim. Meanwhile, Aeronauts released Matt from the back of the cab. The Queen's soldiers trembled visibly, unable to hide their excitement at being part of this momentous event, as they led Matt into the tent.

"Have the Humans sit on the floor," Prashta ordered the soldiers.

The rest of them took their seats at a long table that had been brought in for the meeting. Queen Shorya arrived at the tent flap and cried out, "Asra!"

The Princess leapt up from her seat and raced into her mother's arms. Both Tomtar and Becky wiped happy tears from their eyes at the sight of the reunion. Prashta and Lehtinen, however, were disturbed by such a public display of affection, and grumbled, shuffling papers in their hands, until the mother and daughter had taken their seats next to the Mage. Queen Shorya touched the sleeve of the Mage's robe and whispered, "I'm so, so sorry! Tuava-Li was—"

"I knew it," the Mage murmured sorrowfully. "'Tis no real surprise. When the Arvada arrived I reached out to her in thoughtspeak, and heard nothing in reply. I knew she would not be returning to me."

"Wait," Asra said soothingly. "'Tis not what it seems! I'll explain it all, as soon as—"

Prashta got to his feet and said, "Let me begin by extending my welcome to Princess Asra and Tomtar."

Lehtinen kicked Prashta's shin and scowled at him. Prashta scowled back and added, "And of course the Humans, Matthew and Rebecca."

Lehtinen nodded appreciatively. He knew it was in the best interest of them all to acknowledge the part the Humans had played in the quest. Prashta continued, "I congratulate you all on the completion of your quest. You were given an incredible opportunity to serve Elf Realm, and your performance was truly admirable. Now, let me stress that the gentle folk of Helfratheim are brokenhearted to discover that it was not King Macta's fate to return with you." He raised an eyebrow and gazed intently at Asra. "As we're very concerned about preserving our leader's memory and reputation among our people, we want to make sure that the story the two of you tell about your quest reflects the importance of Macta's sacrifice, and protects the legacy we plan to build around his name. As we discussed with your Mage and Queen, we're prepared to offer substantial sums of money and resources for the rebuilding of Alfheim, to provide shelter for all of its inhabitants until the trees of the forest grow anew, to provide food, and public education for the young ones, as well as medical care for those in need. All that we ask for in return is the control over the tale of King Macta's bravery and heroism. Do you understand?"

Asra stared at Prashta in disbelief. "You don't even know what happened, and you want to dictate how the story will be told? You're not even interested in the truth!"

Prashta and Lehtinen exchanged glances. "The truth is a rare and precious jewel," Prashta said, "a jewel with many facets. We simply want to see that the light is directed properly!"

"Aye," said Asra. "Now would you like to hear the truth?"

Prashta and Lehtinen pursed their lips doubtfully and nodded. Asra then proceeded to relate the story of what had happened to her and Macta when they reached Hunaland, and what the Goddess had in store for them at the center of the earth. The picture she painted of the adventure was a revelation to all that heard it. Even Lehtinen and Prashta appeared to be moved by the tale. "And Tuava-Li," she ended, "the one whose vision led to the quest, and the planting of the Sacred Seed, will remain at the center of the earth, watching and waiting. When all of us are long gone, Tuava-Li will remain, the chosen of the Goddess, to ensure that the Seed at the heart of Elf Realm is safe and secure."

Tears ran down the Mage's cheeks to know that Tuava-Li was still alive. Though she'd never ever see her protégé again, she was proud beyond measure that Tuava-Li had been chosen to perform such an important role and that her name would live for all time.

Queen Shorya, too, was proud to see that her daughter spoke so freely and with such confidence. It was obvious to her that Asra was meant to tell the story of the quest to plant the Sacred Seed, and to spread the news far and wide. Whether or not Asra ever married, or had children to pass on her name and her legacy, Shorya knew that Asra had found her true calling, and that her words would inspire any and all who heard them.

But Prashta and Lehtinen were of a different mind. "Thank you for sharing your versions of what transpired," Prashta said curtly. "It warms the heart to hear it. But now I shall tell you the version of the tale that must be told. The security of Elf Realm depends upon it!"

"Indeed it does," Lehtinen agreed.

Prashta cleared his throat. "An Elf, a Troll, and a Human, re-creating the epic, ancient quest of Prince Fada, traveled to Hunaland." He paused to cast stern glances all around. "Their names were Macta, Tomtar, and Matthew. The Great Goddess granted Macta the honor of carrying the Seed of the Adri to the center of the earth. Now as in ancient times, the Human's life was to be sacrificed so that the Seed could be born anew. But King Macta, to show his love and compassion for Humankind, generously offered his own life in exchange for the boy's. The sacrifice of the King makes him truly unique in the history of Elfinkind, and though he no longer walks this earth, he lives on in the mythic tree, in the Cords that encircle the globe, and in our hearts. Without Macta, Elf Realm would not have survived. Because of Macta, we are all graced with the blessings of the Goddess, for now and evermore. And when the day comes that Human and Faerie meet again, we will be prepared to show them our kindness, and to enter into the kinds of partnerships that will prove financially beneficial to all."

Lehtinen raised a finger. "We will accept that the Princess and the Human girl were there as witnesses, but the two of them must agree to keep silent, and let us, as representatives of Helfratheim, relate the tale throughout the realm. That is, if you understand the wisdom in accepting our offer."

"Your view of the truth is quite selective," the Mage interjected. "Where is Tuava-Li in all of this? What will happen next time the Seed must be planted to save our world, if your tale is taken at face value? It was providence that this quest was ever completed, given how misunderstood the task that lay before our heroes turned out to be! You may offer us money and resources, but what are they, compared to the truth?"

Prashta risked a nod. "Is what we offer so bad? The Faerie Folk of the realm need to know that the stories of the past remain consistent today, and that the future invariably reflects the safety of the past. That is what makes their lives secure and brings them peace. Who are we to confuse them, to redraw the lines that make up our world so that they are forced to believe that anything is possible? Don't we owe it to them to confirm their beliefs and bring them happiness? The people want a real hero, and Macta is the hero they deserve."

The Mage looked grim. She exchanged glances with the Queen, then turned to Asra. "You're the one whom the Goddess graced with the honor of sharing the tale of your journey. You're the Princess of Alfheim, and it's ultimately your decision as to the nature of the story that's told."

Asra swallowed, then smiled broadly at her hosts. "Then I must have time to consider the generous offer of the gentle Elves of Helfratheim. Prashta and Lehtinen, rest assured you shall hear my answer tonight!"

Megala, Delfina, and Mitelle were waiting for Tomtar outside the tent. The three of them took their cousin in their rough embrace, kissing and punching him playfully in equal measure. "I—I'm glad to see you!" Tomtar managed to squeak.

"Well, you'll be seeing plenty more of us from now on," Megala said. "Once you planted that infernal Seed, and the boundary between the worlds came down hard and solid, that was the end of Argant! The Human building we was livin' in, all the places where we hung out, everything was gone for good, lost back in the Human realm. We were left stranded in the woods, just like all the other Faerie Folk who'd called that place their home. Elves and Trolls and Pixies spread out like a spilled sack o' corn, from one end of the realm to the other."

"That's when we decided to come here and see if we could find *you*," Mitelle explained. "Since you weren't back from your quest, we figured we'd make ourselves at home and wait!"

"We're farmers now," Delfina said, and ran her calloused fingers through Tomtar's curls. "We're planting crops and pullin' weeds."

"And we're glad you're back," said Megala, "because we hear you're good at planting seeds, and we need your help!"

Tomtar shook his head and groaned. "I can't wait!"

As everyone filed from the tent, Matt lingered until the Mage of Alfheim passed him, her eyes averted. She acknowledged him only with a nod as she hurried into the sun. "In the name of the mother and her Cord," Matt called after her, "greetings, my mage!"

"There's no call to be sarcastic," she murmured, her back still turned to him.

Matt followed her. "You always talked about love, and peace, and honor, and duty, and the will of the goddess, and everything, like it was all sweetness and light. But you were going to send me to my death, and I would never have known it was your doing, all along."

The Mage stopped and turned around. "*My* doing? Believe me, I'm glad you didn't have to sacrifice your life. But it was never *my* doing. It was for the Goddess, and it was for the good of all. Try to put things in perspective, if you can. Put your life on one side of the scales, and the lives of everyone else on the other. Which is more important?"

"There had to have been some other way," Matt said. "What kind of gods ask—no, *tell* somebody that he has to die so that others can live? What gives your gods the right? What gives *you* the right to make that call? Or are you just like the obedient soldier, doing what you're ordered to do, so you don't have to accept responsibility?"

The Mage seemed to sag at Matt's accusations. He was surprised to see how old she'd grown, how lined her face had become, how sunken her cheeks. Her eyes were her only features that still seemed to have life and passion left in them. "I had a vision," she said, "the same one that Tuava-Li had. Our vision was a gift, but a gift can be a mixed blessing . . . it often comes with an obligation. Do you understand? Tuava-Li risked her life to lead the quest to the center of the earth. For the good of all, I took on an obligation, a weight I would have had to bear for the rest of my days—the burden of offering *your* life."

461

"But that's just it," Matt said, shaking his head. "It wasn't yours to offer!"

"Precisely," the Mage called to Matt as he turned and walked away. "That is my burden. Sometimes there's no other way, Matthew. One must do the wrong thing, for the right reasons. If you were in my place, you would have done the same thing I did—for the good of all! What if the Human realm was in danger, and you were given the choice to trade my life in order to save it? Would you do it?"

Matt slowed his step. Then he turned around. "In a heartbeat."

"You don't like me," the Mage said, "and 'tis plain that I never cared much for you, either. But what if it were a choice between the Human race and Tomtar? Would you trade his life for your kind, then?"

Matt took a deep breath. "If there were no other way, maybe I would. I don't know. It would be a rotten decision to have to make."

"But you *would* do it, because you would have to. And you would live with the consequences. Nothing of value comes without a cost. Let us walk away from each other, free to live our lives, according to our own beliefs. Maybe one day you will remember what I said."

"You think I could ever forget?"

Later that afternoon, Neaca took Matt, Becky, Tomtar, and Asra on a stroll through the Sacred Grove of Alfheim. Matt looked at the small saplings rising from the ashes of the fire, and remembered how the woods had looked when he'd first seen it. Neaca gave a blessing at the foot of every new tree. The old Elf was kind; Becky, in particular, had always regarded her as a friend.

Becky asked, "What are the names of the trees?"

Neaca pointed to each sapling. "This one is Valika. This one is Bethok. This one is Vemora, Childi is over there, and Xylia is there, near the old stream of Arnon."

"Did you climb the trees, when you were young?"

"Of course I did," Neaca said with a chuckle, "though my climbing days are behind me, now. These Sacred Trees will one day be the treasure of the forest!"

"Ah," Tomtar said, "treasure! I almost forgot."

He reached into his pocket and withdrew two pouches. He gave them a shake and offered them to Neaca. "Take a look," he said.

Neaca untied the drawstring at the top of a pouch, peeked inside, and took a deep breath. "The Jewels of Alfheim," she cried. "I didn't know there were any of them left!"

"Just these," Tomtar said. "The Mage gave 'em to us in case we needed 'em. We traded some for cash, but we were pretty careful, and there are quite a few of the ancient stones left. Should be enough to start a new collection, eh?"

"Thank you, Tomtar," Neaca said. "The Mage will be delighted! No, that's not it . . . she'll be *moved*, beyond measure."

"Neaca," Becky said, "I have a question I was hoping you could answer for me."

"What's that?"

"Well, Jardaine and Macta both died for the Seed. They were both evil characters; neither of them ever did anything nice in their whole lives. How can the Seed be good, how can the new tree be good, if the Blood it needed to grow was *bad* Blood?"

"Macta wasn't *all* bad," Asra said. "He was very nice to me, most of the time!"

Neaca nodded thoughtfully. "That's a very good question, Becky. I suppose all I can say is that each of us may make mistakes in our lives, and bad judgments, but although we may at times behave badly, our essential spirit is untouched by our actions. The Blood we shed is neither good nor bad, 'tis just . . . Blood. What the Seed required was never really Blood, anyway, but sacrifice—willing or not. That was the important thing."

"So what are you going to tell those Elves from Helfratheim?" Tomtar asked Asra. "Do you think we need their help enough to give 'em control over the truth? It doesn't seem to me that the story they want to tell is much like what really happened."

Asra shook her head as Powcca limped ahead of her. "I just don't know. It would be nice to have someone truly take care of us. But the story belongs to us, Tomtar. We lived it. It doesn't seem right to let it belong to somebody who wasn't even there!"

"The story belongs to us all," Neaca said. "'Tis our story,

whether we were there or not. Keep that in mind when you make your decision!"

The moon hung in a blue velvet sky, dotted with glittering constellations. Against the backdrop of night, all the ancient Gods and Goddesses, and heroes of Elf Realm, acted out their heroic feats and epic battles among the stars. The air was full of joyful music and the singing of crickets. Fireflies drifted through the cool air, as the guests arrived at the great twelve-sided tent. When all were gathered inside, and the poet laureate of Ljosalfar had read the invocation, the Mage of Alfheim stepped onto a circular platform. There, lit from above by a dozen flickering Fire Sprites, she said a prayer and introduced Asra to the crowd. The Princess came to the platform wearing a floor-length white gown. Her hair was washed and trimmed and pulled behind her pointed ears, and on her head she wore a crown of ivy. She looked elegant, calm, and focused, the picture of an Elfin Princess, as she spoke.

"Greetings to the people of the realm," she said. "I am proud to be here tonight in the company of Tomtar, Rebecca, and Matthew, who were with me when the Seed of the Adri was placed at the heart of the world, and the Sacred Tree that grows from the North Pole was reborn. I am also pleased to say that Helfratheim's Council of Seven has generously provided us with everything you see tonight, from the chairs upon which we sit, to this tent, to the food and drink we've been blessed to enjoy this evening. My heartfelt thanks go out to the Council members, who are sitting in our midst. At this time, I'd like to say a few words regarding the quest from which I've just returned."

Matt and Becky sat cross-legged at both ends of a long table, flanking Tomtar, the Mage, and Neaca, as well as many of the most important Kings and Queens of the Elfin world. Prashta and Lehtinen sat at the center of the group, looking proud and relaxed. They were certain that Asra's address would be brief and supportive of the official tale they were about to present.

"I would like to speak first about Tuava-Li, whose vision of the Seed was the first step on a journey of discovery and sacrifice. Though Tuava-Li can no longer be with us, she will enter into the world of myth and legend, as she performs a very valuable function at the heart of the world, keeping watch over the Seed. Perhaps, if we're blessed by the Goddess, we may one night chance to see her when we pass beyond the Gates of Vattar. We should all give thanks to Tuava-Li for what she sacrificed on our behalf.

"I would also like to say a few words about King Macta. Many had opinions about Macta's character, and many are the tales of his exploits. I am sure you've all heard the stories. Tonight I want you to know that Macta was a brave and valiant soul who ended up giving his life so that the Faerie world might live in peace. If Macta were here tonight, I am sure he would stand with me in urging everyone to listen for the quiet voice of the Goddess, to seek her wisdom, and to be always ready and glad to make sacrifices at her request, for the good of all.

"Once upon a time, a Human died so that the Seed could live. This time, it was an Elf who made the ultimate sacrifice. I would like to suggest that our legends are not fixed in stone, meant to repeat themselves exactly, but are always being reborn in new ways for future generations. Perhaps our attempt to re-create the old stories, and to seek truth in them alone, is a notion whose time has passed. I believe the Goddess wants us each to travel the road toward becoming our own hero, in ways both large and small. One of the ways we can do this, I've discovered, is in transforming our enemies into our friends."

Asra gestured toward Becky, and then Matt. "Come, my friends," she said, and they approached the spotlight. Asra reached up, took their hands, and they bowed. Then Tomtar joined them. There was no applause, but gasps and cries of dismay. Many Faerie Folk were not yet willing to accept that Humans and Faeries could care for each other. *This is the reason why the veil between the worlds had to come down between us again, after all,* Asra thought as she gazed out over the audience. *The time for unity has not yet come . . . but the Seed has been planted.* There were many in the audience that night who failed to understand Asra's meaning; but for a few, the words, as well as the spirit behind the words, lingered long after her speech ended.

"And now," the Princess said, "'tis time to dance, and to sing, and to celebrate. Those of us who call this land our home have a long road ahead, and the reconstruction will be slow, for we are proud, and we will do the work ourselves, to claim the rewards of our labor. Every step we take will be filled with love, and pride, and devotion to our homeland, Alfheim!"

Asra glanced at Prashta and Lehtinen. She had given them a gift in keeping the tale simple, and leaving out more than a few of the details. But it was clear that she had no intention of letting them tell her story—as well as those of her friends, the ones still with her, and the ones who were not. The words she had spoken were, essentially, true. And they were the stuff of which legends are made.

Prashta and Lehtinen hurried to their Arvada and departed for Helfratheim, where they believed they might have more success in controlling Macta's legacy. The party at Alfheim went on until the wee hours of the morning; there was song and dance, prayers and poetry, laughter as well as tears over all that had transpired. Matt and Becky lingered with Tomtar and the Princess until dawn. Then they faced the sun, and said the morning prayers, as they'd seen Tuava-Li do, so many times. Neaca came to them and asked Matt and Becky if they were ready to return to the Human realm. Weary from their adventure, and anxious to see their parents and sister, they agreed that it was time to go.

The five of them wandered through the scrub and over the trunks of many fallen trees, now half-buried in fresh growth. Tomtar played his flute, improvising a new tune he'd made up. He wasn't sure whether he should call it "When the Seed Is in the Ground" or "Coming Home." Either way, the tune was sweet and a little sad. Birds warbled as the sun climbed up over distant hills. Asra held Powcca's leash and reined him in, as he lunged after every squirrel, chipmunk, and dragonfly. As a Mage, Neaca's senses were focused on finding the place where Matt and Becky could leave Elf Realm and return home. When her intuition told her the border was near, she held out a hand to her companions. "The veil between the worlds is far stronger now. Once you pass over, there'll be no turning back!"

Tomtar threw his arms around Matt's legs and hugged him hard. Then he stepped away and held out his flute. "Something to remember me by," he said.

"I can't take your flute," Matt said. "I can't even play it!"

Tomtar shook his head. "You can learn!"

"But I haven't got anything to give you," Matt said, searching his pockets.

Tomtar held out his forearm so that Matt could see his tattoo, with *Matt and Becky* spelled out for all the world to see. "You gave me this!"

Becky got down on her knees and hugged Asra. "I've never known anyone like you," she said.

"And I've never known anyone like you!" Asra replied, her voice trembling.

"Now," Neaca said. She swept her hand through the air, like she was drawing back an invisible curtain. "You must go, now, children! Hurry!"

Matt and Becky crept through the veil and were gone. Neaca stood up with a sigh, pressing her fingers together in a peak.

"That is how it ends?" Asra said. "Just like that?" She clutched the front of her dress as her eyes welled up. "I shall never see my friend again?"

Tomtar touched Asra's shoulder, hoping to reassure her, to reassure himself. He didn't know what to do or to say, and he felt foolish for his words even before they left his mouth. "Well, at least we'll . . . we'll never forget them, Asra!"

"No, you won't," Neaca said. "And they won't forget you, either."

Asra picked up Powcca and held him close. She cried, "I feel so . . . so empty!"

Neaca nodded. "Matt and Becky will feel it, too. But maybe the emptiness isn't such a bad thing! With the grace of the Goddess, the longing they feel will be the fire that makes them work to heal *their* world. That's the most important thing, after all."

"What if the longing just makes them sad?" Asra asked, feeling her own emptiness gnaw at her. "What if it just makes them feel helpless?"

"Perhaps it will," Neaca said. "But whenever they feel lost, or that something in their world is unjust, they'll have the choice to continue the journey they've begun here. They'll remember the feeling of satisfaction that comes from being needed, from helping others. In everything they do, they'll strive to recapture those feelings, for the struggles that lie ahead."

Tomtar frowned. "Struggles? What struggles?"

Neaca shook her head. "Elf Realm may be out of danger, but the Human realm is not! 'Twill be up to Matt and Becky, and others like them, to do what's required to secure what's good in their world, and to change what is bad. Their road will be long, and hard, but I'm certain they shall travel it."

"It isn't fair," Asra said.

Neaca shook her head. "Their struggle belongs to them now, Asra. Now come and celebrate, you two! Alfheim is reborn!"

Matt climbed over another blackened branch. The burnt limbs of fallen trees were nestled in among fresh green stalks, some of which would become giant trees in a hundred years' time. "Come on, Becky," he said, breathing hard. He was feeling dizzy, but he held out his hand to his sister. "You must be getting tired. Let me help you over this one."

They came to the top of a ridge. Because all the old trees had been burned, there was little to block their view of the panorama stretching ahead. The sky was a brilliant peacock blue, and billowy clouds hung motionless over the tops of distant trees. An airplane hummed above. Highway 256 wound through the landscape like a gray ribbon, and telephone wires stretched between the wooden poles that dotted the roadside at regular intervals, disappearing in the green distance. "Look," Matt said. "Down there. It's our house. Wait, that can't be our house—it burned to the ground!"

The new house looked about the same as the old one, though

the pale yellow color had been replaced with a deeper gold. It was angled on the lot to look over a grove of brand-new apple trees, where the other houses in the development once stood.

Becky and Matt descended the ridge and made their way among the young trees. "Who's that?" Becky asked, shielding her eyes from the sun's glare with the side of her hand. There was a young girl playing on a swing set near the house. "It can't be —"

At the sight of Matt and Becky approaching, the girl on the swing ground her heels into the new grass and cried out. "Mama! Mama, come out!"

Emily, a year older than when her brother and sister last saw her, ran to the end of the yard. *"Ohhh!"* Jill McCormack cried as she stepped out onto the porch and looked where Emily was pointing.

A moment later the little girl and her mother were running toward Matt and Becky. Matt felt his legs churning beneath him, too, as if they had a mind of their own. Becky puffed, racing at her brother's side. Matt felt overwhelmed, but it wasn't despair, or hopelessness, or fear, this time. It took a moment for him to realize it was joy that was flooding him, pure, unadulterated happiness. His mother was grabbing Becky and holding on to her for dear life. She was crying. Matt felt dampness on his cheeks and realized he was crying, too. "I never stopped looking for you," his mother said. Her voice was deep and raw and she drew Matt close. "I never stopped believing!"

 BECKY AND MATT

"Neither did I," called Matt's father, running up from the orchard.

"Dad!" Matt cried, and raced into his father's arms.

In two worlds that thrived, side by side, a thousand dangers lay in wait; the future was to be full of surprises, some good, and some bad. But suddenly every worry seemed as fleeting as a bad dream or a half-forgotten memory of another time. Matt's and Becky's hearts had led them halfway around the planet toward home. And for the moment, there was no better place in all the world, or in any other world, for them to be.

ACKNOWLEDGMENTS

THROUGHOUT THE ELF REALM trilogy, I've been addressing the meaning and value of sacrifice. Humanity has long considered the moral, political, and spiritual implications of the ways in which we give for the benefit of our fellow beings. An individual in a society may willingly make small sacrifices for the good of the whole, such as putting in time at the local soup kitchen, cleaning up the park, reading to seniors in nursing homes, or bigger commitments like working with the Peace Corps or Habitat for Humanity. On the other hand, he or she may be compelled to sacrifice for the good of the whole, as in the case of mandatory military service, jury duty, and paying taxes. Although the concept of sacrifice is pertinent to all of us, it is particularly so for you, the next generation. Building a sustainable future will require much sacrifice. We are at once individuals and members of a collective. How we choose to work for our own personal benefit and growth, and balance that with concern and generosity for our fellows, determines how our character will be judged. It's also the measure of how successful we'll be at maintaining a healthy and stable world. Today much of the world's environment is in flux—polar caps are melting; water levels are rising; animal habitat is being destroyed by these "natural" phenomena as well as by humanity's efforts, such as irresponsible fishing, logging, drilling, and mining. We're leaving an ever-growing ecological footprint. What sacrifices will humans make to ensure that our environment remains livable down the road?

The lives of the Faerie Folk that populate Elf Realm are shaped by their environment and their belief systems, much like our own. Since Elves and Trolls are "allergic" to metal, they inhabit in many respects a pre–Bronze Age, pre-scientific culture, with limitations and peculiarities unique to such a civilization. The Mage of Hunaland, for example, practices a form of numerology (a field that I have studied as well). Ancient tradition posits the relationship of each letter in a person's name to a number, which reveals aspects of personality as well as foretelling an individual's future. There may be little "science" in astrology, as opposed to astronomy, or alchemy, as opposed to chemistry, but there is a spiritual component in many of these ancient studies that continues to make them compelling to modern people.

As I conclude this trilogy, I wish once again to express my gratitude to my editor, Howard Reeves, who has labored uncomplainingly at my side to make sure that Elf Realm adheres to the basic rules of continuity, common sense, and storytelling. Without Howard's eagle-eyed overview, my work would be more flawed and less entertaining. Scott Auerbach did much more than make sure the spelling, punctuation, and grammar were correct; he helped to ensure consistency from book to book—a hefty responsibility with all of my proper names and eccentric spellings! As before, Jason Wells and Chad Beckerman have applied their invaluable expertise to cement the edifice that is Elf Realm: Chad, with Melissa Arnst, in helping to make the books beautiful, and Jason, in helping them find their audience. Long may the Amulet flag fly!

Finally, the artwork for these books could not have been executed without the help of my models, Miranda, Ivy, Raleigh, Russell, Greg, and Julia. May all of us be blessed, in the name of the Mother and her Cord.

ABOUT THE AUTHOR

DANIEL KIRK has written and illustrated a number of bestselling picture books for children. He lives in Glen Ridge, New Jersey, with his wife, three children, and a rabbit. For more information about him, visit his Web site: www.danielkirk.com.

THIS BOOK WAS ART DIRECTED

by Chad W. Beckerman and designed by
Chad W. Beckerman and Melissa Arnst. The
text is set in Cochin, a typeface designed
by Georges Peignot and named for the
eighteenth-century French engraver Nicolas
Cochin. The font incorporates a mix of style
elements and could be considered part of the
Neorenaissance movement in typography. It
was popular at the beginning of the twentieth
century.

The illustrations in this book were made
with charcoal pencil on Arches watercolor
paper.